A MEMORY OF EARTH

A Memory of Earth

CHILDREN OF EARTHRISE, BOOK II

Daniel Arenson

This novel is a work of fiction. Names, characters, places and incidents are either the product of the author's imagination, or, if real, used fictitiously.

CHAPTER ONE

Ayumi was helping her father weave rugs when death rolled into their city.

Of course, it wasn't *their* city. Not really. They were humans. Pests. Untouchables. They were kept in the enclave, a dusty hive of misery, walled off from the rest of Palaevia. But this place, a ghetto of poverty and buzzing summers and quiet despair, was home. Was life.

Until the scorpions came.

The day had begun like any other. Ayumi awoke in her small bed, in her small room, in her small house, in this small enclave—barely larger than a true prison—where thousands of humans crowded together. For all her twelve years, Ayumi had lived in the enclave. She knew no other life. Many of the elders, those who had seen the outside city, spoke of wide boulevards, of marble fountains and birds of many colors, of trees and flowers—actual living plants that bloomed and gave forth sweet scents. To Ayumi, those were fairy tales, as unreachable as Earth, the planet they had lost. To Ayumi Kobayashi, the weaver's daughter, Palaevia Enclave was the cosmos entire.

"Ayumi-san!" her mother cried as Ayumi raced across the living chamber. "Slow down and brush your hair! And fix your clothes. You're a weaver's daughter!"

Ayumi paused and blew her mother a raspberry.

"My clothes are simple rags compared to the fabrics Father makes for the aliens," she said. "Why should I tend to them?"

Her mother was a stern, slender woman, her hair still jet black. She stood by the stove, tending to a pot of rice flavored with eel skins. The kitchen, living area, reading nook, and her parents' bed—all shared this single small chamber. Ayumi supposed she was lucky. She had her own room, even though it was barely larger than her bed.

Mother groaned. "I swear, Ayumi-san, on old Earth you'd be mistaken for an urchin."

"Well, this isn't Old Earth," Ayumi said. "This is Palaevia, a stinky old city on Paev, a stinky old planet far on the butt of the galaxy."

"Ayumi, watch your language!"

Ayumi placed her thumbs on her temples, wiggled her fingers, and stuck out her tongue. As Mother swung a ladle at her, spraying rice, Ayumi fled the room.

She leaped over her baby brother, who was sleeping in his crib, and around her dustdog, a fluffy critter who grumbled and shuffled away. She reached the window. Ayumi slammed open the shutters and jumped outside.

For a moment, she flew, legs kicking in midair. The city of Palaevia spread out around her.

Her home was inside the enclave, the city's human ghetto. Thick stone walls boxed her people in. The enclave was only about a kilometer squared. A tiny place. But fifty thousand humans all crowded in here, among the largest human communities in the Milky Way.

They could not leave. They were born, lived, grew old, and died here in this stone box. Here was a miniature Earth, reborn thousands of light-years away from their lost homeworld.

Buildings filled the enclave. There were apartment buildings, workshops, and pagodas that rose many tiers tall, extending tiled eaves, all jumbled together in a haphazard mass. Awnings and balconies hid the alleyways like a jungle canopy hides the forest floor. Ayumi could just glimpse mulers pulling carts. The shaggy animals grunted as they moved down the cobbled streets, occasionally leaving steaming piles. Smithies belched out smoke and sparks. The bells of a bakery clanged, announcing a batch of fresh bread. The voices of actors rang out from the small theater. Hundreds of workshops. Thousands of apartments. Dozens of languages, ranging from old Earth tongues to the Common Human many spoke today across the galaxy. An echo of Earth so far from home.

The humans were everywhere. They filled the alleyways. They toiled on rooftop gardens, shooing away birds. They stood on balconies, tending to herbs, hanging laundry, and beating rugs. They peered from windows. They haggled in bustling markets. Children jumped from roof to roof, laughed in the streets, and communicated between windows using cups and strings.

Palaevia Enclave—a hive of stone and squalor, fabric and steel, imprisonment and life.

Home.

And beyond the enclave walls—a vast, forbidden world.

The rest of the city.

Palaevia was a sprawling metropolis, home to a million Paevins, a race of sentient felines. From here, Ayumi couldn't see much of that forbidden realm. The tops of several towers. The distant palace on a hill. That was all. To her, the rest of Palaevia was as unreachable as Earth.

Ayumi saw all this within seconds as she leaped out her home window. She had seen this view thousands of times. With a thud, she landed on the roof of a neighboring home.

She ran across the adobe tiles, vaulted over an alleyway, and landed on another rooftop. Birds cawed and fled, shedding feathers. Ayumi hopped from roof to roof, waving at her neighbors. A few waved back. Others shook their fists at her, and one mean old woman even pelted her with rubbish, shouting that

Ayumi was scaring her plants. Ayumi stuck her tongue out at the hag and kept leaping.

As she leaped toward the bakery, she gave a loud whistle. The baker, a portly man with a white mustache, emerged onto the balcony and tossed her a roll. Ayumi caught it in midair and dropped him a seashell.

"*Konnichiwa*, Mister Hiroji!" she said, landed on a library roof, and kept hopping onward. "*Arigato gozaimasu*!"

"Slow down, Ayumi-san!" the baker cried, pocketing the shell. "One day you're going to fall down and break your knees."

"*Sayonara*, Mister Hiroji! I'll be careful, I promise!"

She bounded across several more roofs and finally reached the enclave's outer wall. It soared higher than any rooftop, enclosing the ghetto. But Ayumi knew every brick in this wall like every roof in the enclave. She barely had to think as she climbed, her fingers and toes deftly finding the grooves between the bricks. She scrambled up, then pulled herself onto the top of the wall.

For a moment, Ayumi stood, looking at the city beyond.

She heaved a deep sigh.

"Palaevia," she whispered.

She pulled from her pocket the roll Mister Hiroji had given her. It was filled with raisins and nuts, still steaming from the oven. Ayumi chewed thoughtfully, walking atop the wall, gazing upon the city beyond.

She came here every morning to see Greater Palaevia. To dream.

Palaevia was the largest city on the warm, verdant planet of Paev. Its towers of white limestone scratched the sky. Its marble temples soared, filled with hymns and psalms. Gardens bloomed across the city, lush with trees and flowers, plants Ayumi had never seen up close. The boulevards were wide, filled not with shaggy mulers and creaky carts but ornate, steam-operated chariots trimmed with gold. Airships floated leisurely above, delivering passengers between the city and provinces.

The Paevins were a graceful, slender species, bipedal and feline, covered with golden fur. From up here, Ayumi could see several Paevins strolling along a boulevard. The men wore fine red coats embellished with golden thread. They sported red top hats, monocles, and ivory canes, and their whiskers were oiled. The females wore gowns in a dizzying array of colors and patterns. Ayumi's own father supplied many of these fabrics, toiling inside the enclave to produce wonderful gowns and coats for the Paevins.

One of the felines, a guard in a burnished bronze breastplate, stared up from below.

"Back into the enclave, pest!" the Paevin shouted. "We don't want to see your kind."

He raised a crossbow and fired. Ayumi, no stranger to this ritual, leaped aside. The quarrel missed her.

"Go play with some yarn, cat!" She blew him a raspberry, then hopped back into the enclave.

She landed on another roof. She heaved another sigh. How often she had wished to explore that realm beyond! There was an entire city out there. Not just the enclave, this small, walled-off neighborhood, but an entire city of a million souls, neighborhood after neighborhood of wonders spreading toward the horizon. And beyond—an entire world! The whole planet of Paev, a world she had seen only in faded postcards. A world of misty forests, trains that chugged between snowy mountains, soaring castles, and deep caves filled with jewels. A world of wonder and beauty. And beyond Paev—the stars! Countless other worlds, and one among them—a pale blue world called Earth. The homeland they had lost. That all humans prayed to someday see again.

Standing atop a pottery shop, Ayumi lowered her head. She dropped the rest of her sweet roll onto the rooftop. She had lost her appetite. A bird grabbed the morsel, then flew over the wall, heading to the city beyond. Ayumi wished she could follow.

But I'm human, she thought. *I'm a pest. I can't leave the enclave. None of us can.*

Some humans, only a handful, were allowed near the enclave gate. There they could trade their wares—fabrics, tools, leather, and other goods—for water and food. But even the tradesmen could not leave the enclave, only stand at the gate. The Paevins believed that humans spread disease. That they were cursed, twisted beings. Demonic. Evil.

They let us live, she thought. *But they keep us locked up like lepers. Why can't they see that I wish them no harm?*

She raised her eyes and gazed into the sky. The sun was bright. She could not see the stars. But somewhere beyond that sky, invisible to her, shone her star. Sol, the star of Earth. Of all humans. Somewhere their home awaited them. Calling them.

Ayumi sang softly. The song of humanity.

Someday we will see her
The pale blue marble
Rising from the night beyond the moon
Cloaked in white, her forests green
Calling us home
Calling us home

Tears filled her eyes. She rubbed them away with her fists. No more tears. She had cried too many mornings. The enclave was her home, and it was home enough. She had her life here. Her friends. Her dustdog. Her family. And her work.

Ayumi raised her eyes, looked across several workshops, and saw the Weavers Guildhall. She nodded.

Yes, I have our work. I have weaving.

Ayumi tightened her lips and moved toward the guildhall, hopping from roof to roof, jumping with more determination now. The Weavers Guildhall was among the oldest, most venerated buildings in the enclave. It wasn't particularly large. It was narrow and only three stories tall. The bottom floor was a store, the middle floor a workshop, the top floor a storeroom. It wasn't particularly pretty. The facade was simple brick, but the doorway's keystone bore the rune of a loom. The ancient symbol of the Weavers Guild.

For thousands of years, we wove, Ayumi thought. *Wove fabric for gowns and coats. Wove the fabric of reality.*

She hopped onto the guildhall's roof, scrambled down a water spout, and climbed through the window.

The room was shadowy and cool. Dust danced in beams of light that shone between the shutters. Rolls of fabric rose in piles, hiding the walls. There were fabrics of every kind. Rich red wool hung in a beam of light, embroidered with golden dragons that coiled and reared, their sequin scales chinking. Bolts of black fabric lay on a table, as soft and secretive as the night, and stars were woven into them, winking and shining with true light. Green rolls of fabric rose like the lost green hills of Earth, scented of grass. The fabric seemed magical to Ayumi, filled with mysteries and wonder.

She walked downstairs, the limestone steps cool beneath her bare feet. Her family had been weaving here for generations. The steps were well-worn, polished by the passage of many feet, sunken in the middle. She entered the workshop, and she saw him there.

Her father, Hiroto Kobayashi, sat at a wooden loom. An heirloom. It had been in the family for generations. A silver rune glowed upon the loom like molten moonlight, illuminating strands of red and blue wool. Hiroto hummed as he pressed the pedal over and over, moving the loom, weaving a rug. He worked as in a trance, not even noticing Ayumi approach.

Once, other weavers had worked here. Their portraits still hung on the walls, embroidered in cotton—old men and woman in fine robes, faces Ayumi knew as well as her own. But all had passed from the world. Today only her father remained, the last weaver in Palaevia Enclave. There were weavers on other worlds, Father had told her. But what were other worlds to one who could not even leave her neighborhood?

She padded closer. "Father?"

He continued weaving, pushing the pedal, humming, eyes closed. He paused for only an instant to raise a finger, hushing her, then continued with his work. He was a wiry man, his cheeks gaunt, his nose sharp. His hair was long and purest white, the color of starlight on snow, and his skin was deep bronze. To Ayumi, he seemed the strongest, wisest man in the world.

As Hiroto toiled, patterns and figures emerged on the rug. Birds woven of blue and green fibers flapped their wings. Stars of silver thread shone. A stream of blue wool flowed and gurgled. The rug came alive, a vibrant work of art filled with color and movement. Ayumi had seen her father weave many rugs, but she had never seen one of such magnificence.

"Father, it's wonderful!" she said. "The birds are actually flying, and the stream is moving! Who is this rug for?" She gasped. "It must be for the king of Paev himself!"

The pedal froze. Father removed his hands from the loom. Ayumi saw the rune on his right hand, a tattoo in white ink, shaped like a small loom. It glowed with pale light.

The light of aether, Ayumi knew. *The light the weavers can weave.*

Father sighed. "Even when I'm deep in weaving, you disturb me, Ayumi-san. Have you no manners?"

She shook her head. "No. Mother says I'm horrible, that I chew with my mouth open, that my hair and clothes are always a mess, and that I never pray to the spirits. But I think having no manners is fine. I like being wild and rude. It's better than being mild and meek, don't you think, Father?"

"I think you have been spending too much time climbing the wall and taunting the guards below, Ayumi-san."

"They deserve taunts," Ayumi said. "It's horrible how they imprison us humans here in the enclave, don't you think? Someday I will break out of here. I will see wonders."

Father's eyes flared with anger. "Do not speak this way, Ayumi-san. We are humans. The world outside is forbidden to us."

But Ayumi barely paid attention to his words. She had heard them all a thousand times before. Instead, she was watching the glowing tattoo on his hand. Slowly, the rune dimmed. Soon it just looked like any old tattoo, inked in white, barely visible amid the wrinkles on Father's palm. The matching rune on the loom, which had shone so brightly, faded too. Now that rune appeared as but a simple engraving in the wood.

The aether has gone dark, Ayumi thought.

Ayumi never tired of watching that light glow and fade and glow again. The loom was not merely a tool of wood and metal and rope. It was an artifact, filled with a core of aetherstone. Weavers were the guardians of artifacts, after all. Not just here on Paev but across the cosmos. Every artifact had a rune, a keyhole to the plane above, to the realm of aether.

Ayumi reached out gingerly and touched the loom. Nothing happened. The rune engraved into the wood did not light up. The loom did not produce its wondrous patterns. She was not yet a true weaver. She had no rune tattooed onto her hand. She could not unlock the wonders of the artifact.

"I wish I could use this loom!" Ayumi said. "When will I get a tattoo?"

"It's called a rune, Ayumi-chan," Father said, voice softening. Whenever somebody affixed *chan* rather than *san* to her name, Ayumi knew they weren't mad. "Not a tattoo. It's a blessing from the ancients, allowing us to use their artifacts. Tattoos are mere trifles compared to runes."

He brought his hand closer to the loom. Again, both his tattoo and the symbol engraved into the loom shone. When he pulled his hand back, they faded. Only he could use the loom to create rugs of such beauty. Whenever Ayumi tried to use it, she could barely weave toilet paper.

"Well, when will I be worthy of a *rune*, Father?" Ayumi said.

He smiled and mussed her hair. "Be patient, Ayumi-chan. The ancients are wise. They control the aether. They will know when you're ready to weave."

"I'm ready now!" Ayumi said. "I'm tired of waiting. I want to become a weaver like you. Like the great weavers of old, the powerful masters who could weave the fabric of spacetime itself. Old Kioshi says the great weavers of old could move mountains, raise the dead, even destroy entire planets. She says that if I become a master weaver, I could even defeat our enemies and lead us home to Earth."

Father frowned. "Old Kioshi is filled with silly stories and old tales. Do not listen to that crazy old kook, Ayumi-san. We use the aether to toil. To weave fabrics. To weave beauty."

"But Old Kioshi says that—"

"Be silent, Ayumi-san!" Father said. "Must I strike you?"

Ayumi bit her lip, remembering the welt on her hand, the gift of his ruler. She had stolen seashells from his pocket that day, but had never stolen since. She tucked her hands behind her back, still feeling the sting.

"Someday I'll have tattoos on my hands instead of welts," she said. "Sorry, Father. I mean *runes*." She rolled her eyes.

And Father did something unexpected. He laughed.

"Come here, Ayumi-chan. Look at this rug I'm weaving."

She sat beside him on the bench and passed her fingers over the rug. As her fingers moved near, the birds moved their wings. She trailed her fingers over the grassy hills, the flowing streams, the mountains.

"I can feel the grass!" she said. "And the stream is actually wet, and the mountains feel like real stone!"

Father nodded. "That is the power of aether."

Ayumi sighed wistfully. "I wish I owned such a rug! Is this for a great general? A king? An emperor?"

"I weave this rug for you, Ayumi-chan."

Her eyes widened. "For me, Father?"

He nodded, smiling, but there was a tinge of sadness to that smile. He took her hand. His rune was still warm.

"You're my little girl, Ayumi-chan. But very soon, you will be thirteen, no longer a child. I watch you growing up so fast. And so I weave this rug for you, something eternal when all of life is so ephemeral. I weave you a rug with a vision of Earth."

She gasped and turned back toward the rug. Again she touched the grass, the streams, the mountains.

"Earth," she whispered.

"Our homeland," said Father. "Our birthright. I may never live to see Earth. But perhaps you will, or your children, or your children's children. Until that day, may this rug be as a sweet memory. I've never seen Earth. I've never seen paintings or photographs from our homeworld, or even read books written on that world. But we have our tales. We have our legends. This is how I imagine Earth."

Ayumi tightened her lips. She clenched her fists. "I promise you, Father. Someday I will leave the enclave. I will reach Earth. Then I will come back here, and I will tell you if Earth is like this rug." She tilted her head. "Actually, I'll take you with me to Earth. We can live there together, don't you think? We can bring Mother and even the baby."

Father laughed. "That's very generous of you. Can we bring Granny too? Or—"

A rumble sounded outside, so loud the room rattled.

Ayumi started. She frowned. She had never heard anything so loud. Even a thousand mulers pulling carts down cobbled alleyways wouldn't sound this loud.

"Thunder?" she said, her voice barely audible.

She made to dash toward the window.

Father reached out to grab her. "Ayumi, come with me!"

But Ayumi ignored him. She ran upstairs. The entire building was trembling. Ayumi burst out the window and climbed onto the roof.

The sound was rumbling around her. Smoke veiled the sky, and a stench like burning oil filled her nostrils, but she saw no flames. The city was shaking—not just the enclave but all of Palaevia. Humans were running through the enclave and pointing at the sky, and the wails of native Paevins rose beyond the wall. The Paevin airships were mustering in the sky, brass cannons bright. Their small wooden airplanes were taking flight, propellers buzzing. The sky gurgled, the smoke churned, and the rumbling grew louder.

No, this is no thunder, Ayumi thought.

She craned her neck back and saw the sky crack open.

Fire blazed like strands of flame in a burning loom.

And the demons descended.

They had to be demons, these shards of black metal ringed with fire. They were massive beasts, each larger than her entire house. They were triangular like arrowheads, and they moved just as fast, swooping toward the city. Red eyes blazed upon them, and their bellies rumbled, belching out fire.

Machines, Ayumi realized. *They're machines like the airplanes. Like the blimps. Great machines that burn massive engines filled with steam, more steam than powers this entire city.*

She had heard of such machines. The elders still spoke of them. They said that back when humanity had still lived on Earth, brave men and women had flown great flying carriages called starships. They said that Queen Einav Ben-Ari, the Golden Lioness of Earth, had led thousands of starships to smite humanity's enemies.

"These are starships!" Ayumi cried out. "Enemy starships!"

But nobody could hear her. The starships were so loud. More and more emerged from the clouds, hundreds of them, then thousands. The Paevin airplanes attacked, firing their machine guns. But the bullets glanced off the starships like spitballs off a stone wall.

And the black, triangular starships opened fire.

Bolts of searing red flame blasted out and slammed into airplanes. The wooden wings burned. The steam engines shattered. Blimps tore open, and the hydrogen inside ignited and blazed and filled the sky with an inferno. Fire rained upon the world of Paev. Both humans and Paevins screamed.

"We're under attack!" Ayumi shouted. "Aliens from another world!"

"Ayumi!" Father was reaching from the window. "Ayumi, come inside!"

But Ayumi remained on the rooftop. "We have to save Mother and the baby!"

"Ayumi!" He tried to grab her. "Ayumi, come—"

One of the black starships came to hover above the guildhall. Wind blasted back Ayumi's long black hair. Heat bathed her. The machine rumbled above, casting shadows and red light. It was forged of metal, many plates bolted together. There were portholes too, like on an airship, and creatures scuttled inside. Great arachnids. Eyes red and blazing. Shells black.

Scorpions, Ayumi realized. *Scorpions larger than men.*

Cannons extended from the ship.

Fire rained down.

Near Ayumi, a bolt of searing blue agony slammed into the roof, blasting sparks and tiles and heat and flame. It tore a hole into the roof and roared into the building, burning fabrics, toppling bricks.

Ayumi screamed and stumbled backward until her heels hit the roof's edge. Her arms windmilled.

"Ayumi!" Father cried from the window. He was climbing outside, feet wobbling on the windowsill. The Weavers Guildhall was burning.

She reached down to him. "Fath—"

Another bolt slammed into the roof, shattering the building.

The walls crumbled.

Screaming, Ayumi fell through dust and smoke and hailing stones.

Tiles and bricks slammed into her. Smoke filled her lungs. She landed with a thump on bolts of fabric. Rolls of wool tore free and unspooled, spilling everywhere, blazing. Ayumi coughed. She had landed inside the workshop. The roof was gone, and the sky burned.

"Father!" she cried.

The entire building was burning, crumbling. Half the floor was gone, leaving a gaping hole. The staircase remained, and Ayumi ran down to the first floor, calling for her father. The loom lay shattered on the floor. The rug embroidered with Earth scenes was burning. Even through the horror, as the world burned, Ayumi leaned down and tore free a patch of the rug. It showed a white bird on a blue field.

"Ayumi!"

Father stumbled toward her, bleeding and covered with dust. He was limping, and burns spread down his side. She ran and embraced him.

"Ayumi, outside, onto the road!" Father said. "We must find Mother and the baby."

They fled the crumbling guildhall. People filled the streets, screaming, pointing at the sky. The starships were roaring overhead, and ash rained. A muler raced by, bleating, its fur ablaze. A dead man lay by a collapsed building. Above, the wooden airplanes were still launching an assault, and the machine guns rattled across the sky. A plane ignited, crashed down in flame, and slammed into a ropemaker's shop near Ayumi. Shards of wood flew. The wooden propeller detached and rolled across the road, mowing people down.

Ayumi and her father kept going, barely able to navigate through the panicking throng.

"What do they want, Father? Who are they? Why—"

A shriek sounded above.

Words tore across the sky.

"Bring me the humans alive, you fools! I want their skins! Do not burn them. Bring them to me alive!"

Ayumi looked up. Through the smoke and fire, she saw a figure standing on a rooftop.

She gasped.

A human!

But she was not a human like the others in the enclave. Her skin was purest white, the color of bleached bones. Her hair was blue and flowed in the wind. She wore a garment of black webs. Across the distance, the woman made eye contact with Ayumi and smiled. There was as much warmth in that smile as in a steel blade.

Several of the triangular starships came to hover above the woman's head, arranging themselves in the shape of a star. Hatches opened in the ships' underbellies, and the scorpions spilled out.

Ayumi stood frozen, unable to even scream, to comprehend the horror.

The beasts fell onto roofs, streets, and balconies. They were as large as mulers. Gleaming black shells covered them, and their pincers seemed mighty enough to tear through trees. Their stingers curled over their backs, dripping venom.

The aliens swarmed.

They moved like lightning. They pounced onto humans, knocked them down, and grabbed them with their claws. One man resisted, lashing a cleaver. A scorpion snapped his pincers, slicing the man in half under the ribs. The man fell, organs spilling.

"Humans, hear me!" cried the blue-haired woman on the roof. "I am Jade, a human like you! I am your friend! I've come to take you home to Earth. Line up, follow my scorpions, and I will bring you home! Resist and you will die."

Some people began to line up, glancing around, whispering in fear.

"Earth!" a woman whispered.

"She's come to slay the Paevins who imprison us!" said an old man. "She'll take us home!"

Ayumi stared up from the street. Jade met her eyes again and gave her a small nod.

I don't believe you for a second, Ayumi thought. She had heard what the woman had shouted earlier. *She wants our skins.*

"Move, you filthy apes!" rasped a scorpion, shoving a mother and son onto the road.

"Line up and move, pests!" shrieked another, shoving a man, bloodying his back.

Great, so they can talk, Ayumi thought.

Hundreds of people lined up on the narrow road. The scorpions clung to the walls and balconies, venom dripping. Where the liquid hit flesh, it sizzled and burned. Children wept, only for a scorpion to grab one boy, slice through his neck, and toss the severed head onto the road. The other children fell silent, faces pale, bodies trembling.

Ayumi winced and squeezed her father's hand. Tears filled her eyes. This seemed unreal. It had to be a dream. Just a nightmare like the ones she had where her teeth were falling out. Any moment now, she would wake up. She would find herself back in her bed. She would leap out the window, and buy a sweet roll from Mister Hiroji, and visit her father to help him weave, and none of this would happen. None of this could be real.

"Father," she whispered, voice shaking.

"I'll watch over you, Ayumi-chan." His voice was soft and deep. "We will not die today."

A scorpion leaped off a balcony and landed beside them. The beast hissed, stinger raised, red eyes blazing.

"Get into the line, apes!" The creature snapped his pincers. "Line up or I'll slice your limbs and suck your marrow."

Ayumi felt the blood drain from her face. Her limbs shook. She began to move toward the line of humans, but Father refused to budge. He remained on the roadside. Gently, he released Ayumi's hand and turned to face the scorpion.

"Move it, maggot!" the scorpion hissed. "Do you want to die in front of your daughter?"

A gust of wind billowed Father's long white hair. The weaver rolled back his sleeves, revealing gnarled arms. Runes were tattooed onto his forearms with white ink, intricate sigils of circles and filigree—the runes of air. They began to glow.

"I am Hiroto Kobayashi, weaver of aether, servant of the ancient ones," Father said. "And I am a son of humanity, an heir to Earth. You will stand back, foul beast, or you will feel my wrath."

The scorpion hissed and reared.

"A weaver!" the beast said and lunged forward, pincers snapping.

Ayumi screamed.

Father held out his arms, palms pointing toward the scorpion, and his runes shone.

The air rippled.

A funnel of air thrummed forward and slammed into the scorpion.

The alien flew back into a smithy wall, cracking the bricks.

At once, a dozen scorpions pounced toward Father, shrieking.

Ayumi leaped back and cowered, covering her head with her arms, trembling. She watched with eyes narrowed by terror.

Father spun from side to side, his runes shining. Funnels of air blasted from his palms, rippling forward like visible sound waves, pounding into scorpions. The blasts knocked the aliens back, cracking their shells, slamming them against walls. Father's cloak and hair fluttered in the wind. A scorpion thrust his stinger, spraying venom. Father held out his palm, and a blast of air blew the venom aside. Another scorpion swooped from a balcony, and Father swept his arms, knocking it onto the ground, cracking the flagstones. He moved with the studied grace of a dancer.

Ayumi slowly removed her arms from over her head. Her eyes widened.

He's more than a weaver of fabric, she thought. *I always knew he was more.*

She had never been more proud of him. Never loved him more.

Ayumi ran to stand beside him. She had no runes of her own, no power to access the aether, that mystical light from the realm above. But she followed his movements, thrusting out her palms, snarling, as if she herself were a weaver.

"Take that!" she cried. "And that! Be gone, scorpions. We are humans! We are strong!"

With every word, she extended her palms, mimicking her father's movements. And her father kept fighting at her side, his tattoos aglow, knocking the aliens aside with blasts of air.

"Ayumi, get back!" he said.

Scorpions kept descending. They covered the rooftops, scuttled down the walls, and raced across the alleyway. Father could barely knock them aside fast enough. Three of the beasts lunged onto Father at once. He managed to knock two aside, but the third sliced his leg. Father fell to one knee, blood spurting.

Ayumi cried out.

More scorpions raced forward.

Roaring, Father rose to his feet and tore off his robe. An intricate tattoo shone on his bare chest, a masterwork of coiling lines and circles. Now, instead of blasting out funnels of air, he cast beams of light from his fingertips, searing the scorpions, cutting through their shells.

Ayumi gasped.

He's firing pure aether from his fingertips, she realized.

He was terrible to behold, so mighty that even Ayumi took a step back, fearing him, what he had become. His wrath tore through the beasts, slaying scorpion after scorpion.

But his runes' glow was dimming.

He was using up too much power too fast.

The light faded.

Emboldened, the scorpions moved in, climbing over the corpses of their fallen. Another claw tore at Father, slicing his arm. He cried out, voice hoarse. A pincer slashed his leg, severing it beneath the knee.

Father fell.

He hit the bloody cobblestones, bellowing, and his runes lost their glow. They now appeared as mere faded white ink.

"Father!" Ayumi ran toward him.

She pulled him into her arms, weeping. He was trembling, losing blood fast. Already his skin was turning gray.

"Leave him for me!" rose a shriek from above—the voice of Jade. "He's mine! His skin is mine to claim."

Tears in her eyes, Ayumi turned to see Jade leaping off a roof. The strange, pale woman landed on the cobblestones with enough impact to crack them, then walked across the street toward Father. Her blue hair billowed, and claws extended from her fingertips.

"Father!" Ayumi turned back toward him. "Father, you have to fight. You can keep fighting!" Her tears fell. "You have to kill them. You have to save me, save Mother and the baby."

He clutched her with both hands. His arms were shaking. Blood pooled around him. He looked into her eyes.

"Fly, Ayumi-chan," he whispered. "Fly like only you can, roof to roof, and leave the enclave."

"But I'm not allowed to—"

"Fly, Ayumi!" His tears fell. "And know that I love you."

His runes glowed again—soft now, their shine barely visible. But it was enough. Ayumi felt the power surge from him. Father hurled her into the air, and wind blew out from his palms, blowing her higher, thrusting her out of the alleyway, up toward the rooftops.

"Father!" she said, legs kicking in midair.

The scorpions grabbed his remaining limbs and pinned him down.

Ayumi landed on a rooftop, rattling the tiles.

Below, Jade approached Father. She smiled crookedly, looking down at the man.

"I like your skin," Jade purred. "Such lovely tattoos. They will form my new robe."

Father tried to fight, but only weak blasts of air left his hands now, and his runes faded.

He used his last power to save me, Ayumi realized.

"Earth calls us home!" Father cried. "Remember Earth, sons and daughters of humanity! Remember our—"

Jade lashed her claws, slicing his throat open.

His head hit the cobblestones, dead eyes staring.

Ayumi wept. She reached into her pocket and clutched her scrap of rug. A piece of cloth. Of Earth. Of her father.

Father ... No ...

Jade looked up from the alleyway, her claws dripping blood. She met Ayumi's eyes. The creature—surely she was a creature, not a woman—grinned savagely.

"Scorpions, grab the girl!" she shrieked. "Bring me the girl!"

Ayumi turned and ran.

She pattered across the roof and soared into the air, vaulting over another road. She landed on another rooftop, ran, leaped again.

The scorpions were everywhere. They scurried across the rooftops, moving at incredible speed. They jumped off pagodas. They landed before Ayumi, cackling, stingers raised.

But Ayumi had grown up on these rooftops. She knew every slope, ever rickety chimney, every loose tile. Today Ayumi flew.

A scorpion landed before her, and Ayumi swerved and raced down the rooftop of Miss Nori's chandlery. Her feet nimble, she skipped over the loose tiles. But the scorpions hit the wrong tiles, and they detached. The aliens slipped and crashed down onto the road. Ayumi swung around the chimney of Masaki's butcher shop, hurling herself onto the watchmaker's balcony. She raced through an attic, scattering gears and screws, out the window, over an alleyway, and onto the cobbler's shop.

Many of the roofs had been damaged. Some were burning. Ayumi leaped through fire and smoke. Scorpions raced around her, covering the city, but she dodged them at every turn.

Father had told her to flee the enclave. But Ayumi was making her way back home.

I have to save Mother and the baby.

She kept running, a thousand scorpions in pursuit. And ahead she saw it—her street, cluttered with homes. Her own home—a small apartment on the top floor. Mother and her brother were in the window, pointing at her, calling out in fear.

"Mother!" Ayumi vaulted over the rooftops. "Mother, I'm here!"

She leaped over an alleyway, soaring toward her home.

One of the dark, triangular starships descended and opened fire.

Blasts hit the building.

The explosion knocked Ayumi back through the air.

She screamed, hit a wall, and slumped to the ground.

More fire rained. The starship was pounding her home with blast after blast.

Ayumi scuttled backward, her legs burnt, screaming.

Her apartment building collapsed before her.

Her mother's burning corpse fell and slammed onto the roadside. Her baby burned in her arms. An instant later, the wall of the building collapsed, burying them.

Ayumi wept as she ran. She wept as she tore off her burning clothes. She wept as she reached the wall of the enclave and found it crumbling, filled with holes. The gates had fallen. The guards lay dead.

She had scaled this wall so many times. Ayumi scaled it again, finding the old grooves between the bricks, until she reached the top and gazed into the city beyond.

Palaevia—this city forbidden to her, a realm of wide boulevards and lush gardens and soaring temples. So many times she had stood on this wall, dreaming of exploring the wonders ahead, only for the feline guards to shout, to fire at her, to keep her imprisoned.

Now the scorpion starships flew over Palaevia, and the airplanes and airships had fallen, and enemy banners draped over the temples and palaces. The banners were as black as burnt corpses, and red stingers coiled upon them, symbols of the Skra-Shen Empire, the color of fresh blood.

Ayumi looked back into the enclave, her eyes stinging. Smoke and dust hovered over her home. Her family was gone.

Human survivors were being marched down the streets. Scorpions were shepherding them through the enclave, up ramps, and into their starships. Soon the ships were soaring, taking the prisoners past the smoke and into the sky.

Ayumi looked away. She lowered her head, and the smoky wind streamed her hair.

"I always knew I'd leave the enclave one day," she whispered. "But not like this." Her voice cracked. "Not like this."

The scorpions shrieked behind her, on the hunt again.

Ayumi tightened her lips and clutched her shred of rug. She leaped off the enclave's outer wall, flying to freedom, to despair, to a life unknown.

CHAPTER TWO

Corporal Rowan Emery sat on the roof of ISS *Brooklyn*, wearing a spacesuit, gazing into space. The stars shone everywhere, and the Milky Way spilled before her like a dazzling river. Somewhere in that spiral arm, invisible to the naked eye, it waited.

"Earth," she whispered.

Fillister, her dear robot, hovered at her side. He was shaped like a dragonfly with glowing blue eyes and delicate wings. There was no sound in space, but he transmitted his words to the speakers inside Rowan's helmet.

"It's beautiful, ain't it, Row? All them stars. Sure is a sight! What after all them years we spent cooped up in Paradise Lost."

Rowan nodded, smiling thinly. "Remember how we used to climb through the ducts to the top of the space station, curl up by the tiny porthole, and look outside? We saw only one or two stars from there. Nothing like this." She swept her arm at the vista before her. "There must be millions of stars we can see from here. And billions beyond them, invisible to the naked eye."

"Yep, she's a big galaxy, she is," Fillister said. "A beautiful bird, our old Milky Way. Pity them bloody scorpions are knocking about, making a mess of things."

Rowan's mood soured. "Way to kill the moment, Fill."

The dragonfly bristled. "Me, a buzzkill? Blame the bloody scorpions. Never did no good for no one, that lot. The sooner we beat 'em, the better."

Rowan sighed. The stars suddenly seemed less beautiful, the darkness between them more terrifying.

"Beating the Hierarchy won't be easy," Rowan said. "They've been winning every battle against the Concord. They've conquered hundreds of worlds already, and they only invaded a few months ago." She shook her head, wincing. "How can we defeat such evil, Fill? How can we stop such hatred?"

"Chin up!" Fillister said. He buzzed under her helmet and nudged her head higher. "We've overcome evil before, haven't we? We defeated the marshcrabs, the bonecrawlers, and all sorts of nasties. We'll beat them scorpions too, don't you worry."

"I can't help but worry, Fill," she said. "I wish we could just blast off toward those distant stars, find Earth, and build a new home there. But millions of humans still live in exile—behind us. And the scorpions are killing them, Fill. Imprisoning them in gulocks. Skinning them. Slaughtering millions." She trembled. "And Jade is leading them. My own sister."

Tears filled her eyes.

Fillister landed on her knee. "I got no words of comfort for that one, Row. I wish I did. Honestly. All I can say is: I'm with ya, love. Through fire and rain, thick and thin. And so is the rest of our fleet. And a mighty fleet it is these days. That's not too shabby, is it?"

Rowan turned around on the roof of the *Brooklyn*, facing the rest of the fleet.

And yes, she instantly felt better.

Danger filled the cosmos. The scorpions were conquering the galaxy, slaying every human they could find. Thousands of smaller civilizations had joined the scorpions, serving lower in the Hierarchy. Thousands of worlds who resisted, members of the Concord, fell like dominoes. But here before her flew the Heirs of Earth. The fleet of humanity. There were still good, brave warriors fighting for justice. For Earth. For humans everywhere. And that comforted her.

As she gazed upon the fleet, she tapped her music player, and the sounds of Strauss's "Blue Danube Waltz" filled her helmet.

The ISS *Jerusalem*, the flagship of the fleet, flew directly behind her, largest and mightiest of humanity's warships. The *Jerusalem* had been a tanker once, alien-built, used to ferry gasses and liquids between the stars. The Inheritors had bought the aging, rusty derelict and converted her into a mighty warship, coated with shields, bristling with cannons, painted deep blue like Earth's seas. The symbol of the Heirs of Earth shone on her hull: the planet Earth with golden wings growing from her equator.

Admiral Emet Ben-Ari himself, commander of the Heirs of Earth, flew in the *Jerusalem,* the flagship and largest frigate in the fleet. Even from here, Rowan could see the man standing at a porthole, gazing out into space. He was wearing the brown trousers and blue coat the Inheritors took for their colors, and a black cowboy hat shaded his eyes. Emet was a tall, broad man in his mid-fifties, his long blond hair and beard streaked with white. His soldiers called him the Old Lion. It was his roar that led them forth.

Several other frigates flew farther back, all named after ancient Earth cities. The ISS *Jaipur* and ISS *Bangkok* had suffered heavy damage in the Battle of Terminus, but repair crews were clinging to the hulls, welding and mending and painting.

The ISS *Nazareth* brought up the rear. It was a hulking warship, newer than the others—or at least, *less old.* Many believed that the *Nazareth* could someday become the new flagship, replacing the *Jerusalem* when that aging frigate was finally scrapped. Commodore Leona Ben-Ari, Emet's daughter, commanded the *Nazareth.* Many believed that Leona too would someday rise, become the next admiral, would lead the Heirs of Earth, succeeding her father.

Perhaps it will be you, Emet, who leads us home, Rowan thought. *And you, Leona, who rebuilds our world.*

Corvettes flew in the fleet too. Corvettes were small warships, smaller than frigates, but just as deadly. Each was named after a small city or town from Earth. Each was the size of an old sailing vessel from Earth's seas. Many corvettes had fallen at Terminus. Leona's charge at the lead of the Corvette Company was already legendary. Even the ten corvettes that served today were an impressive force, lined with cannons, thickened with shields, ready for war.

The frigates and corvettes formed the main muscle of the fleet, but there were many other ships here too. Firebirds, small starfighters built for a single pilot, escorted the larger starships. There was a medical ship, the ISS *Kos*, and an entire ship dedicated to farming, its hold filled with crops and cattle. Heavy freighters, tankers, and cargo hulls lumbered along too, carrying supplies, munitions, and refugees. There were thousands of refugees in those ships, rescued from the horrors of gulocks or the isolation of exile.

Here was a nation in space. A species without a home. A people clinging to a dream.

"What the devil are you listening to, Row?" Fillister said, interrupting her thoughts.

"Blue Danube Waltz," she said. "Strauss. It's tradition. Homer Simpson listened to it in space."

"*Space Odyssey* did it first," Fillister said. "Listen to something dramatic instead. Some Beethoven! Or Mozart! Or—"

"K-pop it is," Rowan said, switching to a new playlist.

Fillister groaned as the high-pitched voices chirped over dance music so saccharine it could rot your teeth. Hey, call it a guilty pleasure.

A fist banged on Brooklyn's hull from inside, rattling Rowan where she sat.

"Hey, what the hell are you listening to?" Bay shouted from inside the ship, his voice reverberating through the hull into her suit.

"How the hell can you hear that from inside?" she cried.

"There are deaf aliens three systems away who can hear it!" Bay called back. "Put on something good."

Rowan rolled her eyes. "Why does nobody appreciate K-pop? You're all Philistines."

"I don't know that what means," Bay said, voice muffled as he shouted from inside the ship, "but that music is killing off my testosterone as we speak. Put on some heavy metal!"

She hopped on the ship, rattling it. "I'll show you heavy metal."

Now it was Brooklyn's voice that rose. "Hey, ease off, Rowan. I'm a delicate starship, you know, and you weigh a ton, dude. You've been scarfing down too many of those pancakes."

"Great, now even the damn starship is complaining." Rowan rolled her eyes. "I told you a million times, Brook, there's no weight in space."

"Sure there is!" Brooklyn said. "Oh, and—can you put on some smooth jazz instead? Some Kenny G would sure hit the spot."

"I'll stick to the K-pop," said Bay.

With a groan, Rowan shut off her music. Between a talkative dragonfly robot with a Cockney accent, a sassy starship with a phobia of ants, and Bay complaining and banging on the ceiling, it was a wonder Rowan hadn't gone mad.

She floated off Brooklyn's hull and into the airlock. When she pulled off her spacesuit, she shivered. A memory surfaced, unbidden. The Battle of Terminus. Floating in space without a suit. Bay pulling her into this very airlock. Gasping on the floor, barely alive. She could smell space on her suit—a smell like seared steak and welding fumes. Perhaps that smell would always remind her of that battle, of how close to death she had come.

She turned toward a porthole. She looked back outside at the stars.

"Are you out there somewhere, Jade?" she whispered. "Did you survive, my sister, when Emet blew us out into space?"

Rowan shuddered, this time more violently. Yes. That was a big part of her pain. She had not simply fallen into space during the Battle of Terminus. Emet had opened the *Jerusalem*'s airlock, blasting himself, Rowan, and Jade into space. The Old Lion himself, her commander, the very leader of humanity—he had been willing to sacrifice Rowan's life to slay Jade. To slay the Blue Witch, the Skra-Shen commander. His attempt had failed. His intent still stung.

Rowan still loved Emet. She still followed him, fought for him, believed in him.

But now she also feared him.

"You might be a monster now, Jade," Rowan whispered, eyes damp. "But you're still my sister. Still a human, despite what the scorpions did to you. I know you can come back, Jade. That you can remember your humanity. If you're out there, don't despair. I'll find you, sister. I'll make you remember home, and me, and yourself. I'll save you."

Rowan rubbed her eyes. It would not do for Bay to see her crying. She was an Inheritor now, after all. A corporal in the Heirs of Earth. A warrior. She refocused her eyes, looking at her reflection in the porthole.

She was a slender girl, still young; she had just turned seventeen. For most of her childhood, she had lived in the ducts of Paradise Lost, a sleazy space station catering to gamblers and drunks. A lifetime of scrounging for scraps had left her short—she only stood five feet on her tiptoes. Thankfully, she was no longer so skinny. Since joining the fleet, she had been gaining some much-needed weight.

Maybe Brooklyn is right, she thought. *I've been enjoying quite a few pancakes from Bay's freezer. I can't help it. The frickin' things are delicious.*

The rest of her looked the same as always. Her hair was brown and cut short and messy, just long enough for Bay to muss, which he did often. Her eyes were dark and almond shaped, perhaps hinting at some heritage in Earth's far east, and her was skin olive-toned.

Her worst feature, she thought, was not her stature but her teeth. They were white enough, thankfully, but as crooked as a two dollar bill. She rarely smiled or chewed with an open mouth, and even when speaking, she often turned her head away, seeking to hide those teeth.

But who cares about my teeth? she told herself. She was an Inheritor now! A warrior! She proudly wore the uniform of the Heirs of Earth. She had needed to borrow clothes from the children's closet, yes, but she had found the right colors, at least. Her pants were brown, symbolizing Earth's soil. Her vest was blue, worn over a white collared shirt, symbolizing Earth's sky. It had nifty brass buttons too. Goggles perched on her head, holding back her short brown hair.

But her favorite part? Her pistol, Lullaby. It was a large weapon, the size of a power drill. It was carved of real wood, lovingly sanded and adorned with brass gears. The weapon was shaped like a flintlock from ancient Earth, the kind buccaneers used to fire, but far deadlier. The pistol hung against her hip. It was so hefty that for the first few days Rowan had walked at a slant. But Lullaby comforted her. For the first time in her life, Rowan had a weapon. Had power. For the first time, she was proud of her humanity.

She left the airlock and entered Brooklyn's main cabin. Brooklyn was a tiny ship. The hold was cozy, containing a bed, a desk, and Bay's artwork on the walls. Brooklyn had originally been a shuttle craft aboard the ISS *Jerusalem.* Bay had refitted her, installing an interstellar azoth drive, cannons and shields, and an AI system.

A particularly neurotic AI, as it turned out.

"Rowan, check yourself for ants!" Brooklyn said, her voice emerging from speakers in the ceiling. "Did you check for ants? You know I hate ants."

Rowan patted a bulkhead. "There aren't ants in space, Brook. I'm fine."

"There might be," Brooklyn said. "I heard tardigrades can survive in space, and they're kind of like ants."

"Brooklyn, she doesn't have ants!" Bay cried from the cockpit. "For Ra's sake."

He entered the hold, wearing his own uniform, except instead of a vest, Bay had chosen a navy-blue overcoat with brass buttons. The sleeves bore two chevrons each—the insignia of corporal. He was seven years older than Rowan, but like her, he had just recently joined the Heirs of Earth, ending years on the run. His rifle, Lawless, hung across his back.

He was handsome, Rowan thought—his hair dark blond, his eyes kind. He looked a lot like Emet Ben-Ari, his father, but slimmer and shorter, and also somehow … softer? No, not softer. There was nothing soft about Bay. But maybe more thoughtful, more kind. More sensitive, maybe. Rowan knew that he was sensitive about his left hand, at least. He often kept it in his pocket, hiding the fingers that were always curled into a malformed fist. Rowan didn't mind his disability. No more than he minded her teeth.

Our flaws always seem magnified to our own eyes, Rowan thought, *even if others barely notice them.*

"How was your little space meditation?" Bay asked. "Come to any deep insights about mankind?"

She nodded. "I did! I came to the conclusion that *man*kind is your concern. Womankind is going to have a shower." She headed toward the bathroom. "I'll sing K-pop really loudly, don't worry!"

Bay groaned. He put a hand on her shoulder. "You'll have to stay stinky for a while longer. My dad called a meeting. He wants us on the *Jerusalem* in fifteen minutes. He said it's really important. Something to do with the fate of mankind—I mean, *woman*kind—and the universe. And I know that womankind needs at least an hour to get ready."

Rowan scoffed. "I can get ready in ten seconds. And I'm not stinky! I'm just … well-seasoned." She pulled off her vest.

"You smell like a seared steak." Bay headed back into the cockpit.

"That's the smell of space!" she cried after him. "It's not me."

"Space doesn't have a smell!" he yelled back, settling down at the helm. "You said so yourself."

"I said space doesn't have *weight*." She groaned.

Brooklyn snorted, entering the conversation. "You said space doesn't have ants, but what do you know?"

Rowan tugged her hair in frustration. "Ants have more brains than you two!"

She hopped into the shower. Within seven minutes, she was washed, dressed, and ready, and they were flying toward the ISS *Jerusalem*, flagship of the fleet.

Brooklyn flew toward the *Jerusalem*'s airlock, and the larger ship extended a jet bridge. Bay made to climb aboard, but Rowan grabbed his arm and held him back.

"Bay, wait." She checked her watch. "We have another minute."

He raised an eyebrow. "Thought of watching a very, very short movie?"

She hugged him. "Just hold me. For a minute, hold me."

He held her. His arms were thinner than his father's, but they were still strong, and she felt so safe in them. She laid her cheek against his chest. Bay was not a tall man, but the top of her head barely reached his shoulders.

"Are you all right, Row?" he said, voice soft.

She closed her eyes. "Every time your dad calls us for a meeting, it's some horrible news. Another Concord world falling to the Hierarchy. Or another human enclave liquidated. Or another Inheritor who died from his wounds. And every time, I get so scared, so worried that we'll lose this war. So for a minute, hold me. Let me feel safe in your arms."

He stroked her hair and kissed her forehead.

"You're safe now, Rowan. With us. With your kind. You'll never be in danger again."

She looked up at him, smiling sadly. "You're a horrible liar, do you know that?"

He laughed. She stood on her tiptoes and kissed his cheek.

I love you, Bay Ben-Ari, she thought. *I dare not say it. But I think you know.*

"Come on, hobbit." He mussed her hair. "We're late."

She gasped. "I am not a hobbit!"

"You look just like one."

She groaned. "If we weren't late, I'd prove to you that I'm elven warrior." She grabbed his hand. "Now come on, let's go hear your dad talk."

A meeting to do with the fate of humanity and the cosmos, she thought, stepping into the flagship. *Well, what else is new?*

CHAPTER THREE

Admiral Emet Ben-Ari stood in the ISS *Jerusalem*'s war room, watching his soldiers enter and salute.

Perhaps I'm seeing some of them for the last time, he thought, his heart heavy.

As always when troubled, he placed his hand on his weapon—a beast of a rifle, double-barreled, the stock lovingly carved of real wood. He had named the weapon Thunder, for it fired bullets with booming fury. Its sister weapon hung from his belt, an electric pistol called Lightning. Both weapons had shed much blood. They would shed far more before this war ended.

His most trusted officers gathered before him. Commodores. Captains. Leaders representing the refugee communities who had joined his host. A few young, enlisted soldiers were here too. Among them stood his son Bay, new to the Heirs but not to war, and the girl Rowan, keeper of the Earthstone. Some of these people Emet had known for decades, others for only weeks. He trusted each one. These men and women, Emet knew, would give their lives for Earth.

Finally they were all here. All but Leona.

Emet saw the others glance around, seeking her, the famous Commodore Leona Ben-Ari. Since the Battle of Terminus, she had become something of a legend—the officer who had led the vanguard, who had carved the way out of the wormhole, forging a path for the Concord fleet. Even in alien civilizations, they were speaking of Leona the Lioness.

Yet Leona was not here aboard the *Jerusalem.* Not yet.

Emet cleared his throat.

"My fellow humans! We stand here together, refugees from many worlds, united in one army, fighting for one cause. To find Earth again!"

"For Earth, woo!" Bay cried out, raising a fist. The boy still had some protocol to learn.

Emet nodded and continued. "Yet while we do not forget our main cause, we fight another battle too. The Hierarchy, led by the cruel Skra-Shen scorpions, has invaded peaceful Concord space. Within the past few months, they have spread through the Tree of Light, the network of wormholes connecting the galaxy. They have won every battle. They have conquered every world they invaded. Before them, the Concord is crumbling."

"What do we care about the Concord?" said a gruff, mustached man, a leader of fifty refugees who had just recently joined the Heirs. "My people and I lived on a Concord world for years. The Concord aliens treated us as pests. They kept us imprisoned. Enslaved us. Brutalized us. You call the Concord peaceful? Bah! I say let the scorpions kill them all."

Mutters of agreement rippled through the group, especially among those recently saved from Concord worlds. Emet understood. The Hierarchy was brutal, but life in the Concord was not easy for humans either. On most civilized worlds, humans were treated somewhere between rat and cockroach. They were sometimes caged, sometimes tolerated if they kept out of sight, often killed. Concord aliens had slain many humans throughout history, destroying entire communities.

They're right to be angry, Emet thought. *They're right to hate the Concord. But right now, the enemy of our enemy must be our friend.*

Emet spoke over the crowd. "Friends! I understand. You suffered on Concord worlds. Some of you languished in enclaves. Others survived in hiding. I do not discount your suffering. It's why I, a human who also suffered in the Concord, founded the Heirs of Earth. But the Hierarchy is worse! The scorpions seek not only to imprison us, to enslave us, but to butcher us all. Already they've killed millions of our brothers and sisters across the galaxy. We survivors must help the Concord fight them."

"I refuse to choose a lesser evil!" said the mustached man. "I care only for Earth."

"As do I!" said Emet, his voice overpowering the crowd. "All my battles, all that I do, my life's purpose—it is for Earth. I spoke to Admiral Melitar, commander of the Concord fleets. He has recognized our courage at the Battle of Terminus. And he has recognized our ambitions for Earth. Should the Concord survive this war, Melitar will speak on our behalf. We'll have a powerful voice in Concord Hall, one that recognizes our independence, our right to live on Earth as a free people."

Another Inheritor, this one a tall, bald man, snorted. "I don't need anyone to give me Earth. I don't need any alien's approval. Earth is ours by right, not by privilege. It's our birthright!"

"It is!" said Emet. "And Earth will be our home again. Yet we cannot neglect this galactic war. All free people must choose sides in this war. All must fight. And we will fight against the Hierarchy! We will strike those who strike us! And more importantly—we will save some of the humans who might still live behind enemy lines, who might still need us."

This time, everyone agreed. Perhaps they didn't like the idea of fighting an alien war. Perhaps they hated the Concord as much as the Hierarchy. But they could all get behind saving more humans. A few people raised their fists, bragging of how many scorpions they would kill.

But one in the crowd remained somber.

She stepped forward, her blue coat rustling.

Emet recognized her. It was Coral Amber, the weaver.

They had only one weaver among them, one member of the Weavers Guild, that ancient and mysterious cult. Emet had never trusted weavers. Their theology seemed laughable. Ancient beings living in a higher plane of existence, sending down mystical aether? Glowing tattoos that could summon magic? If you asked Emet, it was a bunch of hogwash.

Coral raised her chin. She spoke to him, her voice surprisingly sonorous for one so young.

"You cannot defeat the scorpions with your starships, mighty as they may be, Emet Ben-Ari! Only the light of aether can defeat evil."

Emet glared at the young woman. Her skin was dark brown, and white tattoos coiled across her arms, cheek, and forehead, the symbols of her cult. She wore an Inheritor uniform, but she had embroidered silver sigils into the fabric. Instead of a gun, she bore an elaborate dagger carved of white crystal. It pommel was apple-sized and scrimshawed with runes.

"Corporal Amber, this is not the time," Emet said. "We have freedom of religion in the Heirs of Earth. But this is a council of war, not a worship service."

That much was true. Emet himself traced his ancestry back to ancient Jewish warriors. Some in the fleet worshiped the Christian god. Others worshiped Ra, the sun god, a popular deity in many human communities. There were pagans, Buddhists, Sikhs, Cosmians—a variety of faiths from ancient Earth, as well as newer religions born in exile. Many Inheritors had no faith at all; they too were valuable soldiers. Emet accepted them all, so long as they did their job.

Yet he had to admit—weavers were different. Weavers seemed too fanatical. Too dangerous. Too obsessed with their symbols and lore, likely to ignore the reality around them.

Did I make a mistake accepting Coral into our ranks?

Coral scoffed. "Religion? No, dear admiral, I do not practice a religion. I do not rely on faith but on ancient knowledge. I am a weaver, a member of a guild that existed even before we lost Earth. I know the secrets of the aether, the forbidden knowledge of the Guild. And I tell you: There is a great weapon in the galaxy, a weapon forged by ancient weavers. A doomsday weapon. It is called the Godblade, and it can win this war. Do not engage the enemy with your guns. Seek the Godblade, Admiral, and you shall be victorious! But you must seek this artifact with all your haste, for the scorpions seek it too. And whoever finds the Godblade will find eternal glory!"

Mutters passed through the crowd. A few people rolled their eyes. Somebody laughed.

"Corporal Amber," Emet said, his voice softer now. "You said this weapon is ancient?"

She nodded. "Many eras old. Human weavers sought it even during the reign of the Golden Lioness, your own ancestor, thousands of years ago."

"All right," Emet said, "so surely, somebody would have found it by now, yes? If nobody has found it in thousands of years, why should—"

"Its location has only now been revealed," Coral said, interrupting him—actually interrupting him, the admiral of the fleet. "The alien Melitar has given you a map, Emet. A map showing the location of Earth. I've seen this map! It shows many hidden secrets, among them—the path to a planet called Elysium, a holy world in weaver lore. Elysium's location has long been lost, as was Earth's. But now we know the way! On Elysium, we'll find the Weeping Weaver Guildhall, the resting place of our greatest sage, the founder of our order. According to legend, the Godblade is buried there."

Emet grumbled. "Corporal Amber, enough. These are old legends. These—"

"The Hierarchy is expanding!" Coral said, eyes flashing. "Soon it will absorb Elysium too. The Skra-Shen know the Godblade is there, Emet. There are weavers among them. I faced a weaver scorpion myself in the swamp of Akraba. Your daughter saw him too." Coral stepped closer and grabbed Emet's arms. "Forget your war in space, and send your entire fleet to Elysium. You must reach the Weeping Guildhall before the scorpions! You must find the Godblade!"

More mutters rose in the crowd. Some gasps. Many rolling eyes.

"She's a nutter," mumbled one man.

Emet gently pried Coral's hands off. "Corporal, I've heard your advice. I will consider it. Now please return to your place."

"Do not dismiss me like a child!" she snapped. "Don't you understand? If the scorpions find the Godblade first, they—"

"Corporal!" Emet said. His patience was fraying. "I've spent enough time listening to this talk of ancient spells, magical artifacts, and fairy tales. Return to your cabin. Now."

Coral inhaled sharply. She gripped his arms again—and this time she shook him. "You must understand, Emet! The Godblade is real! Aether is real! You're being obtuse. If you refuse to listen to me, I will—"

"You will go to your cabin now, Corporal! And you will refer to your commanding officers as 'sir' from henceforth. Be thankful I don't court-martial you for your insubordination."

Coral's eyes widened. "Admiral! Sir! Whatever you want to be called, you must listen to me. Don't be a fool! You don't understand what we're dealing with. We—"

"Guards, remove the weaver," Emet barked. "Let her cool off in the brig."

Guards stepped forward and grabbed Coral's arms. She kicked wildly as they dragged her away.

"You must listen to me, Emet!" she said. "You must find the Godblade before the scorpions! You must or all is lost!"

Then the guards dragged her out of the room, and her cries faded in the distance.

Awkward silence filled the room. People glanced at one another, then at Emet.

"The weaver is passionate," Emet said. "Perhaps I treated her too harshly. After this council, I'll meet with her in private, and I'll hear more of her tale. But right now, we must focus on the physical universe, on saving our brothers and sisters from the gulocks."

People nodded, voicing agreements, and soon Coral was forgotten.

Bay stepped forward and spoke up. "And what about Earth? We finally know where Earth is! After thousands of years, we know Earth is real, waiting for us. Will we just forget our world until the war is over?"

The doors slammed open.

A tall figure stepped into the room.

"No, brother," said Commodore Leona Ben-Ari, smiling thinly. "A few of our ships will fly to Earth. And I will lead them there."

CHAPTER FOUR

As Leona entered the war room, all eyes turned toward her, and a hushed silence fell.

They still see me as the heroine, Leona thought. *The famous commodore who led the Corvette Company. They don't know how hurt I am. How scared I am.*

On the surface, she was all strength. She wore tall leather boots, brown trousers, and a blue overcoat with polished buttons. Her rifle, Arondight, hung across her back. Her mane of brown curls spilled from under her cowboy hat, cascading halfway down her back, thick and untamed. She could see herself reflected in the portholes. She had a proud face, much like her mother's, the skin olive toned, the eyes dark. If she lived on old Earth, she might have looked Mediterranean, maybe Latin American, unlike her father and brother who were fairer. But the old distinctions no longer mattered. They were all one nation in the darkness of space.

Yes, she appeared strong. She was strikingly tall, muscular yet graceful, and she walked with squared shoulders, a straight back, and a raised chin. She carried the aura of authority and of her legend.

Nobody knew of the pain inside her. The grieving widow. The haunted, broken warrior.

She dared not show them that side of her. She had to be a leader now. She would lead the mission to Earth. Someday, she would lead the entire fleet, inherit this war from her father. The people had to believe she was a heroine, a legend, as strong as a pillar of stone.

Or perhaps a pillar of fire, Leona thought.

In an old legend from Earth, one recounted in the Earthstone, the ancient Israelites had followed a pillar of fire out of captivity. It had led them to a promised land of milk and honey.

Today I must be like that pillar, Leona thought, *and lead my people home. Not to a holy land but to a homeworld. To our planet. The only home we have.*

"I will lead an expedition to Earth!" Leona said to the crowd, crossing the room. "I cannot take all of you. We're not ready to settle Earth yet. First we must see if Earth can still support human life. No human has set foot on Earth in two thousand years, not since the Hydrian Empire destroyed it, butchered billions of us, and exiled the last few humans into space. The Hydrian Empire fell long ago, but Earth might not be safe. Perhaps the soil or air are now toxic, poisoned by war. Perhaps other aliens have settled there, have claimed Earth as their own. The cruel Basiliska civilization, a race of giant serpents, now flies across that sector of space. Perhaps they will allow no humans in their empire."

"Then we'll take Earth from them!" a man cried. "Earth is ours! Nobody can forbid our return."

Cheers rose from the crowd.

"First we must know what we face!" Leona said. "We will not fly to Earth with our entire fleet, carrying thousands of refugees, only to find a world overrun with serpents, or with disease, or with radiation. I will take several brave warriors with me. We will find Earth! If the way is blocked, we will fight our way through. We will not turn back. If Earth is still hospitable to life, we will establish a colony. We will build walls and towers, but also plow fields." Her voice softened. "Thousands of human refugees might need to find a home on Earth very soon. Maybe millions, if we can save them. We will plant our flag. We will make Earth safe."

Bay stepped closer to her. Her younger brother's face was pale. There was fear in his eyes, but courage too.

"And what if Earth isn't hospitable to life?" Bay said. "What if it's overrun with serpents, or what if aliens nuked it, and it's just a radioactive wasteland now?"

"If Earth is truly gone," Leona said, "a lifeless rock that can support no life, we'll have to find another home. A planet nobody else has claimed. Such a journey could take generations. But let's not lose hope yet. Let's pray to find a good, green planet, the home we lost so long ago. Earth is still calling us home."

"Calling us home," Bay repeated softly.

Lyrics from *Earthrise*, the anthem of humanity.

Rowan stepped forward, small and slender. The girl was normally a wallflower, hiding away, shy as a mouse. But now Rowan raised her chin and sang in a soft, clear voice.

Someday we will see her
The pale blue marble
Rising from the night beyond the moon
Cloaked in white, her forests green
Calling us home
Calling us home

Leona joined her song. They sang the next verse together, woman and girl, officer and corporal. Two humans far from home.

For long we wandered
For eras we were lost
For generations we sang and dreamed
To see her rise again

Blue beyond the moon
Calling us home

The entire crowd joined them. Their voices rang out, filling the starship.

Into darkness we fled
In the shadows we prayed
In exile we always knew
That we will see her again
Our Earth rising from loss
Calling us home
Calling us home

The song ended. Everyone had tears in their eyes. None of them had seen Earth—aside from a single blue pixel on Rowan's telescope, an image thousands of years old. But to every one of them, it was home.

Leona stepped closer to Rowan, held the girl's hands, and looked down into her eyes.

"Rowan, you've carried the Earthstone for years. You know more about Earth than anyone. Will you join my expedition?"

Rowan's eyes widened.

"I'd be honored, ma'am!" she said. "To travel to Earth! With Commodore Leona Ben-Ari herself, descended of our queen! To see the green hills, the blue seas, the sky of our home that I dreamed of so often …" Her eyes dampened, but then Rowan pulled her hands back. She lowered her head. "I thank you for your offer, ma'am, but I cannot accept." Rowan turned toward a porthole and gazed out at the stars. "My sister is out there. Leading the Hierarchy fleet. I won't flee while she's butchering our people, while I can still, perhaps, bring her back."

A tear rolled down her cheek.

Several mutters rose in the crowd.

"The Blue Witch."

"Jade's own sister is among us!"

"A traitor?"

"No, the girl is kind."

Rowan rubbed her tears away and raised her chin. She faced the crowd, and her voice shook, but she refused to look away. "Yes, my sister is the Blue Witch, the huntress who slays humans across the galaxy, who leads a host of scorpions. She is evil. There is blood on her hands. Sin Kra, the scorpion emperor, has broken her body and mind and reformed them. He controls her like a puppeteer. But I believe that I can bring her back. And if I can't …" She sniffed. "Then I'll fight her. Even …" Her voice dropped to a whisper. "Even kill her."

Bay stepped through the murmuring crowd and took Rowan's hand in his.

"Then I'm staying too," he said. "With you, Rowan. You won't face her—or anyone—alone." Bay glared at the crowd, as if daring anyone to question Rowan's loyalty again.

Leona looked at her brother and smiled to herself.

Years ago, brother, you lost a woman you loved, Leona thought. *I remember. I remember how it broke you. Let Rowan heal you. Be happy with her. Both of you—find joy and healing together.*

Leona nodded. She came to stand by her father and faced the others.

"The road to Earth is long and dangerous," she said. "I will fly the *Nazareth*, a full sized frigate. And I will take with me three corvettes: the ISS *Rosetta*, the ISS *Stratford*, and the ISS *Kinloch Laggan*. On the way, we'll face many dangers. On Earth herself, we might face war. It might be a year or two before we return with news of Earth—and hopefully a colony waiting for the rest of you. By then, may we defeat the scorpions. And may Earth rise again!"

Bay slammed his fist into his palm—the Inheritor's salute. "Earth will rise!"

Across the hall, everyone repeated the gesture. Their voices rang out. "Earth will rise!"

Emet raised his hands and spoke in a booming voice. "Let us accompany the heroes to the airlock, from where they will depart to their ships. Let us see them off with honor, with prayer, with all our blessings and hope."

Leona led the way, walking along the *Jerusalem*'s central corridor. Doorways lined her sides, leading into the living quarters of refugees. The survivors all came to their doorways, cheering for her, blessing her, reaching out to shake her hand or just touch her coat. They were still frail, haunted, withered after surviving the brutality of the gulocks. But for Leona, they cheered.

Behind Leona walked three captains, those who would fly the corvettes. They were the best pilots in the fleet.

Captain Ramses "Pharaoh" al Masri walked directly behind her. His uniform was sharp and perfectly tailored, and he held a small porcelain cup of black coffee. He was a tall man with brown skin, a goatee, and sharp eyebrows. He looked and moved like an aristocratic cat. He nodded his head at those he passed, lingering to kiss the hands of ladies. Many of the women blushed. He blew kisses to several, sending them into fits of giggles. Ramses was still young, not yet forty, and devilishly handsome. He was also a damn good pilot. Leona had seen him fight in battles, shooting down many enemy ships.

"Do not worry your hearts, my lovely ladies!" Ramses said. "I shall be back, triumphant, a hero for the poets. By this time next year, we'll be sharing hot, bitter coffee by the Nile River, brewed from the best Arabian beans and seasoned with cardamom. Have I told you that I'm descended of the great pharaohs?"

"You never stop telling us!" somebody cried from the crowd.

"And I never will, for their reign was glorious, as shall be our new reign on our world." He raised his coffee cup like a wine goblet.

"Muck your damn coffee!" rose a voice behind him. "Give me booze and cigars. Coffee is for stuck up sissies."

The woman who had spoken was following Ramses, chomping on a cigar. She wore a jumpsuit but no helmet, revealing her wild red hair. Her face was impish and strewn with freckles. Her eyes were green, her nose upturned, her smile wide. She was the youngest captain in the fleet, only twenty-three years old, a wunderkind. Mairead "Firebug" McQueen, daughter of the late Doc Duncan, had been born here aboard the ISS *Jerusalem*, among the first Inheritor babies born in space. She had been flying starships since she was a toddler. Many called her a maverick and the best pilot in the fleet.

"That's right, bitches, we're gonna conquer Earth!" Mairead flashed the devil horns and stuck out her tongue. "Any mucking alien who gets in our way—I'll kick his ass!" She swung a wild kick in the air.

Yes, the Firebug was young and brash. But Leona needed her. She could think of nobody better to fight at her side.

Behind the Pharaoh and Firebug walked the third and final captain of the expedition. Christopher Smith was a tall, serious man in his forties. He was still a captain, able to command a corvette, but was likely to become a commodore upon his return and command a full-sized frigate, the largest class of warship. Many thought that Smith could someday make rear admiral. His uniform was old, his cheeks stubbly, but intelligence and determination filled his eyes. His soldiers called him the

Philosopher, and indeed Smith was wise and well-read, always carrying a book along with a gun.

Behind the captains walked their soldiers, two hundred humans. Some were starfighter pilots, others marines, and some were scientists, medics, and mechanics. A few were farmers. All wore the colors of the Heirs of Earth.

For the first time in thousands of years, humanity has an army, Leona thought. *For the first time, we're going home.*

"Hail to the heroes!" said a young lieutenant.

"Hail to the heroes!" replied the crowd.

They reached the airlock and pulled on spacesuits and helmets. Normally Inheritors used shuttles or jet bridges to move between starships. Today they would jump into space, using jetpacks to fly toward their starships. It would be a show for all to watch. The grand flight of heroes setting out on a quest.

Leona zipped up her jumpsuit, pulled on her helmet, and opened the airlock door. She jumped out of the ISS *Jerusalem* into open space. The others followed, one by one, two hundred warriors diving into the black. Mairead, in a particularly showy display, somersaulted her way out.

The stars shone. The Milky Way spilled before the heroes, hiding within its brilliance a pale blue marble. Leona ignited her jetpack and flew, gliding between the other starships. Warships. Cargo ships. Transport holds. People watched from the portholes, saluting the heroes.

"I could fly the entire way like this," Leona said softly. "Out in the open, nothing but a helmet and jetpack. This is freedom."

Beside her, Mairead smirked. "Not me, sister. Give me a warship with roaring engines, cannons as hot as dragonfire, and a crew of filthy warriors in my hold, all ready to kick alien asses. That's how this bitch flies."

Ramses came floating toward them, wheeling his arms as if doing the backstroke. "Sounds positively primitive, dear girl. I fly with some class. Give me a gilded ship with all the decadence of an Egyptian palace. Murals. Bitter black coffee as thick as mud. A few belly dancers. That's how a pharaoh should fly."

"Ancient Egypt didn't have belly dancers," Leona said.

Ramses cocked an eyebrow. "And how would you know, my dear?"

Mairead interjected. "Because her people built the damn things!"

"Kids, enough," said Smith, eldest of the captains. He flew toward them. "We're here to do a job, not banter."

"Banter makes the world go round," said Ramses. "Well, banter and the swaying hips of a belly dancer." He shot Mairead a smug look.

Leona smiled as she flew. Let them banter. Let them joke. The galaxy was filled with horror, with death and suffering, with millions crying out in agony.

Let us cling to whatever joy, whatever laughter we can find, she thought. *There's always time for joy.*

She saw their starships ahead. The *Nazareth*, a full frigate, nearly as large as her father's flagship. With her flew three corvettes: the *Rosetta*, the *Stratford*, and the *Kinloch Laggan.*

"Many years ago," Leona said softly, transmitting her words to the entire fleet, "Columbus led wooden sailing ships across an ocean, seeking a new world. Today we sail with ships of metal across the cosmic ocean, seeking an old world. Today we seek our homeworld. Today we fly for Earth."

She glided toward the *Nazareth*, and behind her flew her two hundred fellow travelers.

Lights appeared above.

Red lights.

Leona looked up and inhaled sharply.

Dozens of starships were emerging from warped space, swooping toward the Heirs of Earth. Black. Triangular. Roaring out fire.

"Strikers!" she cried.

CHAPTER FIVE

The strikers charged toward the Heirs of Earth, engines blazing, cannons firing, vowing the death of humanity.

Leona floated in open space, only a thin spacesuit protecting her, gazing upon the horror.

They shouldn't be here, she thought. *They can't be here. Not so deep in Concord space. Not so soon.*

And yet the scorpion warships swooped, plasma firing.

The inferno slammed into the Inheritor fleet.

Holes blasted open across the ISS *Bridgetown*, and the starship blazed. Plasma rained across the ISS *Bangkok*, melting the shields. More bolts slammed into cargo freighters, ripping them open. A barrage hit an ammunition ship, and the explosives inside detonated. A massive explosion tore across the fleet, showering shrapnel and chunks of the starship. Behind Leona, two hundred of her soldiers were still flying through open space. Debris slammed into them, and they screamed, their cries filling her helmet.

For an instant, Leona was paralyzed, staring at the destruction.

The instant of horror ended.

She yanked the lever on her jet pack, pushing the engine to maximum power.

"To our ships!" Leona cried. "Earth expedition, to our ships!"

Their jetpacks roared at full power. They shot forward, leaving behind streams of flame. Ahead, the expedition's ships—

the *Nazareth* and her three corvettes—awaited with a skeleton crew aboard. Already the ships were turning to face the enemy.

Emet's voice filled Leona's helmet. He was transmitting his words on an open signal to every comm in the fleet.

"Full defensive formations!" the admiral said. "Firebirds, charge! Warships, give them cover! And damn it, Leona, get your people out of there!"

She raced toward the *Nazareth*, body a straight line, eyes narrowed, teeth bared. She was three kilometers away, then two, then almost there …

A striker plunged down before her, blasting fire.

Leona screamed and soared.

Plasma blazed under her feet and washed over her warriors.

Men and women screamed, burning.

Leona aimed Arondight. It was shaped like an ancient Earth rifle, complete with a wooden stock, but was actually a railgun with enough power to punch through steel.

She fired. Her aim was true. She hit the striker's cannon just as a plasma bolt was emerging. The cannon exploded, and the striker careened and slammed into an Inheritor freighter.

Both ships exploded.

Shrapnel flew around Leona, ripping her spacesuit.

She yowled and soared higher, her jetpack thrumming.

More shards pattered against her. One pierced her jetpack, and the fuel began leaking.

"Muck!" Leona said.

The *Nazareth* was fighting ahead, blasting shells toward the enemy. The three corvettes were fighting too. The ships were trying to reach Leona and her warriors, but strikers kept charging at them. Explosions rocked the ships' hulls, denting the shields.

"Keep flying toward them, Earth company!" Leona said. "Make your way to those ships!"

She jiggled the lever on her leaking jetpack, trying to boost her speed. But the pack sputtered and she corkscrewed through space. Fuel spilled around her, forming rings of liquid. The fuel caught fire, blazing around Leona in a halo, then petering out within an instant.

She floated, helpless.

A Firebird streamed above her, charging toward a striker, only to take heavy fire and disintegrate. Shards rained.

Leona's spacesuit was leaking.

She was dying.

No, she thought, turning away from the *Nazareth. No! I cannot die. Not now! Not after all this. Not before I see Earth.*

She held her breath as a striker swooped toward her.

She aimed her rifle into empty space and fired.

A bullet flew. Leona flew backward—heading closer to the *Nazareth.*

Thank Newton, she thought.

The striker spewed its fury. Leona fired again, propelling herself backward through space. The plasma rained before her, missing her. A warrior screamed below, still floating in space. Two more Firebirds charged, firing missiles at the striker, and searing white light filled space.

Another warrior died.

Another human ship shattered, and the surviving warships battled all around her.

Leona fired her rifle. Again. Again. She was freezing, maybe dying. Where her spacesuit was torn, her skin was blistering. She kept firing, emptying her magazine, and hurtled backward through space. She dared not even turn her head for fear of changing her trajectory.

Before her she saw the devastation. The dead floated. Her soldiers. Sons and daughters of Earth who would never see their home.

Her back hit something hard with a crunching *thud.* Pain bloomed.

She turned her head. She had slammed into a starship hull.

She had hit the Heirs of Earth symbol—golden wings growing from a blue planet—which was painted onto the starship. With her back to the hull, they seemed like her own wings.

She had reached the *Nazareth.*

A striker charged toward her, firing.

Leona scuttled upward, and the fire slammed into the *Nazareth* below her feet, burning the symbol, melting the paint and the metal beneath it. The flaming torrent rose toward her, searing the ship's shields. Leona had no more bullets. She unstrapped and tossed her broken jetpack, propelling herself upward until she reached the airlock.

Below her, the *Nazareth*'s cannons were firing, trying to hold back the enemy ship, but the striker kept advancing, cannons spurting flame, and Leona realized: *It's going to ram into us.*

She had no more air.

She was instants from death.

She grabbed the airlock door and yanked it open.

Below her, the striker glided into the *Nazareth*, almost graceful.

Leona curled her legs upward, missing the enemy ship by centimeters.

As the *Nazareth* shook and jolted and spun through space, Leona clung to the open airlock door. Air streamed across her, nearly blowing her back into the void. Fire blazed around her boots.

With all her strength, she pulled herself into the airlock, yanked off her helmet, and took a deep, ragged breath.

"Come on!" she shouted, beckoning her fellow warriors who were still outside.

They flew toward her, crying out, bleeding, burning. Three men tried to fly around a floating chunk of debris, only for a striker to fire, to burn them down. One woman reached the airlock, then a man, then a third warrior. More died, only meters away. Nearby, other survivors were scrambling into the three corvettes.

Hundreds of Inheritors had left the ISS *Jerusalem* as heroes.

Maybe half made it into their ships.

Our journey hasn't even begun yet, Leona thought, *and already they're slaughtering us.*

She had saved everyone she could. She yanked the airlock door shut an instant before plasma slammed against it.

Leona ran through the warship as klaxons blared, as gunners fired the cannons, as mechanics raced to fix breaches in the hull. She leaped onto the bridge, still wearing her charred spacesuit.

A scorpion was waiting on the bridge, hissing over the corpses of her flight crew.

"Hull breach, hull breach!" intoned a robotic voice. "Enemy aboard!"

No shit, Sherlock, Leona thought.

The scorpion pounced.

Leona swung her rifle.

The blow slammed into the scorpion's pincer, knocking the claw aside. But the beast still slammed into Leona, easily twice her weight. It knocked her onto the floor, hissing and clawing. A pincer grabbed her rifle and yanked it aside.

Leona yowled, struggling beneath the alien. The *Nazareth* was listing, no pilot at the helm. Through the viewport, Leona saw them dipping through the battle, plowing through debris. They glided toward a freighter, and Leona winced.

"Die now, pest," the scorpion hissed above her. His drool fell onto her, sizzling hot, and she screamed. "Your skin will be mine, and your screams will—"

The *Nazareth* slammed into the freighter.

The bridge jolted so madly control panels cracked.

The scorpion fell off Leona.

She rose, lifted her rifle, and loaded a fresh magazine.

The alien lunged toward her, shrieking.

She filled its mouth with lead.

This railgun could punch through steel. The bullets barely penetrated the scorpion's palate. It took an entire magazine to finally shatter the alien's head. The creature fell down, leaking yellow blood.

Leona ran to the helm and pulled the dead pilot aside. Through the viewport, she saw the battle still raging. A striker was charging toward the *Nazareth*. She raised her prow and unleashed the fury of a dozen shells.

The striker broke apart before her, and Leona tugged the yoke, flying over the debris. Chunks of metal skimmed the *Nazareth*'s underbelly. Behind her, she heard her fellow warriors—those who had made it aboard, at least—battling more scorpion invaders.

Leona checked the monitors around her, surveying the battle. Her heart sank. Several human ships had already fallen. The *Jerusalem* was still flying, and Firebirds were mustering around it, firing their machine guns, desperate to hold back the enemy.

The dashboard communicator crackled to life. Emet's voice emerged, staticky.

"Leona! Leona, damn it, can you hear me? Leona!"

"I hear you, Dad!" she said. "Damn bastards broke the comm in my helmet."

"Get your ships out of here!" Emet said. "Continue your mission! To Earth!"

"Kinda busy now, Dad!" She pulled the *Nazareth*'s yoke, swerving aside from a charging striker. She fired her starboard cannons, hammering the enemy. "Got a battle to win."

"You got a planet to find!" Emet shouted. Screams and thundering cannons rose in the background from the *Jerusalem*'s bridge. "Fly out—now! We'll keep the enemy busy."

"I won't leave you!" Leona said.

"You must! You must find Earth. Go now, before the enemy rallies! We'll hold them off."

"Dad, I will not flee from battle, I—"

"That is an order, Commodore! Engage your warp drives and fly out!" His voice softened. "Don't you worry. We'll take care of these buggers. Godspeed, daughter."

Leona's hands shook on the yoke. Her breath was heavy and fast. Her head spun.

Could she truly do this? Flee from battle?

She checked her side viewports. Her three corvettes were arranging themselves in formation around her. They had received the order too.

Ahead, a dozen new strikers emerged from warped space, blocking their path.

Leona sneered and fired her cannons.

"Break through them!" she said. "Charge!"

The strikers opened fire.

Chunks of spinning, semi-molten metal flew toward them. The enemy was firing a new type of artillery, one Leona had never seen.

The fusillade slammed into the *Nazareth* and her corvettes with the fury of gods.

Leona screamed. Her shields cracked. A breach tore through her hull. At her side the corvettes were spinning, pounded by the enemy.

"What the hell are those assholes firing?" Mairead cried. The young maverick was flying the ISS *Kinloch Laggan.*

"Send them to hell!" said Captain Smith, flying the *Stratford.*

"Onward, for the glory of Ra and eternal life!" said Ramses, piloting the *Rosetta.*

They charged toward the enemy, cannons blasting.

Leona's cannons took out one striker, a second, a third. Mairead flew high and swooped, her corvette smaller and faster than the hulking *Nazareth*, and her cannons took out another striker.

But the enemy kept charging. Blasts slammed into Leona's ships, tearing off more shields.

"Leona, Mairead, Ramses, fly high!" Smith yelled. "Fly over them! I'll keep them busy!"

His ship, the *Stratford,* stormed toward the enemies. The corvette swung into a mad spin, firing cannons in every direction like a whirling firework.

"Smith, you crazy son of a bitch!" Mairead said.

Leona tugged back on her yoke, and her frigate soared, engines rumbling. Mairead and Ramses followed in their corvettes. Below them, the *Straford* was spinning faster and faster, a mad top, spraying fire, pounding the enemy.

"You're going to get yourself killed, Smith!" Ramses cried out.

Captain Smith shouted from inside the spinning *Stratford.* "Fly, friends! Fly to Earth! Win that planet for me. Go! Go—"

Globs of molten metal slammed into the *Stratford*, cutting off his communicator. Still his ship spun faster, overheating, whirring like a pulsar. It took more fire. The *Stratford* careened madly, flying at the enemy like a throwing star, and rammed into the strikers.

Leona kept flying, sailing over the battle.

Mairead and Ramses followed.

Behind them, the *Stratford* exploded, showering shrapnel over the enemy ships. The strikers burned.

He died for us, Leona realized. *To let us fly free.*

She looked behind her. Smith had taken out many strikers, but the battle still raged. Her father was still fighting aboard the *Jerusalem*, and other human ships were fighting at his side. Missiles and plasma and bullets filled space. Leona wanted to fly back, to join her father.

But Smith died for me, Leona thought. *For this mission. I cannot let his death be in vain.*

"Mairead, Ramses, you with me?" she said.

Their two starships flanked her.

"We're here, Captain," Ramses said.

"Here and ready to go, Cap," said Mairead.

Tears burned in Leona's eyes. "Activate azoth drives. Forward!"

She pushed a lever, igniting her interstellar engine.

Deep inside her ship shone an azoth crystal, able to bend spacetime like a diamond could refract light. The fabric of reality curved around the *Nazareth*, forming a bubble. Leona's head spun, and she felt disconnected from her body, floating by the ceiling, past and present blending together. She was a child. She was a grieving bride. She was a warrior. She was an old woman. She was time and space and light.

The warp engine kicked into gear.

The stars stretched into lines.

The *Nazareth* blasted forward, engulfed in curved spacetime, flying faster than light.

Within a second, they were millions of kilometers away from the battle.

Leona sat at the helm, lowered her head, and shed tears.

I'm sorry, Dad, she thought. *I'm sorry, Bay and Rowan. I'm sorry, everyone. I didn't want to leave you. I didn't want to run ...*

Ramses flew at her starboard side, captaining the *Rosetta.* Mairead flew at her port side, commanding the *Kinloch Laggan.* Each ship carried warriors—some wounded, some dying, some already dead.

We were supposed to fly out as heroes, she thought. *We fly out as bleeding, haunted warriors.*

"Commodore?" Ramses's dark, sharp-featured face appeared on a monitor. "You fought well, Commodore. You truly have the heart of a lion."

"Damn right, you kicked ass, Leo," Mairead said, appearing on another monitor. The young pilot passed a hand through her fiery red hair and chomped on a cigar.

"Don't you worry, Commodore," Ramses said. "Your father will take care of the scorpions that remained. We killed plenty for him."

"Wish we could have killed more." Mairead leaned back in her seat and slammed her boots onto her dashboard. "But hell, we'll find plenty of buggers to kill on Earth. Lookin' forward to it! Love me a good fight."

I don't, Leona thought, eyes stinging. *I hate fighting. I've fought too many battles. I've been fighting this war for ten years, and I've hated every battle. But I fight on. For a dream of Earth. For a dream of peace.*

The three starships flew on in silence, the stars stretched into lines at their sides. It would be six months, maybe longer, before they reached Earth, and Leona didn't know what dangers lurked on the way.

"May we find nothing but darkness and light on our journey," she said softly. "And then a pale blue dot that slowly grows into a world, clement and kind, calling us home." She wiped her eyes, and her voice dropped to a whisper. "Calling us home."

CHAPTER SIX

Coral Amber, Journeywoman of the Weavers Guild, stood in the *Jerusalem*'s brig as enemy artillery hammered the warship.

"Guards!" Coral pounded at the door. "Let me out!"

Another blast hit the ISS *Jerusalem*. The flagship jolted. Klaxons wailed. Smoke seeped around the door. There was no porthole in the brig. She couldn't see the battle. But judging by how violently the *Jerusalem* was shaking, it was bad.

Coral pounded on the door again. "Boys, you there?"

Shouts answered her.

A shriek tore the air.

Gunfire rattled through the halls.

The scorpions boarded us, Coral realized. *And I'm locked in a prison cell. Damn it!*

The guards outside screamed. Blood trickled under the brig door.

Another blast slammed into the warship, denting the bulkhead near Coral and tossing the *Jerusalem* into a tailspin.

I have to get out of here, Coral thought. *I can't die here. Not now. I must find the Godblade or we're all doomed.*

She threw herself against the door again and again, unable to break it. The brig had once been a regular crew cabin. The door had been reinforced, but there was still a control panel, keeping it locked. Coral tapped buttons, but the panel kept insisting on a password.

Coral had grown up on Til Shiran, a desert world where the idea of high technology was a bucket that didn't leak. Until Leona had rescued her from that hellhole, Coral had never even been in an automobile, let alone a Ra damn starship. Hell, she had never even ridden on a muler; back on Til Shiran, humans were considered lower than those beasts of burden. She could pick locks, but this? Buttons and passwords and electronics? It was like sorcery to her.

But I'm more than a lockpick, she thought. *I'm a weaver, a wielder of the ancient light. No door can stand in my way.*

She took a deep breath and closed her eyes. She tried to ignore the klaxons, the shrieking scorpions, the booming cannons.

"Be with me, ancient ones," she whispered. "Bless me with your aether."

And Coral felt their presence. She knew they were here. The ancients did not live in this plane. Theirs was a realm of pure light and majesty. Here, in this reality, there was only their shadow, only the vast stains of black matter upon the cosmos.

"Let your light seep through," Coral said. "Let it shine."

She held out her arm. One of her white tattoos, shaped like a key, began to glow.

She was a conduit to the aether, guiding it from the Empyrean Plane to her reality. Its power filled her.

Coral approached the doorway and turned on the control panel.

She began to type.

She entered a password. Rejected. Another password. Rejected again.

She began to type faster and faster. Her rune glowed. She typed in hundreds, then thousands of passwords, her fingers moving so rapidly they blurred. She reached tens of thousands of passwords, and the keys were cracking, and—

"Password accepted."

The door's lock clicked.

Coral breathed out a shaky sigh and released the aether. Her tattoo dimmed.

For a moment, she stood in place, dizzy, struggling for breath. Using the aether always left her winded. If she used too much, she was likely to pass out, even die. Playing with aether was like playing with fire—powerful and dangerous.

Finally she placed her hand on the doorknob and allowed herself a smile.

"Yes, these electronics are like sorcery," Coral said. "But I have my own tricks."

Before opening the door, she drew her runeblade. The dagger was the length of her forearm, carved from a single block of white aetherstone—the solid form of aether. The blade was triangular and shimmering, the hilt narrow. The pommel was the size of her fist, so large the weapon almost looked like a scepter. On that pommel appeared a sunburst rune. In the early days, weavers only used one type of artifact—the ceremonial lume, used for weaving wondrous rugs. Even today, thousands of years later, most weavers dared use no other artifacts.

But some, like Coral, dared.

Because I'm more than a weaver of fabric, she thought. *I'm a weaver of the cosmos.*

A rune on her palm began to glow—a starburst tattoo. The same rune as on the pommel. As Coral held the dagger, the matching runes connected, the aether flowing through her and into the blade. The power crackled, raising her hair as if she floated underwater.

Coral opened the door and stepped into the corridor.

A scorpion knelt there, feasting on a dead guard. The beast hadn't noticed Coral yet. It ripped off a chunk of flesh and ribs, tossed its head back, and guzzled the bite.

Coral winced. She nearly lost her connection to the aether.

They are so cruel. They are so evil.

Her eyes watered. When she used aether, she always had heightened empathy. Often she could see an enemy's frailties and buried goodness, bringing pity to her heart. Perhaps the ancients had given weavers this curse, forcing them to gaze into the hearts of their foes, to see goodness there. Perhaps without this empathy, the ancients feared, weavers would be too dangerous, a terror upon the cosmos. Coral had faced cruel enemies before—aliens who had tried to abuse her, demean her, even rape her. In every one, she had felt at least a kernel a goodness, often buried deep but still glowing softly.

In the scorpion ahead—nothing.

No goodness. No pity. No compassion.

It was a being of pure evil.

It doesn't just want us dead, Coral realized, trembling, eyes damp. *It wants us to suffer. It wants us to suffer so much.*

The scorpion finally noticed her. It lifted its head and grinned. Shreds of bloody human skin dangled from its jaws.

"Ah, lovely young flesh." The scorpion licked its chops and shoved the half-eaten corpse away. "This one died too soon. You I will keep alive as I feed."

The scorpion pounced.

Such terror filled Coral that she could barely move.

She raised her runeblade.

The scorpion flew across the corridor.

A beam of searing, thrumming aether blasted from the blade and slammed into the alien.

A hole tore through the scorpion and the bulkhead behind it.

The beast crashed into Coral, knocking her down, dead before they hit the floor.

She groaned, crushed under its weight. She struggled to free herself, finally shoving it off. Her tattoos had gone dark, and her head spun. She paused for a moment, nearly vomiting. It would be a while before she could summon more aether.

The *Jerusalem* shook again. Bulkheads dented. Heat blazed through the corridor.

Coral knelt and fished a rifle out from a puddle of gore. Her insides churned, and she nearly gagged, and for a moment Coral could only breathe, willing herself not to pass out. Finally she straightened, bloody rifle in her hands. She had never fired a gun before, but she clung to the weapon and ran.

Doors stood alongside her, leading into living quarters for refugees. Screams sounded from one cabin, and Coral skidded to a halt and kicked the door open. A scorpion was inside the room, cornering several refugees. One man lay on the floor, half-devoured, while the others wept and begged.

Coral fired her rifle, hitting the beast's back. The bullet embedded itself into the shell but did not reach the flesh. The scorpion spun toward her, shrieking, and she fired into its open jaws.

It didn't stop.

The scorpion pounced onto her, and claws tore at Coral's arms.

She screamed and fell, her blood spurting.

Teeth dug into her shoulder, and she yowled. Her rifle hit the floor.

At once, the refugees leaped onto the scorpion, tugging it back, pounding with their fists. One boy slammed a bread knife into its eye, blinding the beast.

Coral managed to rise, dripping blood.

She closed her eyes and summoned more aether.

She slashed her glowing runeblade, severing the scorpion's head.

At once, she collapsed into a puddle of her own blood.

Please, ancients. Her eyes were rolling back. *A little more. For humanity. For the sake of goodness in the cosmos.*

She could barely sense them anymore. She was a mere journeywoman, not a master. She was not meant to use this much power.

But she felt it. An inkling. A mere feather of aether. She clung to it, and a rune on her wrist glowed, this one shaped like a serpent coiling around a staff.

She was trembling, losing blood, but managed to pass her hand over her wounds. Her rune shone. Her wounds closed.

"Help me up," she whispered. "Please."

The refugees pulled her to her feet. Coral could barely walk. Another blast hit the ship, and the floor tilted. She stumbled toward the viewport and looked outside.

Her heart sank.

The strikers were everywhere.

The enemy starships were pounding the human fleet. Inheritor warships were fighting back, but they were woefully outgunned.

Bullets cannot defeat these creatures, Coral thought. She tossed the rifle aside. *Only the Godblade, the greatest artifact of our order, can cast these beasts back into the abyss. And I will find it!*

She left the cabin. She ran down the corridor, heading toward the back of the ship. Above the thrumming engine room, she burst through a doorway into the hangar.

A battle had been fought here too. The corpses of both scorpions and humans lay across the floor. The Firebirds which normally docked here were gone; the small starfighters were outside now, engaging the enemy. There was only one vessel left: a small shuttle, a dragon painted on its hull. A shuttle equipped with an interstellar engine.

The ISS *Brooklyn.*

"Perfect," Coral said.

She had to get out of this place. She had to find the Godblade. And this shuttle would take her there.

Sorry, Bay, Coral thought, running across the hangar toward the shuttle. *I know this is your ship, but I need to save the universe.*

She was a few steps away from the *Brooklyn* when the shuttle jostled. A scream rose from inside—a human scream—followed by a scorpion's screech.

Coral burst into the shuttle, runeblade raised.

Bay stood inside, back to the wall. He was bleeding. Blood stained his shirt and pooled on the floor. A scorpion was hissing at him. Bay was swinging his rifle like a club, perhaps out of bullets, perhaps just too close to aim.

The scorpion leaped onto him, knocking him down, and drove a claw into his chest.

Bay screamed, then lay still. His blood spilled.

Bay. No.

Coral stared, heart cracking. She didn't know Bay well, but she liked the young man. He had always been kind to her, even when other Inheritors mistrusted the strange weaver among them. In many ways, Bay too was an outsider, a former druggie and grogger who struggled to fit in among soldiers.

Don't you dare die, Bay.

The scorpion opened its jaws, prepared to feast.

A scream found Coral's lips. She lunged and thrust her runeblade.

She had no more aether, and her runes did not shine, but traces of the substance still clung to the blade. It was just enough. The white blade sank into the scorpion's head, piercing the thick exoskeleton.

Yet the creature did not die.

The alien turned toward her, screaming, a sound so loud Coral nearly dropped her blade to cover her ears.

She stared at the scorpion, lips peeled back.

"Leave this place!" she said, runeblade held before her.

The creature hissed, drooling. Blood filled its mouth. Bay lay on the floor, still, maybe dead.

"Leave!" Coral repeated, voice louder now. "By the light of the aether, by the honor of weavers, I banish you from this place!"

The scorpion took a step toward her, laughing. It spoke in a guttural voice. "You have nice drawings on your skin. I will hang your pelt in my emperor's hall."

Coral refused to back away. She held the blade before her. The scorpion was not attacking yet.

It's afraid, she thought.

She had no more aether to summon. She was so weak she nearly fell. But she was still a weaver. Still a human. Still far from powerless.

"I am Coral Amber of Til Shiran, Journeywoman of the Weavers Guild! I am a servant of the ancients, a wielder of the aether, a warrior for light! Leave this place, beast who dwells in shadows. You are not welcome here. Leave now or burn in the Empyrean light!"

It hissed. It took a step closer. She pointed her dagger, and it retreated a step.

"Leave!" she said. "Leave now! I banish you from this place."

She thrust her dagger into the air. Again. Again. With every thrust, the scorpion took another step back, until the alien backed out of the *Brooklyn*. The creature sneered at her from the hangar floor.

"The scorpions rise," the alien said. "You cannot stop this, weaver. Humanity will fall."

"But not today," Coral said.

She slammed the airlock door shut, sealing the alien outside.

Immediately, Coral leaned over Bay. He was unconscious but still alive, breathing shallowly. Possibly, Coral could heal his wounds with aether, could still save his life. But not like this. She was too weary, drained of the power. It would be a while before she could summon that light.

She ran into the ship's washroom, opened the cabinet, and found a first aid kit. She did what she could with gauze and bandages, stopping the blood flow, but Bay remained unconscious. The wound on his chest worried her the most. He seemed to be breathing well enough. Did that mean his lungs had not been pierced, that the wound was not deep? Coral hoped so. Perhaps blood loss was his greatest threat now, not internal injuries.

"Hang in there, Bay," she whispered. "Until I can summon more aether."

Booms sounded outside. Shrieks rose. The strikers were still pounding the *Jerusalem*, and scorpions were still aboard.

She had to fly out now.

Leaving Bay in the hold, Coral raced into the cockpit. The dashboard spread before her, covered with buttons and monitors and levers and switches. The system was off, and Coral had no idea how to use it. She'd have to figure things out on the fly. She hit buttons at random, and the dashboard came to life. Lights turned on. The monitors began to display stats. The engines purred.

And the ISS *Brooklyn* shuddered.

"Bay!" A feminine voice emerged from the ship's speakers. "Bay, oh Ra, Bay!" A camera swiveled toward Coral. "What happened? Who are you? Did you do this? Is he dead? You killed him! You killed him, you murderer! Bay!"

Coral blinked. Talking machines? Truly space was a place of sorcery.

"It was not me, but a scorpion who stabbed him," Coral said, facing the camera. "I can save his life, but we must fly out. Now! Can you leave the hangar?"

"Yes, but—" the shuttle began.

"Then fly!" Coral said. "Fly away from this battle. Fly into deep space! Go now, and I will heal Bay when I can."

Brooklyn hesitated. "I'm not allowed to leave. I—"

"If you want Bay to live, we must go!" Coral said. "I'm a weaver. Do you know what that means?"

Brooklyn gasped. "A weaver! I thought they were all gone. The legends speak of the Weavers Guild. They say you can fight like gods! That you can heal the wounded, even raise the dead. You must heal Bay! Please!"

"Brooklyn, you must fly out—now!"

"And you will heal him?"

Coral nodded.

The shuttle spun toward the exit, the hangar doors opened, and Brooklyn shot outside.

As they raced away from the *Jerusalem*, Coral looked around her. Several human ships had shattered. Leona and her starships were gone, perhaps destroyed, perhaps already traveling to Earth. The rest of the fleet was beginning to retreat. Ship after ship began blasting into the distance at warp speed. Soon even the large frigates were turning tail and vanishing with streaks of light.

We lost this battle, Coral thought. *But we live to fight another day.*

"They're fleeing to the Diluvian sector," Brooklyn said. "Admiral Emet has called for us all to fall back."

"We won't join them," Coral said. "We have a different mission. I need you to fly to the Elysium system."

Brooklyn's camera spun toward her. "What? My comm is receiving no such orders."

"The order came from the admiral himself," Coral lied. "He told me in person. It's too secret to transmit through open space. Head there now, and hurry! Those strikers are charging toward us."

Brooklyn made a small, choked sound, and a deep hum rose from her engines. Blue light filled the cockpit. The ship's warp drive turned on.

Coral grimaced as spacetime bent around them.

Past and present blended together.

Coral saw herself a child in a desert. Saw the scaly aliens laugh as they killed her parents. Saw the wise old weavers take her into their guildhall, teach her the ways of the ancients. And she saw herself an old woman, wizened, mourning a horrible loss.

The stars stretched out around her like strands of aether.

The shuttle glided through different space, moving in a bubble of warped spacetime.

Coral blinked and rubbed her temples, bringing herself back to the present. In many ways, entering warp drive felt like accessing the Empyrean Firmament, discovering a different reality.

When she could walk again, Coral stumbled back into the hold. She knelt over Bay. He was waking up, eyes sunken, skin pale. Blood soaked his bandages.

"Rowan," he whispered hoarsely. "Where is Rowan . . ."

His eyes closed.

"I'm here," Coral whispered, stroking his hair. "Stay strong, Bay. Stay alive until I can heal you."

"I love you, Rowan," he whispered, then lost consciousness.

Coral held him in her arms, not knowing if he'd live or die.

If I fail in my mission, she thought, *we all die. Every last human. I must find the Godblade. I must find it before the scorpions do. And I must win this war!*

CHAPTER SEVEN

The fleet limped through space, battered and scarred. The Heirs of Earth had fought another battle and lost. Hope seemed as far and dim as Earth herself.

Emet stood on the bridge, head lowered, thinking of the dead.

Of his wife, buried on a distant world.

Of the hundreds who had fallen in the recent attack.

Of the hundreds who had fallen at Terminus.

Of the millions who were crying out in gulocks, desperate for aid.

"Wherever there are humans in need," Emet said softly, "we will be there." He clenched his fist. "Those are our words. But we are so few. And so many cry out."

Silence filled the bridge.

Nobody was there to answer.

Emet missed Duncan, his dear friend, but he was gone. He missed David Emery, co-founder of the Heirs, but the man had betrayed him, and his bones now lay in a cave across the galaxy. Leona had flown to seek Earth, and Bay was missing with the *Brooklyn*.

Emet had no way of knowing if his children were alive. They were beyond the range of comms. Had Leona escaped on time? Had Bay fled the battle, or had he gotten lost in the chaos? Were both still breathing?

Emet stood there, alone with his despair, a demon that clawed at his throat.

"No." He placed his hand on his pistol. "Not alone."

He raised his head.

He stared through the viewport, and he still saw a fleet.

They had lost ships at Terminus Wormhole, lost ships in the ambush, and lost ships in many other battles. But the Heirs of Earth still flew. Emet still stood aboard the ISS *Jerusalem*, a mighty frigate. Two more frigates flanked him. Cargo holds still flew among them, still sheltering thousands of refugees from many worlds. A hundred smaller ships, ranging from heavy corvettes to agile starfighters, circled the fleet.

It was a small fleet. Barely an army. In a galaxy where mighty civilizations clashed, where millions of starships battled in the dark, the Heirs of Earth were hardly more than a flotilla of haunted, powerless refugees.

But we're not powerless, Emet thought. *We have a secret weapon.* A thin smile stretched his lips. *A weapon that can win this war.*

He hit the comm on his lapel, calling her cabin.

"Corporal Emery?" he said. "This is Admiral Ben-Ari. Report to the bridge at once."

He could hear Rowan gasp through the comm. "Be right there, sir!"

He ended the call.

In the silence, guilt filled him.

He liked Rowan. She was young, brave, and intelligent. She cared deeply for Earth. Yes, she was the daughter of the traitor, but Rowan was different. She was decent.

And a few weeks ago, I blasted her out of an airlock, Emet thought. *And now I must sacrifice her again.*

He clenched his fists. The guilt weighed on his shoulders. It was a struggle to keep his back straight.

Could he truly do this? Truly lead the girl into danger, into nearly certain death?

"Yes," he hissed through clenched teeth. "Yes! A thousand times—yes!"

The weight would forever crush him. So be it! Military leaders had always borne the weight of their dead. This was the game Emet was playing. Sacrifice a pawn to win a queen.

Rowan was dear to him. In another life, he might have seen her as a daughter.

But Rowan, you are still a pawn, and your sister is a queen, and I'm sorry. But to save the millions, I must send you into the fire.

"Sir?"

Emet turned to see Rowan enter the bridge.

A bruise spread across the girl's cheek, and a bandage clung to her temple. Her brown trousers were torn, revealing scratches on her legs. The girl had fought bravely when the scorpions had boarded the *Jerusalem*, slaying one of the beasts herself. Her hand now rested on Lullaby, her pistol.

Emet gazed at the Earthstone that hung from her neck, the treasure she had guarded for years. He looked into her eager eyes, at the courage and love for Earth he saw there. The weight seemed even heavier now.

Why must the brightest stars burn to hold back the night? he thought.

"Sir, you wanted to see me?" Rowan said. "Is there any news of Bay?"

"I've sent out three space-racers, the fastest ones we have, to seek him," Emet said. "It'll be a while before we hear back. Bay has flown off aboard Brooklyn before. We must be hopeful."

Rowan bit her lip and nodded. "Yes, sir."

But Emet could see the fear in her eyes. The same fear filled Emet.

Had Bay truly fled again? Or had he died in the battle? So many were missing, blasted into space during the battle. Even Coral the weaver was gone. The icy terror filled him. Emet forced it down. Right now, he had a duty to his people. To Rowan. To humanity.

"Come, Corporal, stand beside me," Emet said. "Look with me at the stars."

She came to stand beside him, not even half his size. The galaxy's spiral arm spread out before them.

"It's beautiful, sir," Rowan breathed. The stars shone in her eyes. "And somewhere among those millions of stars is Earth."

"We're not looking in Earth's direction," Emet said. "We're flying toward the front line now. Away from Earth. Toward the fire."

"Oh." Rowan bit her lip. "It all looks the same, doesn't it? All of space is so beautiful, even if it hides so much ugliness." She took a shuddering breath and tightened her grip on her pistol.

"Are you afraid, Corporal?" Emet said.

"Of course." Rowan nodded. "I'm terrified, sir. But I won't run." She looked up into his eyes. "I know that my father ran. I don't know what his reasons were. I know many say he was a coward. I think he just wanted to save me and Jade. But know this, sir: I will never run. I will never abandon Earth. I will fight for you. Always. Whatever sins stain my father's memory, I will redeem him."

If would be easier to sacrifice you if you hated me, if you were disloyal, Emet thought. *Once you learn what I want, you might learn to hate me like David did.*

That old pain and guilt resurfaced.

Of course, David was not a coward. He had a reason to hate me. To run from me. After I …

Emet shoved that memory aside. He had vowed to forget. It hurt too much. It was another weight he would always bear.

"Corporal, look at the ships flying around us," he said. "What do you see?"

"Pride!" she said. "Strength! Humanity! I see Earth painted on the hulls of mighty warships. I see humans who will no longer hide in ducts or caves. I see warriors."

Emet nodded. "Brave warriors. The finest in the galaxy. But too few. Most of us are refugees. Too young or too old or too wounded to fight. We have only a few hundred fighters. Corporal, we cannot win this war with strength of arms."

"Then we will win it with courage!" Rowan said, eyes shining. "Like the Rohirrim charging toward the orcs at Pelennor Fields!" She bit her lip. "Sorry, sir, you probably don't know them. I grew up learning about life from movies and books."

"Maybe courage is enough in movies and books and other old tales," Emet said. "But in our day, we need more than bullets and bravery. We need deception." He turned away from the viewport. He stared into her eyes. "Corporal, your sister is leading the assault on humanity. She is carrying out the Human Solution, the genocide of our people. We cannot defeat her in open battle. But we can trap her. I will set the trap. You will be the bait. And we will end this."

Rowan inhaled sharply. "A trap!" she whispered. "Like Admiral Ackbar flew into!"

"Admiral Ackbar?" Emet frowned. "Does he serve in the Aelonian fleet?"

She winced. "Sorry, sir, I did it again. Earthstone reference." She nodded, and her eyes were damp. "Of course, sir. I will help you. I'll gladly be the worm on your hook. Jade will come to me. She hates me, sir. How she hates me! I felt her hatred, so strong, so hot …" She took a shuddering breath. "But she loves me too. In the airlock, she embraced me. She was coming back to me before …"

Her voice trailed off, and her cheeks flushed.

Emet nodded. "Before I blasted her out of the airlock. Along with you and me. You understand why I did it, Corporal Emery."

She took a deep breath. "I do, sir. You wanted to kill her. You were willing to sacrifice my life and hers. But you were wrong, sir. There is still goodness in Jade. Still humanity. The implants in her skull—they crackled and glowed when she was killing. They're controlling her." Her tears fell. "We can remove them. We can save her. Please, sir, promise me that you won't try to kill her again. Promise me that you just want to trap her, to bring her back alive, not to kill her."

Emet stared into her eyes, face hard. "And if I tell you we will kill her? Will you disobey my orders?"

Roan gasped. She looked down, clenched her fists, then raised her chin and stared straight into his eyes.

"Yes."

Damn the girl, Emet thought. He had not wanted that answer. He had wanted to hear undying loyalty.

His anger rose. His chest tightened. Rowan refused to look away, and now there was defiance in her eyes. She had her father's eyes.

Yet the Earthstone still shone around her neck. And she was still here. She was not running.

Emet felt his anger fade.

He placed a hand on her shoulder.

"Good," he said. "Perhaps that's best. Perhaps I don't need blind loyalty from my soldiers. Perhaps I should not ask a soldier to sacrifice somebody they love, even if I would make such a sacrifice. I promise you, Corporal Rowan Emery, I will make every effort to capture Jade alive." He smiled grimly. "I'm not sure I could kill the woman if I tried."

Rowan did not return the smile. She maintained eye contact, but now sadness filled her eyes.

"I know you want her alive to interrogate her," Rowan whispered. "Maybe even to torture her. She has information about the enemy. She is a tool for you, as am I. Pawns in your war. Know that I understand these things, Admiral. The fate of humanity itself rests on our shoulders. But know this, sir: Jade can be saved. She can become human again. She can be my sister. We fight to save millions. But I also fight to save her."

Emet saw himself reflected in her eyes. A large man. Weary and worn. His hair shaggy and graying, no longer the proud golden mane. An aging lion. Perhaps to Rowan a villain.

Noble heroes cannot save us now, Emet thought. *Bitter old lions might still roar.*

"Go back to your chamber, Corporal," he said. "I'll summon you again tomorrow for briefing. Until then, get some sleep. You'll need your strength."

"Sir." She saluted and left the bridge.

Emet turned back toward the viewport. He stood in silence, one hand on his pistol, gazing into the darkness.

CHAPTER EIGHT

Ayumi huddled in an attic, hiding, praying.

Please. Please don't let them find me. I want to live.

The attic was a place of whispers and shadows. Beams of light fell through cracked walls, sparkling with motes of dust. Holes peppered the wooden floor. A baby bird hid amid the cracked rafters, cheeping, hungry, calling out again and again until Ayumi trembled.

"Be quiet," she whispered. "Please. Hush."

Ayumi cowered in the corner. She almost never left the corner, daring not creak the floor. It was dark in the corner. Maybe safe. A heavy rafter hung overhead, shadowing her.

A few paces away, a hole gaped open in the roof, letting in cold wind and rain. If Ayumi had to, she could flee. She could climb through the hole, emerge onto the roof, yet what was there outside for her? Nothing but a fallen city. A realm of scorpions. Death. Nothing but death.

Ayumi huddled deeper into the shadows of the attic.

They took the others, she thought. *All the humans. The scorpions took them into their ships, flew them into the sky.*

She trembled. Jade's ghostly white face haunted her dreams. Her voice wouldn't stop echoing.

I want their skin!

The baby bird started cheeping again.

"Quiet!" Ayumi whispered. "Please. The scorpions are everywhere. They'll hear you."

The animal kept mewling—a pitiful, hungry sound. Ayumi rose to her feet and padded across the attic. She moved slowly, step by step, fearful of cracking the wooden boards.

The house had suffered damage in the attack. Half the place was charred and filled with holes. And yet a family of native Paevins still lived below. They did not know Ayumi was hiding in their attic. If they knew, would they shelter her, bring her food? Or would they turn her over to the scorpions?

Ayumi did not know. Her father had warned her about the Paevins. The bipedal felines were perhaps graceful, what with their golden fur and gleaming eyes, but their claws were sharp, their fangs deadly. In many ways, the Paevins were like humans from ancient Earth. Certainly they were more humanoid than the scorpions. The Paevins built homes, wove fabric, and had begun to use steam engines before the war.

Yet despite their similarity, they hated humans. Ayumi knew this.

They imprisoned us in the enclave, she thought. *They called us pests. Perhaps the cats hate the scorpions. But not enough to protect me from them.*

She took another careful step forward, wincing when a floorboard creaked. She froze. From the house below, she heard Paevin cubs squealing and laughing. They were playing a rowdy game despite the scorpion invaders in their streets. The family had not heard her footfalls.

"But they will hear *you*!" Ayumi whispered, reaching the nest in the attic.

The nest was wedged between two rafters. The mother bird had fled the house, or perhaps she had died in the invasion. Lizards had claimed most of the hatchlings, but one baby bird still remained in the nest.

He was naked and pink, mewling pathetically. His beak was like the soft skin under one's fingernails, opening in search of food that would not come. The bird's bulbous eyes were still closed, the eyelids downy. But the animal seemed to sense Ayumi. He chirped with more fervor. For a creature so small, he was damn loud, like a living squeak toy.

The voices downstairs died.

Then one of the children spoke up.

"Momma, I hear something upstairs."

Ayumi's heart burst into a gallop.

Down the street, she heard scrapes and clatters—scorpions on patrol.

Ayumi closed her hand around the baby bird.

Her tears were hot and salty, pouring down to her lips as the bird struggled in her fist, as she kept his cries contained, as the children resumed playing below, as the scorpions clattered on.

Be quiet. Please. Please be quiet.

And the bird kept struggling. And she kept him wrapped in her fist, and her tears flowed.

When she finally opened her hand, the bird was silent. She placed the little animal on the floor, where he lay still, lifeless. The lizards would return for the morsel.

We are all links in a chain of death, Ayumi thought, shrinking back into her shadowy corner. *Scorpions. Cats. Girls and birds. At least I'm not on the very bottom.*

The beams of light moved through the attic, crossing the floor, climbing a wall, then fading. The night was hot and humid, and the sounds of scorpions rose louder outside—the screeching, scuttling, grunting as the creatures rutted and killed and feasted. A few times, Ayumi had dared peek through a hole in the wall. She had seen the city, once fair and forbidden, smoldering in ruin. Hierarchy banners hung from temples, palaces, and city squares. A few blocks away, the human enclave lay barren and burnt.

Paev had fallen. From a fair, bustling Concord world it had become a planet of the Hierarchy. A world of scorpions and cats, masters and servants, fear and barely any hope.

I'm the last human here, Ayumi thought. *Maybe the last in the universe.*

She curled up and closed her eyes, and she found herself jumping over rooftops, moving through the enclave, trying to find her way home. But she was lost. How could she be lost? She had been traveling these rooftops all her life, but the labyrinth was shifting now, and the rooftops sloped down toward a distant shore. Ayumi had never seen the ocean, yet it spread below her, gray and foaming, and a great wave was rising in the distance.

"Do you know the way home?" she asked a bird.

The creature stood on a rooftop before her, taller than her, pink and moist and wet, its beak like soft cartilage.

"Feed." It stared at her with small, pink, rheumy eyes with downy lids. "Feed."

They were standing in her father's shop. Rolls of fabric hung everywhere, embroidered with dragons and stars and flowers. When Ayumi touched the fabrics, she recoiled. These were not fabrics after all, but human skins. These were not embroideries but tattoos. Weaver tattoos.

"Father!" she shouted. "What are you doing? Why are you weaving human skin?"

She raced downstairs and found him working at his loom, weaving a rug made from skin. From her skin. Her face was still attached. He looked up at her, and he was the naked bird, pink and staring.

Ayumi blinked and sat up. She was back in the attic, and it was still dark.

She dared not sleep again, fearing the dream should return. She huddled in the corner until dawn spilled through the holes in the roof. The dead bird was gone. The lizards had fed.

Ayumi sat in the corner, watching the sunbeams move across the floor.

She caught the lizard, but its tail broke off, and the rest of it fled. Ayumi shoved the wriggling tail into her mouth, winced, and chewed until it stopped moving. She swallowed.

The light faded. She closed her eyes.

She leaped over the roofs, and this time she leaped in the darkness, and the sea was a distant frozen sheet like black glass. The bird stood on a rooftop, watching her from the shadows, ten feet tall and eyeless but still staring. Its stare bored into her.

She woke.

She watched the beams trail across the floor, and she listened to the scorpions outside. She caught a fly. She chewed.

"All dead, I tell you!" The voice rose from downstairs—one of the Paevin children who lived in the house. "Scorpions took 'em to skin 'em, boil 'em, and eat 'em. Mama, Papa, can I have some humans to eat too?"

Ayumi was so weak with hunger she could barely move. But she flattened herself on the floor, pressed her ear against the dusty wood, and listened.

The feline family was eating at the dinner table. The delicious smells wafted into the attic, intoxicating, spinning her head, searing her body. Cooking meats. Stewed vegetables. Conversation. She had to listen. She had to hear the words.

"Nonsense," said the family father, his voice deep and buttery. "They took humans to enslave them. To work them for the war effort. Why kill good slaves?"

The mother of the family laughed—a trilling sound. "I think it's positively delightful what the scorpions are doing. Cleaning this city of pests. Best thing that ever happened to us."

Papa Cat harrumphed. Newspapers rustled. "Good point, darling. It's been nice to live without the stench of the creatures. The enclave was too good for them."

"I told you!" rose the first voice—the eldest son. "They took 'em to boil 'em and skin 'em." Lips smacked. "Yum yum."

"Well, it's more than they deserve," said Mama Cat. "But must those scorpions scuttle about so much? Their claws raise a bloody racket."

The newspaper rustled again. "Yes, well, that's life in the Hierarchy, dear," Papa said. "If you want peace and quiet, you can return to the Concord, and you'll have human pests up to your eyeballs. I say bring on the claws!"

Ayumi kept lying on the attic floor, insects crawling around her, until the family slept.

That night, for the first time, Ayumi dared creep downstairs into the house. The family was sleeping, and she tiptoed down the corridor. She rummaged through the trash and pulled out some fish bones. She ate in silence and shadows, hunched over, feeding on bits of flesh and skin, a carrion bird. She returned to the attic.

The sunbeams moved across the floor and along the walls, and the days came and went, and she wasted away. Her limbs were like the limbs of birds, stick-thin. Sometimes at dusk, when the shadows were deep, Ayumi climbed to a hole in the wall and peered outside. The scorpions were always there, hundreds of them in the city, maybe thousands. Many scorpions had built hives upon roofs, and Ayumi lived in constant fear that they would choose this house.

She kept waiting to see another human. Maybe somebody she knew. Sometimes, in her hunger and delirium, she thought that her family still lived, that she might see them again. She sought them in the alleyways outside, but the scorpions crawled everywhere, and she pulled herself away from the window. Again she curled up in the corner.

When the smells of food rose below, Ayumi placed her ear against the floorboard, and she listened. The newspaper rustled, and the children bickered, and Papa Cat reported news of the war.

A harrumph. "Scorpions took over another star system this morning."

A wicked laugh. "The Corvid Empire surrendered. Well, that's a blow to the damn Concord, isn't it?"

A deeper belly laugh. "Entire human community on Corvidia Ceti liquidated. A hundred thousand of the pests burned, it says."

"Not burned!" said the higher voice. "I told you, Papa. Boiled and skinned and eaten, yum yum."

"Be quiet, Junior, and eat your damn rat. You think meat comes cheap with the war on?"

"My friend's papa says the humans are to blame for the war," the son said.

"Your friend's papa is wise." Papa Cat rustled his newspapers.

"Must you two talk about the war every mealtime?" Mama Cat said, voice close to snapping.

"Well, it's not every day a big war like this rolls through," said Papa Cat. "Whole new Galactic Order, they're calling it. Damn Concord is falling like a house of cards, galaxy cleaned of humans, finally some law and order."

Mama Cat was nearly whining now. "Butter costs ten times what it used to."

A paw slapped the table. "Well, that's the cost of war, isn't it? Paying more for butter sure beats going out to fight. Now, if I were a young cat, I would—"

"Yes, yes, we've heard all about it before."

Papa Cat harrumphed. "It's not my fault I've got a gammy paw and am too old."

"And too fat!" said Junior, and Papa Cat laughed.

Ayumi had heard enough. She huddled in her corner, digesting the news. Every mealtime—more snippets from below. Another Concord civilization fallen to the scorpions. Another human community liquidated.

When she peered out the window, Ayumi no longer saw young male Paevins. The Hierarchy had drafted them all, sent them out to fight in the war. It wasn't only the scorpions fighting now. On every world they conquered, it seemed, they captured the humans and drafted the natives.

Am I the last human? Ayumi thought, sitting by the hole in the wall, watching the rain.

Night fell, and she stared out at the stars, and she prayed to see Earth. Prayed that someday a spaceship would arrive, would carry her to that distant homeworld.

"I promise you, Father," she whispered, tears falling. "I will see Earth. For you."

She pulled the scrap of fabric from her pocket. A piece of the rug he had woven her. A rug featuring the mountains and rivers of Earth. A bird was embroidered on her scrap with white thread, and she held it close.

That night she rode on a great bird, an animal the size of a whale, its feathers dyed with the indigo blood of mollusks, the same dye her father used for his blue fabrics. The bird's eyes were pale and small and covered with a pink, downy membrane, but it flew confidently through the night. As Ayumi rode on this animal, she felt no fear, no pain, no hunger. The scorpions scattered before them, and he carried her to Earth, her painted blue bird, and she fed upon his feathers.

The days went by. The newspapers rustled. The war went on and the Hierarchy kept winning, and the cold winds and snow of winter came. She sat in the corner under the rafters, her knees pulled to her chest, frost in her hair. She thought of nights in her family home, sitting by the fireplace, snug between her parents, a blanket wrapped around her. She could almost taste Mister Hiroji's steaming rolls again, warm cider, and her mother's ginger soup.

The wind shrieked.

The snow fell.

Ayumi shivered, and she moved across the attic, desperate to keep her body warm. She finally found the other hatchlings from the nest. They had fallen behind the rafters where even the lizards did not reach, and they were frozen and pink, and Ayumi thawed them in her hands but they were hard and rotten and inedible.

At night, she still sneaked into the kitchen below, but the fish bones were picked dry most nights. All of Paev, the whole planet, was hungry.

"Once the war is over, the harvest will be rich again," Mama Cat said one evening.

"Blame the damn humans," said Papa Cat. "They're the ones who started this whole damn mess of a war."

There was no more butter, no more turnips, and the fish were smaller, and Ayumi shriveled away. She was so thin, always so cold. The scorpions still patrolled outside, more of them every day, their military bases rising in the city, their strikers forever in the sky. And the snow kept falling, and Ayumi could no longer see the stars.

"Come to me, painted blue bird," she whispered, reaching toward the window, her fingers numb. "Fly with me … Fly …"

Her eyes closed, and she dreamed again. She was flying on a bird through the night, but this time it wasn't the painted blue bird but the naked hatchling. It had grown to monstrous size. The animal's skin was sticky and cold, and she melted into it, becoming nothing but skin. Skinned. Skin 'em. Boil 'em. Cook 'em. Eat 'em. They flew into darkness, an endless voyage through the eternity of space.

The bird's claws clattered.

Her bones clacked together.

The sounds grew louder, and she opened her eyes.

Footsteps.

Her heart thrashed.

"Damn it, I knew it! Holes in the roof, attic almost certainly filled with snow." Footsteps thumped. Papa Cat harrumphed. "Damn humans probably burrowed holes into the attic."

Ayumi was lying in the snow, freezing, maybe dying, so weak. But as the attic trapdoor opened, she managed to rise. She scurried like a scorpion, like a small naked bird, and hid behind the rafters in the back.

She peered around a wooden beam and saw Papa Cat entering the attic. He was a burly Paevin, twice Ayumi's size. His fur was graying and shaggy. The aliens were not true cats, of course. Ayumi didn't know what actual Earth cats looked like, had only heard of them in tales. But she imagined that this was one of those fabled animals, that she was a mouse, hiding, so quiet, daring not peep.

"Damn it, Mama, I told you!" The Paevin peered back down through the hatch. "Damn holes in the roof. Snow everywhere. That's why it's so damn cold." He turned back toward the attic. "It'll cost a fortune to fix, and—"

He voice died with a grumble.

And Ayumi realized: *I left a trail in the snow.*

Papa Cat padded forward, breathing heavily, and Ayumi ran.

She burst out from behind the rafters, making for a hole in the roof.

A paw reached out and grabbed her.

Ayumi screamed.

The beast pulled her back, and she found herself facing him. His fur bristled, gray and rough like cheap wool. His eyes were yellow suns, his fangs like the sharpened bones of dead things left to rot. No, this was no cat. No humans would keep such creatures as pets. This was a demon, a monster, and Ayumi struggled and cried out but could not break his grip.

"A human!" he rumbled. "A human in the attic!"

Ayumi kicked him, but his fur was thick and matted, and she was so weak.

Pain bloomed.

She realized a paw had struck her. Another blow hit. Her eyes rolled back, and she felt him carrying her, his fur rank and foul but warm. So warm. For the first time in weeks she was not cold.

Footsteps creaked the stairs, and he tossed her down, and she hit the floor, banging her hip. The kitchen. She was in the kitchen, the place where she had scrounged for food so many times. She lay on the floor, bloody, head spinning.

"My God, don't bring that creature into the house!" shrieked Mama Cat.

"What the hell do you want me to do with her, leave her to freeze in the attic?" said Papa Cat. "Come spring, she'll thaw and stink up the place."

"Boil her, flay her, cook her!" Junior danced around her, a hideous cat with sharp fangs, mad yellow eyes, and bright orange fur. "Human, human! Good catch, Papa! Yum yum."

Ayumi tried to rise, but a blow knocked her down. She lay on the floor as the burly, furry creatures stared down at her, eyes yellow and bloodshot, paws large and heavy and callused. How had she once thought the Paevins fair and graceful? They were like the blue painted bird, heavyset and strange and carrying her in shadows, calling out with deep, guttural cries.

"Please," Ayumi whispered. "Please. Help me. Help me …"

Mama Cat took a step back. "Get that thing out of my house! Call the scorpions! Hand her in! Get her out of—"

"Calm yourself!" Papa rumbled. "What do you think will happen if the scorpions find out we were harboring a human?"

"Harboring?" Mama's fur bristled and she hissed. "The damn thing sneaked through the roof. We didn't know—"

Papa Cat scoffed. "Try telling that to the damn scorpions."

"I thought you said the scorpions were a splendid race," Junior said.

Ayumi struggled to her knees. She trembled. Her heart pounded against her ribs, and the room spun around her.

"Please," she whispered. "I'm scared. Don't hurt me. I'm not bad." Her tears flowed down her cheeks. "I'm not a pest. I don't want to hurt you. Just let me back into the attic, and I won't make a sound, I promise."

"My God, the things actually talk," Mama Cat said, taking a step back.

Papa growled, fury in his eyes. "I'll take care of this *thing*."

He grabbed her. He bound her with rope, then stuffed her into a burlap sack. She was too weak to resist. As he carried Ayumi out of the house, she could hear his son behind them, laughing, dancing around.

"Boil her, skin her, cook her, eat her! Boil her, skin her, cook her, eat her!"

Papa Cat carried her through the cold streets. The wind moaned and Ayumi shivered in the sack, seeing nothing, hanging across Papa's back. And she felt like she was flying again on a great bird, dyed blue and large as a whale, blind in the darkness, a bird that would carry her to a distant star.

Papa seemed to walk forever, grumbling and trudging through snow. Finally he tossed down the sack.

"They'll take good care of you, vermin." His voice rumbled. "God damn pests in my attic. Thank God for the scorpions. Fantastic race. Fantastic. War will be over soon, and butter will be back. Finally some law and order ..."

His footsteps shuffled away. His voice faded into the storm.

Ayumi wriggled out of the sack, her limbs still tied, and fell into the snow. She lay on a dark roadside. Buildings rose around her, their walls draped with Hierarchy banners. Above she could see churning, roiling clouds, shedding snow like the ashes of burning souls. But when Ayumi, lying in the snow, craned her neck back, she could see a patch of clear sky. She could see the stars. And she imagined that great blue bird carrying her there, taking her to Earth.

Claws clattered.

The scorpions crept down the walls and across the snow.

The creatures loomed above her, saliva dripping, and Ayumi closed her eyes and trembled. As the beasts grabbed her, she clutched her scrap of torn rug. A piece of wet old cloth. An embroidered bird. A shred of her family and a memory of Earth.

CHAPTER NINE

Bay opened his eyes, bolted up in bed, and banged his head against the ceiling.

He winced, stumbled off the bed, tangled the blanket around his legs, and crashed down. At once he leaped up, pawing for his rifle.

"Scorpions!" he cried. "Scorpions attacking! Rowan! Dad! The scorpions are—" He blinked and looked at his legs, then up again. "Where are my pants?"

A woman sat in his swivel chair, watching him. "I took them off you. Pretty undies, by the way. Hearts. Nice touch."

Bay grabbed a pillow and covered his underwear, his face flushing. "Who the hell are you? And what are you doing on my ship?" He looked out the porthole, then back at her. "And where the hell is the rest of the fleet?"

She sighed. "Sit down, Bay, before you fall again. You're probably still woozy. You were hurt pretty badly."

He *was* woozy. His head spun, and he half sat, half fell back on his bed. The woman had removed his shirt too, he noticed, and there was a bandage on his chest, more bandages on his legs.

Bay looked back up at her, blinking. She looked familiar. He had seen her on the ISS *Jerusalem.* A young woman, about his age, but with an older wisdom in her lavender eyes. Her hair was long and smooth and the color of starlight. Tattoos coiled across her skin, the ink silvery-white like her hair. Despite her odd appearance, she was an Inheritor. She wore the uniform, though she had embroidered more runes onto the fabric.

Of course. He remembered now. He had spoken to her several times aboard the fleet. She was friends with Leona. But right now, it was hard to think, to remember details. The past seemed a blur—not just meeting this woman but everything before this moment.

Bay pointed at her. "You're a weaver. You're ..." He rubbed his temples, struggling to remember. "Coral. Coral Amber. My sister enlisted you."

"I come and go as I please, Corporal Bay Ben-Ari," she said. "Nobody enlists me."

Bay rolled his eyes. "Yeah, I kinda noticed that, what with you coming into my spaceship and stealing it." He rose to his feet. "Brooklyn! Yo, you there, babe? Where are we?"

He tried to rise from bed, to stumble into the cockpit, but his head spun again. Coral rose from her chair, crossed the small hold in two steps, and pushed Bay back onto the bed.

"Rest!" she said. "That is *not* a suggestion. I healed your wounds, Bay Ben-Ari, but you still need time to recover. I'm a weaver, not a miracle worker."

"You're a bloody thief," he said.

Her eyes flashed. "I am a servant of the ancient light, a weaver of aether, a guardian of justice, and I am *not* a thief!"

"Well, you stole my pants," he said.

Coral rolled her eyes. She grabbed his pants from under the bed and tossed them at him. "Here. For pity's sake."

He pulled on his pants. "Now will you give me some answers?"

She sat beside him on the bed. "Mind if I sit here? Your chair squeaks."

"I thought you come and go as you please," Bay said. "So sit. And talk!"

She heaved a deep sigh. "The scorpions attacked our fleet, wounded you, and knocked you unconscious. I stole your ship. I didn't mean to steal you with it, but I couldn't leave you to bleed to death on the hangar floor. So I stole you too."

He blinked. "You defected from the Heirs of Earth?"

"I didn't defect," she said. "I just escaped from the brig and went AWOL. Totally different. And I would again in a heartbeat. Because your dad is a stubborn, ignorant old fool."

"You're preaching to the choir, babe," Bay said. "But he's still fighting the good fight. Battling the scorpions. Saving humans. And I'd sort of like to rejoin that fight. Ra, the old man must be worried sick about me. Or he thinks I fled the battle and he's pissed. Either way, not good. So what say we fly back now? But let's stop for pancakes on the way. Rowan got me hooked on the stuff. Buy me a stack of flapjacks at the nearest space station, and I might just forgive you for kidnapping me."

Coral gripped his shoulders—painfully. Her fingernails dug into his skin. She sneered at him, eyes glaring.

"You do not understand! I don't flee from battle. I seek a weapon! The Godblade! A weapon that can change the course of the war. The scorpions are chasing it too. It's an ancient artifact, forged by weavers thousands of years ago. We must find it first! We must beat the scorpions to the Weaver Temple and retrieve the Godblade! Your father refused to believe me. He thinks weavers are like parlor magicians. His arrogance will kill us all. But I will find the Godblade. I will learn its secrets. And I will defeat the Hierarchy!"

Bay blinked at her. His mouth opened and closed several times in silence.

"So," he finally said, "it's a no to pancakes."

Coral groaned and rose from the bed. "I'm returning to the cockpit. Sleep."

"Wait!" He reached out to her. "Coral, wait." He rubbed his aching head. "Dude, I'm going to have to agree with my dad here. Ancient, magical artifacts? Spells and myths? It doesn't sound very ... scientific."

She sat back down. "Bay." She placed a hand on his knee and stared into his eyes. "There's no magic here. I'm not a magician. I'm a weaver. I gaze into the Empyrean Firmament."

"The what now?"

She slapped her forehead. "You really are ignorant, aren't you?"

"About mucking spells and magic—I mean, sorry Imperial Furballs or whatever? Um, yeah, I tend to be kind of ignorant when it comes to voodoo like that."

She groaned again, louder this time. "Ra above! I liked you better unconscious. Fine. Crash course. Listen up, all right? The Empyrean Firmament is another universe. A universe parallel to our own. You do believe in parallel universes, right?"

He nodded carefully. "Yeah. I think so. I mean, scientists talk about them sometimes. But I thought parallel universes are beyond our reach."

"Well, weavers can access the Empyrean Firmament—to a degree. Imagine it as a bright universe, filled with light, hovering in a dimension above our own. It's filled with a luminous substance called aether. In fact, we see evidence of the Empyrean Firmament everywhere in our reality. Dark matter? That's the shadow aether casts onto our own universe. Wormholes? Those are passageways that lead through the Empyrean Firmament. Ever traveled through a wormhole?"

Bay nodded. "Yeah. A few times."

"Well, buddy, you were traveling through the Empyrean Firmament. The light you saw around you inside the wormhole tunnel? Aether."

He blinked. He opened and closed his mouth like a fish again. Finally he found words. "But the wormholes are ancient!

Nobody knows who built them. People say they're a million years old."

"They are," Coral said. "A race of ancient aliens constructed them. They were powerful beings. Eventually they became so powerful they left our universe. Today they dwell in the Empyrean Firmament, where they have no physical forms. At least not how we understand physical bodies. But the ancients still watch over our universe. And we weavers found a way to communicate with them."

Bay blinked. "So you talk to invisible ancient aliens living in another dimension. Got it. Yep, makes perfect sense. How could I ever think it was magic and spells when really it's so simple?"

Another groan. "Ra, you are a sarcastic little bugger. It's not like I can pick up a comm and give the ancients a call. It's not that direct. See, thousands of years ago, the first human weavers were, well, literally weavers. They wove rugs, spun fabric, embroidered garments, and so on. One day they discovered that by using silver threads, by embroidering specific shapes into fabric, they could open a portal. Think of it as a tiny wormhole to the Empyrean Firmament. Using these symbols—which we call runes—the weavers could access the ancients. And the ancients gave them bits of aether. Bits of power."

Bay looked at the silvery tattoos on her body. He pointed. "So those are …"

"Runes." Coral nodded. "Like the first weavers embroidered on their fabric. I have only basic runes. I was an apprentice only a year ago. My current rank in the Weavers Guild is journeywoman. It's the lowest rank above apprentice, sort of like a lieutenant in the Heirs of Earth. Some weavers are masters, even sages, and they have mighty runes I haven't yet earned. The ancients grant us these runes. The wisest among us gain the greatest powers."

"So ..." Bay chewed his lip. "Why do you need this Godblade? Just pray and ask these ancient buddies to smite the scorpions for us."

She sighed. "Not that simple. See these runes on my body? They're called *power runes.* And yes, they are powerful, as their name implies. This rune?" She tapped a tattoo shaped like a serpent coiling around a staff. "This is a healing rune. It's how I healed your wounds." She pointed another tattoo, this one shaped like an eye. "This rune gives me stronger eyesight. Power runes often amplify our own human abilities—healing, eyesight, hearing, strength, and so on."

"So no pancake runes, I imagine."

She gave him a thin smile. "Look, Bay." She raised her hand. Another tattoo appeared on her palm, shaped like a sunburst. "This is a *key rune.* Key runes are different from power runes. Key runes let us unlock artifacts. With the rune on my palm, I can unlock my runeblade."

She drew a dagger from her belt. It was carved from a single block of gleaming white material. It looked like crystal. The blade itself was small, barely longer than a finger, and the pommel was the size of an apple. The same sunburst tattoo was engraved into the pommel.

As Coral brought her tattooed hand near the weapon, both runes began to glow—the one on her palm and the one on her dagger. The blade too began to shine, gleaming as if starlight were trapped inside.

"See how they glow?" Coral said. "That means the rune on my hand is unleashing the power in my runeblade. Now you hold it."

She handed Bay the weapon. As soon as he took it, the light vanished.

"Creepy stuff," Bay said. "So this weapon is an artifact? And the tattoo on your hand unlocks it?"

"A rune," she said, "not a tattoo. A key rune to unlock artifacts. The earliest artifacts were looms used to weave wonderful rugs, works of art that were beloved across the galaxy. Even today, most weavers—the few of us who remain, at least—only use their abilities for actual weaving. But some—we call ourselves *battle weavers*—have been expanding our abilities. Gaining many power runes and key runes. And seeking artifacts."

"And I suppose you can't just build a new Godblade," Bay said.

She shook her head. "No. Only sages—that is the highest rank of weaver—can forge artifacts. No sage has lived in this cosmos for thousands of years. My order has lost the ability to forge new artifacts, but we still seek the ones forged in antiquity. And the Godblade is the greatest artifact ever forged. It's a runeblade, like my own, but infinitely more powerful. The legends say it can destroy entire planets, shatter entire fleets."

Bay leaned back in bed. "So here we go. Back to legends and myths."

Coral sighed. "I suppose. I give you that one. But tell me, Bay, have you ever heard of Chrysopoeia Corporation?"

He frowned. "From Earth? Yeah. I heard about them in the Earthstone. Big corporation in the twenty-second century. If I remember my history lessons, they became the biggest company in history, surpassing Walmart and Amazon. They built starships and mines and just about everything else. They built the entire army Einav Ben-Ari led in battle."

Coral smiled thinly, and a secret light filled her eyes. "They were weavers."

"Pull the other one," Bay said.

"They were! Everything they built for humanity—from warships to refrigerators—that was just a front. Just a decoy. Their real purpose was to seek the Godblade. But they failed."

"Oh, I see." Bay finally dared rise from bed and test his wobbly legs. "So a giant, massive corporation with fleets of starships couldn't find the Godblade, but the two of us—in this tiny shuttle—are going to succeed."

"We have something they didn't. The location of the Weeping Weaver Guildhall." Coral stood up, grabbed his arms, and stared into his eyes. "The planet Elysium. It's a holy place. It was there that Gadriel the Good, the greatest of weavers, lived and worked and forged his artifacts. For thousands of years, nobody knew where the Weeping Weaver Guildhall is. But now we know! I saw its location on map Admiral Melitar gave your father. But we must hurry. The scorpions are racing forward. They too will be seeking the Godblade."

He frowned. "There are scorpion weavers?"

Her eyes darkened, and she looked away. "Yes. I would not have believed it myself. But I saw one. In the swamps of Akraba. Your sister and I battled it." She looked back into Bay's eyes. "His name was Sartak. He is the scorpion who killed Jake Hawkins, your brother-in-law. I saw him, Bay. I fought him. A scorpion with a white shell—white like my hair. When weavers gain their first rune, their hair turns white. With scorpions, it's their shell. I saw the power runes on that shell. If there is one weaver scorpion, there will be more." She shuddered. "We must find the Godblade first."

Bay had to lean against the wall. "So these ancients of yours. They're not too picky about who to bless, are they? I mean, if they're giving power to scorpions too."

She sighed. "There is a truth I don't like contemplating, let alone speaking of. But Bay … not all the ancients are benevolent. They too have nations, empires, good and evil. The ancient I speak to is named Sandalphon, and he is wise and kind. But there are ancients who are evil beyond what you can imagine, creatures of searing fire and eternal torment." She shuddered. "As there is a war waging in our universe, there is a war raging in the Empyrean Firmament as well. All that happens in our universe is a shadow of theirs."

Bay's head hurt. He was skeptical about all this. And yet, he had seen Coral's runes glow. And she had healed his wounds. When he peeked under his bandages the cuts seemed weeks old already. There was true power to her. Could she be speaking truth?

Bay heaved a sigh. "Brooklyn is going to freak out. I assume you placed her in sleep mode, yes?"

Coral nodded. "I had to. She was babbling on about ants."

Bay couldn't help it. He laughed. "Oh Ra. Oh Ra above. Giant scorpions are flowing across the galaxy, I'm on a quest with a crazy tattooed lady to find a magic sword, there are ancient angels and demons of eternal fire living above us, and my talking starship has a phobia of ants. What the hell happened to my life?"

Coral laughed too. An actual laugh that made her seem almost like a normal human. She embraced him.

"It's crazy, Bay. I know. But thank you. For being here. For not strangling me for stealing your starship. And your pants."

"And my sanity." A sudden shadow seemed to pass over him, a chill to his belly, a tremble to his heart. "Coral, I don't remember how the battle ended. My family. Rowan. Are they … Did you see …?"

"When I left, they were still alive," Coral said. "The other starships were fleeing the battle. I don't know how it ended."

Brooklyn was flying on autopilot through warped space. Bay could see the curve of starlight through the portholes. They were too far to communicate with the other Inheritors now. Even a signal broadcast at light speed would never catch up with the fleet. Some starships had wormhole generators, able to open tiny tunnels—only a few atoms wide—to other ships and communicate faster than light. Some ships used quantum entanglement portals to communicate instantly across any distance. Such devices were called ansibles, and they were tremendously expensive. Even the *Jerusalem* didn't have such technology, let alone little Brooklyn. They were all alone here, cut off from the rest of humanity.

Worry for his family and friends filled Bay like bad grog.

I miss you, Dad, Leona, Rowan. I miss all of you. Stay safe.

He looked back at Coral.

"I don't suppose you have a walkie-talkie rune, do you?" Bay said.

She shook her head. "Sorry. No runes for pancakes or walkie-talkies. Our best hope for saving the others is to find the Godblade. We will return with it to the Heirs of Earth. We will have a weapon that can defeat the scorpions—and any other enemy of humanity."

Bay looked into her lavender eyes. There was a strange light there, a deep eagerness, and Bay wondered. *Are you truly interested in saving humanity, Coral Amber, or in the secrets of your order? Where do your loyalties lie—with Earth or with the Weavers Guild?*

He did not know, and he dared not ask.

"All right." He nodded. "I think it's time to wake up Brook. She can navigate a hell of a lot better when she's awake. Just get ready for her to freak out."

Bay and Coral stepped into the cockpit and took the two seats. Space spread out before them, and the galaxy's spiral arm shone above, smeared through the warp bubble. They woke up Brooklyn and spent a few moments calming her down, assuring her that no ants were aboard. Then they flew onward. They flew across the light-years. They flew toward the front line—toward the scorpions, toward a distant world with an ancient temple, toward myth and the hope of humanity.

CHAPTER TEN

The three starships flew across the darkness, seeking a distant blue world, and the enemy followed.

Leona sat on the bridge of the *Nazareth*, flooring her throttle. The frigate surged forward, rattling and grumbling. The *Nazareth* used to be a cargo freighter, and she was still slow and lumbering. And the enemy was inching closer every hour.

"Damn it," Leona muttered.

She glanced at the controls. The strikers were too far to see with the naked eye, but they appeared as dark triangles on her monitor. Fifty of them. Too many for Leona and her companion ships—two small corvettes—to defeat.

The strikers inched closer.

Every time she looked, the bastards were closer.

Damn.

"I'm telling you, Commodore, you should abandon that flying mule cart of yours. It's slowing us down. Who needs a big, slow, lumbering frigate? Come fly with me aboard the splendorous and speedy ISS *Rosetta*! She flies with the grace of a pharaoh's chariot."

The voice emerged through her speakers, rich and smooth as aged wine, coming from the starship to her left.

Leona looked out the viewport. She could see the *Rosetta* flying there. She was a slender, graceful corvette, and her captain had painted her hull with ancient Egyptian hieroglyphs. The *Rosetta* was barely larger than the ship Columbus had sailed thousands of years ago—smaller than the lumbering *Nazareth* which Leona was flying. *Rosetta* was just large enough to be considered a warship, but small enough to be fast and agile, almost as fast as a starfighter.

Captain Ramses "Pharaoh" al Masri sat on the *Rosetta*'s bridge. He waved at Leona through a porthole.

Leona tapped her controls, initiating a video feed. The Pharaoh's face appeared on the monitor before her—dark and sharp, ending with a pointy beard. A handsome face, but there was always something cocky about those arched eyebrows.

"You've suggested that already, Pharaoh," Leona said. "And I said no. We need the *Nazareth*. She's the toughest ship we have."

Ramses raised a small, porcelain cup of steaming coffee. "And the slowest." He took a sip and sighed with satisfaction. "Ah, perfect! Thick and black and seasoned with cardamom." He lowered the cup. "Sooner or later, Commodore, those scorpions are going to catch us. Now, you know me. A proper pharaoh is always up for a fight. And yet I feel some discretion behooves us. If Earth is truly our mission, we need speed more than firepower. A wise pharaoh, like any wise leader, chooses his battles."

A snort sounded through the comm—coming from the second corvette, the one that flew to Leona's right.

A new voice emerged through the speakers. "Well, I must be a Ra damn idiot, because I say we fight every last mucking scorpion. Choose battles? To hell with that! I'll fight 'em all, anywhere, anytime. Speed's only good for one thing—charging at the enemy, all guns blazing. Say the word, Commodore, and I'll blast those scorpions so hard they'll regret ever hatching."

Another monitor flickered to life, and Mairead appeared on the screen, chomping on a cigar. Her fiery red hair was in disarray, and she had smeared war paint beneath her green eyes—but not enough to hide the freckles that covered her impish face. She rested her feet on the dashboard, and she was twirling a pistol in her hand. She blew a ring of smoke.

Each captain was allowed to customize his or her ship, and Mairead had painted flames across the *Kinloch Laggan*, a snarling mouth filled with teeth, and furious eyes. Mairead had claimed it was the Loch Ness monster, but it looked more like a dragon. In either case, it suited the Firebug.

"We've been over this," Leona said. "Ramses, we're not ditching the *Nazareth*. There will be enemies on the way. The *Nazareth* might be slow, but she's tough as nails with furious firepower. Mairead, we're not engaging the enemy yet. I know you're eager for a fight. But we're three warships. They have fifty."

Mairead snorted and puffed out more smoke. She scratched her chin. "Hell, I've faced worse odds. I'll take 'em all out myself. You two can keep choosing your battles."

Ramses sipped his coffee. "As much as I'd love to watch your freckled posterior kicked in a fight, we need your ship. For the true battle—the battle for Earth. Fighting scorpions is for other Inheritors now. We're on the mission to Earth."

"Well, ain't this a pickle." Mairead cracked open a bottle of beer with her teeth. "The Commodore says we can't fight. But the scorpions will catch us soon. She says we can't ditch that giant turtle she's flying. So we can't outrun the bastards." She looked at Leona. "So what'll be, Curly? Fight or flight? You gotta choose one."

Leona glared at the younger woman. "Captain McQueen, you might be a wunderkind, a maverick pilot, and the youngest Inheritor to ever command a warship, but you will still call me *Commander* or *ma'am*. Not *Curly*." She passed a hand through her hair. "Besides, my hair is wavy, not curly."

Mairead snorted. "Ma'am, I've seen fewer curls on a pig's ass. Pardon my French."

Ramses took another sip. "So crude. Your mouth is filthy."

Mairead leaped to her feet and raised her fists. "Say it to my face, mate. I'll smash your mouth across space!"

The Pharaoh scoffed. "Firebug, if I were face to face with you now, rather than talking through the comm, I wouldn't smash your mouth. I'd wash it out with soap."

"That does it!" Mairead grabbed her yoke, tilting her corvette toward the *Rosetta.* "I can't smash your mouth, but I can smash your Ra damn flying piece of—"

"Enough!" Leona roared. "Captain McQueen, resume formation or I will relieve you of duty!"

"But—"

"Silence!" Leona said. "Damn it, McQueen, you are a captain in the Heirs of Earth, not a street fighter." When Ramses chuckled, she spun toward him and glared. "And you should know better than to goad her, Pharaoh."

Ramses had the grace to look remorseful. "I suppose you're right." He set down his porcelain cup. "We're all edgy, torn between fleeing and fighting. So what *is* the plan, Commodore? Which path do we choose—fleeing, as I recommend, or a fight that will almost certainly end with our deaths, as the crazy little imp suggests?"

"You better believe I'm crazy, you bastard." Mairead glared through her viewport. "They call me the Firebug, and I'll burn your ass if you ever try me again."

"Splendid." Ramses poured himself another cup of coffee and swallowed. He seemed to be swallowing a retort as well.

"Yes, we're slower than the scorpions," Leona said. "Yes, yes, Ramses, close your mouth—fine, *I* am slower than the scorpions. So we'll lose them in the wormholes. We're near a wormhole portal. We can be there within hours. We'll shake them off along the Wormhole Road."

"If we can get there fast enough," Ramses muttered.

They raced onward at top speed.

Three warships. Inside them—over a hundred warriors and a handful of starfighters. Before them—the vast emptiness of space.

Even flying as fast as they could, even using the wormholes, even if everything went smoothly, Earth was still six months away. It seemed an infinity.

They flew in silence.

Leona checked her monitor.

The strikers were closer.

Damn it.

She reduced life support to a minimum. She carried a hundred warriors in her hold, and she moved them to one section, then shut down life support entirely in the other rooms. She switched off her cannons. After a moment's hesitation, she switched off power to the shields too, disabling the electromagnetic field that surrounded the graphene plates. She figured she could withstand a few hours of space dust hitting her. Every drop of power she could squeeze out—she diverted to the engines. To speed.

And the strikers were closer still.

She should never have flown on this mission in a full-sized frigate. Her father needed the *Nazareth*, a heavy warship. She needed small, fast vessels. A mistake. A damn mistake. But she could not turn back now. And she would not abandon this ship, not a single cannon or missile or soldier.

Our mission is Earth. A fight might await there. And I will arrive well armed.

"Commodore." Ramses on the comm again. "Those strikers—"

"I know, I know!" Leona said.

"I hate to pester," Ramses said, "but according to my calculations, even at this speed, we're still an hour away from the nearest wormhole. And the enemy will be upon us in fifty minutes."

"So it's a fight." Mairead joined the call. She had replaced her cigar with a strip of jerky. She ripped off a piece like a wolf ripping flesh off a bone. "I'm ready. Let's show those bastards human pride."

Ramses winced. "There is no pride in how you're devouring that cheap meat. On my ship, we enjoy fine dining. I cook for my troops—all the delicacies of ancient Egypt."

Mairead belched and flipped him off. "Cook this."

The Pharaoh winced. "What are the Inheritors coming to? Riffraff piloting starships. Heavens above, how standards here have fallen. This would have not passed along the Nile, I can tell you that."

Leona tried to ignore them. She ran her own calculations.

Her heart sank.

"Captains," she said, "looks like you both get your wishes. New plan: fight *and* flight."

"Um, yay?" Mairead said. "Boo?"

"The scorpions are gonna hit us ten minutes before we reach the wormhole," Leona said. "That means that for ten minutes, we're gonna fight them—while simultaneously fleeing toward the wormhole. Fight *and* flight."

"Well, my dear Firebug, we should both be happy," Ramses said.

"Don't wet your pants in the battle, mate." Mairead tore off another strip of meat.

"I assure you, my darling, my pants are quiet safe unless there are lovely ladies around. And aside from Leona Ben-Ari, who is my commanding officer, I see none."

Mairead rolled her eyes. "Haha, very funny, Casanova. What say we make it interesting? Whoever kills more scorpions wins. Loser pays ten scryls for each scorpion less killed—fewer killed, that is—than the other person killed scorpions, if you subtract the total number of scorpions killed."

Ramses blinked at her. "I have no idea what you just said, my dear. But I'm on. I'm Egyptian, after all. We've been killing scorpions for thousands of years."

"Yeah, well, this ain't your ancient desert, mate. I'm going to kick your backside so hard that—"

"Enough," Leona said. "This isn't a game. These scorpions have killed millions of our people. Millions still need us. This isn't a time for banter."

Both captains were quiet for a long moment.

Finally it was Mairead who spoke. For once, her voice was soft. "Ma'am, I've seen the Earthstone. I know about the genocides humanity faced in the past. I know how serious this is. I know how mucking awful things are. Humor is how I cope with the terror."

Ramses lowered his head, sounding unusually contrite. "Yes, perhaps I too have been using humor as a defense mechanism. My homeland on ancient Earth fell, and all that remains is memory. We all lost our home. We all lost Earth." He raised his chin and squared his shoulders. "But we will regain it. We, my friends, will be the first humans in two thousand years to set foot on Earth. I believe this. The enemy cannot stop us. Nobody can."

They flew onward.

The minutes ticked by.

And the enemy drew closer and closer.

Leona diverted power back to her cannons and shields. The three warships took defensive positions. Battle was near.

She left the bridge.

She walked down a corridor, boots thumping. She passed by the hangar, where her Firebirds waited, then stepped into the hold.

A hundred warriors were there. The best and bravest Inheritors. They ranged in age from youths to graybeards. They wore no proper uniforms, just assorted garments. Brown trousers, cargo pants, leggings, even a skirt or two. Blue shirts, vests, cloaks, and coats. Most of the clothes were second or third hand. Some of these warriors were bald, others had long shaggy hair, A few sported Mohawks and piercings and tattoos. They carried a variety of weapons, no two alike—rifles, pistols, even swords and hammers. The Heirs of Earth were rebels and refugees, not a true military, and they scavenged and scrounged for their uniforms and weapons. But to Leona, they were the best warriors in the galaxy.

"Inheritors," she said. "I handpicked every one of you to accompany me to Earth. Yet the scorpions seek to slay us before we reach our homeland. Within moments, they will be upon us. They will attack. They will try to board us. Perhaps they will make it into our ships. But we will fight them! We will never surrender! For Earth!"

"For Earth!" they cried, voices thundering across the *Nazareth.*

When Leona returned to the bridge, the strikers were only minutes away.

"All Firebirds—launch!" she said. "All warships—prepare to give our birds cover!"

The *Nazareth* opened her hangar. The Firebirds emerged. The *Kinloch Laggan* and *Rosetta* each released two Firebirds of their own. The dozen starfighters took battle formation.

Klaxons began to blare. Red lights flashed.

Leona could see them now, closing in rapidly in her rear viewport.

Fifty strikers.

Leona's throat tightened. She forced herself to swallow.

Fifty strikers. Each the size of the *Nazareth.* Each a machine built to kill humans.

Her hands shook.

She was back on the beach. Seventeen years old. A grieving bride. Blood on her thighs and her husband dead and tears on her cheeks and—

No.

She inhaled sharply.

That was eleven years ago. I am a woman now. A commodore. A warrior for Earth. And I will see my homeworld again.

The strikers stormed closer.

Blasts of plasma hurled forth.

The Firebirds charged.

Leona gripped the *Nazareth*'s yoke, flying as fast as she could as the battle exploded around her.

CHAPTER ELEVEN

They fled, and they fought, and fire filled the darkness.

Ten minutes to the wormhole.

The strikers stormed toward them, plasma roaring, and the inferno bathed the sterns of the human warships. The ships fired their back cannons, shelling the enemy. The Firebirds charged, unleashing missiles. Plasma washed over a starfighter, and it burned and shattered, and missiles and shells exploded against the dark hulls of the scorpion ships.

Leona leaned on her throttle, desperate for more speed. She still raced forward, moving as fast as she could. No power to the front shields or cannons. Barely any life support. She kept firing as she raced across the darkness.

Another Firebird burned. The pilot screamed into the comm, then went silent.

Nine minutes to the wormhole.

More blasts hit the warships. The *Nazareth* shook. The strikers were closer now, right on their tail, meters away, nearly ramming into them. Leona fired shell after shell, pounding them back. Plasma washed across the two corvettes, burning their sterns.

"That does it!" Mairead shouted, spinning the *Kinloch Laggan* toward the enemy.

"Damn it, Captain McQueen, keep flying toward the wormhole!" Leona said.

"I am!" she shouted. "Fight *and* flight, remember?"

The *Kinloch Laggan* began firing her front cannons, pounding the enemy with full fury. Every blast propelled the corvette backward—toward the wormhole.

"I'm with you, Firebug!" Ramses said, spinning the *Rosetta* around. His cannons joined the bombardment.

"Bullshit!" Mairead shouted. "You only want to beat me at killing them!"

Her corvette soared, spun over a striker, swooped, and fired a barrage of missiles into the enemy's exhaust pipes.

The striker exploded, showering shards of metal across space.

Mairead whooped.

As the two corvettes fought, Leona focused on flying toward that wormhole.

"Remember, it's fight and *flight*!" she shouted.

Five minutes to the wormhole.

Leona still couldn't see it. But she kept flying. She was almost there.

Another Firebird exploded.

Mairead screamed as a striker pounded the *Kinloch Laggan*, tossing her corvette into a tailspin.

Leona frowned and leaned on the throttle, willing the ship to go faster.

"Come on, come—"

A striker rammed into her.

The *Nazareth* jolted forward.

Another striker slammed into their side.

The enemy warship extended spinning, shrieking drills.

Sparks rose from the *Nazareth*'s hull.

Three minutes to the wormhole.

Three eternities.

"Scorpions aboard!" rose a cry from the hold. Gunfire rang through the frigate.

Bolts slammed into the *Rosetta*. The corvette spun madly, hull breached. The *Kinloch Laggan* was trying to right itself, but enemies rammed her. The strikers were everywhere. A Firebird crashed onto the *Nazareth* and burned against the hull. A striker charged overhead, another from below. Both came to fly before the *Nazareth*. Leona screamed as she plowed into them, and the frigate shook and burned.

Two minutes to the wormhole.

She fired her cannons. Again. Again. Desperate to knock the strikers aside. She drove between them, and her shields screeched, and their plasma washed over her viewport.

Leona fired shell after shell.

Ramses and Mairead came from above and below, slamming into the strikers, finally knocking them back.

Ahead she saw it.

The wormhole.

From here—a distant light, barely more than a star.

Just a minute away. Just an eternity.

She stormed forth.

Behind her—a clatter. A screech.

A scorpion burst onto the bridge.

Leona spun around and raised her rifle.

The creature leaped toward her.

She fired.

The bullet hit.

The scorpion slammed into Leona, snapping its jaws, knocking her against the helm.

The *Nazareth* swerved madly, slamming into the *Rosetta*.

"Commodore!" Ramses said through the comm.

"Ra damn scorpion on my bridge!" Leona cried.

A claw lashed at her. She screamed and swung her barrel into the creature's head. It didn't even leave a dent.

"I will wear your skin, Leona Ben-Ari," it hissed.

She tried to aim her rifle, but the barrel was too long. A claw pinned her arm down. The scorpion opened its jaws, ready to feed.

Leona reached into her boot, pulled out her pistol, and fired into the open jaws.

The scorpion's brains splattered the wall.

The sounds of battle still rose from the hold. There were more scorpions deeper in the ship. The marines would have to handle them. Leona rose to her feet, bleeding, and limped toward the controls.

The wormhole loomed ahead, only seconds away, a glowing sphere.

Leona grabbed the yoke and raised the ship's prow.

A striker slammed into the *Nazareth*, nudging her off course.

Leona howled and tugged the yoke with all her strength. She skimmed the edge of the wormhole, fell out into open space, then blasted her cannons.

The shells flew, shoving the warship back toward the portal.

For an instant, Leona saw the two corvettes ahead, fighting the strikers.

The *Nazareth* fell into the wormhole sideways.

Light flowed across her, and space was gone.

She tumbled through the tunnel of light.

The *Rosetta*, *Kinloch Laggan*, and the remaining Firebirds plunged in after her.

The starships tumbled down the tunnel, spinning. One burnt Firebird careened toward the edge of the wormhole, tore through the shimmering wall, and vanished. Leona was bleeding, panting, dizzy, but she grabbed the yoke, desperate to steady the *Nazareth*.

The wormhole shimmered all around them. The frigate was barely large enough to fit. She was sliding down the wormhole at dizzying speed, moving a light-year every second, and the ship was damaged, cracked, still spinning. Leona cried out, tugging the yoke with all her body weight, pulling the prow to the left, and—

The frigate grazed the wormhole wall.

The prow of the ship ripped through curtains of light.

Leona found herself staring—not into space but into another universe.

Blackness. Endless blackness and dark gray clouds and blobs the color of old bruises. Lightning flashed—endless storms of lightning spreading into the distance. Figures moved between the clouds, great black beasts, larger than warships, lumbering whales of tar.

Another universe.

Leona screamed and yanked the yoke sideways, blasted her thruster engines, and careened back into the ripped wormhole.

She kept sliding forward, finally flying straight. The *Rosetta* and *Kinloch Laggan* overshot her. The corvettes were charging ahead now, moving toward a distant portal. The end of the wormhole was near. A shadow at the end of the tunnel—a gateway back into her universe.

Engines shrieked behind her.

In her rear viewport, Leona saw them.

The strikers.

There were still forty scorpion warships, and they were charging down the wormhole in pursuit. Their plasma fired, and the blasts slammed into the *Nazareth*, nearly knocking the warship against the tunnel wall again. Another blast. The frigate jolted. She was only seconds away from the portal now.

Leona inhaled sharply.

She gripped the controls.

"Goodbye, assholes," she whispered.

She fired the cannons lining her starboard and port.

But she was not aiming at the strikers behind her.

She fired to her sides.

Around Leona, the wormhole tore open.

She charged toward the portal.

Behind her, the tunnel of light crumbled, exposing the black vastness and lightning storms. Thunderbolts slammed into the strikers, and the vessels blazed white, filled with lightning, revealing the scorpions inside. The creatures screamed. Their strikers tumbled, crackled, tore open, then vanished into the storm. In the abyss beyond, the monsters bellowed.

Leona stared, frozen in horror.

I tore through our universe. I doomed us all.

The *Nazareth* shot through the portal back into space.

She floated in sudden silence.

The *Rosetta*, *Kinloch Laggan*, and the surviving Firebirds joined her.

The ships turned to face the portal, gazing into the wormhole they had just plunged through.

Inside, Leona could see that dark realm of purple storms and lightning. The tunnel was gone. The wormhole was now a portal, not to another location in this universe—but to another dimension.

Leona kept waiting for the entire structure to collapse, for the portal to become a black hole and suck them in. But it remained stable. A doorway in space, leading to a realm of storms and monsters.

"All right," Leona said, feeling faint, "nobody use this wormhole anymore."

"Sort of like the toilet after Ramses uses it," said Mairead from the *Kinloch Laggan*.

"At least I know how to use modern plumbing," the Pharaoh said from the *Rosetta.* "Do you still squat in the bushes like a barbarian? With the amount of grog you drink, I'm surprised your captain's seat isn't a toilet."

She scoffed. "Shut it, coffee cake."

"Shut it both of you," Leona said, still shaken. "We lost men in there. Good men. Humans." She lowered her head. "Friends."

The corvette captains too lowered their heads. For a moment, they sat in silence, mourning.

"Rest in peace, sons of Earth," Leona said softly. "Your courage will forever guide us, and your light will—"

A striker burst from the wormhole, cracked, burnt, revealing the scorpions inside but still firing plasma.

The three human warships opened fire.

Artillery slammed into the striker, shattering scorpions, blasting the hull apart. Severed claws and stingers flew across space. Shrapnel thudded against the *Nazareth*, scratching the shields.

Leona slumped back in her seat, her legs shaky.

"That one was mine," Mairead said. "My shell hit first."

Ramses glowered. "How the devil do you know?"

"Because I paint dragons on my shells," Mairead said. "Easy to recognize."

Ramses fired his corvette's machine guns, tearing through a living scorpion that floated through space. "Well, you cracked the ship open, I killed the scorpions. You owe me some scryls."

The war raged, and Earth awaited, but Leona lingered here for a day. She repaired her ship—and prepared a beacon. The glowing, egg-shaped pod emitted a signal, warning ships not to enter the wormhole. She released the beacon around the wormhole, where it began to orbit, beeping out its signal. A galactic *Out of Order* sign.

I will tear the universe apart if I must, Leona thought. *But I will reach Earth. I will bring humanity home.*

They flew on through space—battered and burnt, low on ammo, still so far from home. The light-years stretched before them, filled with darkness and raging war.

CHAPTER TWELVE

He was a light-year from the front line, so close Emet could practically smell the battle. He flew toward the ancient alien relic, the place of his deepest nightmares.

I should not be here. He gritted his teeth, and his fists clenched around the yoke of his starship. *I swore to never return.*

And yet there it was. The Relic hovered before him. And here Emet stood on the bridge of the ISS *Jerusalem*, his flagship, flying back to this place of deceit and old pain.

The Relic was a starship the size of a small country. Nobody knew who had built it. Myths from a million years ago still spoke of the Relic floating in the darkness, dead and barren, its halls whispering with wind and ghosts. The original builders were long gone. Their civilization was lost to time. Yet the Relic remained, pocked with holes, dented, burnt, an old ruin that would never fly again. It floated through space, dead but bustling with new life, like a whale's skeleton covered in crabs.

For thousands of years now, new inhabitants found shelter here. Shops clung like barnacles to the top of the Relic, known as the Sunny Side, selling everything from cutlery to androids. Shantytowns grew across the Relic's underbelly, a neighborhood called Barrel's Bottom. Here were crude huts of rusting metal, barely airtight, bristling with electrical wires, bulging with water domes and terrariums. Sandwiched between them rotted hives of sin: drug dens, brothels, fighting pits, and grog houses. Twenty million aliens from a thousand worlds lived in the Relic. This ancient, decaying starship had become a world of its own, a home to smugglers, druggers, bounty hunters, refugees, and countless other galactic lowlifes.

I should never have brought Alexis here, Emet thought. *I'm so sorry, my love.*

"Sir?" Rowan looked up at him. "I know this must be hard for you. Bay told me what happened here. I'm sorry. If you need anything, I—"

"Corporal, we're on duty," Emet said. "Concentrate on that. Our emotions don't matter now."

Rowan's cheeks flushed. She nodded. "Yes, sir."

Emet looked at the girl. She stood at a control panel, staring ahead at the Relic, eyes somber.

For the past few weeks, Rowan had barely left his side. Emet had insisted on it. He took her to meetings. On missions. He stationed her here on his bridge.

You must learn wisdom and strength, Rowan, he thought. *You must become a true Inheritor. Someday, very soon now, you will win or lose this war for us. I must mentor you until then. But Rowan, I cannot be your friend.*

Emet had known friendships before.

All those friends had died.

Duncan—his dear old Duncan McQueen, wise doctor, listening ear. Duncan—slain in the Battle of Terminus.

David Emery—an old friend, more like a brother. David—who had shared this dream. David—who had betrayed him, who had defected, who had died in a distant cave.

And Alexis. Emet's dearest friend. The friend he had married.

A friend who had died inside this ravaged, ancient starship that hovered before him.

Emet looked again at Rowan. A young, petite woman. Barely more than a girl, her hair short, her eyes serious, eager to learn and fight. A kind soul.

I loved your father, Rowan, but I cannot love you. I cannot be your friend, only your teacher, your commander. I almost sacrificed your life once. And I might need to sacrifice you again. Someday you might win this war for us. The cost will be your life. I cannot learn to love you. It will hurt too much.

He thought too of his children. Of Leona—on a quest to Earth. Of Bay—missing. Were they alive, or had they too fallen? The fear for his children was a constant demon in his belly, coiling and icy.

As the *Jerusalem* flew closer to the Relic, Emet slowed down. He navigated between many other starships. Thousands of vessels flew around him and docked at the Relic.

Most aliens here were of Type A2: solid, organic, and air-breathing. Type A2 species tended to congregate together, able to share space stations and worlds. Humans were of this type. But Emet saw starships carrying other types of aliens too. There were starships filled with water for aquatic species, known as Type A1—the most common type in the Milky Way. Other starships looked like huge airships, filled with thick gases. Within them flew air-dwelling floaters, aliens that commonly evolved on gas giants with no solid surface. These floating, balloon-like aliens were of Type A3, bizarre to Emet but still biological. A few of the Type A aliens were silicon-based. Nearly all, like humans, were built of carbon.

There were also drones for Type B aliens—species who had left their organic bodies behind. These aliens had uploaded their consciousness into machines. They controlled robots to navigate the stars. Some still had physical brains kept in jars. A handful even had vestigial biological bodies in storage, withering away. But most had no organic components at all; they had converted their minds into software. To Type B aliens, physical bodies were primitive, mere sacks of meat. Given enough time, many Type A aliens eventually evolved into Type B. Those who survived that long, at least. Most Type A's never made it that far, destroying themselves too soon in devastating wars.

If there were any higher types around, Emet wouldn't know. Aliens of Type C and above would be invisible to him. They had no solid form, not biological *or* mechanical. They were beings of energy and consciousness, living on a higher plane. According to weavers, the ancients who had built the wormholes had become a Type C civilization. They now dwelt in a realm beyond. Some believed in hypothetical Type D aliens, but little was known about them, and their existence had never been proved; they would be as gods.

Will we humans ever become Type B or C? Emet wondered. In truth, he hoped not. It disturbed him. He did not want to move humanity toward another existence, only to bring them home to an older, better life. Emet did not look to the future. He gazed toward the past.

He kept flying the *Jerusalem,* pushing such contemplations aside. He headed toward Rawside, the Relic's industrial neighborhood.

Here was a seedy landscape of scrapyards, warehouses, docking stations, refineries, and smuggling guilds. If Sunny Side offered a glittering front of high rises and boutiques, and Barrel's Bottom housed the lowlifes, the Rawside kept this world operating.

The *Jerusalem* had been a tanker in her old life, built to haul liquid and gas. She stood out in most battles, larger and bulkier than a typical warship. But here the *Jerusalem* seemed like the smallest kid in the playground. Freighters and tankers rumbled around her, three, four, even ten times the size.

Rowan looked around with eyes like saucers. "I never imagined starships could be this big."

Emet smiled thinly. "I never imagined your eyes could grow that big."

Her cheeks flushed. "Sorry, sir. I'm not used to seeing such wonders."

Sadness touched Emet at those words. Rowan had never seen the singing waterfalls of Lerinia, the diamond towers of Mazil, or the rainbow birds of Alisium. To her, this rundown old port was a wonder.

May you survive this war, Rowan, he thought. *And may you see beauty in this galaxy. May we all survive this darkness and see light again.*

Emet navigated the *Jerusalem* toward a scrapyard that clung to the Relic's hull. Hundreds of scrapped ships decayed here, piled up into towers, bristly with space barnacles. There were ships of every kind—freighters, tankers, cruise ships, slavers, starwhalers, even a few old warships. Not one looked younger than a century or spaceworthy. They formed an entire neighborhood, rising like fortresses, their portholes dark. Parasitic aliens clung to them, feeding off the metal. Between the stacks of ships, like a courtyard, gaped the hatch of an airlock.

It was here. Emet winced. *Here that the scorpions attacked us. That Emperor Sin Kra grabbed my wife, tore her apart. That I held Alexis in my arms as she bled. That I sang to her until the light left her eyes.*

He inhaled deeply and clenched his jaw.

No memories now. No pain now. I'm on duty. I'm an Inheritor. I've had years to grieve. Today I fight.

Yet he felt Rowan gazing at him with soft eyes. He clenched his hands around the yoke and flew onward.

He paused over the scrapyard. The *Jerusalem* hovered above hundreds of other old ships.

He switched on his communication monitor.

"Luther," he said. "Luther, it's me."

A video feed appeared on the monitor, displaying an old man in a tattered armchair. His skin was dark brown and wrinkled, and white stubble covered his cheeks. He wore a flannel shirt, a flat cap, and cargo pants stained with grease. Luther didn't look up at the camera. He was smoking a cigarette, strumming blues chords on a beat-up guitar.

Rowan gasped. "A human!"

Luther grunted, busy strumming his guitar. He still didn't look up.

"Been a while since anyone called me human, girl." His voice was as gritty and raw as his blues. If a slab of dry meat soaked in whiskey could talk, it would have such a voice. "They call me a starling. Silly name, if you ask me. Heard it's the name of an old bird. But I can't control how folks are talkin'."

Rowan's eyes widened.

"A starling!" she whispered, turning toward Emet. "Half human, half—"

"Half alien, it's right, girl," Luther rasped. "Said my DNA's got all sliced up and mixed." He finally looked up, revealing luminous golden eyes, the irises shaped like stars. When he pulled back his cap, he revealed small horns.

"You went bald," Emet said.

Luther turned to look at him through the monitor. Those golden eyes widened, and he let out a chuckle.

"Well I'll be damned. Emet Ben-Ari is back. The Old Lion himself. How long has it been? A decade?"

"Two decades," Emet said.

Luther whistled. "Ra damn, time goes by quick when you're old and forgetful like me. And Ra damn, you're still flying that old piece of junk I sold you."

Emet patted the dashboard. He spoke softly. "She's a good ship."

"Damn right. Among the best I've sold." Luther placed aside his guitar. "You turned her into a fine warship, I see. What are those, electro-shields?

"I'd rather not say over an open comm."

Luther nodded. "Of course. 'Scuse my manners. You still got a shuttle on that thing? Come on in. I'll rustle up some flapjacks. Little Bay with ya? The boy used to love my flapjacks."

I don't even know if Bay is alive.

Emet shoved down the pain. He had to believe. That Bay was safe aboard Brooklyn. That he would return again.

"He's not here," Emet said. "But I have a hungry soldier with me."

They boarded a shuttle—the only one that remained with Brooklyn missing again—and flew into the Relic.

Luther greeted them in the airlock. What little hair he still had was white now, but his back was still straight, his shoulders still broad. Tools hung from his belt, but he carried no weapon.

"Ra damn, twenty years!" Luther said, holding out his arms. "Dammit, Emet, look at ya. Your beard is more white than blond now." He barked a laugh.

Emet couldn't help but smile. "And your beard has gone completely white."

"Age'll do that to you. Sneaks up on you, she does." He pulled Emet into a hug and slapped his back. "Good to see you again, old man. How are the kids? Last I saw Leona and Bay, they were about yea high."

"Adults now," Emet said. "Leona is twenty-eight, Bay is almost twenty-five."

Both far from me, he thought. *Maybe dead.* But he dared not articulate those fears.

Luther shook his head in wonder. "Ra damn. As I said, sneaks up on ya." He turned toward Rowan. "And who is this lovely, hungry-looking soldier?"

Rowan grinned, then covered her mouth. "Rowan Emery, sir."

Luther snorted. "Sir? I ain't no fancy sir. Call me Luther or Big Blue. That's what my friends call me. Come on, come on, outta the airlock! We got some pancakes to fry up and stories to swap."

Rowan's eyes widened. "Pancakes! My favorite!"

He led them through a hangar filled with countless scrapped starships. A handful of robots bustled about, working at repairing what could still be salvaged, disassembling what could not. Dozens of deactivated robots lay stacked up inside crates. Rowan looked around with wonder at all the machines around her. The girl was always enthralled around engines, gears, and anything mechanical. But Emet lowered his head as he walked.

This was the place.

The pain stabbed him.

Again he saw the blood wash the floor, heard the bullets fly, saw the scorpion claws. Saw the bloodlust in Sin Kra's eyes.

"What is this, Big Blue, a nuclear twin-turbine engine?" Rowan asked, walking toward a derelict starship that stood on the hangar floor. "Sweet! How many Carvs does it run?"

"This old dog?" Luther said. "Aye, you got a good eye. She used to run fifteen hundred Carvs, but she's busted now."

"You should try replacing the copper coils," Rowan said. "Get silconian coils instead, and you can prime her by attaching her to a good hydrox generator. Might still be life in her."

Luther barked a laugh. "I should hire you, girl. Want to switch careers?"

"Sure," she said. "You can pay me with pancakes."

As the two conversed, Emet walked toward a spot in the hangar. Where once blood had spilled, there was only a dark stain on the floor. Before him, on the wall—a framed photo. A woman with kind eyes and curly black hair.

She looked so much like Leona, Emet thought.

The conversation behind him died. Luther approached and placed a hand on Emet's shoulder.

"I look at her whenever I walk by," Luther said in a soft, raspy voice. "She was a good friend."

"This is the place, isn't it?" Emet said. "Right here. Where I'm standing."

"Aye." Luther nodded. "She died here. Too young. Far too young. A tragic day."

Emet turned around slowly and stared into Luther's strange golden eyes.

Somebody tipped off the scorpions that day, Emet thought. *Somebody betrayed me, told the scorpions that I—their most hated enemy—was docking at the Relic. For a long time, I thought it was you.*

And standing here, gazing into his old friend's eyes, that suspicion finally faded.

It wasn't you, old friend, Emet thought.

"Thank you," Emet said, voice hoarse. "For hanging up her photo. For remembering." He clasped Luther's shoulder. "Thank you, old friend."

Duncan is gone. David is gone. Alexis is gone. But not everyone from my past is lost.

They stepped into a kitchen—just a corner of the warehouse with a stove and plastic table—where Luther began to fry up the pancakes. Old electric blues played from an old stereo. Posters of bluesmen hung on the walls.

"This is Earth music," Rowan said in wonder. "Pre-Hyrdian. It's on the tip of my tongue." She frowned, raised her finger, then smiled. "Bootstrap and the Shoeshine Kid! Mid-twenty-first century duo, from just before the Cataclysm."

"You know your Earth lore." Luther glanced down at the crystal that hung around Rowan's neck, then up at Emet. "This one is entrusted with a special gift."

Emet nodded, staring steadily into his friend's eyes. "As are we all."

Luther stared for a moment, silent, then pulled the pancakes off the griddle. He placed them on the table, along with slabs of butter and syrup.

"Tuck in," he said. "You look hungry."

But there was something subdued and cold in his voice.

Rowan didn't seem to notice. She began to feast. For somebody so small, she put a serious dent in the platter of pancakes. Syrup dripped down her chin, and she reached for more, eating so fast her cheeks puffed out.

"What?" She blinked at Emet and Luther, who were looking at her in shock. "I like pancakes."

Luther laughed, and soon Emet was laughing too, and some of the tension dissipated. They ate and the old electric blues played.

"You know, Big Blue," Rowan said between bites, "I can let you copy more blues music, if you like. I have a lot on the Earthstone. How many Bootstrap and the Shoeshine Kid albums do you have?"

"Both," said Luther. "Best damn albums ever made."

Rowan gulped down another bite and licked her lips. "Both? Dude, they released three albums, you know. And I have hours of their live recordings as well. Not my usual music. I'm a K-pop girl, but I like all sorts of music. I can't actually copy files digitally off the Earthstone—the data is stored in crystals, not bits—but I can probably rig up an analog recorder."

Luther's strange golden eyes widened. The star-shaped irises shone.

"Rowan!" Luther walked around the table and knelt at her side. "You have no idea what a precious gift that would be." His eyes dampened, and he had to dab them with a napkin. "Barely anything from old Earth ever comes rolling in. I would Ra damn *love* to hear your music."

Rowan swallowed a last pancake, then pulled out a pocket watch. She detached its thin golden chain. When she hit a button, wings, legs, and a head emerged, forming a robotic dragonfly.

"Fillister," Rowan said, "we've got an audio interface to build."

Soon new music filled the warehouse. To Emet, it sounded the same as before, but Luther was bobbing his head, almost in a trance.

Emet wanted to interrupt. There was little time. The front line was moving closer, and Emet could not waste more precious moments on pancakes and music. But he also wanted to butter up the old man, as surely as Rowan had buttered up her flapjacks.

And you're doing a better job than I could, Rowan, Emet thought.

Luther and Rowan were now sitting on a tattered couch. He was teaching her to play a bass guitar, laughing and mussing her hair.

Finally Emet had waited long enough.

He walked up to the tattered couch.

"Luther, we need to talk."

Rowan looked up, hands on the bass, and smiled. "I'm slamming the bass!"

"Slapping," Luther said, lighting another cigarette. "Slapping the bass."

She plucked a reverberating note. "Slap. Rowan Emery, goddess of thunder!"

Luther rose to his feet, joints creaking, and placed a hand on Emet's shoulder. "Aye, friend, I know you didn't come here for flapjacks and blues. You want another ship."

"Another tanker like the Jerusalem," Emet said. "In fact, I need the same model. Modified the same way. Painted the same. I need an exact replica."

Rowan stopped playing and looked up, curious. Emet had not told her of his plan. He had told nobody.

It was a plan that could save humanity. And right now, it all depended on Luther.

The old man nodded and scratched his chin. "Aye, old friend, might be I got another T-class tanker lying around. But the things ain't cheap. Aren't many left in the galaxy. They cost a splendid scryl."

Emet frowned. "When you sold me the *Jerusalem* twenty years ago, you said it was a hunk of junk. The cheapest freighter you had."

"Aye, that's before the civilization that built them went extinct," Luther said. "They're a classic now. A collector's item."

"I'll pay you a million scryls," Emet said. "That's a lot of money. I know it's less than what I paid last time. I know there's inflation. I need a favor."

Luther winced. He scratched his chin. "Now, Emet, there's a war going on. Big one. There are certain risks involved with selling ships to terrorists—and that's what they're calling you. Prices have been going higher to handle those risks. You're an old friend, Emet. A good friend. But I'm gonna be honest with you. I haven't heard from you in twenty years. Now you swing by and want a favor. Well, I'm happy to do you a favor. I support what you're doing. You're fighting for a cause, and I can appreciate that. But these ships ..." He gave a whistle. "They're going for ten million on the black market these days."

Emet didn't have ten million. He could barely scrape together one.

"We'll set up a loan," Emet said. "Name your rate, and—"

"Now, Emet, you know I don't do loans," Luther said. "I deal in cash only. Everyone in my line of work does. This place is in no man's land. We get both Hierarchy and Peacekeeper goons here. You know how much it costs to bribe them, keep them away?"

"Whatever you paid last time, it wasn't enough," Emet said, unable to keep the bitterness out of his voice.

Luther went very quiet. He lowered his head.

"I know, Emet." His voice was low and raspy. "And I'm sorry. Ain't a day go by that I don't think about that night. How the damn scorpions blasted in here, tore up the place, killed Alexis. I lost people that day too. And earned this scar on my side." He lifted his shirt, showing a long scar that stretched under his ribs. "And the damn Hierarchy has been getting fanatical. Lots of them flying by the Relic these days, causing trouble. We're half a parsec from the front line. Too many damn scorpions. I'm sorry, Emet, I really am, but I'm going to have to insist on the price."

Rowan leaped from the couch. "But Big Blue, you don't understand! This isn't about money. This is about Earth!"

"Corporal, sit down," Emet barked.

"I will not, sir!" Rowan placed her hands on her hips. "Big Blue, you listen to me. I don't care what the damn Peacekeepers say. Emet Ben-Ari is not a terrorist. He is a noble, brave man. He sacrifices so much every day for humans. And you're one of us! He fights for you too!"

"Corporal!" Emet roared.

Rowan took a step back, paling at the sound of his fury. But then she tightened her lips and clenched her fists. Silent, she turned to glare at Luther.

Luther stared at her. His eyes softened. He put out his cigarette. "Now, Rowan, that's mighty kind of you, calling me human. But I ain't one. Not fully. I'm a starling, only half human, half of me a mix of Ra knows what else. We starlings used to be men. But we flew too deep into space. Lost our humanity. Came back with our genes spliced and woven with alien strands.

Human?" He barked a raspy laugh. "Humans never accepted me. Never wanted me among them."

Rowan's eyes softened too. "I do." She stepped closer and embraced Luther. "I want you with us. To teach me the bass. To fry me pancakes. To listen to music with me. You might have strange eyes, Big Blue, but you're a human. And a good one. I don't need to see your DNA to know that."

Luther held the girl in his arms. A sigh ran through him.

"Girl, you know how to warm an old man's cold, shriveled heart." He laughed, though there was pain in his eyes. "You remind me of my own daughter. Haven't seen her in thirty years, but Ra above, you remind me of her." He looked up at Emet. "I'll give you the ship. On the house. Do good by this girl, Emet. You promise me you do good by her."

Emet exhaled in relief. "Thank you, old friend. Let me pay you the mil—"

"I don't want to launder your damn money!" Luther said. "Just you promise me that you kill some damn scorpions, and that you bring this girl to a good place to live. Or Ra above, I will chase your ass across the galaxy."

Emet smiled wryly. "Join the club." He clasped his friend's shoulder. "Come with us, Luther. The scorpions are going to annex this sector soon enough. I know it. You know it. The days of bribing them are over. The scorpions will tear this place down. We all must fight now. So fight with the Heirs of Earth. We could use a guy like you."

Luther lit another cigarette. He stared into the distance, thoughtful. Finally he shook his head.

"I got the cancer in my belly, Emet."

Emet inhaled slowly. The news spun his head. "I'm sorry, Luther."

"Yeah, I am too, Emet. Doc says I only have a few months to live. Maybe only weeks. Thousands of years of doctors tinkering around, and still ain't nobody got the damn cure. Fight?" He shook his head. "I'm too old, Emet. Too damn old and too damn sick. I've lived here in the Relic all my life. Let me die here."

Rowan approached slowly. She held the old man's callused hand.

"Or you can die fighting for a cause," she whispered, gazing up into his eyes. "You can die among friends. Me. Emet. And many other humans who will accept you. Don't die alone here, Luther. Don't die alone in space, so far from Earth." She smiled and her tears fell. "Besides, who will teach me to smack the bass?"

"Slap the bass, child, slap the bass." Luther heaved a sigh. He looked at Emet. "You sure you want an old fool flying with you?"

Emet nodded. "That's all we are, friend. A bunch of old fools with an old dream."

Luther huffed. "Well, seems you got one more old fool with you." He winked at Rowan. "At least this one can fry up some flapjacks."

Rowan grinned, too happy to even cover her teeth. "And we'll listen to lots of blues together. Wait till you hear everything on the Earthstone!"

A few hours later, they flew out.

Emet had come here to buy another T-class tanker, one that could be refitted with shields and canons, made to look like the *Jerusalem*, a decoy he would need in the battle ahead. That old tanker now flew behind the *Jerusalem*, Luther at the helm. And behind it flew fifty other ships, every spaceworthy old beater Luther had, robots at their helms.

Emet stood on the bridge of the *Jerusalem*, and Rowan stood at his side.

"Corporal," Emet said, "today you were disobedient, insufferable, and impudent. You spoke out of turn. You contradicted me, your superior officer. And you also might have saved humanity."

He gave her a thin smile, but she stared at him, face blank, fear in her eyes.

"I didn't save humanity," she whispered. "But I saved Luther's life, didn't I?"

Emet lost his smile. "What do you mean?"

"What would you have done, sir?" Rowan stared steadily into his eyes, a feat few in his fleet dared. "If Luther had refused to sell you his ship. You would have stolen it, wouldn't you? If he fought back, you ..." Her eyes strayed toward the rifle hanging across his back, then she looked into his eyes again. "I intervened, sir, not because I was afraid we wouldn't get the ship. I knew you wouldn't leave without it. I was not afraid for us." Her voice dropped to a shaky whisper. "I was afraid for him."

Emet looked ahead into space, jaw tight. "I would not have harmed him."

"And if he had fought you? Pulled a gun, tried to protect his—"

"You forget yourself, Corporal," Emet said. "It's not for you to question my motives, plans, or decisions."

"I will always question them, sir," Rowan said, voice cold. "Because they affect me. They affect my sister. They affect all of us. You chose to take me on your missions. To put me here on the bridge. To mentor me. And I will not be silent, not when I see you veer into immorality."

Emet felt rage flare in him. His fists tightened. He took a deep breath and looked at Rowan.

"Emery, suppose Luther had resisted. Suppose I killed him, stole his ships. Horrible crimes. Horrible. Theft. Murder. Betrayal. Enough to get me into hell if such a place exists. But if I had left without the decoy ship I need? We could lose the war.

Millions could die. Would I not be a greater monster if I allowed millions to perish?"

Rowan hesitated. "I don't know."

"These are the decisions soldiers must make," Emet said. "These are the decisions soldiers have had to make since the dawn of history. Sometimes we must take one life, even an innocent life, to save many. We are soldiers. We deal in death and life. We kill to save. And it is a heavy burden."

Rowan gazed ahead into space, silent for a moment. "Today goodness won," she finally said. "Today I was kind, and I swayed him with my kindness, without needing your gun." She looked at him. "Sir, perhaps I'm naive. But I believe that goodness always wins."

Emet nodded. "You are naive. Your father was like you. He believed in goodness. Rowan, I admire your kindness. You have a deep sense of justice. But do not let your compassion lead you to weakness. Cling to your righteousness. But burn away the innocence. Burn away the girl. Become the soldier."

She nodded. "You're good too, sir. I know it. I can see it. You were hurt many times, and you saw more than I can imagine. But there is goodness inside you. I forgive you, sir." Her eyes dampened. "For blasting me out of the airlock. I forgive you."

They flew on through the darkness. The front line loomed before them, a scar of light across space. The Heirs of Earth flew toward it.

CHAPTER THIRTEEN

Bay was flying through space, seeking the Weeping Weaver Guildhall, when he saw the front line ahead.

At first he mistook it for a galactic spiral arm. The stream flowed across space, gleaming with countless lights, blue and white and beautiful. He put down his drawing—the paper featured an elven archer battling a dragon—and leaned back to admire the view.

I've never seen the spiral arm look so bright, he thought. *It almost looks like—*

He frowned and leaned forward.

The small lights were swarming, swirling, flashing bright then vanishing. It looked as if the galaxy were breaking apart, supernova after supernova raging with white fury.

That was when Bay realized: this was not the Milky Way. It was a battle. The largest battle he had ever seen.

Thousands—maybe even millions—of starships were flying, firing, and exploding ahead.

"The front line," he whispered.

He stared, for a moment struck by how oddly beautiful it was. Horrifying. A tragedy. But sickeningly beautiful from a distance.

And it was blocking their way.

Both Brooklyn and Coral were asleep. Brooklyn was humming in sleep mode, running her background threads to clean up databases, scan for corruptions, archive old files, and tweak her algorithms. She called it dreaming, and she often woke up with memories of her various files.

Coral was back in the small hold, curled up in Bay's bed, her silvery hair spread out around her head. They had been taking shifts at the helm, alternating between cockpit and hold.

Bay had been trying to avoid her. Which was almost impossible on a ship so small. Even with him in the cockpit, and her in the hold, they were only a few feet apart. There was no privacy aboard Brooklyn. And Coral was the last person Bay wanted around. Flying with the weaver was intolerable.

She betrayed my father, he thought. *She stole Brooklyn!*

The irony of that thought struck him at once. Had he himself not stolen Brooklyn once, using the shuttle to defect?

No, it wasn't that Coral had stolen Brooklyn—with Bay himself aboard.

He looked at the weaver. Her smooth, dark skin decorated with silvery ink. Her hair like molten moonlight. Her full lips and graceful form. She was beautiful. She was intoxicating. She was ethereal like a fairy from an old book.

Bay was young and hot-blooded, and he was not blind to Coral's beauty. He didn't like how she heated his blood, how she stirred desire inside him.

I wish it were you here with me, Rowan, he thought.

He looked at the bulkhead, where he had hung a portrait of Rowan, one he had drawn only last week.

"Draw me like one of your French girls," she had said.

Bay had never heard of France, and he assumed it was a reference to one of Rowan's movies. Half of what the girl said made no sense to him. She had grown up in a duct, learning about humanity from books and movies, the most recent ones two thousand years old. Even her accent was nearly impossible to understand, the same accent humans had in the old films. Yes, Bay barely understood Rowan, but whenever he was with her, he felt good. Felt at peace. It was only with Rowan that he felt truly happy, that he could forget his past.

In the portrait, she was wearing her Inheritor uniform, leaning against a starfighter, smiling. A tight-lipped smile. She only ever smiled with her lips closed, hiding her crooked teeth. Bay didn't mind her teeth. So what if they were crooked? He didn't mind that her hair was short and messy and brown, not long and silvery and shiny like Coral's. He didn't mind that she was so small. When he called her a hobbit, he was only teasing. Today he would have readily swapped the fairy in his bed with the hobbit in his drawing.

I miss you, Row.

But there was no time for navel-gazing now. Not with the battle so close. He approached Coral and touched her shoulder.

"Coral?"

She rose in bed, blinking, her hair tousled. "Never wake a weaver for anything less than the end of the universe."

Bay nodded. "Good, so I was right to wake you. Come into the cockpit. You better see this."

She followed him, stared through the viewport, and gasped.

"You weren't kidding," she said.

The battle spread before them, a glimmering scar across the darkness. A million starships or more swarmed ahead.

Bay licked his dry lips. "We'll have to give this battle a wide berth. It'll add a few days to our journey, but—"

"No." Coral narrowed her eyes. "The front line has moved to encompass Elysium, the planet of the Weeping Guildhall. The scorpions will be there soon, if they're not there already. We cannot delay!"

Bay stared ahead. The battle was closer now. When he zoomed in, the lights revealed themselves to be warships. Countless warships. The entire Inheritor fleet would disappear here. On one side, closer to Brooklyn, flew the Concord armada. On the other side—the Hierarchy. But the border between them was blurry. Both fleets were swirling, clashing, blending together in a chaotic dance.

"You want us to fly through *that*?" Bay said. "We'd have better luck flying through a minefield."

Coral took a shuddering breath, then nodded. "The ancients will guide our way."

"If the ancients want to help, they can teleport the Godblade into my hand right now." He held out his hand. "Nope, didn't think so."

Coral glowered. "Do not mock the ancients. And yes, we will fly through the battle. I'd rather fly through a battle of a million starships than a scuffle between ten."

Bay tilted his head. "Explain that logic."

She groaned. "Bay! We're flying a tiny shuttle barely larger than a bathroom. And barely cleaner, by the way."

"Hey!" Bay said, then looked around him at the piles of laundry, sheafs of paper, and snack wrappers. He sighed, conceding the point.

"They won't notice us," Coral continued. "We'll be like an ant scurrying under battling elephants."

"That's what I'm worried about," Bay said. "Ants tend to get crushed in that situation."

Lights flashed on the dashboard. Monitors turned on. Brooklyn's camera swiveled toward them.

"Did somebody say ants?" The ship shook. "Are there ants inside me? I knew it!"

"Good morning, Brook," Bay said. "We're flying toward a massive battle with a million warships and Coral wants us to fly right between them."

"That's fine, but what about the ants?" Brooklyn said.

"No, it's not fine!" Bay tugged his hair. "Why is everyone fine with this? Flying between a million warships blasting missiles and plasma is *not* fine!"

The battle was even closer now. It wasn't only that Brooklyn was flying toward the front line. The front line was moving toward them. The Hierarchy was pushing deeper into Concord space.

Brooklyn's sensors began picking up signals from the ships ahead. Her monitors scrolled through stats on countless starships. Dozens of species were fighting here. On the Hierarchy side, most were scorpions. But many slave races had come to fight under the stinger banners. There were giant spiders, electric trees, gargantuan centipedes, and a host of other monsters. Even the marshcrabs had come to fight for their masters. Each Hierarchy race flew their own warships, nightmarish machines that sprouted claws, spikes, and cannons.

On the Concord side, the Aelonians formed the bulk of the fleet. The glowing, translucent humanoids flew in graceful, silvery ships shaped like leaves. But many other civilizations had come to help. There were glassy ships filled with water and intelligent fish, rocky ships that contained intelligent crystals, the pod ships of the Esporian mushrooms, round ships filled with soil and sentient mosses, and other species Bay didn't recognize.

It was, by far, the largest battle he had ever seen, ever imagined. Not since the First Galactic War a thousand years ago, the war that had destroyed the Galactic Alliance and birthed the Concord and Hierarchy, had such violence filled the Milky Way galaxy.

And Brooklyn was charging right toward it.

"Are you sure this is a good idea?" Bay said, wincing.

Coral nodded. "Like an ant between—" She paused as Brooklyn trembled. "Like a bee between elephants."

Bay grimaced. The battle was closer, closer, the starships soaring, tumbling, blasting fire. Within seconds, Brooklyn would be flying through the gauntlet.

"Brook, you wanna take the wheel?" Bay said.

"Dude, I'm not programmed for this!" Brooklyn said, voice rising to a panic. "I vote to get the hell out of here. Take the long route! We—"

"Too late!" Coral pointed.

A massive frigate, torn open and burning, came tumbling toward them, trailing smoke and shrapnel.

Brooklyn squeaked and her camera retreated into the dashboard like a scared turtle. Her monitors went dark.

Great, Bay thought. *I think my spaceship just fainted.*

Wincing, he grabbed the joystick. He'd have to fly.

The ruined frigate rolled toward them. Ra, it was huge. It was the size of an office building. Two more warships chased it, blasting cannons, filling space with light and red-hot metal. Just beyond them swarmed a thousand more ships.

Bay yanked the joystick all the way back. Brooklyn soared.

The burning warship tumbled toward them. Closer. Closer. Only a heartbeat away.

Bay and Coral both screamed.

Bay tugged the joystick harder. He shoved on the throttle, rising higher. He overshot the spinning frigate, grazing its cracked hull. Brooklyn jolted and shouted and careened.

Bay didn't even have time to release his breath.

They rolled into the inferno of war.

Space burned.

To their right, two starships slammed together and shattered, showering glass and metal. Scorpions and squid-like aliens spilled out.

To their left, a cruiser plowed through a storm of starfighters, blasting cannons, then exploded with a furious shock wave that tossed Brooklyn into a spin.

Bay clung to his joystick, nearly falling from his seat. He righted himself and flew onward.

Below them flew a flat, rectangular vessel lined with circles and towers. It was nearly the size of Paradise Lost. Drones rose from the colossal machine, reaching out robotic arms. Starfighters swooped toward the behemoth, raining fire. Bay swerved from side to side, evading the drones, then dodging the blasts of fire from the mechanical monster.

Above them, warships shaped like crabs scuttled across the darkness, reaching out claws, grabbing smaller starships and crushing them. A pincer reached toward Brooklyn, and Bay floored the thruster, shooting between the claws before they snapped shut.

"This was a stupid idea!" he shouted, swerving left to right, escaping a swarm of missiles.

"You're doing great," Coral said.

"I'm mucking terrified!" Bay swooped, dodging several scorpions in mech suits, then vaulted over a warship lined with a thousand cannons like porcupine quills.

"We're almost through!" Coral said.

"Don't you have any magic that can help?" he cried as shells burst around them. A striker slammed into an Aelonian leaf-ship above, and Bay dived through, barely avoiding the debris.

"I told you, it's not magic!" Coral shouted over the roaring battle. "It's aether."

"Whatever the hell it is, can you help?" Bay shouted.

Coral nodded. "Sure, let me just activate my 'defeat the entire Hierarchy' rune."

Grimacing, Bay swerved past two starfighters. "Gee, would ya?" He fired his shells at a missile flying their way. It exploded before them, and he flew through the flame. "Activate your 'generate new underwear for Bay' rune while you're at it."

Another missile flew their way.

Bay cursed and fired, destroying the missile in space.

A third missile flew, and Bay fired again, missed it. Cursing, he charged toward a warship and flew in rings around it. The missile slammed into the larger vessel's hull. The warship opened fire—at Bay. He flew, zigzagging.

More missiles came flying their way.

"All right, this is definitely not crossfire," Bay said. "The bastards are firing on us."

"Which side?" Coral asked, gazing across the battle. Thousands of warships of a dozen species spread around them.

"Both!" Bay said. "Everyone!"

He swerved around a hulking destroyer, zigzagging around its cannons. Shells burst behind him.

Strikers streamed toward them, blasting plasma.

"Bay, I don't like this," Coral said.

"Gee, you think maybe flying into the Ra damn front line was a bad idea?" he said. "Really?"

"There's no need to be sarcastic." Coral pointed. "We're almost at the end. We can do this."

Bay pressed his thruster to the max, roaring toward the edge of the battle. That was Hierarchy space ahead, but anything would be better than this gauntlet.

The strikers kept chasing him. Three. Then ten. Then a hundred.

"Dammit, dammit, dammit." Bay shoved himself against the thruster, desperate for more speed. "I think they know we're humans. Why else would they send so many strikers after a shuttle?"

"I am not a shuttle!" Brooklyn said, waking from slumber. "I am a micro-ship. There's a huge difference. Well, a micro-difference. But a significant one."

"Well, look who decided to wake up!" Bay said. "Rise and shine, princess. Care to use any of that staggering micro-ship intelligence to increase our speed?"

"I told you, dude, if you ever bought me premium fuel, I—"

"Enough about the premium fuel! Give me extra speed, Brooklyn!"

The camera on the dashboard nodded on its stock. "Put on your air masks, dudes."

Masks dangled down from the overhead compartments. Brooklyn shut off life support, and their speed inched up.

They were nearly through the battle now.

Bay could see open space ahead.

A wall of enemy warships, shaped like writhing octopuses with metallic tentacles, rose to block their passage. The tentacles unfurled, revealing hundreds of round holes like suction cups.

From each hole flew a whirring, blinking bomb ringed with blades. They looked like saw blades glued onto grenades.

Bay stared in horror as hundreds of spinning bombs flew toward them.

Brooklyn screamed.

Coral closed her eyes. A rune on her forehead began to glow.

As Bay clutched the joystick, Coral placed her hand over his. Light flowed from her rune, down her arm, and into her hand.

She began to move the joystick.

The spinning bombs reached them. Hundreds of them.

Eyes closed, Coral jerked the ship—down, up, side to side.

Blades scraped against Brooklyn's wings, hull, and roof, sawing grooves into the metal—but missing the cockpit. Missing the engine. Failing to cut all the way through.

Behind Brooklyn, the saw blades slammed into the pursuing strikers, embedded themselves into their hulls, then detonated.

The strikers exploded.

Shock waves blasted out, hitting Brooklyn, propelling her forward.

The shuttle spun through space, hurtling closer to the octopus ships.

"Coral, I need my hand." Bay struggled to pull his hand free from under hers; she was pinning it to the joystick. "Coral, I need my hand to fire!"

But she seemed to be in a trance. Her eyes were still closed. Her glowing hand still covered his, moving the joystick. Her grip was iron; Bay couldn't free himself.

He raised his left hand—the bad hand, the one with the stiff fingers always curled into a deformed fist.

He screamed as he uncurled one finger—just a centimeter—the joints creaking, the muscles spasming. He grabbed the cannon's trigger.

He fired.

Shells flew into the octopus starships, exploding against tentacles, tearing off the appendages. More explosions rocked the enemy ships—perhaps their armaments. Flame and metal showered. True octopuses spilled out from the burning vessels, flailing, and more bombs exploded, and a wall of fire rose in space.

Bay winced, holding his breath, as they flew through the inferno.

They shot through the fiery curtain.

Bombs and blades whirred everywhere around them, and Coral flew madly, her eyes closed, whipping between the projectiles, streaming up and down and sideways at speeds Bay had never seen from the shuttle.

And it ended.

They broke through.

They hovered in open space.

Behind them, the last few strikers attempted to fly through the inferno, only to shatter and burn and scatter in pieces. A few scorpions, ejected from their strikers, tumbled through space, flailing, then finally falling still.

Brooklyn flew onward, leaving the battle behind.

"We did it," Bay whispered. "We actually flew through the front line. We emerged in one piece." He spun toward Coral. "*You* did it, Coral! You used your magic! You—"

Her rune dimmed, her eyes rolled back, and she slumped in her seat, unconscious.

"Coral!" He turned toward her but dared not release the joystick. He kicked the dashboard. "Brooklyn! Brooklyn, wake up, you useless hunk of junk!"

Her camera propped up and dilated.

"Is it over?" the starship asked, then swiveled toward Coral and gasped. "What happened to her?" Her voice dropped to a worried whisper. "Did she get ants?"

"She doesn't have ants!" Bay said. "She used too much of her magic, I think. Or aether. Or whatever you want to call it. But she got us out of the battle alive. And by the way, lots of help you were, Brook."

Bay didn't think cameras could roll their eyes, but Brooklyn came close.

"Dude, I'm only a shuttle," she said. "I'm not made for battle."

"I thought you were a micro-ship."

"Whatever!" Brooklyn said. "I'll take over now, though. You take care of the weasel."

"Weaver," Bay said. "She's a weaver, not a weasel."

Brooklyn tilted her camera. "You sure?"

"Almost certain."

"Well, I'll be damned. You lifeforms all look the same to me."

As Brooklyn flew onward, leaving the battle behind, Bay turned to Coral. She was out cold, but he could find no wounds, and her pulse was strong, her breath deep. He lifted her in his arms, surprised by how light she was. He carried her into the hold and laid her down in his bed.

"Coral?" he said softly, kneeling beside her.

Her eyes fluttered open. "Did we … make it through?"

He nodded. "We did, Coral. *You* did."

A faint smile touched her lips. "Good. I'm tired. It'll be a while before we reach the Weeping Guildhall. I need to …"

Her eyes closed, and she slept.

Strands of her hair lay across her nose and mouth. Bay brushed them back, marveling at how silky the strands were, how they shone like snow under moonlight, and how soft her skin felt when his fingertips brushed it.

He pulled his hand back.

"Sleep well, Coral the weaver, you nut," he said softly. "You're either going to save the galaxy or drive me mad. Or both."

He returned to the cockpit. They flew on into the darkness. Into Hierarchy space. Into the realm of scorpions, untold danger, and the faintest shred of hope.

CHAPTER FOURTEEN

For a long time—darkness and pain.

Ayumi thought it would never end.

The scorpions carried her in the sack. She felt their claws—poking, cutting. She heard their laughter—hissing, crackling, cruel. She smelled the stench of them, the acidic smell of burning oil and dead things. Their saliva ate through her sack, her skin.

The scorpions shoved her into a vehicle. She could not see, but she heard engines rumbling, her ears popped, and she vomited. She trembled, and blows struck her, and she passed out.

Hours passed, maybe days, maybe years. A blur of shadows and pain and beatings.

Once she thought she saw light. She peeked through a hole in her sack, and she saw a rattling window. Through it—grassy plains in the night, silvered with moonlight. Towns and cities and roads below her, clusters like stars, strands of pale gray between them. She was flying. Then more claws, and a scorpion shaking her, and she screamed and passed out again.

She fell. She spilled out of her sack, hit the floor, and woke up with a scream. She was in a bustling, grumbling, oily station, a place of pipes and smoke and bricks. When she tried to stand up, the scorpions knocked her back down. They kicked her, stabbed her, yanked her up by the hair. Ayumi looked around her, dazed, swaying, struggling to focus her eyes.

She had worried the scorpions had taken her into space. But she was still on Paev, the planet Ayumi had been born and raised on.

This had once been a train station, it seemed. Ayumi could still see the train tracks and a few locomotives, their steam engines cold. There was a ticket booth, a platform, a few kiosks, but they were deserted.

The station had been converted into a spaceport.

A handful of rectangular starships stood across the train tracks, and several more hovered above, engines rumbling. They were built of black metal, the hulls emblazoned with Hierarchy sigils. Skra-Shen ships. But these were no strikers, no slick warships, but boxy cargo vessels.

Deathcars, Ayumi realized. She had heard of such ships. *Human cattle cars.*

Posters hung on the station's brick walls, displaying caricatures of twisted, ugly humans. Captions appeared under the drawings, written in the Paevins' sharp script.

Humans go home!

Blame humans for the war!

The Hierarchy wins when humans die!

Seen a human? Report!

There were several scorpions moving about the station, but there were Paevins too. The bipedal felines wore military uniforms with Hierarchy symbols on the sleeves, and they held muskets and batons. They stared at Ayumi, disgust in their eyes.

"I'm not to blame," she whispered to them, bleeding. "I didn't cause the war. Please. I'm Paevin too. I was born here. Help me."

The felines approached her, and hope sprang in Ayumi. They would help her, shelter her, feed her, tend to her wounds.

But instead the cats grabbed her. Their claws were smaller than scorpion pincers but still drew blood.

She screamed and they laughed.

One cat leaned in close. He hissed into her ear.

"You ruined our planet, pest. Now you will pay. Hail the Hierarchy!"

The cats dragged her along the train tracks toward a waiting deathcar. They manhandled her up a ramp and opened a hatch.

Humans were inside.

A lot of them.

The deathcar wasn't large, no larger than a steam train's railcar. But there must have been hundreds of humans packed inside. They began spilling out, only for the Paevin soldiers to shove them back in, to shock them with electric batons, to laugh. As the cats worked, the scorpions watched from a distance, cackling.

The humans were crammed together, limbs entwined, bodies crushed. They gasped for air. They tried to reach out, to beg, but could barely move their arms. A mother raised her baby overhead, trying to save it from being crushed. Several children lay dead underfoot, trampled.

"Get in."

The soldiers shoved Ayumi against the mass of humans. Ayumi fell back out, only for a baton to slam into her back. Electricity crackled across her. She yowled.

The door slammed shut behind her, banging against her back, squeezing her in, shoving her more tightly against the people inside.

Darkness fell.

Ayumi stood, trapped between the door and a man in front of her. Her face pressed into the man's chest. She couldn't breathe. He was crushing her. They were all crushing her. Her lungs didn't have room to expand. She tried to cry out, could not. Across the deathcar, the others were crammed in just as tightly. Blood and human waste pooled on the floor.

"Where are you from?" the man asked, the one who was crushed against her.

"Palaevia City," she whispered, hoarse, barely able to speak.

"We heard the scorpions liquidated Palaevia last year," the man said.

"I hid," Ayumi said. "In an attic. For a long time. Months, I think. Maybe a year."

The engines rumbled.

The deathcar rose.

This time Ayumi knew: they were leaving Paev behind.

Tears flowed down her cheeks.

She was twelve years old, maybe thirteen by now, and she had never known another planet. For her first twelve years, she had known only Palaevia Enclave, that prison inside the cats' city. For another year—the attic only a few streets away. That had been her life. A lifetime spent within a kilometer.

Now they were taking her to another world. To a fate unknown.

Jade's voice echoed in Ayumi's ears.

I want their skin!

The starship flew for hours. Maybe days. It felt like years.

Ayumi fell asleep, maybe she passed out. There was no room to lie down, to sit. The crowd pinned her against the wall. A hive of misery, of death, of despair. Piss and shit and blood and vomit on the floor. Bodies on the floor. An old woman dead on the floor. A woman giving birth on the floor. A baby dead on the floor. Feet on corpses.

Thirst.

There was so much thirst.

Heat.

It was so hot.

Disease. Fever. They coughed, trembled, swayed. The disease spread through the ship, and they emptied their bowels and coughed and trembled, and more died. More bodies on the floor. There was no more floor now, just an oozing pool of filth and death. Feet on rot. Ayumi stood on bodies, but still the crowd pinned her to the wall, and she struggled to breathe. So much thirst. So much heat. No air. No air. And more dead.

Days. It had to be days. It had to be years.

She lost consciousness again, and this time she slid between the sticky flesh of the people around her. She thudded onto the floor. Splashed onto the floor. Lay among the dead until hands grabbed her, pulled her up, shook her.

"Stay alive, Ayumi," they said. "Stay alive!"

She nodded, eyes rolling back.

"I promised to see Earth," she whispered. "I promised."

"Stay alive."

"I will, Father. I will …"

Days. Eras.

And the engines rumbled and the deathcar shook.

And they landed.

The hatch opened, and her nightmare began.

CHAPTER FIFTEEN

"Again!" Emet barked. "Faster this time."

Rowan brushed back her damp hair and wiped sweat off her brow. "I can't—"

"You can!" Emet said. "You must. Faster!"

The girl glared for a second. But then she nodded.

"Bloody hell, you are a slave driver," Rowan muttered. "*Sir.*"

The sun beat down, filling the ravine with heat and light. Grass carpeted the canyon floor, and vines covered the walls. Insects buzzed everywhere, as thick as raindrops. Helios was a hot, humid moon. It orbited a hot blue gas giant which, in turn, orbited a hot white sun. No sentient life lived here. They were half a parsec from the front line. And that front line was moving closer every day.

Emet peered up at the searing white sky. He could just make out his fleet, tiny white specks like pale satellites. The Heirs of Earth were up there, orbiting just beyond the atmosphere, waiting for allies and enemies. Neither had yet arrived.

He looked back down at Rowan. She stood before him, the grass rising past her knees. Burrs clung to her vest, and sweat dampened her short brown hair. Scratches, bruises, and mosquito bites covered her exposed arms.

Farther back, the metal cage rattled. The leafy vines covering it rustled madly. The stench of the animal within wafted through the ravine.

"You're Ra damn right I'm a slave driver," Emet said. "And you'll be thankful. As mean as you think I am, your sister will be worse. Ready?"

"Just a min—"

Emet hit a button on his controller, and the cage door opened.

The hellbull emerged, bellowing and kicking.

Rowan winced and scrambled back, cursing.

Hellbulls weren't much larger than people, but damn, the animals were mean. Coarse green fur covered them, providing camouflage on this grassy world. Not that the beasts needed it. Emet doubted any predator would mess with these creatures. They didn't have a real name. As far as Emet knew, no other humans had ever seen these animals, endemic to Helios. Emet had dubbed them hellbulls because they resembled small, muscular bulls, complete with horns. And because, well, they were hellish.

Cursing up a storm, Rowan retreated from the animal. She held up her magnetic blanket like a matador holding a red *muleta.* The hellbull kicked at her, and Rowan stumbled back, dodging the hoofs. She retreated another few steps, tripped over a tree root, and fell down hard.

"Damn it, on your feet!" Emet barked.

"You're worse than the hellbull!" she said, struggling to rise.

She tossed the magnetic cape.

The hellbull dodged the cloth and drove his horns into Rowan.

The girl screamed, falling backward.

"Damn it, Corporal!" Emet said. "How are you going to trap your sister if you can't even trap a dumb animal?"

She lay on the grass, eyes wide, and the bull charged again, hoofs about to crush her bones.

Emet cursed and fired his rifle, putting a bullet through the hellbull's brain. The animal thumped onto the grass, a smoking hole in its skull.

Rowan struggled to her feet, wincing, and opened her shirt. Two dents pressed into her bulletproof vest. She was trembling.

"It hurts," she said.

Emet sighed and lifted the magnetic cape. It had coiled shut. Tufts of grass and twigs and a handful of insects peeked from folds in the cloth.

"Congratulations," he said. "You've managed to trap some grass. You can eat it as salad tonight. I'll be eating that dead bull." He shook his head in disgust. "If this had been Jade attacking you, we'd both be dead right now."

Rowan winced, tugging off her bulletproof vest. "Ow. Damn. I think the animal might have cracked a rib." She grimaced. "Damn."

Emet sighed. "Let me see."

The bull had hit her bottom ribs. The skin was tender and red, but no ribs had been cracked.

"You're fine," he said.

"It hurts."

"So?" Emet glared at her. "So what if it hurts? Are you going to curl up and cry, girl? Are you going to give up because of a little pain? This isn't Paradise Lost. You can't hide here in a duct, whimpering in the shadows. You're an Inheritor now. A warrior of Earth. Act like it!"

Rowan stared at him, mouth open, rage in her eyes. Her cheeks flushed.

And then her eyes dampened. She began to cry.

Ra damn it.

Emet cursed her tears. Cursed himself for the pity that rose in him. He had not trained the girl properly. He had given her too much responsibility too fast. Yes, she was an Inheritor now. But still just seventeen. A girl who, until a few months ago, had never met another human.

He sat down on a boulder. He patted the stone beside him, and Rowan joined him.

"Do you think me harsh?" Emet said.

Rowan wiped her eyes. She shook her head. "No." She thought for a moment, then nodded. "I lied. Yes. You *are* harsh, sir. You're tough and terrifying and …"

She looked him, voice trailing off. She didn't need to say more. Emet saw the rest of her words in her eyes.

And you blasted me out of an airlock.

He gazed at the tall grass and creeping vines. Wind blew through the canyon, rustling the vegetation.

"My parents died when I was only twelve, did you know?" Emet said.

She shook her head.

"I was lucky," Emet continued. "I knew them for twelve years. Longer than you knew your parents. We lived on a cold, icy world. Nothing like this place. Barely a scrap of vegetation anywhere. We hunted local wildlife and ate the meat and organs raw. Ice and snow and rock everywhere. We had no fuel for fire. There were thermal springs on that planet, but the native sentient species had claimed those spots. They built domed cities there, filled with heat and life. We humans were cast out into the cold."

"I'm sorry," Rowan said softly.

"We were happy enough," Emet said. "I was, at least. My father taught me to hunt, and by age ten, I'd be going out to the icy plains alone, a rifle on my back. I would travel for hours on a motorized sled, hunting. Nothing but me and white mountains and sheets of snow for hours, sometimes days. Quiet solitude and stark, startling beauty. As I got older, I would go out longer and longer. I said it was to catch larger beasts, but in truth, I needed that solitude. I was always a solitary one. I think you know something about that."

Rowan bit her lip. "For a long time, I was like that. Even now, with humans around me, often I want solitude."

"One morning I set out on a hunt," Emet said. "I loaded my sled with gasoline and supplies, and I headed across sheets of ice toward the mountains. For days I stalked a great bear the size of a whale, following its tracks across valleys and hills and icy planes. It was a landscape untouched by sentience, primal and pure. Four days later, I returned to my village and found it gone. Wiped out. Every man, woman, and child slaughtered. Including my family."

Rowan looked at him with pity. "The scorpions?"

He shook his head. "No. This was years before the war. The natives had lost a child. Days later, they found out he had fallen into a lake and froze under the ice. But at first, they had blamed the humans outside their heated domes. So they came to our village. A mob. They slaughtered everyone, stole everything, burned what they couldn't steal. I remained alone in the world. As far as I knew, I was the last human in the galaxy."

She lowered her head. "I'm sorry, sir."

"That day, my childhood ended," Emet said. "For months, I survived alone in the wilderness. I was a good hunter. A survivor. But winter was coming, and I knew I could not survive the storms on my own. And the solitude, which I once craved, was even worse than the cold. I sneaked into a trading ship and smuggled my way off the planet. For years, I traveled between the stars, doing odd jobs on starships, serving as janitor, gunner, mercenary. By age seventeen—your age—I was already good at killing for hire."

She blinked. "I'm not very good at that yet."

"Whenever I could, I visited human communities," Emet said. "All of them had hard stories. Every one. Some were walled off in enclaves. Others suffered attacks from mobs. Some humans were slaves. Many communities had been wiped out. When I arrived, I found nothing but ashes, sometimes just a lone survivor huddling in the ruin. My wife was such a survivor. I found her on an asteroid colony, curled up among the dead."

"And … my father?" Rowan whispered, daring to meet his gaze. "Where did you meet him?"

"Ah, your father." Emet leaned back, and a thin smile tugged at his lips. "He was a wild one. David Emery was another mercenary. One of the few men I met who wasn't cowering, afraid, hiding in shadows. Your father was a fighter. A damn good soldier. We fought well together. For years, we fought side by side. Your father, Rowan, became more than a friend. He was like my brother."

She stared at her feet. "Until he betrayed you."

Emet sighed. "David Emery did what he felt was right. After years of war, he didn't want to fight anymore. We led the Heirs of Earth together as equals. But he grew weary of battle. No, not weary. That's the wrong word. David was never weary. He became … optimistic. He believed that humanity could still find peace, could find a place to hide, to live free. Not on Earth. We both knew Earth was thousands of light-years away, that other civilizations had claimed it, that many battles lay between us and our homeworld. But David believed we could find a new world, maybe a small moon like this one, and settle down, hide away from the galaxy." Emet sighed again, a deeper sigh this time. "I called him an idealist, a dreamer, a fool. He called me a warmonger. We fought. And he left. He left with a hundred others. With Jade. With your mother—and you in her belly. With the Earthstone."

"And he died," Rowan whispered. "My dad found a world to hide on. And the scorpions found him. I remember."

Emet placed a hand on her shoulder. "Rowan, I am harsh, and I am tough on you, because I still believe what I believed then. That our war is not over. That we all must become hard if we're to survive. The weak perish in this galaxy. Only if we're strong, if we fear no pain, can we hope to win, to bring about a generation that will grow up on Earth, that will know freedom and peace. We are the last generation of exile. We are the greatest generation. And therefore our curse—and privilege—is to suffer hardship and keep marching on. Despite the pain. Despite anyone who stands in our way."

Rowan rose to her feet. She stared at him, eyes damp, lips wobbly, and Emet thought she would weep again. But Rowan tightened her lips and saluted, slamming her left fist into her right palm. The Inheritor's salute.

Emet returned it.

"For Earth," he said.

"For Earth," Rowan repeated.

She walked around the hellbull carcass and lifted the rolled-up cape. Emet pressed a button on his controller, and the blanket released its magnetism and unfurled. Rowan shook off the plants and dirt inside, then looked at the nearby cage. There were still three hellbulls inside, snorting and pawing the ground.

"Ready?" Emet said.

Rowan assumed a fighting stance and raised the cape.

"Ready, sir."

He hit another button on his controller.

The cage opened again. Another hellbull emerged, charging toward Rowan.

She sidestepped with a dancer's grace, raised her cape, and draped it across the animal.

The magnetic cape wrapped around the animal and tightened, trapping its legs.

The animal crashed down, wrapped up inside the cloth. It thrashed madly, moving across the grass, but couldn't escape.

Rowan looked up at Emet, grinning. "I did it, sir!"

"Now hurry!" He ran forward and grabbed one end of the writhing animal. "With me, grab the other end, into the tunnel! Go, go!"

Rowan gripped the other end of the trapped hellbull. They lifted the heavy beast. It flailed, and they nearly dropped the bundled animal. They managed to haul the thrashing creature toward the canyon wall. Emet parted the vines, unveiling a stone door worked into the cliff.

He shoved the door open, revealing a tunnel. They carried their burden inside, then slammed the door shut behind them. It locked. They placed the struggling hellbull on a waiting gurney, then rolled it down the tunnel as it flailed.

A hundred meters down the tunnel, they reached a chamber and a waiting shuttle.

"Faster!" Emet said.

They shoved the struggling animal into the shuttle, leaped into the cockpit, and fired up the engine.

They tore through a curtain of vines and soared into the sky. The shuttle rattled. Emet's ears popped. Rowan grimaced, clinging to her seat, turning green. The shuttle clattered, roaring out fire. Within three minutes, they were in space.

The rest of the Inheritor fleet awaited them there.

"Go, go, faster!" Emet said.

Rowan gripped the controls, directing the shuttle toward the hangar of the *Jerusalem*. She slid into the hangar—moving too fast. She winced and hit the brakes. The shuttle banged onto the floor, chipping metal, raising sparks.

The hangar door slammed shut.

"Warp speed, go!" Rowan shouted into her comm.

In the hangar, a blue light turned on, emulating warp speed.

Rowan let out a shaky breath. She looked at Emet.

"Time, sir?" she whispered.

He checked his watch. His heart sank, and he grumbled.

"Thirteen minutes and ten seconds since we caught the animal. Too slow. Too damn slow! If this were your sister, her strikers would have pulverized us before the jump to warp."

Rowan glanced behind her. In the back of the shuttle, the hellbull was still kicking in its trap. It floundered in the cape like a fish in the net, banging against the shuttle walls.

"Sir," Rowan whispered, "if this were my sister, she would recognize me. She would listen to reason. She was coming around last time, and—"

"Corporal, enough," Emet said. "We've been over this. This is our plan. We will wait for Jade's fleet to arrive. We will battle her in space. We will pretend to crash the *Jerusalem* into the ravine. Jade will follow us down onto Helios to investigate. She'll want to capture us herself, whether we're dead or alive. When she approaches you, you'll sing your song. The one from your childhood. When Jade is disoriented, you'll trap her in the electric cape."

Rowan nodded. "Then into the tunnel, then into the shuttle, then up into space, then into the *Jerusalem*, then to warp speed. Yes. I know. But I think, sir, that if I could just talk to her, we can—"

"No!" Emet said. "Jade is dangerous, Rowan. More dangerous than you realize. This is the creature—not a woman anymore but a creature—that murdered millions. She is no longer your sister. She is a hybrid, part humanoid, part scorpion, part machine. No longer human. We're capturing her so that we can interrogate her. That is all. Not to bring her back into humanity's embrace." His voice softened. "I'm sorry, Corporal. I know you want your sister back. I want my own slain family back."

"Jade was not murdered like our parents," Rowan whispered. "She's still alive. She's still inside that hard white skin they gave her. Somewhere inside that cyborg, that creature, Jade Emery is weeping and begging for help. I know it. And you'll see, sir. I'll help you trap her. Like you planned. And I'll help you interrogate her for information on the scorpions. But sir, I know that we can bring her back, that we can return her sanity, that we can make her human again. Or at least, I believe. I hope." Her eyes dampened. "All my life, I've run on hope. It hasn't let me down yet."

Emet stared at the girl. They sat together in the shuttle, quiet for a long moment.

Yes, let her believe this, he thought. *Let her have this hope. It will motivate her. She needs to believe.*

He nodded.

"All right, Corporal. We'll see. Now come, down onto the planet. We have time for another few drills. This time, we'll use a tougher, stronger animal." He smiled grimly. "I'll be throwing all sorts of beasts at you over the next few days."

Rowan winced. "Are you sure we can't just tranquilize Jade?"

"Rowan, I've seen railgun bullets shatter against Jade's skin. A tranquilizing dart isn't going to work. Nor will gas. Our rebels report that Jade can breathe in anything we lob at her. It has to be you—with a trap. Ready for another round? I want this done under ten minutes. Think we can crack ten?"

She nodded. "We'll get it done in seven minutes, sir. I know we can do seven. From canyon to warp—seven minutes. Let's do this."

Emet gave her an approving nod. "There's fire in you. Good. How are your ribs?"

"They hurt, sir. Badly. But so what?"

He smiled. "Come on, Emery. Fly the shuttle down to the planet. I want you to become an expert pilot by the end of today, as well as an expert trapper. In case anything happens to me, you need to complete the mission yourself—including flying this shuttle. Let's—"

Before Emet could complete his sentence, Rowan fired up the shuttle and burst back out into space. Fire filled her eyes, and her lips were tight. They dived into the atmosphere, wreathed in flame, and back into the canyon.

They got it down to seven minutes.

Then to six.

Within only days, maybe hours, the scorpions would arrive.

They would be ready.

CHAPTER SIXTEEN

"There it is." Coral pointed, tears in her eyes. "Elysium. The birthplace of weaving."

"They must sell great baskets," Bay said.

Coral glared at him. "Don't joke. This place is holy to us weavers." She returned her eyes to the planet ahead. "Long have I wished to gaze upon ancient Elysium, a world of myth and wonder."

They sat together in Brooklyn's cockpit. The small ship rattled across space, badly damaged but still flying fast. The planet floated before them, green and mottled with white clouds. Elysium was just slightly smaller than Earth, its atmosphere rich with oxygen, her temperature just above water's freezing point. Most planets were hellholes—barren deserts, flaming ovens, frozen wastelands, or jungles filled with bacteria that would eat your flesh faster than piranhas. Here was a rare clement world.

"It's here," Coral whispered. "On this planet's surface. The Weeping Weaver Guildhall. It's here that Gadriel the Good founded the order. Here that we'll find the Godblade, the weapon that can defeat the Hierarchy."

"Are you sure this place is abandoned, Coral?" Bay stared at the green planet. "It looks beautiful. A Goldilocks planet."

She frowned. "Goldilocks?"

Bay nodded. "Yeah, like the chick from the fairytale. She wanted porridge that's not too hot, not too cold, just right. Goldilocks planets are just right. The temperature keeps water liquid. The gravity is just right. The atmosphere is rich with oxygen, but not so thick that it'll crush you. Goldilocks planets are rare. One in a million. Usually you see a bunch of aliens fighting over them."

Coral stared ahead, a small smile on her lips. The planet's light reflected in her eyes.

"Only weavers may enter the skies of Elysium. In ancient legends, all others are cast away."

"Great." Bay leaned back. "Another planet I'm not welcome at. I'll add it to the list. At least this one isn't because I got drunk in the pool."

Coral rolled her eyes. "You're with me, Bay. You'll be fine. But do try not to drink until you fall into any bodies of water."

"No promises," Bay said.

As the planet came closer, Bay barely noticed any bodies of water. There were certainly no oceans or lakes. The world of Elysium was a single continent, its mountains towering, its canyons deep. Vegetation covered most of the world, receding only from the poles and tallest mountains. Soon the planet filled their field of vision.

"Um, dudes?" Brooklyn woke up from sleep mode. "I'm detecting something weird ahead. Whole lotta radiation hitting me."

"Divert more power to shields," Bay said.

"Done." Brooklyn shuddered. "Dude, I feel all tingly. Like a million space ants hitting me. I—coming from—can't—"

Her monitors began to crackle with static.

Her camera wilted.

The starship all but shut down.

Gravity seized Brooklyn and began pulling her toward the planet. At this angle, they wouldn't even survive atmospheric entry, let alone a crash on the surface.

Bay grabbed the controls, desperate to pull them back up. But the engines were dead. Life support shut down. Oxygen masks dangled from the overhead compartment.

"What the hell?" Bay said. "Coral, what did your damn planet do to my starship?"

"It's not my planet!" she said. "Your starship is just old and broken."

"Hey! Brooklyn is not old. Well, okay she is, but she's not broken. Okay, she's broken too, but your planet still sucks." Bay yanked a lever, switching on emergency power. Life support came back on, but the monitors remained dead. "Brook! Brook, can you hear me, girl? I—"

A shimmer of light caught his eye.

He stared toward the planet.

Oh hell no.

"A shield!" Bay cried, pulling the joystick.

He managed to slow Brooklyn, to raise her prow, but not pull free from the gravity well.

They slammed into the transparent shield engulfing Elysium in a huge bubble.

Brooklyn jolted and skidded. The floor dented. Sparks flew. If not for their seat belts, Bay and Coral would have flown through the windshield. The starship careened back into space, tumbling, rolling back into the distance.

Once they were far enough, the power came back on.

Lights blinked and Brooklyn's camera rose.

"Whoa." The starship moaned. "I feel like a frigate ran over me. What the hell happened?"

Bay glared at Coral. "*Somebody* neglected to tell us that an invisible shield encloses Elysium."

Coral grimaced and rubbed her neck. "I didn't neglect to tell you anything, Corporal Bay Ben-Ari. I didn't know. I've never been here." She winced. "Rattled every bone in my body. At least now we know what the old legend means. The shield must be what casts out anyone who isn't a weaver."

"Um, last I checked, Miss Coral the Weaver, you got your ass cast out pretty bad too."

She ignored him. "Brooklyn, can you turn back toward the planet? I need to take another look."

"Sure thing, dude," Brooklyn said, turning back toward Elysium.

Bay raised an eyebrow. "Why do you obey Coral right away, and it's always an argument with me?"

"She doesn't demand obedience," Brooklyn said. "She just asks, doesn't order."

Bay groaned. "She doesn't own you! You *are* my starship, you know."

"Actually, Bay, I was reading the Galactic Charter of Android Rights, and according to that, I'm an EFA. That's Electronic Free Agent. And according to the charter, *you* are a slave owner."

"Yeah, well, according to your user manual, you're a shuttle that belongs in the ISS *Jerusalem*'s hangar. Which, I am told, is a breeding ground for ants. But if you want go back, I can—"

"I'll be good!" Brooklyn said.

Coral glared at them. "Will you two be quiet? I'm trying to focus." She took a deep breath. "I hesitate to spend aether so soon, but … I must see."

She began unbuttoning her shirt, revealing a tattoo between her breasts. The rune was shaped like an eye. It began to glow, and soon Coral's real eyes shone too, filled with starlight.

Bay found himself staring. He quickly looked away, cheeks flushing.

Brooklyn's camera lens dilated. She gaped at the weaver but said nothing.

"I see," Coral whispered. "A sea of radiation shielding the planet. A force field. An impenetrable wall. And … a door." Coral smiled. "Brooklyn, can you take us closer to the pole? And over the horizon. Yes. We're closer now. A gateway reveals itself. But the door is locked. It ..." Her eyes and rune went dark. She buttoned up her shirt. "I dare not use more."

She slumped in her seat, winded.

"You all right, Coral?" Bay said.

She nodded and closed her eyes. "There is always a cost to summoning aether. I'm not yet a master. It wearies me."

"I know what you need," Bay said. "A nice, strong cup of coffee, black as a moonless night."

"That would be nice," she whispered. "But add some creamer. Black coffee is just hot bean water, you know."

Bay left the cockpit and brewed some coffee in the kitchenette. As he worked, he tried very hard to ignore the memory of Coral unbuttoning her shirt, revealing the sides of her breasts.

Don't, Bay, he told himself. *She's a damn weaver. You don't want to get into this mess.*

Brooklyn's voice emerged from the kitchen's speakers. "Dude, why don't you ever make me coffee?"

"I fill you up with fuel. That's your coffee."

"Yeah, but you're never nice about it," Brooklyn said.

He rolled his eyes. "Fine, next time I'll serve your fuel in a mug with creamer, happy?"

"And make sure you add crumpets," Brooklyn said.

He poured a mug of coffee. "Brook, you don't even know what a crumpet is, and neither do I."

"Well, we don't know what a Godblade is either, but we've let Coral take us to this planet in search of one."

"Touche."

Bay added creamer to the mug, then brought the drink to Coral. She took a few sips, and some life returned to her eyes.

"Thank you, Bay," the weaver said. She held the mug in both hands, waiting for the drink to cool. "All right. The shield around the planet? Weavers built it. It's woven of aether and air and energy. There's a gateway, large enough for a starship to fly through, but it's locked. The gateway is a giant weaver artifact. Remember what I told you about artifacts?"

Bay nodded. "Yeah. Like your dagger. Like the old weavers' looms. Like the Godblade we're seeking. You need the right rune to unlock them."

"Exactly." Coral reached for a notebook and pencil, which Bay had been scribbling with during the journey. "May I?"

He nodded. "Go ahead."

Coral began to draw, tracing an elaborate sigil. It was shaped like a filigreed circle, enclosing stars and keys.

"When I was using the sight, I saw this rune engraved into the gateway, glittering with aether," Coral said. "It's called a skylock rune. This rune can open the door."

"Great," said Bay. "So after your coffee, can you turn on your skylock tattoo and open the gate?"

Coral sighed. "I don't have a skylock rune."

Bay's mouth hung open. "Are you sure? Maybe if you unbuttoned your shirt a bit more?"

Her smile was tight. "I'm sure you'd love that, Bay, but I assure you—I've never been inked with a skylock."

"All right." Bay nodded. "No problem. We take a little detour. We find a tattoo parlor, we get you a skylock tattoo, and Bob's your uncle."

"Bay!" Coral's eyes flashed. "Have I taught you nothing? It's not that simple. A weaver can't just stroll into a tattoo parlor and get a new rune. These are ancient sigils of power, inked with aether. A weaver must *earn* each rune. Only the ancients, when they deem us worthy, may bestow the runes upon us."

Bay grimaced. "Well, that certainly puts a damper on things. So how do you earn a rune?"

"Depends on the rune," Coral said. "The one I just used, the sight? I had to meditate and pray for a week in the wilderness, gazing into nature and into myself. My rune of healing? I had to serve for a year in a hospice, tending to the dying, before the ancients granted me a rune to save lives. Often, the ancients demand a task, a mission, something to help a weaver learn the true value of a rune."

"I'm almost afraid to ask," Bay said, "but what quest do you need to complete for a skylock rune?"

"I don't know," Coral said. "I must meditate and pray to the ancients for wisdom. It might take a while."

"Coral, I thought we didn't have time," Bay said. "The whole thing about, you know, this planet being behind enemy lines, and the scorpions flying here to find the Godblade too, and Jade hunting humans everywhere, and us basically needing the Godblade really, really soon? You know, that thing?"

"Oh, don't worry, Bay, we can defeat the scorpions with your sarcasm, I'm sure." Coral rolled her eyes. "I'm aware of the time concerns. But unless you have a few antimatter weapons on Brooklyn, or a fleet of warships armed with hydrogen bombs, a skylock rune is the only way to open the door."

"Brook, any anti-matter weapons?" Bay asked. "Hydrogen bombs? Nope? Well, as I thought, the only doomsday weapon around here is somewhere in the Weeping Guildhall down on that planet. All right! Get to praying, Coral. While you're at it, can you pray for some crumpets?"

Coral tilted her head. "Crumpets? You mean the old English griddle cake made from flour and yeast?"

"So that's what they are!" Brooklyn said.

Coral went into the hold, sat cross-legged on the floor, and began to meditate.

She meditated for a long time.

Brooklyn went into sleep mode, shuddering sometimes in a dream, mumbling in her sleep about ants. Bay kept to the cockpit, wanting to give Coral privacy, but soon grew antsy and began to pace the small starship. Brooklyn was only a few meters long, but Bay made the most of them.

All the while, Coral remained still, eyes shut, meditating.

Bay lounged on the bed, reading a book.

He paced again.

He made more coffee.

He drew a few elven warriors.

Still Coral meditated, seemingly in a trance.

Don't you even have to use the bathroom after that mug of coffee? he thought, daring not disturb her.

He yawned. He hadn't slept in a long while, but he felt too anxious to nap, knowing the scorpions might arrive at any moment.

Brooklyn woke up and whined. "What's taking her so long?"

"Hush, you'll disturb her," Bay said.

"Good." Brooklyn rocked from side to side. "I'm bored."

Bay grabbed a bulkhead, nearly falling. "Brooklyn, do you want me to shut down your AI?"

"I'll be good!"

Coral kept meditating.

Bay yawned again. He looked at the drawing of Rowan on the wall. He had covered his walls with his artwork: scenes of starships battling dragons, wizards and elves on adventure, and curvy space princesses. But his favorite drawing was his portrait of Rowan. Her sparkling eyes. Her impish smile. Her messy brown hair.

I miss you, Row, he thought. *If you were here, we'd watch one of your movies. Or you'd read me the script you wrote for* Dinosaur Island II.

We both have to survive this, Row. You still need to write Dinosaur Island III *and act it out for me.*

He took his sketchpad and began to draw Rowan again, only this time he drew her on an island, facing a dinosaur among the trees. While various small animals fled, Rowan held a video camera, filming the beast.

"Someday you'll film your movies, Row," he said softly. "*Dinosaur Island* and all the other ones."

He was putting the final touches on the drawing when Brooklyn screamed.

"Striker!" The starship rattled and her red alert lights flashed. "Bay, Bay—striker incoming!"

He whipped his head toward a porthole.

He saw it in the distance—a triangular warship, black as the space between stars, its afterburner blazing.

His heart sank.

The scorpions were here.

CHAPTER SEVENTEEN

"Bay!" Brooklyn cried.

"I see him!" he shouted, then looked at Coral. The woman was still meditating, eyes closed. "Coral, you better wake up now!"

"Bay!" Brooklyn shouted. "Take over my controls! You're better at battle than me."

"Coral, wake up!" Bay shook the weaver, but she wouldn't emerge from her trance.

With a groan, Bay abandoned Coral, raced into the cockpit, and scrambled into his seat. He grabbed the joystick and spun Brooklyn around toward the charging striker.

Ra, the size of the thing. It flew alone here, perhaps a scout, but it loomed as large as a frigate. Brooklyn was like a minnow facing a barracuda.

The striker charged toward them, plasma blazing.

Bay shoved the throttle with his bad hand. He had recently installed a harness there, allowing him to slip his bad hand into a leather grip, then operate the lever. With his good hand, he tugged the joystick, soaring above the inferno. The fire grazed Brooklyn's underbelly, and she yowled.

"I've been savaged!" Brooklyn said. "We have to flee!"

"You're too slow." Bay gritted his teeth, whipping around another blaze of plasma. "Look at the engines on that ship. We'll never outrun it."

More plasma bolts flew toward them.

Bay plunged down so quickly his heart leaped into his mouth. He dived under the plasma, then rose high, flying toward the enemy ship.

"What are you doing?" Brooklyn screamed.

"Improvising!" Bay said.

He soared toward the sun, then spun, the light at his back, and swooped toward the striker.

"Bay!" Brooklyn screamed. "I changed my mind. I'll fly!"

Bay ignored her. He narrowed his eyes, diving toward the enemy, and fired his cannons.

Shells flew out, rattling Brooklyn, and slammed into the warship below.

The shells exploded against the striker's hull.

Fire blazed and gushed upward like geysers. Bay tugged the joystick, swerved, and dodged the inferno. He flew away, orbiting the green planet below, racing a hundred kilometers over the force field.

Behind them, the striker was dented but fully operational. The lumbering warship spun toward them, extended new cannons, and released an inferno of blazing metal bullets the size of swords.

Bay had no time to rise above or dive below the rapid projectiles.

Instead, he plunged headlong toward the striker—into the hailstorm of bullets.

Brooklyn and Bay both screamed.

He yanked the joystick all the way to the side, barrel-rolling.

Bullets flew all around him. They scratched the roof, grazed the starboard hull, and perforated the wings.

"What are you doing?" Brooklyn cried.

"Dodging bullets!" he shouted. "Coral did this back at the front line, remember?"

"She's a weaver!" Brooklyn said. "You're an idiot! You're gonna gets us killed!"

He kept flying, spinning madly, and fired his own cannons.

The artillery tore through bullets, exploding in space. A few shells made it to the warship and blasted against its prow.

Bay soared.

Brooklyn was clattering now. Bullets had dented her all over. Some had nearly broken through her hull. Smoke rose from their stern.

"Brook, you all right?" he said.

"No!" she said. "I've got holes in me! Left engine is leaking, Bay. I'm hurt. We gotta run."

Bay glanced behind him. Coral still sat in the hold, cross-legged, meditating. Her eyes were closed, her face serene.

"Coral, you really need to wake up and use some magic!" Bay shouted, but she remained in a trance.

The striker turned back toward him. Brooklyn wouldn't withstand another hit. The plasma blazed through space, searing white and blue, and Bay flew madly, zigzagging around the assault. He tried to flee, but the striker pursued doggedly, and Bay was too close to the planet's gravity to activate his warp drive. A blast slammed into their stern, and Brooklyn wailed.

Smoke filled the cabin.

"Coral!" Bay shouted.

The weaver still sat, silent, eyes closed, even as the smoke wafted around her.

More plasma flew. The striker charged, about to ram into them. Bay rose high, firing bullets at the enemy, but they shattered against the shields. He had to reach the striker's exhaust pipes. To fire into the enemy's engines. But he couldn't make it across the striker's stern. Whenever he approached, the striker spun its prow toward him, and more plasma fired.

"Brook, hang tight, I'm gonna try something."

"Does it involve not dying?" she asked.

"Hope so!"

Brooklyn shuddered. "I love your optimism."

He took a deep breath. He shoved both joystick and throttle forward.

He swooped toward the planet.

The striker followed, cannons firing.

Bay jerked left, right, dodging the incoming plasma, diving closer, closer, closer . . .

"Bay, the radiation! It's—"

Brooklyn began shutting down.

That was his signal.

With the last drop of power, Bay jerked the joystick back, leveling off.

Brooklyn's belly grazed the invisible shield around the planet, showering sparks. They skipped forward like a rock on ice before careening off the force field. They tumbled back into space.

Behind them, the massive striker slammed into the shield with full force, afterburners blazing.

For an instant, Bay thought the warship would break through, would rip the shield like a knife through a soap bubble.

But the shield was stronger.

It was almost a thing of beauty. The striker's prow crumpled first, flattening against the shield, casting out a cloud of debris. Then the body cracked open, ripping like an overripe fruit, and the thrusters kept shoving, kept plowing what remained forward, into the shield, until the body of the striker shattered into millions of pieces. The engines tore free, spinning through space, pounding against the shield, then flying off into the distance, still spewing fire. A cloud of metal blasted outward, interspersed with bits of scorpion exoskeletons. Below the shield, the sky rippled with the impact.

Bay flew away from the explosion, roaring out from the cloud of debris and fire. Shards of metal slammed into Brooklyn, and she awoke, wailing. A shock wave of debris slammed into them, and they careened through space, tumbling, alarms blaring, before finally Bay managed to steady their flight.

They came to a stop, barely alive, and looked down at a blackened patch on the transparent shield.

The rest of the striker floated away in countless pieces.

Coral stumbled into the cockpit, rubbing her eyes.

"What the hell happened?" She blinked. "I go for one short meditation, and it looks like a nuclear war went down."

"Oh, Princess Pillows is awake!" Bay raised his hands. "Hallelujah! We're saved. Did you enjoy your nap, Your Highness?"

She took her seat, frowning. "What are you talking about? What did I miss?"

Bay groaned. He spent a moment describing the ordeal. His stomach was still lurching, his knees still weak. He had to pause and swallow several times, and his heart wouldn't slow down. The encounter had rattled him—badly. Perhaps his father and sister blew up spaceships every day, but to Bay this was still new, and cold sweat trickled down his back.

"So that's my story," Bay said. "What about you, Coral? You dream up a solution?" He glanced down at her body, then back up to her eyes. "Any new tattoos, ones that can open the shield gate?"

"Runes, not tattoos," Coral said. "And not yet. Remember what I told you? The ancients demand that weavers *earn* each rune, prove themselves worthy. The mightiest runes require great tasks. A battle rune might demand victories in war. A rune to unlock knowledge might require the weaver to read certain books, even write a book of her own. In my meditation, I reached out to the ancients. I spoke to one who called himself Sandalphon, an ancient who has been guiding my path. I asked him for the skylock rune, which can open the gate in the shield. And Sandalphon explained how I can prove myself worthy."

Bay steeled himself, preparing for the worst. "It involves something on the other side of the galaxy, doesn't it?"

"Well, hopefully not," Coral said. She blushed and looked at her lap.

Bay frowned. "What is it? It can't be that bad."

She looked up, then down again. She twisted her fingers in her lap. "It's … not that bad."

"Great." Bay exhaled in relief and wiped his forehead. "I was worried for a sec. Can you do it here? From aboard Brooklyn? Before more strikers arrive, preferably? If you need to study something, Brook can patch you into Wikipedia Galactica."

"It's not something … I can learn … from a monitor." Coral bit her lip. She met his eyes, then quickly looked away.

"Coral." Bay frowned. "Look at me, buddy. What did the ancients tell you? What must you do to earn the skylock rune?"

She sighed. "Don't hate me, all right?"

"Coral, out with it!"

"Fine!" Coral said. "The ancients speak in riddles. Here is what he told me."

She cleared her throat and recited what sounded to Bay like a poem.

The heart is like a house
With many chambers, locked
Some are dark and secret
Others filled with light
Ghosts haunt and cry and moan in some
While sweet visions laugh in others
Dancing like light through rain
The heart is like a house

Its doors are often locked
And many hearts have burned
And risen from ashes to blaze
And burn again
Their locks grow heavy
Forged with many fires
They are tempered and hardened
Trapping ghosts and angels
The heart is like a house
With a door that can still open
To light and life and love
And chambers filled again
When she who has closed her heart
Opens her secret garden gates
No locks will hold her back
For she can cross through stone and air
Into houses of light

Coral finished her poem and lowered her eyes.

Bay frowned. "I'm not sure I understand. Actually, I'm sure I don't understand."

Coral sighed. "Bay, the ancients want weavers to grow as people. To walk along a path of fulfillment, experience, and wisdom. In the past, I've had to cross deserts under the searing sun, learning about solitude and spirituality. For other runes, I've had to face battle, to know fear and courage. Weavers don't just learn knowledge. We grow as people. We gain life experiences. As we grow, as we become wiser, we gain runes."

"Okay," Bay said.

She winced. "Now the ancients want me to open my … secret gate."

Bay frowned. "What do you mean?"

"They want me to know love," she said. "To open my heart and body to you." She placed her hands on his shoulders. "To make love to you. The poem, Bay. It's about me. How my heart has been closed, locked up, filled with secret pain. How it burned." Tears filled her eyes. "I've known much pain in my life, Bay. Pain I haven't told you about. Memories that still hurt me so much. And now I must learn joy. Learn love. Make love to me, Bay. Teach me the pleasure of lovemaking. This is what I must learn."

"But ... why?" Bay learned back. "What does that have to do with locks?"

"It's about me unlocking myself," she said. "My heart. My soul. My body. It's about finally opening up."

Bay's mouth hung open. He forced it closed. With a sigh, he took Coral's hand in his.

"Coral, you shouldn't feel compelled to sleep with me." He looked into her eyes. "It shouldn't be forced. That's not how love works."

She trembled. "Bay, I'm a virgin. I've never had time for men. I've dedicated my life to the Weavers Guild. I'm a human—I grew up hunted, oppressed, beaten and enslaved. In the Weavers Guild, I found strength and purpose. But never love." Tears filled her eyes. She touched his cheek. "When I met you, that changed. Spending time with you has changed me. The ancients wouldn't force me to do anything I didn't want to. They know my heart. They know its secrets and whispers. They know what it yearns for, and how it can grow. They know that my heart beats for you. Make love to me, Bay."

She pulled him into the hold and undressed. Her body was slender, her skin smooth and dark, adorned with silver runes. Her platinum hair cascaded around her breasts and down to her rounded hips. Bay had never seen a sight more beautiful. He had made love to women before, but none had seemed so ethereal, so intoxicating.

Coral stepped closer to Bay. Her breasts pressed against his chest. She stroked his hair and whispered into his ear.

"Make love to me, Bay." Her soft breath caressed his ear. "My secret gates are yours, those of my heart and my body."

She began to undress him, her fingers deft, until he stood naked before her. Suddenly he felt self-conscious. Bay normally wore draping sleeves and deep pockets, clothes he could hide his left hand in, but there was no hiding his flaws like this.

He turned away, abashed. He found himself looking at the drawing of Rowan on the wall.

"Do you love her?" Coral said, following his gaze.

"Yes. I mean, not like … that poem the ancients recited. She's very young."

Coral pulled his face back toward her. "But I'm older, and I'm here, and I want you, Bay." She kissed his lips. "Make love to me. Teach me."

She lay down on the bed, pulling him down with her.

"Will you teach me?" she whispered into his ear.

He nodded. It had been so long since he had loved a woman of flesh and blood, not just a hologram.

"I will teach you," he whispered.

He had always known Coral to be confident, bordering on arrogant, but in his bed she was meek, trembling at first, shy when she kissed him. But soon the ice broke, and she kissed him deeply, hungrily, and Bay knew that she had spoken truth. She was not only doing this for her rune. She wanted him, and she gasped when he kissed her neck, when his lips trailed down to her breasts, and she buried her hands in his hair.

As Bay made love to her, she moaned, and he felt her heart beat, and her breath was soft against him. Bay realized that the androids and holograms never had beating hearts, warm breath, and tremble in their lips. It had been years since he had loved a real woman. A woman of flesh and blood. A human. And this was good. This was humanity. And in her kisses there was love.

Afterward, she lay by his side, nestling against him, and ran her fingers across his chest.

"Thank you," she whispered. "You're an excellent teacher. What grade do I get?"

He smiled. "You should ask the ancients. They're the ones who need to grade your project."

Her hand strayed lower, moved under the blanket, and wrapped around him.

"Teach me again."

His eyes widened. "So soon?"

She nodded, grinned, and bit her lip. "Yes. I demand it."

They made love again, slower this time, gazing into each other's eyes, laughing, smiling, kissing.

Finally they lay side by side again, covered in sweat.

"That was good," Coral said. "Maybe the ancients wanted me to learn what it's like to be human. This is what humans did back on Earth, isn't it?"

"I think they might have done it a few times since, too," Bay said.

"I don't just mean sex. I mean happiness." She kissed his cheek. "I am happy. For the first time in years, I'm happy."

He rolled onto his side to face her.

"Coral." He stroked back a lock of her hair. "You told me earlier that you suffered pain in your life. Would you like to tell me what happened?"

She lowered her head. "Okay."

Bay cursed himself. "I'm sorry. You just said you were happy, and I had to ruin the moment."

She looked back up into his eyes. "No, really, it's all right. This is about opening up, right? So I'll open up." She took a deep breath. "My story is not unusual. Not these days. I was born on Til Shiran, a desert world on the fringe of the galaxy. My first few years were happy enough. My parents owned a vegetable cart. We were poor but happy. But when I was three years old, a native child went missing. The natives are called Tarmarins, scaly creatures, similar to pangolins or armadillos from Earth."

"I've met a few Tarmarins before," Bay said. "Never drink with them. They're mean drunks. Nasty things."

"Some are," Coral said. "The young Tarmarin was soon found, dead. His body lay on a roadside, holding half a fruit. The natives accused my parents of poisoning him. Never mind that the child had been sick for years, dying of inner rot. Never mind that we sold vegetables, not fruit. My parents were human. That's what Tarmarins do—blame humans for their troubles. They took my parents into the city square, nailed them to wagon wheels, broke their bones with a hammer, then left them to die." Her voice was soft, her face expressionless. "They forced me to watch. They would have killed me too, broken my limbs and slung them through the spokes of a wheel."

"That's horrible," Bay said. He put a hand on her waist. "I'm so sorry."

"The weavers saved me that day. Not human weavers. Tarmarins. They're not all evil. They took me to their guildhall. There are weaver guildhalls on many worlds, operated by many species. The weavers raised me, taught me to weave, to earn my runes. It was a hard life. Even among the other weavers, I was an outcast. Many apprentices bullied me. Beat me." Her eyes hardened. "And yet I became stronger. Strongest among them. By age twenty, I had gained more runes than any other apprentice. I became a journeywoman."

"A weaver rank," Bay said. "Like a lieutenant."

She nodded. "Once I earned that rank, I left my guildhall. I could have remained, risen in the ranks. But I moved back in with the small human community on Til Shiran. I wanted to protect them. But I watched so many slain. Every week, the natives killed another. Every time a well ran dry, or a child died, or a crop failed, the aliens punished us humans. Every week, the mobs attacked. I tried to fight them. To defend my community. To save human lives. One time the Tarmarins grabbed me, and ..." She winced. "They stripped me naked, Bay. They marched me naked through the streets, pelting me with trash. And one of the Tarmarins, he ..." Her eyes flooded with tears.

He held her close. "You don't have to tell me," he whispered.

She wept. "I lied to you, Bay. I wasn't a virgin. But I had never made love to a human. When the ancients gave me this task, I knew. I understood. They didn't just want me to lose my virginity." She wrapped her arms around him. "They wanted me to heal, Bay. To learn that sex can be joyous too. To make me whole again." She smiled through her tears. "And you made me whole."

Bay kissed her tears away. "Coral, I'm sorry for all those times I was a smartass, when I bickered or scolded you. You're a wonderful, brave, and wise woman. I'm happy that you stole my ship and kidnapped me."

She laughed. "I am too."

A sob sounded above. "And me too!" Brooklyn said.

Bay and Coral leaped up in bed. They tugged the blanket up to their chins.

"Brook!" Bay said. "I thought you were in sleep mode! How long have you been listening?"

"Not long!" the starship said. "Since that pretty poem."

Bay groaned. "Brooklyn! I'm going to wipe your memory clean."

"I mean—I just woke up!" Brooklyn said. "I'll go back to sleep now. Oh, and Bay? You have a cute butt."

He gasped. He turned toward the cockpit, where he saw her camera staring through the doorway.

"You were watching too?" Bay cried.

Brooklyn vanished into sleep mode. Bay flopped back onto the bed. Coral looked around, slack-jawed, then shook her head and sighed.

"Well, she's right, you know," she said.

Bay sighed. "I'm definitely wiping her memory."

Coral lay back down, curled up against Bay, and kissed his cheek. Suddenly she gasped.

"Bay!" she whispered. "Look."

A white dot was glowing on her chest, just above her heart. The light moved, coiling in silvery lines, drawing a rune. Coral watched, smiling, the light in her eyes. Bay held her, watching too.

The ancients are drawing it, Bay thought. *They* are *real.*

Finally the light faded, leaving a white tattoo on her chest—a skylock rune.

Coral looked up into his eyes. She rose from the bed, wrapped a blanket around her nakedness, and walked into the cockpit. Bay paused to pull on his clothes, then joined her.

They flew closer toward the planetary shield.

"Can you sense the gateway?" he said.

Coral nodded and pointed. "There."

As Bay flew, the skylock rune on her chest began to glow. Down on the planetary shield, a matching rune—a circle filled with symbols like stars and keys—began to glow too. The rune on the shield was the size of a crop circle, glowing bright.

Bay had seen Coral unlock her runeblade before. The pommel had the same rune as on her hand. When she used her blade, both runes shone, connecting through the aether.

Now strands of aether rose from the shield below, flowed across space, and entered Brooklyn. The light connected to Coral's chest. The shimmering strands of aether flowed between the two runes.

She's plugged in like a damn toaster, Bay thought.

And below, where the rune appeared on the shield, a gateway opened.

Bay realized that the planet was even greener than he had thought. The opening revealed the true, vibrant colors of Elysium. He guided the ship through the gateway and into the rich atmosphere and blue sky. Behind them, the skygate slid shut and locked with a thud.

The aether floated away. The rune on Coral's chest faded to white ink.

"Most locks just need a password," Bay said. "You know, I prefer the sex-locks."

Coral rolled her eyes. "You would."

Bay's eyes strayed toward his sketchbook on the dashboard. It was opened to the drawing of Rowan on Dinosaur Island, filming one of the beasts. And sudden guilt filled Bay.

It was strange. He was not Rowan's boyfriend or lover. He was just her friend. Besides, she was far too young to romance. Why was Bay feeling guilty for making love to the beautiful Coral?

He descended through the sky, approaching the verdant landscapes below.

"Let's find this Weeping Weaver Guildhall," Bay said. "Let's find this Godblade and learn how to use it. If one striker already got here, others will follow, and I wouldn't count on this shield holding for long. Not with a Hierarchy fleet bombarding it. They won't need sex. They'll nuke their way through the door."

Coral nodded. "We must hurry." Her eyes lit up. "We'll find the Godblade. I'll learn what rune I need. And then we'll have a weapon that can kill them all." She placed a hand on his thigh.

"For Earth, Bay. For humanity. For happiness." She grinned impishly. "And for sex."

Bay wanted to grin too, to laugh, but he remembered how the striker had fired on him. How he had nearly died. He imagined thousands of those warships arriving here, and his hand shook on the joystick, and he couldn't stop seeing the fire.

CHAPTER EIGHTEEN

Everything hurt.

Rowan stood in her cabin, rubbing her shoulders, wincing. "Ouch."

Fillister buzzed around her. "Training hard? Or hardly training?"

Rowan glared at him. "That's a horrible joke. Yes, I've been training hard. Emet is a slave driver. He works me ruthlessly. Day after day—battling hellbulls down on the planet, climbing cliffs, racing down tunnels, lifting weights, flying shuttles, running, climbing, jumping, shooting ..." She grimaced and rubbed a sore muscle. "Bloody hell, Frodo never had to train like this."

Thankfully, Emet had given her a private cabin. This was a rare luxury aboard the ISS *Jerusalem,* normally reserved only for senior officers. Rowan was only a corporal, the second-lowest possible rank. But in the looming battle, she would be the most important soldier in the fleet.

It will be my task to capture Jade, she thought. *To save humanity. If I do that, Emet better promote me!*

Rowan looked through the porthole out into space.

The Inheritor fleet floated around her. Several warships. Barges and freighters filled with refugees and supplies. Starfighters with bright engines. There were also the starships Luther had given them, more than fifty old vessels. They were rusty and falling apart, but mechanics were floating around them, patching them up, readying them for battle.

Below the fleet, Helios was lazily orbiting its swirling gas giant. A yellow haze clung to the large moon, shimmering in the starlight. Rowan had spent much of the past few weeks on that hot, damp world, training for battle. Training to capture the Blue Witch, the architect of the Human Solution.

Rowan raised her eyes. She stared into the depths of space.

"You're out there somewhere, Jade," she whispered. "But you know I'm here. You'll come back to me. Soon we'll meet again. One day. Doomsday. You'll try to kill me. But I will make you remember who you are. I'll make you my sister again."

Rowan lowered her head, and a tear rolled down her cheek. She had been only a toddler when the scorpions had stolen Jade. Fifteen years had passed. A lifetime for Rowan. She didn't remember much from that time. But some memories remained. Playing with toy swords. Laughing. Singing in a cave with stalagmites that glittered and glowed. Hugging her sister. Being happy. Living with love.

But they captured you.

Rowan winced, remembering that day, how Sin Kra, the scorpion emperor, had gripped Jade in his claws, pulled her away.

They broke you. Turned you into a monster.

"They say she murdered millions," Rowan whispered. "But it's not her fault. I know this, Fill. It's not her fault. Sin Kra broke her. Implanted something in her brain. Forced her to kill. So she killed. She killed millions. But deep inside, she's still Jade, a scared girl, my sister. Still good. And afraid. And begging for help. We have to save her."

Fillister nodded. "Chin up, Row! We'll save her all right."

Rowan raised her chin, tightened her lips, and rubbed her eyes. "We'll save everyone. We'll end this war. We'll find Bay, wherever he is. I have to believe."

She stepped into the shower and stood for a long time under the hot water. Showers were a luxury. Back on Paradise Lost, she could only shower during the brief moments before artificial dawn, sneaking into the communal showers outside the brothel, places that reeked of mold and sex. Here aboard the *Jerusalem*, Rowan lingered under the stream, eyes closed, letting the water flow over her, steam against her skin, sear away her pain.

I live in comfort now, Rowan thought. *I have a bunk of my own, a real bed, a chair and desk, not just an HVAC duct. I own real clothes, the uniform of a proud military organization, not merely a blanket I turned into a ragged dress. I eat real food, not scraps stolen from the trash. I have real friends, not just friends from books and movies.* Her tears mingled with the water. *But I wish none of this had happened. I wish I could go back to Paradise Lost. Back home. I wish I could stop being so afraid.*

Her doorbell rang.

Rowan started, sure that the attack was here. Yet no klaxons wailed. When she peeked from behind the shower curtain, she saw no red lights.

"Be right there!"

She hurriedly pulled on her uniform, passed a hand through her wet hair, then slipped on her goggles, which she used as a headband.

"Coming!"

She rushed toward the door, then paused and reached for her pistol, her beloved Lullaby. Its stock was carved of aromatic wood, and brass gears shone above its trigger. She strapped a belt around her waist, then holstered the gun.

Just in case it's a scorpion ringing the doorbell, she thought with a wry smile.

When she opened the door, she saw Emet there.

"Sir!" She stumbled back and saluted. He had never visited her cabin before.

He nodded. "Corporal. I have an offer for you today. A surprise, if you will. I thought that you might like to—" He froze and frowned. "Are your pants inside out, Corporal?"

She glanced down and her cheeks burned.

"Ra damn it!" she blurted out. "I mean—sir! Will you excuse me, please?"

She rushed into the bathroom, fixed the mistake, then rushed back to the front door. She saluted again.

"Sir, ready for duty!" Her wet hair dripped across her face, but she dared not flick it back.

Emet gestured with his eyes.

Rowan flushed again and zipped up her fly.

"Sorry, sir," she whispered, too mortified to speak any louder. "I don't look much like the savior of humanity, do I? I'm so awkward and goofy."

As if on cue, her goggles slipped down her forehead and settled, crooked, across her face.

Emet smiled, and his smile eased her terror. "Sometimes, it's not the brave big heroes who save humanity, not the shining knights or legendary warriors. It's the simple people, awkward, endearing, and brave."

She pushed her goggles back up. "Well, I don't know about endearing and brave." She began tugging on her boots, wobbled, and fell. She looked up with a groan. "But I've got the awkward covered." She rose to her feet. "Sir, how can I serve today?"

"It's your day off, isn't it?" Emet said.

Rowan nodded. "Yes, sir. I thought I'd spend it watching movies, but sir, I'm glad to train today." She winced. "Truth is, I need to keep my mind off things. I'm worried sick. About meeting Jade again. About Bay missing. About this whole damn mess. I know you are too, sir."

Emet nodded. "I worry about my children every minute of every day. With every breath." Suddenly such pain filled his eyes. He seemed almost vulnerable, almost fragile. Then his face hardened, and he was the Old Lion again. "Corporal, for your day off, I wanted to show you something. Follow me."

They left her quarters and walked along the *Jerusalem*'s central corridor. As they walked between other bunks, soldiers stood at attention. There was a nervousness in the air. The men's knuckles were white around their rifles. The gunners stood stiffly at their posts, ready to fire their cannons. The shields stayed at maximum power, and the Firebirds were flying outside in tight patrols.

The Inheritors had not kept their location secret. In fact, they had been broadcasting it across the galaxy, chattering of an Inheritor base on Helios, of Emet Ben-Ari and Rowan Emery aboard the flagship.

We're calling you, Jade, Rowan thought. *Soon enough, maybe even today, you will come. Soon our fleets will clash. Soon thousands will die. Soon you and I will meet again. And I will spring the trap.*

Emet took her to a hatch near the back of the ship. He opened the door, revealing a shaft and ladder.

"You like machines, don't you?" Emet said.

"I love them, sir."

"Then come. Today I will show you the *Jerusalem*'s engine room."

Rowan gasped. She took a step back and gaped at him.

"Sir! The engine room of a starship!" Her eyes dampened. "For so many years, I dreamed of seeing one. Thank you, sir!"

He gestured at the shaft. "After you."

Grinning, Rowan scurried down like a monkey. She emerged into a vast chamber. She walked forward, jaw hanging open, staring around with huge eyes.

"Oh, sir," she whispered. "It's beautiful."

Massive pistons, as large as bathtubs, were pounding. Gears like dinner tables were turning. Pipes ran across the walls and ceiling, hissing and rattling and humming. Cables, sprockets, and fuel tanks rose like miniature cities. At the back of the room, a nuclear reactor was humming, encased with steel, rising as tall as a house. Everywhere were levers and buttons, hundreds of them. Rowan walked through this mechanical city, eyes like saucers, listening to the hissing and rumbling and humming, gazing at the moving gears and pistons, feeling the heat and cold and vibrations.

"I could live here," she said, turning toward Emet. "Can you let me live here?"

"Usually my soldiers hate engine room duty."

"Not me, sir. I love it here. Once this war is over, I'd love to become a mechanic, if you'll let me. Well, a mechanic or a film director. I still haven't lost hope of filming *Dinosaur Island.* That's the movie script I wrote. I—" She cringed. "Sorry, sir. I sound like a proper nut."

He gave her an odd look, then sighed. "I'm used to it, Corporal. And yes, once this war is over, I will send you to an engineering class. Alien universities don't accept humans, but we have our own teachers. Would you like that? The fleet always needs more engineers."

She gasped, then leaped forward and hugged him. "Sir, thank you! I promise to become the best engineer in the fleet." She bit her lip, then stepped back, her cheeks flushing. She looked around her. "I recognize a lot of this machinery. The nuclear reactor powers our conventional, sub-light speed engines. The pistons pump up the engines. Those furnaces give us life support, and that's an air filtration system. That's a water tank, isn't it? Wait, two water tanks, one to cool the reactor, one for drinking. But sir." She frowned. "Where is the azoth crystal?"

Emet led her toward the center of the room. A graphene pipe rose here from floor to ceiling, and smaller pipes branched off from it, leading to turbines near the exhaust. Emet typed a security code into a keypad on the pipe, then swung a latch open. Inside hovered a lavender crystal the size of a heart.

"An azoth crystal," Rowan whispered. The crystal shone, casting its purple light upon her.

Emet nodded. "A crystal that can bend spacetime the way a diamond can refract light. With this crystal, we can form a bubble of spacetime around us, the very fabric of the universe, and travel faster than light. This little piece of azoth, mined from a moon called Corpus, is worth more than the ship it's installed in."

Rowan reached out to touch out, but Emet grabbed her wrist.

"Careful," he said. "It's quite hot."

She pulled her hand back.

She stared at the pipe. It was large enough that she could have squeezed inside. She raised her eyes. The central pipe connected to other pipes on the ceiling, which in turn branched off, forming a labyrinth. She stared at ducts above. Rattling. Whispering with cold and hot air.

"I want to go back to my cabin," she whispered.

"Rowan, are you—" Emet began.

She ran. She ran across the engine room, reached the shaft back to the main deck, and began to climb.

She was halfway up when her head began to spin. She froze, clinging to the ladder. The shaft seemed to constrict her, closing in. She was stuck in the throat of a metal monster. Below her the engines were rumbling, clattering, shrieking. Bonecrawlers were screeching, waiting below, crawling toward her. Marshcrabs lurked above, ready to pounce. She clung to the ladder, trapped between the beasts, trembling. Trapped for years. Trapped in the ducts. Trapped in darkness. Pest. Pest! And she couldn't move, and her tears flowed.

"Rowan?"

A deep voice bubbled up, echoing in the engine room. Demonic. The voice of Belowgen the marshcrab, hunting her. The voice of Sin Kra, Emperor of the Hierarchy. She wept.

I'm trapped. I'm trapped. Help me. Leave me alone. Leave—

A hand tapped her foot.

Rowan screamed and released the ladder. She slipped, banged against the shaft, and landed in Emet's arms.

He pulled her back into the engine room, and Rowan panted, weeping. Emet held her at arm's length, staring at her, eyes narrowed.

"Rowan, what's wrong? Are you hurt?"

"I . . ." She gulped. "I thought I was back in Paradise Lost, trapped in the ducts. I'm fine now. I'm . . ." Tears flowed over her words.

Emet hesitated, then pulled her into an embrace. She held him tightly, her cheek against his chest. He kept his arms around her until her heartbeat calmed, until she no longer heard the marshcrabs among the engines. Emet had always scared her—this tall, beefy man with the shaggy hair, this old lion with the hard eyes. This man who had blasted her out of an airlock, whom she sometimes thought a monster. Yet now she felt so safe in his wide arms, with his heart beating so close to her cheek, a warm and comforting rhythm.

She looked up into his eyes.

"I hid for fourteen years in a duct," she said to him. "Life here still takes some getting used to."

"Most people would be catatonic after what you've lived through, Rowan," Emet said softly. "You're doing remarkably well. I'm proud of you."

She leaned her cheek against his chest again, feeling his heartbeat. "I used to be so scared of you, sir. When I first saw you, you terrified me. I thought you were more a beast than a man. And after the Battle of Terminus, when you almost killed me, I hated you. For a long time, I hated you." She looked into his eyes. "But I was wrong, sir. To fear you or hate you. You're a good man. I was two years old when the scorpions killed my father. But you're like a new father to me. I feel safe when I'm with you."

Emet looked down at her, his arms still wrapped around her.

"My job is to train you." His voice was low and comforting like distant thunder. "To harden you. To prepare you for battle. To be your commander, to send you into hell if I must. That is the sacrifice we must make. But know this, Rowan. Your father was like a brother to me. And you are like a daughter."

She smiled and wiped her eyes. "Thank you, sir. I feel better now. Shall we train some more?"

"Not today." He shook his head. "Go rest. Watch your movies. Read your books."

"With all due respect, sir, I prefer to train," Rowan said. "I've had years to read and watch movies. Today I will prepare for battle. May I take a shuttle down to Helios?"

Emet nodded, and soon Rowan was flying down to the planet. She landed in the canyon, the place where they planned to capture Jade. For hours, Rowan ran through the brush, climbed the cliffs, lifted heavy stones, and hunted the hellbulls. Soon enough, Jade would come. Doomsday would be here.

Rowan hoped she could bring her sister back to sanity.

But if I cannot, Jade, if you are beyond my help, I will fight you. She wiped sweat off her brow and stared at the sky. *And I will win.*

CHAPTER NINETEEN

All around Leona, the galaxy was falling apart.

Three human starships. The *Nazareth*, the *Kinloch Laggan*, the *Rosetta*. Three beacons of hope. They flew through a fraying universe, seeking a home.

At every wormhole, the scorpions were emerging.

At every major star system, fleets clashed.

Even the vast emptiness of space, the light-years of darkness and nothingness, now brimmed with agony, with charging fleets, with the husks of burnt starships and the floating corpses of soldiers.

"The war is everywhere now," Leona said softly. She sat on the bridge of the *Nazareth*, guiding the frigate onward. "The front line might be far behind us. But the battles are everywhere. No place is safe."

Ramses's face appeared on the monitor to her left. He was flying in the *Rosetta* off her port side. The pharaoh stroked his pointy beard. "Maybe it had to be this way. Only out of chaos can new order be born. Only from ashes can the phoenix arise, reborn. From this horrible tragedy, this inferno, this bloodshed, Earth will rise."

Leona smiled sadly at her dear Pharaoh. "From devastation to reclamation." Her voice was soft. "But it hurts. That millions of our brothers and sisters perish in the gulocks. That thousands of worlds are blinking out. Sometimes it feels like there can be no light after so much darkness."

Ramses nodded. "Those in darkness always feel this way. In the twenty-first century, a race of alien centipedes devastated

Earth, slaying three billion humans. Those in the darkness that followed saw no light. Yet from that destruction rose President Einav Ben-Ari, the heroine who elevated Earth to glory, who built a human empire. Your own ancestor. After her death, only two centuries after the centipede attack, the Hydrian Empire attacked Earth. The squids butchered six billion—nearly all of us. Only a handful of humans fled into exile. Some think only a few thousand humans made it out. In that shadow, they saw no light. Yet they flourished. From those few frightened refugees rose new human communities across the galaxy, and we multiplied into millions. Now new darkness falls. Now the scorpions kill millions of us. Now they destroy entire civilizations. Now again we struggle to see light. But dawn will rise. Earth will rise."

Leona's smile widened. "You are wise, my dear Pharaoh. And ever the optimist."

A grin split his face. "The optimists build futures. And I intend to build a new world on Earth, a civilization to rival the grandeur of ancient Egypt."

A second monitor turned on. Mairead's freckled face appeared, a cigar in her mouth. She was flying the *Kinloch Laggan,* smallest but fastest of their three ships.

"You and your pyramids," said the young pilot. "You only had pyramids because slaves built them. What are you gonna do, enslave Leona and me?"

"I'd have better luck taming a pair of honey badgers," Ramses said.

"You better believe it, mate." Mairead winked. "Ain't nobody gonna tame us. Optimists can muck off. So can pessimists. It's warriors who build worlds." She raised her pistol and twirled it around her finger. "And I'm the deadliest killer in the galaxy, bub. It's from the ruins of battle that we shall arise. From the ashes of war—glory! You said it had to be this way? Damn right. Let the old universe burn. Was a mess anyway."

Leona glared at the young redhead. "Millions are dying, Mairead."

She glared back, but now Mairead's green eyes were damp. "Millions always die, Commodore. Throughout all of Ra damn history—it's genocide after genocide, destruction after destruction. The centipedes. The spiders. The squids. Now these damn scorpions. Ramses says he's an optimist? Not me. I'm a killer. Because you need killers. Because only killers can survive. This is a cosmos of death, and I'm an agent of death."

"I fight for life!" Leona said. "Always for life."

"Is that why you're flying a warship armed to the teeth with missiles?" Mairead asked. "Life? Life is a luxury. We soldiers kill and die and slog through blood so that others may live. So be it." She turned away. "I'd rather be a living killer than a dead dreamer."

Mairead cut off the transmission. The monitor went dark.

Somebody hurt you, Leona thought, gazing through the porthole at Mairead's warship. *May you someday find peace, Captain Mairead "Firebug" McQueen. May we all find peace.*

"Well, that certainly put a damper on my upbeat message of hope," Ramses said, breaking the awkward silence. "Anyway, Commodore, what say we organize a feast tonight for the troops? We need a morale boost. I'm well stocked with Arabian coffee beans on the *Rosetta.* Well, synthetic powdered beans, but we must make do in these times of privation. I'll be glad to share with the soldiers in your and Firebug's ships. I'll cook too. For everyone. First time we'll have a proper meal—Egyptian delicacies, of course—and after dinner, we can—"

He frowned and shut his mouth.

"What?" Leona said.

Ramses stared ahead. "There. What's that? A nebula?"

Leona stared too. She saw it now. A sphere in space, black yet shimmering with a ring of light. No, not a nebula. Her ship's sensors were going wild. The object ahead was close. And growing closer and larger.

"It looks almost like a black hole," Leona said. "But it's right ahead of us. And it just popped out of nowhere. Impossible." She shuddered. "We better give it a wide berth. Turn to our port. Follow me."

She turned the *Nazareth*, and the bulky frigate creaked and groaned in protest. The two corvettes followed, smaller and more agile.

The black hole expanded.

Lighting flashed around it.

It soon grew large enough to swallow a warship.

Leona stared at the thing. "What's that inside? It's—"

Her breath died.

It's not a black hole, she realized. *It's* …

"A wormhole!" she shouted.

And from inside, the strikers emerged.

Dozens of them. A hundred, maybe more.

The scorpion ships fired their guns.

"All power to shields!" Leona said. "Ramses, Mairead, shiel—"

The plasma slammed into them, spraying across the three warships like red waves against boulders.

The *Kinloch Laggan* turned toward the enemy first, blasting its cannons. The corvette raced toward the strikers.

"Mairead, defensive position!" Leona said, but the corvette was already charging.

The *Kinloch Laggan* slammed into a striker, ramming the warship, blasting out shells.

An instant later, a striker rammed into the *Nazareth*, and Leona cried out and fell to the deck, and the bridge shook.

Another striker plowed into her other side.

Leona cursed. In a real warship, there would be a gunnery station, a helmsman, a crew of officers, both living and robotic. But the *Nazareth* had been a freighter only a few years ago, and an old, clunky one at that. The Heirs had quickly modified her for war, but she was still too damn slow, built for hauling cargo, not fighting a battle. By the time Leona pulled herself back into her seat, more plasma was slamming into the *Nazareth*, melting the shields, and the frigate spun through space.

Leona grabbed the triggers for her cannons.

She fired all her guns, port and starboard, not even aiming, just blasting out a hailstorm of death.

The shells flew and slammed into the strikers at her sides, exploding so close they rocked the *Nazareth.*

As the debris cleared, Leona saw the *Rosetta* and *Kinloch Laggan* battling hundreds of strikers. The enemy ships were still streaming out of the strange dark wormhole.

This isn't one of the ancient wormholes, Leona thought. *The scorpions figured out how to build their own tunnels.*

"Fall back!" she shouted. "Ramses, Mairead, back! We're getting out of here. Now!"

The strikers were still mostly organized around the wormhole. Only seven or eight blocked the humans' retreat. The three Inheritor warships turned to flee, cannons firing.

Perhaps the *Nazareth* was slow and clunky. But now her girth was all Leona wanted. The freighter-turned-frigate plowed into the enemy strikers, knocking them aside, as the corvettes hammered them with hellfire.

The Inheritor ships broke free.

Engines roaring, they charged into the distance.

Behind them, the enemy followed, plasma firing.

"Where the hell did those buggers come from?" Mairead shouted, her face reappearing on the monitor by Leona.

"I don't know," Leona said. "But they knew we were here. They were able to open a sort of wormhole. Damn it!"

She fired her aft-cannons, knocking a striker back into its comrades. But the other strikers still pursued. The *Nazareth* could not outrun them for long.

"Well, mates, looks like we go down in glory," Mairead said, speaking around the cigar in her mouth. "I always knew I'd go down in a brawl. Figured it would be pissed in a pub, but this'll do."

"No," Leona said. "No! We do not die here! Our mission is to reach Earth. We will complete our mission."

They raced forward, unable to divert full power to speed. Their cannons still fired. Their shields still took heavy punishment. The scorpions chased in a mass of metal and fire, the hundreds of ships forming a triangle in space.

"Commodore!" Ramses said. "You remember my suggestion to ditch the *Nazareth*? We can extend a jet-bridge in midflight. You and your crew can join me on the *Rosetta*."

"Extending a jet-bridge will slow us down," Leona said, firing more shells from her stern. Her ammo was getting dangerously low. "And we'd be too vulnerable if we space walked."

"Then we die in glory!" Mairead said. "As warriors for Earth! It's good to die for our homeworld."

"Nobody is dying today," Leona said. "Today we live!" She pointed. "There. Make for that star. With me."

She swerved, turning toward a nearby red dwarf. The corvettes turned with her, and the enemy followed. They raced onward, exchanging fire with the enemy as they flew. Another plasma blast hit the *Nazareth*, rattling the frigate. The *Kinloch Laggan* took a blast to the underbelly. The plasma left seared, ugly scars.

"Commodore Ben-Ari!" Ramses said. "My scanners are showing an active battle in that star system. A massive battle."

Leona smiled grimly, leaning forward in her seat. "Exactly."

"Hell yeah!" Mairead whooped. "That's what I'm talkin' about. You are a crazy hooch, Commodore! I approve."

Leona stared ahead, something halfway between smile and grimace on her face. A purplish-gray alien planet came into view.

"Esporia," Leona said. "Homeland of the Esporians."

"Ra damn mushrooms," Mairead said. "Ramses, you wanna cook us mushrooms tonight?"

On the monitor, Ramses looked queasy. "Esporians. I hate Esporians. Commodore, these creatures hate humanity. These creatures killed . . ." He grimaced. "People who were dear to me."

Pain twisted his voice. Leona remembered reading the Pharaoh's files. Ramses came from a nearby system, one in the Esporian's sphere of influence.

"Hang in there, Ramses," she said. "This is the only way. The Esporians might hate us humans. But they're still part of the Concord, and right now, they hate the scorpions more."

The Inheritors raced toward the purple planet, taking continuous fire. The back shields were nearly gone now, and Leona kept firing at the enemy, desperate to hold them off. She had to reach Esporia, that moldy planet ahead.

It grew larger in her viewport. Esporia was a damp world with a dense atmosphere of carbon and oxygen. Moss, mold, and mushrooms covered the entire planet in a thick rug. Some said the fungus roots dug for hundreds of kilometers under the surface, maybe even reaching the planet's core. It was a single ball of decay.

On this planet, the Esporians had evolved.

Leona had seen a few Esporians on her travels. The mushrooms stood taller than humans, grayish and purple and malodorous. They were freakishly intelligent, probably more so than humans, but theirs was a cold, calculating, ruthless intellect. They did not hide their ambition for domination, and many worlds had fallen to their rot, had become balls of mold and fungus like Esporia.

Many human communities had been lost to these attacks. Leona had been to a human village overrun with Esporians. She had burned the mushrooms and fished out the bones of children.

But the Esporians still fly under the Concord banners, she knew. *They are scorpion killers.*

As she approached, she saw the battle ahead.

Esporia was under attack.

Wormholes were opening around the planet—not the shimmering ancient wormholes, the stations in the Tree of Light, but the new black portals of the enemy. Strikers were spilling out, firing at the planet.

The Esporians were not a meek species. They fought back—hard.

Their pod ships surrounded their planet, millions of them. These were not ships of metal like most species flew. Here were organic, fleshy vessels, round and rancid. The pods opened pustules and fired countless spores. The spray hit strikers, clinging to the starships and eating through the metal. On Esporia's surface, organic volcanoes opened their vents and spewed pus into the atmosphere. The geysers slammed into strikers in orbit, tearing through the ships.

"It's disgusting," Mairead said. "Their entire planet is like a huge ass pimple."

"You would know something about those," Ramses said.

Mairead glowered. "Yes, from that time we served together on the *Jaipur* and I saw you naked in the shower."

"Oh please." Ramses rolled his eyes. "My nude divinity was the most glorious sight you have ever seen. Savor the memory, Firebug."

They flew toward the battle, and the strikers followed.

And the Esporians noticed.

A hundred of the fleshy pod-ships came flying toward the Inheritors. Their pustules bloomed open, revealing fiery innards.

"Commodore, are you sure this is smart?" Ramses said, wincing. "The mushrooms look angry."

"They look delicious," Mairead said. "Fresh risotto, coming right up!"

"Do not attack them," Leona said. "Fly! Forward! Fly between them."

She flew toward the pod-ships, wincing.

The pustules blasted out spores.

Leona screamed and tugged on her ship's yoke, raising the *Nazareth*. The two corvettes soared at her sides.

The cloud of spores flew beneath them like pollen and coated several pursuing strikers.

At once, the scorpion starships began to rust and break open. Whatever those spores were made of, they were terrifyingly corrosive, eating through the metal within seconds. The strikers veered madly, slamming into each other, crumbling, spilling out scorpions.

Leona kept flying forward, passing over the pod ships. She stormed into the battle.

All around her, strikers and pods clashed.

Plasma blazed like dragonfire, torching pods, peeling open the fleshy ships and exposing the Esporians within. The sentient mushrooms screamed as they burned. More jets of fire rained onto the planet's surface, burning through the forests of fungus and lichen. The organic volcanoes below—massive lifeforms the size of Everest—belched up sizzling globs, and the streams tore through strikers. Clouds of spores flew through space, clinging to hulls, eating through the metal. Everywhere—fire and flesh, metal and meat, death and destruction.

Through this inferno, the three human starship flew.

The strikers chased them. But the Inheritor ships zigzagged between geysers of acid, and the rancid pillars slammed into strikers, carving through them. The human ships shot under clouds of spores, then over swarms of pod ships, then around raining storms of plasma.

Leona flew like she had never flown, making turns she hadn't known the *Nazareth* was capable of. Spores grazed her hull, corroding a corner of her ship. A geyser from the planet below sprayed her, sizzling across her shields, ripping off chunks of graphene. The corvettes were flying madly at Leona's sides, dodging the massive assault.

Behind them, the last scorpion pursuer perished.

"We're going to make it!" Leona said. "Now fly out of this hellhole. Back to open space!"

"Capital idea," Ramses said. His *Rosetta* was showing ugly scars. "Nasty place, this."

Mairead laughed from the bridge of the *Kinloch Laggan*. "What's a matter, Pharaoh? Scared of a few harmless little mushrooms? Not me! I'm going to roast a few of these buggers. These moldy bastards have been killing humans." She aimed her cannons. "Time to—"

"Mairead, watch out!" Leona cried. "Below you!"

Mairead looked up. "Commo—"

A volcano on the planet below bloomed open.

A geyser blasted and slammed into the *Kinloch Laggan*.

"Mairead!" Leona shouted.

Ramses stared, eyes wide. "Firebug!"

The geyser engulfed the *Kinloch Laggan*, surrounding the ship, blazing across it.

Mairead's transmission died.

Her monitor went dark.

"Captain McQueen, can you hear me?" Leona said into her comm. "Mairead!"

The geyser died down.

The ISS *Kinloch Laggan* was gone. Only a lump of molten metal remained. Nobody could have survived that.

"Mairead . . ." Leona whispered.

Ramses hung his head low. "Mairead. Oh Ra. Mairead, I'm sorry. Farewell, my beloved friend."

A moment of silence.

And the comm crackled to life.

"I knew you loved me, dumbass."

Leona and Ramses gasped.

"Mairead!" they cried out together.

And there they saw her. She was flying through the battle in a spacesuit, blasting fire from a jetpack. A handful of her soldiers were flying with her, along with two Firebirds who had managed to escape the *Kinloch Laggan*'s hangar.

"Thanks for the warning, Commodore," Mairead said, flying toward them. "We ejected just in time. Lost a few good men, though. Heroes."

Ramses was closer. He flew the *Rosetta* toward them, opened the airlock, and Mairead and the others climbed in.

Fifty humans had served on the ISS *Kinloch Laggan*. Leona counted only seven that made it into the *Rosetta*.

A heavy loss. Too heavy. But now was not the time to mourn.

All around them, the battle still raged, the strikers and pods fighting over the moldy planet below.

"Let's get out of here," Leona said as the volcanoes bloomed again.

"Best idea I've heard all day," Ramses said.

They flew through the battle, dodging assaults from every direction, until they soared into open space. The two starships—the *Nazareth* and the *Rosetta*—activated their warp engines. The stars stretched into lines, and they blasted off, leaving Esporia far behind.

They flew on into the emptiness, leaving their fallen.

Earth was still far, and the road seemed darker than ever before.

CHAPTER TWENTY

"You are ready," Emet said, standing before her, the stars at his back.

"I am ready," Rowan repeated, facing him, half his size but standing tall.

"You are lightning in the dark," Emet said, staring into her eyes.

"I am lighting in the dark," Rowan repeated, staring back.

"You are an heiress of Earth," Emet said.

Rowan raised her chin. Her eyes stung. She spoke in a steady voice. "I am an heiress of Earth."

Emet saluted, slamming fist into palm. "For Earth."

She returned the salute, and her eyes dampened, but she kept her shoulders squared. "For Earth."

They stood on the deck of the ISS *Byzantium*, a twin to *Jerusalem*. Luther had given them the old tanker, and over the past few weeks, the Heirs' mechanics had been toiling, installing shields and cannons, painting the hull, and turning the *Byzantium* into a clone of her older sister. The words ISS *Jerusalem* even appeared on the hull. On the inside, she was a cavernous ship, her crew minimal. On the outside, she was a perfect imitation.

Rowan approached a porthole. The rest of the fleet floated around them. The vessels proudly bore the Heirs of Earth symbol—the planet Earth with golden wings. They were all old ships, bought from Luther's scrapyard. But they would all fight bravely today.

Doomsday was near.

The day when we win or lose this war, Rowan thought. *The day when I bring Jade back to humanity ... or die at her hands.*

Rowan lowered her gaze. They were orbiting Helios, a sweltering moon, green and yellow and unforgiving. From up here, she could even see the canyon stretching across the land, thin as a hairline from this distance.

There it would happen. There below. In that canyon.

There we will meet again, Jade. And I pray that you remember me.

Emet came to stand beside her. He gazed down with her at the moon.

"Do you remember the plan, Rowan?" he said.

"Of course, sir."

"Tell me."

She nodded. "We've been sending out a signal with an old code, announcing our presence here. Jade will pick up the transmission. She'll know you and I are here. She'll come with a fleet to meet us." She took a shuddering breath. "And we'll fight her above the sky."

"And then?" Emet said.

"She'll try to attack this warship, the *Byzantium*, thinking it's the *Jerusalem*," said Rowan. "We'll let her hit our shields. We'll pretend to crash. But we'll actually land in the canyon below—right where we planned. Jade will follow us down there, hoping to retrieve us—either wounded or dead."

Rowan hesitated, suddenly too afraid to continue.

"And then?" Emet insisted.

Rowan patted the cylindrical container that hung across her back. Rolled up inside was the magnetic blanket.

"When I see Jade, I'll capture her in this blanket. Its power is immense, ten times the strength of steel links. It'll hold her. You and I will lift her, drag her into the tunnel we carved. Then into our waiting shuttle. Then into space. Then into the true *Jerusalem.*

Then—warp speed. We'll do this within ten minutes, sir. And we'll have her. We'll have Jade."

Emet nodded. "You know the plan. But are you ready, Corporal? Deep inside you, in your heart and gut—are you ready?"

She lowered her head. "I—"

"Raise your head!" Emet said. "Look into my eyes."

She raised her head. She looked into his eyes.

"I don't know, sir." She inhaled shakily. "This will be the most important day of my life. Maybe the most important day of humanity. We have a large army now, but it seems so small compared to the Hierarchy. Jade might not only kill me and you today. She might destroy our entire fleet. We might lose this war, our dream of Earth. Sir, I'm scared."

Emet nodded. "Good."

"Good, sir?" She frowned. "How is being scared good?" She tilted her head. "Are you going to tell me something like …" She dropped her voice, imitating him. "One can only be brave when scared, young Rowan, for true courage means fighting even when you're afraid."

Emet struggled to stifle a smile, then failed. "I was going to say: Good, at least you're honest."

"Oh, you want honesty, sir? Well, in that case, truth is, I'm so scared I'm about to piss my pants." She grinned. "Marco Emery, my ancestor, once said that to Einav Ben-Ari, your ancestor, before a great battle. I read it in Einav's memoirs."

Emet placed a hand on her shoulder. "We are descended of heroes, Corporal. Not just you and me. Every human in our fleet. And this is our great battle. Doomsday, as you call it. It will be here soon. Maybe tomorrow, maybe even today. The turning point of the war."

"But no pressure, right?"

"No pressure," Emet said, smiling thinly. "Now come. We have time until the enemy arrives. Let's train."

Rowan nodded and assumed a fighting stance. "Let's train, old man."

Emet snorted. "Try to keep up, pipsqueak."

He was forty years older than her, but Emet was a capable fighter. They trained at self defense, practicing throws and blocks and thrusts. They trained with rifles, swinging the barrels like blades. They trained with the magnetic cape, capturing bounding robots and knocking them to the floor. Slowly, with deep breaths, they practiced sweeping movements to stretch their limbs and clear their minds. They trained for hours, as they trained every day, as outside the portholes the stars shone and the fleet waited for battle.

Their training ended, and Rowan was about to go shower and eat, when an alarm wailed.

Rowan spun toward the porthole and stared outside.

Her heart burst into a gallop.

"Warships," she whispered. "Hundreds of warships. They enemy is here."

As the Inheritor fleet began taking defensive formation, Emet and Rowan raced onto the *Byzantium*'s bridge. Alarms were flashing. All around the frigate, Firebirds were emerging from hangars, preparing for war.

Rowan trembled.

It's here. The battle is here. It's—

A message came in through the comm.

"Sir, they're Menorians!" said the commander of the ISS *Jaipur*, the warship that flew beside them. "They come in peace."

Rowan gasped and leaped forward. She pressed her hands and face against the viewport like a child gazing out the window at winter's first snowfall. She watched the incoming ships.

"These aren't the scorpions." She spun toward Emet, grinning, then back to the viewport. "Menorian ships, sir!" Her eyes dampened and she laughed. "I read about them in Einav's memoirs. I never thought I'd see them."

Hundreds of ships were flying toward them. They looked to Rowan like huge geodes. They were round, craggy, and grayish-blue. Their middles were hollow and filled with glowing purple crystals.

"Azoth crystals!" Rowan said with wonder. "Huge ones! Azoth crystals the size of boulders!" She whistled. "I never knew they grew that large."

She had read all about azoth crystals. Rowan loved dealing with technology—gears, microchips, cables, anything that could power a machine, be it a tiny robot like Fillister or a warship the size of the *Byzantium.* More than anything, even more than the prettiest fiber optic cable, Rowan found azoth crystals fascinating.

Crystals that can bend spacetime, she thought.

Even the azoth crystal inside the *Jerusalem*'s engine—the largest such crystal in the fleet—was only about the size of Rowan's fist. Each of the Menorian ships ahead had a hundred azoth crystals larger than her entire body, filling their centers.

For a moment, all her terror faded, and Rowan felt like her old self—filled with wonder.

"Do you think they'll let me onto their ships to take a closer look?" Rowan asked, turning toward Emet.

But he didn't acknowledge her. He stood at a control panel, opening a video call with a geode ship.

An image of a Menorian appeared on the monitor. The alien reminded Rowan of an octopus. It floated in a tank of water, eight tentacles reaching out to eight control panels. The alien's skin was purple, but suddenly changed color to yellow, then flashed with blue and green lines.

They communicate with color, Rowan remembered. *Einav described that in her memoirs.*

The *Byzantium*'s computer could translate over a thousand alien languages. Including, it seemed, Menorian. The computer picked up the color changes on the monitor, then spoke in Common Human.

"Many colors and beams of light to you, humans! I am being Aurora, pod leader of this shimmering Menorian school of many. We have heard the murmur of waves and the songs in the great dry depths. They vibrate with your tales. So courageous you swim, no rock nor coral for shelter, to face the hunters in the blackness! We have flowed upon the currents to fight at your side, as we did once before."

Rowan frowned. She wasn't sure she understood all of that, but she suspected that translating colors was challenging, even for computers.

"We thank you kindly, Admiral Aurora," Emet said, relief clear in his voice. "You are most welcome."

The Menorian looked at him and blinked. Her body turned cobalt, and azure circles spread across it, fading to yellow. The translator spoke.

"You are Admiral Emet Ben-Ari! We have heard your song in the depths. Are you truly the podling of Captain Einav Ben-Ari, mistress of the tides, whom I served as navigator in the deep black?"

"I am descended of Einav Ben-Ari," said Emet, "though it's been many generations."

"I do forget how fast time travels for you beings of land and legs!" said Aurora. "For me, it has not been so many tides, for we travel fast upon the currents, moving nearly as fast as the light shines through the water. For me, it has not been so long. I still remember Einav Ben-Ari, mistress of the tides, and her memory is dear to me like sweet seaweed and plentiful plankton on a summer's dawn."

Rowan gasped. She stepped closer to the monitor. "You're her!" Rowan said. "*The* Aurora, the one from the books! You knew Einav Ben-Ari herself! You flew with her on the legendary HDFS *Lodestar*, humanity's greatest flagship! She wrote about you in her memoirs."

The octopus nodded. "Yes, young dry podling! I knew her well. She was kind and brave and feared no rushing currents nor predators. We Menorians hold her in high regard, and we still sing songs of Einav in our shimmering schools. Long ago, we Menorians fought with humans against the cruel predators in the dark. We are proud to fight with you again."

The Menorian ships arranged themselves in formations alongside the human fleet. The two forces formed one army, as they had long ago. They orbited Helios, facing the darkness, waiting.

Rowan took a shuddering breath and placed her hand on Lullaby. The brief moment of wonder faded into fear. With the extra ships here, there could be no doubt: Jade would pick up their signals. She would be heading this way. The greatest battle of Rowan's life awaited.

"I'm ready, Jade," Rowan said, staring into the darkness. "I'm waiting. I love you, my sister. I love you so much. And I'm terrified that you'll kill us all."

The darkness did not answer. Rowan stood, staring, waiting, her stomach knotted and her heart like a stone.

CHAPTER TWENTY-ONE

They flew across the darkness—two starships, dented, scarred, barely flying at all.

The *Nazareth*. The *Rosetta.*

They had set out on this journey with four warships. Only these two remained.

The two most important ships in the cosmos, Leona thought. *Two who must find Earth.*

The crew had been working around the clock, repairing the hulls, replacing the ravaged shields, and working in the bowels of the *Nazareth* to produce more ammunition. But Leona knew: One more battle could end this dream.

The emptiness spread around them, endless, pitiless. Leona sat on the *Nazareth*'s bridge, staring at the vastness before her. They had been flying for nearly half an Earth year. They flew far faster than light, traveling millions of kilometers per second. And still the enormity of the cosmos spread before them. Sol, Earth's sun, was still too far to see with the naked eye.

"All my life, I've been a wanderer," Leona said. "I grew up in space, never had a home of my own. For twenty-eight years, I've traveled from star to star. Yet I've never seen space in all its infinite vastness. Not like this."

Ramses was sitting beside her. In one hand, he held a small, porcelain cup full of black coffee so thick it was practically syrup. In the other hand, he held a book—*The Rise and Fall of Ancient Egypt*, featuring the pyramids of Giza on the cover. He lowered the book, looked at Leona, and raised an eyebrow.

"Never had a home of your own?" the captain said. "My darling, you've always had a home. We all have. It's called Earth."

Leona scoffed. "Your home is just Egypt, I'd say. At least that's the only part of Earth you've ever shown interest in."

"On the contrary, dear," Ramses said. "For the splendor of Egypt belongs to the entire globe."

A monitor turned on. Mairead's freckled face appeared.

"Oh yeah, dumbass?" She puffed cigar smoke at her camera. "So why's your book called *The Rise and Fall of Egypt*—stress on Fall?"

Ramses stiffened. He stared out the viewport toward the *Rosetta*, which Mairead had commandeered. Across the distance, she flipped him the bird. Ramses cringed.

"Have you been eavesdropping, Firebug?" he said.

"Muck yeah, I'm bored as hell here on the *Rosetta*. Your damn spaceship's boring and far too clean. Want a shift flying her?"

Ramses rolled his eyes. "My shift is not for another hour. I intend to spend that hour sipping coffee, being far away from you, and reading my book. And, also, planning Egypt's rise to new glory."

He switched off the monitor and sipped his coffee. Outside in the *Rosetta*, Mairead flipped him off again.

Leona looked at the Egyptian. "You know, Pharaoh, you two need to learn how to get along."

He grimaced. "Get along? With that wild, red-haired hooligan? Commodore, I've seen her bite her own toenails. It's barbaric. I even offered her my pedicure kit, but she said only pansies filed their toenails. I asked her what flowers have to do with it, but she only laughed."

"Ramses, we're barely three hundred humans between these two ships," Leona said. "We don't know what's happening back on the front line. Traveling this fast, we can't talk to them.

There's a chance that we, just three hundred, might be the only humans left. If that's true, it'll be our task to rebuild humanity on Earth. We need to get along."

Ramses looked like he had drunk sour milk. "Heavens. Up to us to rebuild humanity? We'd have to breed."

Leona cocked an eyebrow. "Is that so horrible? I recall you being something of a womanizer back at the fleet."

He cleared his throat. "My genetic material demands a certain standard. I certainly hope you don't expect me to breed with the Firebug."

Leona couldn't help but laugh. "For now, you two just don't murder each other. How's that?"

The Pharaoh sighed. "Perhaps I've been something of an ogre. I'll try to make peace with the girl. I suppose she isn't that bad after all."

The monitor lit up again. Mairead smirked in the video feed, her feet on the dashboard—toenails freshly chewed.

"You damn right I ain't that bad." She spat out a toenail, then lit a cigar. "Nice to hear you admit you're an ogre. Cute that you think I'd breed with you."

Ramses leaped to his feet, cheeks flushing. "What the—? I thought I turned you off!"

She flipped him another bird. "You bet you turn me off, dumbass."

Ramses seemed ready to explode. With effort, he calmed himself. "Firebug, I hereby extend my hand in a peace offering." He reached his hand toward the monitor. "You can pretend to shake it."

She reached her own hand toward the monitor. They mock-shook through the video.

"Nice fingernails, mate," she said. "Filed to perfection like a true lady."

She laughed, stuck her tongue out at him, and shut off the video feed. Ramses fumed.

Leona sighed. "I suppose that's the best I could hope for."

"I need more coffee," Ramses said. "Join me in the kitchen, Commodore Ben-Ari?"

She gave him an uneasy look. "Somebody should man the bridge."

"Commodore, we've been flying for months through the emptiness. I believe the auto-pilot can handle ten minutes on her own. She'll alert us if any danger approaches." He waggled his eyebrows. "I make authentic Egyptian coffee. Best in the universe."

Leona rolled her eyes. "It's not authentic Egyptian coffee if it's from a synthetic powder."

"Next best thing, at least."

She hesitated and glanced at her controls. According to the ship, there was nothing interesting for light-years around, and she could use a caffeine boost.

"Five minutes," she said. "Not a second more."

They entered the *Nazareth*'s galley. The warship's Firebird pilots were already here, eating rations at the table. All were lieutenants, none older than thirty. Leona was a commodore, commander of the expedition, and Ramses was a captain, an officer senior enough to command a warship. The young starfighter pilots rose to salute, but Leona waved them down.

"At ease, boys," she said.

The Heirs of Earth was a band of rebels and freedom fighters, lacking the strict discipline of a true military. After nearly half a year in space, the last semblances of protocol were fraying. Often it was hard for Leona to see her soldiers as mere ranks, pawns in a war. They were friends. They were, perhaps, the last humans in the darkness.

Ramses opened a cabinet and pulled out a decorative wooden box, a masterwork engraved with old animals of Earth. He placed the box on the table, closed his eyes, and whispered a prayer. Reverently, like a man opening a holy ark, he opened the box, revealing the artifacts within. The objects inside were silver and adorned with sapphires. There was a tray, a pot, and small mugs barely larger than eggcups.

"This belonged to my father," Ramses said, "and to his father before him, and to many generations of the al Masri family. It comes from ancient Earth."

"Bullshit," Leona said. "From Earth?"

Ramses nodded. "This is Earth silver." He lifted the pot. It tapered in the center, flared out at the top, and had a long, curved spout like a beak. "This is called a dallah, a traditional pot used for thousands of years." He sighed. "I wish I had coffee beans. True beans grown in Earth soil, aromatic and bitter. For now ..." He pulled a plastic bag from his coat pocket. "We have powder from the ship's organic printer."

He prepared the coffee in a slow, meticulous way like a ritual, and soon it was steaming in the pot. He was about to fill the mugs, then paused.

"Wait," Ramses said. He hit his comm. "Mairead? Get your freckled ass over here."

They waited while Mairead donned a spacesuit, flew over, entered the *Nazareth*, and finally joined them in the kitchen. The young captain removed her helmet and shoved a hand through her hair. She frowned.

"Did I just execute a spacewalk for ... coffee?"

"The best damn coffee in the universe," Ramses said.

"It better be." Mairead slammed a wooden box onto the table. "Because I brought the best damn cigars in the universe, bitches."

Ramses filled their mugs, and Mairead distributed cigars.

"A toast, Commodore?" Ramses said to Leona.

Leona raised her small silver mug. She looked across the group. Her two captains. Her lieutenants. Her friends. She smiled.

"For Earth."

Mairead raised her mug in salute. "For killing Ra damn aliens."

Ramses raised his mug high. "For the glory of the pyramids, may they never fall."

A young lieutenant raised his mug. "For my daughter and wife, both on the front line."

Another pilot raised a mug. "For someday drinking beer instead of coffee."

Cheers rose. More toasts were given.

"For someday drinking pina coladas instead of coffee. With parasols!"

They laughed.

"For someday smoking cigars on a beach."

"For someday seeing the beaches of Earth."

"For all our brave warriors fighting the Hierarchy."

"For the refugees who survived the gulocks."

"For those who fell."

"For the millions who died."

Now the laughter was gone, and they were solemn, still holding their mugs, not yet drinking. They lowered their eyes.

Leona rose to her feet. She held her mug before her.

"For Earth," she repeated, voice softer now, and drank.

Around the table, they drank.

Mairead swallowed and grimaced. "Tastes like piss. But it kicks like a mule. I like it."

Leona took a sip. It was bitter and hot and wonderful. Around the table, the officers lit cigars, and smoke filled the kitchen. They began to swap tales, to laugh, to refill their mugs. But Leona was silent. She thought of the terrors she had seen in the gulock. She thought of her husband, dying on their wedding day. She thought of all those waiting for them, depending on them.

She began to speak softly. The others fell silent, laughter dying, and listened.

"In the darkness, it's hard to see light." Leona held her mug with both hands. "Millions of us died. I don't know how many humans are still alive. Maybe millions still hide or fight across the cosmos. Maybe we're the last. I don't know what we'll find when we arrive at Earth. I don't know if we'll find a verdant planet, ready to recolonize, the same home we lost, or whether we'll find a wasteland awash with radiation and disease. But I know that I'll never forget the gulock, the horrors I saw there. I know I'll never forget the sacrifice of those who fought with us, who gave their lives for our cause. And I know that we—we few in the galley, we three hundred on this expedition, and all humans who still live—will never stop fighting, never stop dreaming of Earth. I know that Earth is our home. We're close now. I know that soon we'll see our planet rise."

Mairead rose to her feet. She glanced out the porthole, to where the *Rosetta* flew; the corvette was now flying on autopilot. Mairead looked back at the group and raised her chin. For once, the young captain was not cursing, bragging, or chomping a cigar. There were tears in her eyes. Mairead began to sing, her voice uncharacteristically soft.

Someday we will see her
The pale blue marble
Rising from the night beyond the moon
Cloaked in white, her forests green
Calling us home
Calling us—

Outside the porthole, the *Rosetta* exploded.

Fire blazed.

Debris hammered the *Nazareth*, rattling the frigate. The coffeepot clattered to the floor, spilling its steaming contents.

Everyone in the galley turned toward the porthole. They gazed upon an inferno.

There were fifty people aboard the Rosetta, Leona thought.

She ran.

She burst onto the *Nazareth*'s bridge and saw two starships looming ahead. Leona leaped into her seat, grabbed the controls, yanked the ship out of autopilot, and opened fire.

Her shells slammed into one enemy starship, knocking it back. A second vessel rose before her. Both enemy ships dwarfed the *Nazareth*.

My God, Leona thought, gazing at them.

These were no strikers.

She had never seen such starships. They were tubular, covered with patches of green and black armor like scales. Red portholes blazed at their prows like eyes, and cannons thrust out like fangs. The ships looked like serpents, each large enough to constrict the *Nazareth*. As they moved through space, the ships undulated like true snakes.

"Mucking hell," Mairead whispered.

"What *are* they?" Ramses said, staring with a mixture of hatred and disgust.

Leona switched on her communicator. "Alien vessels! We come in peace! Lower your weapons, and—"

The two scaly starships turned toward her. Their cannons heated up.

"Incoming!" Leona shouted, diverting all power to the shields.

Searing laser beams flew from the enemy starships.

Leona tugged the yoke, veering sideways. The *Nazareth* lurched into the cloud of debris left over from the *Rosetta.* They managed to dodge one of the laser beams. The other grazed the *Nazareth*, searing their port-side shields.

The frigate hurtled backward. If Leona hadn't diverted full power to shields, they would have cracked open like an egg. She shoved on the throttle, steadied their flight, and opened fire.

Her missiles flew toward the enemy, leaving trails of light across space.

The serpentine warships fired their lasers, taking out three missiles. A fourth slammed into one of the ships, knocking it back.

"Firebirds, fly!" Leona shouted. "Take them out!"

The hangar on the *Nazareth* opened.

Five Firebirds emerged—shrieking, furious starfighters, firing their missiles.

Leona sneered, sending forth a fury of shells, concentrating all fire on one of the two enemy ships.

Another laser hit the *Nazareth,* carving into a hull and breaching a deck.

Leona gritted her teeth as her ship jolted. She kept firing, pounding the enemy ship with shell after shell. The Firebirds were swarming, raining death onto the same vessel.

The serpentine ship exploded.

Fire and debris spurted, hitting the remaining starships. The Firebirds flew high, fleeing the shock wave.

One enemy ship now remained.

Now we're even.

They faced each other in the darkness—a human warship, clunky and battered, and an enemy vessel several times their length.

"Firebirds, cease fire," Leona said, and the starfighters flew back and arranged themselves around her.

She stared at the enemy ship.

It faced them, still, not making a move. Its red portholes seemed to be staring.

Leona hailed the ship again.

"Alien vessel," she said. "I am Commodore Leona Ben-Ari of the Heirs of Earth. You have attacked us on a peaceful expedition. Identify yourself or we will be forced to destroy you."

For a moment—silence.

Then the enemy ship accepted the call.

A video appeared on Leona's screen, showing the enemy ship's bridge and crew.

Mairead, standing at her side, cringed. "Ugly sons of bitches."

Leona rose to her feet, frowning. She stared at the video on her viewport.

"Who are you?" she said.

The aliens stared at her. They looked like Burmese pythons, their scales dark green, their eyes yellow and baleful. But unlike pythons, they had thin arms tipped with long, clawed fingers. In addition to their scales, the serpents wore black armor bristly with spikes, the plates embedded with rubies. Their bridge looked like a medieval dungeon—shadowy, rocky, and filled with chains. Slaves of several alien species cowered in cages, bodies whipped.

One of the serpentine aliens slithered closer. He was longer and thicker than the others, and he wore a black helmet topped with crimson spikes. He stared at Leona, eyes narrowed, and a forked tongue flicked out from his jaws. The serpent almost seemed to be smirking.

"Are you the captain of this vessel?" Leona said. "I am Leona Ben-Ari, commander of the Inheritor Starship *Nazareth*. We are on a peaceful mission. You have attacked us without provocation. Identify yourself and—"

The alien captain spoke. For a few seconds, all Leona heard were hisses, clicks, and grumbles. Then her computer translated the serpentine language into Common Human.

"We are basilisks." The alien captain stared at her, hunger and amusement in his eyes. "We are hunters. We are masters. We are the rulers of this sector, and you are invaders."

Basilisks.

Yes, Leona had heard of these beings. Their true name, in their own language, was a series of hisses and clicks. The translator had chosen a name from old Earth mythology, originally used for a monstrous snake in folklore.

Humanity had never encountered these serpents. Two thousand years ago, back when humanity still lived on Earth, a different alien race had ruled this sector of space. The Hydrian squids had dominated the Milky Way's Orion Arm in those days. The Hydrians had destroyed many worlds—including Earth.

But the Hydrian Empire, for all its might, had not lasted forever. Long ago, the squids had died off, leaving a power vacuum. The basilisks, it seemed, had risen to fill that void.

We humans have never met these snakes, but they're our enemies, Leona thought. *They surround our homeworld.*

Leona glanced at Ramses. He gave her a slight nod and took a step toward a control panel. Leona looked back at the basilisk captain.

"According to the United Intergalactic Treaties," Leona said, "this sector is neutral Concord space. We are a Concord vessel. If you do not move aside, we—"

"This is no longer Concord space," hissed the basilisk. "We basilisks care not for the weakness and frailty of the Concord. We have joined the Hierarchy! We fight alongside the mighty scorpions! Identify your species, enemy vessel, so that we may know how to brag when we drink blood from your skulls."

Leona struggled not to roll her eyes. She heard Mairead scoff.

"We are humans!" Leona said to the basilisk. "And if you think that your threats will intimidate us, you—"

"Ah, humansss," the basilisk hissed. "Yes, we know your soft, succulent kind. Delicious prey animals, though too easy to hunt. No challenge." He hissed rapidly, tongue flicking, perhaps the basilisk way of laughing. "You once came from the world you know as Earth. A disgusting wasteland in the backwater of our empire. Yet still our territory. Turn back, humans! Turn back and flee like the prey animals that you are. Tell your fellow vermin weaklings that you may never enter this sector. Earth will never be yours."

He's afraid, Leona realized. *He's not sure he can defeat us. He's trying to scare us off. That's why he hasn't attacked yet.*

She cleared her throat. "We humans come from Earth. That is our homeworld. We will not turn back, basilisk. Give me your name, rank, and serial number, so that I may report you to Concord authorities. Then stand down."

The basilisk sneered. His mouth opened wide, revealing fangs that dripped venom. His eyes burned, the pupils mere slits.

"Earth is ours, vermin. Die now. Die like the cowards that—"

Leona fired her cannons.

While the creature was talking, Ramses had gradually lowered the *Nazareth*'s shields and life support, diverting full power to the cannons.

The shells now blasted out with twice as much fury as before, pounding into the enemy starship.

Instantly, Ramses pulled the shields back up, and Leona yanked on the yoke and shoved the throttle, flying over the enemy ship.

As the *Nazareth* soared above the basilisk vessels, the Firebirds unleashed a hailstorm of missiles, bombarding the enemy.

The basilisk ship rocked and tilted. Its scaly armored plates cracked. Its cannons blasted lasers, hitting one Firebird, slicing the starfighter in two. Another beam hit the *Nazareth*, rocking the frigate. Leona kept flying. She shot forward, spun, and charged back toward the basilisk warship, all guns blazing.

The Firebirds attacked from one side, the *Nazareth* from the other, pounding the ship with shell after shell. The basilisks tried to flee, only for Firebirds to block their escape, to surround their starship in a ring of fire. Leona leaned forward, snarling, concentrating all her fire toward a crack in the enemy's shields.

The crack widened.

She unleashed a missile.

The missile entered the crack at hypersonic speed, and the basilisk ship exploded.

The shockwave knocked back the human vessels. A sphere of debris expanded through space, pattering them.

Leona took a deep breath, struggling to calm her pounding heart.

Mairead slapped her on the shoulder. "Good work, Commodore. Those bastards are ugly sons of bitches, but they ain't too tough."

But Leona felt a tightness in her chest.

"They destroyed the *Rosetta*," she said. "They destroyed one of our Firebirds. They killed over fifty of our people." She looked at Mairead and Ramses, and her voice was soft, barely louder than a whisper. "We left on this expedition with four warships. We're down to just the *Nazareth*. We're damaged. Badly. And thousands of these basilisk ships might be waiting between us and Earth."

For once, Mairead and Ramses were silent. Leona saw the worry in their eyes—even in Mairead's.

"Well, we're not turning back now, are we, Commodore?" Mairead said, and suddenly she sounded very young. It was easy to forget that Mairead, despite her rank and bluster, was only twenty-four.

Leona shook her head. "No. We won't turn back. But we can't fight more battles either. Not with a single warship—and a battered one at that, her shields cracked and her ammo low. We'll have to rely on stealth, our wits, and luck." She placed her hands on her captains' shoulders. "We were entrusted with a sacred mission. We vowed to become the first humans in two thousand years to set foot on Earth. We will continue toward our home. We will see Earth rise again."

"Or we'll die trying," Mairead said.

As they flew on, diving into the darkness, those words echoed in Leona's ears.

Or die trying.

They glided through the darkness, heading closer to Earth, toward death or legend.

CHAPTER TWENTY-TWO

The gulock gates rose before her, formed of jagged metal and draped with human skins.

Ayumi stumbled along with the others, so weak she could barely walk.

The deathcar idled on the rocky ground behind her. Ayumi had only just emerged from that hell. How long had they spent crammed into the deathcar, transported like cattle to this world? It seemed like eras, like she had aged years. Yet now she craved to return into that dank, hot ship. It seemed like shelter compared to the nightmarish gates before her.

Ayumi had never known coldness. She had been born and raised on a warm, sunny world, but here was a dark, freezing wasteland. Was this a planet, a moon, a mere asteroid? Ayumi didn't know. Icy wind sliced through her, freezing her bones and organs. Her bare feet ached on the rocky ground, and sharp stones cut her soles. Clouds hid the sky, grumbling, thundering, shedding flakes of black snow like ash. On distant mountains, fires blazed.

But more than this frozen, dark, rocky terrain, the gates before her terrified Ayumi.

The gates to the underworld, she thought. The skins hung from them, eyeless faces staring, toothless mouths screaming silently.

Once more, Jade's words returned to her. *I want their skins!*

"Move, maggots!" a scorpion hissed.

As more humans emerged from the deathcar, famished and trembling, scorpions moved alongside. The creatures raised crackling, electric whips.

"Move, damn it, though the gates!"

The humans shuffled forward. Too weak. Too slow.

The whips lashed.

A thong slammed into an old woman, and electricity raced across her. She fell, screaming. Another lash hit a young mother, electrocuting both her and her baby. When the baby stopped breathing, the mother wailed, only to be stung again, again, until finally she limped forward, weeping, her child dead in her arms.

Ayumi walked with them.

They headed toward the gates.

"That's right, into your new homes, worms," said one of the scorpions, raising a crackling lash.

We have to fight, Ayumi thought. *We'll be slaughtered in there. They'll skin us alive. They—*

"Move it!" a scorpion screamed and swung his whip at Ayumi.

The lash hit her, and electricity coursed through Ayumi's young, frail body.

She screamed.

She fell onto the rocky ground, bloodying her elbows. She gasped for air, and her eyes filled with tears.

The scorpion scuttled toward her, raising his whip again.

Trembling, barely able to breathe, Ayumi rose to her feet. She passed through the jagged gate, under the curtains of skin, and into the gulock.

Hell spread before her.

A nightmare, Ayumi thought. *It must be a nightmare. It can't be real.*

Yet the pain was real. Her hunger and weakness were real. The screams around her were all too real.

This wasn't just a prison, wasn't just a concentration camp.

This was a factory.

A gravelly road stretched ahead, leading toward a brick building with tall chimneys, taller than any building Ayumi had ever seen, as tall as the pillars of creation. The chimneys pumped out black smoke that unfurled skyward like demons waking from slumber, spreading wings, opening black jaws. Here was an inferno that could burn nations, that could swallow worlds, that spread across the sky with black shrouds. Standing before these chimneys, Ayumi felt smaller than a mouse, her soul crushed, her consciousness shattering until she was like a fleck of ash.

Huts lined the roadside. Hundreds of huts. As Ayumi walked, she saw aliens cowering within. They were pathetic figures, a race she did not recognize. Their skin was rubbery, sallow, clinging to bones. They were barely more than skeletons, bald and withered, ribs prominent, eyes sunken in dark sockets. Then Ayumi realized: these were humans. These were humans ravaged, starved, beaten, tortured, reduced to animals, to barely more than quivering remains of flesh, to primal fear wrapped in skin and desperate to hide within hutches of bones.

This is what I will become, Ayumi knew.

With scraping claws, with cracking whips, the scorpions drove Ayumi and the other prisoners forward.

The scorpions herded them past the huts and into a courtyard. Poles surrounded the square, and chains stretched between them. On these chains hung human skins. Hundreds, maybe thousands of skins, drying in the cold air. The skins were intact, still with faces and limbs and hands and feet, lurid laundry billowing in the wind. And beyond them—the piles of skinned corpses, some still twitching, and Ra above, some still whimpering, begging. Ayumi saw prisoners collect the writhing, skinned victims into carts, then haul them into the brick building, and the smoke rose from the chimneys, and this had to be hell, hell or a nightmare, and Ayumi fell to her knees in the courtyard and prayed.

"Please, ancient ones," she whispered to the spirits her father had worshiped. "Please, descend from the Empyrean Firmament. Please help us."

A scorpion scuttled toward her, laughing. "No help will find you here, daughter of man. If you are lucky, you can work the carts or ovens." He sniffed and licked her. "Though your skin is soft."

The scorpion ripped off her clothes. Ayumi whimpered, tried to keep the scraps of cloth on her body. But the claws were relentless, stripping her naked, cutting her skin. Across the courtyard, other scorpions were undressing the other prisoners, and the aliens burned the clothes in a pile.

Their hair was next. The claws grabbed, sheared, tugged, ripped, until the prisoners were bald. Ayumi trembled as the claws sliced her hair, sliced her scalp, leaving her bald and bleeding.

A few prisoners had tattoos. "Skin them, skin them first!" the scorpions said. "Beautiful rugs with beautiful art!"

A striker tore through the sky, roaring, and spiraled down, leaving a corkscrew of fire across the sky. This was not a warship but a small, agile starfighter, a triangle of black metal and roaring heat and thrusting cannons. Belching out flame and smoke, it landed in the courtyard, an angel of retribution descended from the sky. The prisoners recoiled from the smoldering triangle of metal. The stench of burning oil and sulfur filled the air.

A hatch on the striker opened, and she emerged.

Jade.

She wore her garment of black webs, and a thin smile danced on her white face. Ashy wind gusted, billowing her long blue hair. She wore a cape of human skin, the leather dyed black and painted with red scorpion tails, sigil of the Hierarchy.

"Hello, humans!" Jade cried, arms spread out. She inhaled deeply and sighed. "Ah! The delicious smell of death. Savor it, humans! It's the smell of our glory."

Jade walked across the courtyard, smiling, her cape fluttering. Her boots crushed bones, and the implants on her skull shone and buzzed and spun. She was a creature of glory, of luminous white skin and glass and metal, magnificent in her triumph, while at her feet groveled the wretchedness of man.

As she walked through the crowd, Jade pointed at one human after another.

"Skin this one! Make a coat. Skin this one! Upholstery. This one is wrinkly—put him to work. Skin this one, skin, skin! This one is too frail—to work, to work! Skin, skin, sweet skin!"

One by one, Jade separated the humans into two groups. Some—to the right. Others—to the left. Some—to be skinned. Others—to toil. All the while, the implants embedded in her skull shone bright blue, turning, humming, buzzing with electricity.

The group on the right—those to be skinned—was far larger.

And the work began.

Ayumi had not even been sorted yet, and already she watched the scorpions begin their grisly work.

The claws gripped people's skin and began to peel. Screams filled the gulock.

Ayumi wept. She looked away.

The scorpions laughed as they worked. One child tried to flee, and the scorpions grabbed him, tore him in two as his mother begged. One father fell to his knees, crying out for mercy. The scorpions began torturing his children slowly, removing bit by bit of flesh, until the man agreed to slay them himself with a rock for the amusement of the aliens. A few scorpions tossed human babies back and forth, skewering them on their stingers, forcing their parents to watch. A scorpion mounted a human girl, copulating with her in the dirt until she died. All the while, the skinning continued, and the skins were hung on chains.

"To skin, to skin!" Jade was walking between the last few prisoners, sorting them. "To toil—to work the ovens, the carts, to mop, to work, to serve. Skin, skin! Toil, toil!"

Finally the strange woman reached Ayumi. A woman? No. Jade was not human, could not be human. She was part machine, wrapped in alabaster skin. A creature. A monster. Madness in her eyes.

Ayumi looked up into Jade's eyes.

But there is some humanity there too. Evil, twisted humanity. But humanity nonetheless.

And that terrified Ayumi more than anything.

Jade walked toward her, eyes narrowing. She reached out to caress Ayumi's bleeding scalp, then licked the blood off her fingers.

"You're an interesting one," Jade said. "Not as cowardly as the others. Not yet broken. What should it be? Skin or toil, skin or toil …"

"Toil," Ayumi whispered. "Please, ma'am. Let me toil."

Don't skin me alive. Please. Please. Ayumi could hear the others screaming. Smell the stench of it. From the corner of her eye, she could see the skinned humans being carted—still alive!—into the merciful furnaces.

"Toil," Ayumi repeated, tears in her eyes. "Please. I'm not afraid to work hard."

I must live, she thought. *I must see Earth. I cannot die. I cannot die. Please. Please, ancients.*

Jade caressed Ayumi's cheek, her claws sharp and cold and scraping her skin.

"You're not yet broken," Jade said. "Not yet insane. I like breaking my victims before skinning them. Should you toil at the carts, loading the dead? No, you're too thin for that. Should you work in the crematorium, perhaps the tanneries? No. You're too delicate a flower for such dirty work of ash and blood." Jade tilted her head, eyes narrowing. "I think, for you … Ah, yes!" Her eyes lit up. "I know. You, child, shall go to the doctor."

Across the camp, prisoners glanced at one another. A whisper rumbled through the crowd.

"Doctor Death."

"The White Angel."

"Mercy!" An old woman ran toward Jade and fell to her knees. "Spare her. Take me to the doctor. Not her. Not one so young …"

The scorpions dragged the old woman away.

Jade laughed. She placed her hands on Ayumi's slender shoulders.

"Yes, the doctor will be pleased with you." Jade leaned closer, cruel fire in her eyes. "In the Red Hospital, he will break you, child. When I see you again, it will not be you."

The scorpions grabbed Ayumi.

They dragged her away from the courtyard and down a dirt road.

Cackling, they pulled Ayumi toward a red building behind a black fence. The Red Hospital.

Prisoners stared from their huts, eyes sunken in their gaunt skulls. They reached out skeletal hands.

"Mercy," they pleaded. "Spare her."

But the scorpions dragged Ayumi on toward that waiting red building, and she was too weak to struggle.

As they drew closer, Ayumi sang softly.

Someday we will see her
The pale blue marble
Rising from the night beyond the moon
Cloaked in white, her forests green
Calling us home
Calling us home

From across the camp, the others sang. The song called Earthrise. The song of home.

The scorpions shoved Ayumi into the red building, and the door slammed shut behind her.

CHAPTER TWENTY-THREE

They flew over Elysium, fabled planet of the first weavers, seeking the mythical Weeping Weaver Guildhall.

"Is that the guildhall?" Brooklyn asked, pointing a laser beam to the surface.

"That's a mountain," Bay said.

"Is *that* the guildhall?" Brooklyn asked, moving her beam.

"That's a tree," Bay said.

"Is *that*—" Brooklyn began.

"Brook, shut up!" Bay said.

For long moments, the starship was silent. They kept flying through the atmosphere, watching the landscapes roll below.

Then: "Is *that* the guild—"

"Brooklyn, shut up now, or I will shut you off!" Bay said.

"I'll be good!"

Finally she shut up.

Bay looked at the landscape rolling below. Elysium was a verdant world. Forests covered most of its surface, giving way only to rivers, lakes, and the poles. There were many kinds of trees here. Near the equator, the trees had broad, bright canopies. Near the poles, the trees soared, tall and thin and dark green, reminding Bay of the pines he had seen in the Earthstone. He saw no sign of civilization. Not even old ruins. It was a beautiful world—a world of misty valleys, snowcapped mountains, icy rivers, and rolling wilderness. Yet there was a quiet loneliness here.

All this beauty and nobody to see it, he thought. *This world is pristine, while we humans suffer in the darkness.*

He wondered. Should humanity even seek Earth? They said Earth lay in ruins. Civilizations had been fighting for that world for thousands of years. The *scolopendra titaniae*, giant centipedes from deep space, had attacked Earth long ago, humanity's first contact with aliens. Since then, it seemed, the attacks had never stopped. The marauders—giant spiders. The grays—wretched humanoids. The Hydrian Empire—a cruel civilization of monstrous squids. Even after humanity had fled the ruins of Earth, aliens kept fighting over the smoldering planet. Even now, they said, the Basiliska Empire ruled over what remained of Earth.

Would that distant planet never know peace?

Bay spoke softly. "Why should we return to Earth when a pristine, untouched planet awaits us here? We could use the planetary shield to protect us from our enemies. Why fight and die and suffer for Earth, when we can settle Elysium?"

Coral sat beside him in the cockpit. She looked at him, a strange glow in her eyes.

"This planet is holy to weavers, Bay. Its song called me here from the darkness. But it's not holy to humanity. Humans are not merely creatures of logic, nor of animal instinct for survival. Humans heed the songs of their hearts. And Earthrise, our song, calls us to our home. To Earth."

Bay frowned. "Even if thousands die fighting for Earth?"

"Millions are dying now," Coral said softly. "In gulocks across the galaxy."

"I know." He lowered his head. "And I want to save them. To give them a homeworld. We need to unite, find a planet of our own, defend ourselves from the bastion of a world we own. So long as we live in hiding—in space stations, asteroids, caves, and enclaves—we'll be weak. But Coral, *this* can be our world. Elysium can be our planet. Earth lies beyond thousands of light-years. Beyond evil empires. And even if Leona can reach Earth, can form a colony, it would be a life of war. We'd have to defeat the aliens who control that sector of space, maybe many other civilizations who would come after. But here? This place? This is a planet on the edge of nowhere. Forgotten."

"Not forgotten," Coral said. "Not by weavers. Not by the striker that attacked us here. And many more strikers will arrive."

"So we will fight them! We have the shield!"

"Bay." She placed a hand on his knee. "There are millions of humans who might still be alive. But they're scattered across thousands of colonies. They will not follow your father here to some distant world, no matter how fair. They will follow him to Earth. The world all humans have been dreaming of for generations. Our homeworld. Even if thousands die for Earth, even if millions perish, even if Earth is a wasteland, as ugly as Elysium is fair—that will always be our world. Our birthright. Stories matter. The heart matters. That has always been the way of humanity."

"Sometimes the heart can get a whole lot of people killed." Bay sighed. "My dad has always been good at this. Contemplating future paths. Doing the math. Sacrificing some lives to save others. He made a choice long ago to abandon a community of humans. He enlisted those who would join him. He left the others behind. He could have stayed on their world. It was a peaceful world. But he left them." Bay lowered his head, eyes stinging. "They died. All those he left behind. My father let them die, because he had a dream of saving many others. Of finding Earth. He let some humans die to save humanity."

Coral was gazing at him with soft eyes. She placed a hand on his knee. "Somebody you loved died there. On that world your father left."

He nodded. His throat was tight. "Her name was Seohyun. I loved her. I understand the math." His voice caught. "But it still hurts when the sacrifice is somebody you love."

"I'm sorry, Bay." She embraced him. "You're a good man."

Brooklyn cleared her throat—or at least, made the appropriate sound.

"Is *that* the guildhall?" the starship said.

"Brooklyn, I told you to shut up," Bay said.

"But Bay!" she said. "I really think that—"

"Brooklyn, be quiet!"

"But—"

"Brook!"

The starship groaned. "Fine! But I really think this time it *is* the guildhall, and if you insist, I'll shut up, but you're going to miss something that's almost certainly not just a tree."

Begrudgingly, Bay looked down at the planet surface. He narrowed his eyes.

It almost looked like …

"Brooklyn, can you zoom in?"

She was silent.

"Brooklyn!"

The starship said nothing.

"Brooklyn, I told you to—"

"You told me to shut up, Bay," she said. "And that wasn't very nice."

"You're right." Bat patted her dashboard. "I'm a horrible, hideous ogre. Now can you please zoom in?"

"An ogre that smells bad," Brooklyn said.

"Not that you would know, not having a nose, but okay."

"And an ogre who probably has ants in his hair, and who spends far too long in the shower, and really needs to learn how to chew more quietly, and—"

"Brooklyn, zoom in or I'll shake all my ants out!" he shouted.

"Zooming in!"

The viewport zoomed in on a cliff below. Coral and Bay both leaned closer, eyes widening.

"This is the place," Coral whispered, eyes dampening. "The Weeping Guildhall."

Bay grabbed the joystick and began spiraling down. The atmosphere thickened, and water drops clung to the windshield. Winged aliens flew around them, featherless and furless, wings translucent. They reminded Bay of dinosaurs, and he wished Rowan had been here to see them. He flew down toward a river below the cliff. Clouds of mist. Trees, moss, and vines grew everywhere, draping over boulders, hills, and the cliff.

Brooklyn thumped down on a patch of dry leaves between fallen logs. After weeks aboard the tiny starship, cramped together and slowly going mad, Bay and Coral dashed outside.

For a moment, Bay just stood, eyes closed, and breathed the air.

Fresh, real air. It was a bit cold. His breath frosted. But it was wonderful.

After a few breaths, he opened his eyes, then drank in the other wonder here.

The Weeping Guildhall rose before him.

Brooklyn had been right. This had to be the place.

"It's beautiful," Coral whispered. She fell to her knees. "I never imagined anything so beautiful."

Bay nodded. "It's beautiful, Coral. I wish the others could be here to see it. Rowan would have loved this place."

A sour look passed over Coral's face, but it quickly vanished. They gazed together upon the wonder.

A man had been carved into the cliff. He must have been a hundred meters tall, as large as a warship. The sculpture was clearly ancient. Eras of wind and water had smoothed it, and shaggy patches of moss bedecked it. Perhaps due to its elevation, the statue's face was still clear and smooth, gazing upon the land, stoic and noble.

The most striking feature, however, was not the statue's size.

Two waterfalls flowed from the statue's eyes, rolling down the man's chest and feeding the pool below. The colossal statue was weeping.

"Here stands Gadriel, the Weeping Weaver, the greatest sage of our order," Coral said. "According to legend, he weeps for the fate of the cosmos."

"He's human," Bay said, gazing in wonder.

Coral nodded, smiling softly. "Though the Weavers Guild has spread among the stars, the first sages were human. Weaving was humanity's gift to the cosmos. According to legend, the Weeping Weaver fled Earth after the Hydrians destroyed it. A refugee, he went on a spiritual journey. He sought a new world, a place of solitude and silence where he could meditate and study from the ancients. He was the wisest among us. He's still the only weaver who rose above the rank of master, becoming a sage. This statue, Bay, is two thousand years old, as old as our memory of Earth. Gadriel's disciples carved it only several decades after Earth's fall. Some of them, like Gadriel, might have been born on Earth."

Bay took a few steps closer. He noticed that runes had been engraved onto the statue. Hundreds, maybe thousands of runes. Flecks of silver still clung to a few. Long ago, the runes must have shone like starlight.

"Brooklyn." He turned toward his starship. "I see a cave behind that curtain of lichen and vines. Hide there and wait for us. Coral and I are going to investigate."

"Dude, I want to come with you," Brooklyn said.

He patted her. "Sorry, girl, I think you'll have to sit this one out."

The starship grumbled, "You know, you really should buy me a robotic body, then copy my software there. You know, my AI was originally built for androids, not bloody shuttles. I want to be able to walk around with you. Hell, even just a robotic dragonfly body like Fillister would work."

"Once we're millionaires, Brook. I promise."

She groaned. "And buy me a finger so I can flip you off."

Muttering, Brooklyn taxied toward the cave, wriggled past the curtain of vines, and vanished.

Bay stepped closer toward the Weeping Weaver. He walked over moss, passed through mist, and reached the foot of the statue. The foot was huge, each toe the size of a couch. On the largest toe, Bay saw a small, bumpy shape, no larger than a dinner plate. He approached and touched the ridges.

"A fossil," he said.

Coral's eyes widened. She stepped toward the heel. "There's another fossil here."

Bay climbed onto the foot and reached the statue's ankle. Here too he found fossils in the stone. They were oval and ridged, no larger than footballs.

"They're some kind of trilobite," Bay said. "Like the earliest fossils on Earth. When the weavers carved this statue, they must have uncovered them. I wonder if life begins this way on every planet."

Coral craned her head back. She pointed. "More fossils up there."

Bay looked up. He pulled out his minicom, aimed the camera, zoomed in, and slowly panned up. Coral stood beside him, peering over his shoulder at the view on the monitor. Fossils covered the cliff. At the lower levels, they appeared like trilobites, shells, jellyfish, worms—simple organisms. But as they looked higher up, the fossils began to develop spines, skulls, limbs. Some even showed the shapes of feathers.

"Dinosaurs." Bay smiled. "Yes, Rowan would have loved this place. A real Dinosaur Island."

Coral frowned. Again, it seemed like anger passed across her eyes, quickly dissipating.

"All right, enough," the weaver said. "We need to find a way inside. This isn't just a statue. It's a guildhall. If the legends are true, there's a temple inside this cliff, and we'll find the Godblade there."

They walked along the base of the statue. Moss, vines, and lichen covered the statue's limestone robes. Bay and Coral worked with sticks, scraping off the green coat, revealing the craggy stone beneath. They sought a doorway to the secrets within the cliff. As they worked, scraping off moss and leaves, they revealed more fossils embedded in the statue.

As Bay scraped a stubborn patch of moss, he glanced at Coral. She was wearing her Inheritor uniform, but Bay couldn't help remembering her naked body, lithe and warm in his arms. The galaxy was burning. Humanity was dying. Any moment, more strikers might arrive. Yet he couldn't stop remembering their lovemaking. A deep need filled him to hold her, to kiss her again.

"Bay!" She frowned. "That moss won't scrape itself off."

He blinked, realizing that he had been daydreaming. He nodded and returned to his work.

Foolishness, he thought. *She only slept with me because the ancients demanded it. I only care about one woman. Rowan. That's it. I will focus on my mission. On getting back to Rowan. Not on the memory of Coral's warm, eager body and the joy she brought me.*

He returned to brushing the moss and vines from the cliff. Snails and beetles fled as he worked, and again Bay marveled at how evolution took similar paths on similar worlds. This fauna and flora would not seem out of place on Earth.

"We all start the same way," he mused. "Carbon molecules in a primordial ooze, self-replicating, growing more and more complex, taking shapes to fit our environments." He plucked a snail off the wall, admiring the Fibonacci curve of its shell. "The laws of chemistry and physics, the laws that create life, are universal."

Coral glanced at him. "I have no idea what you're talking about."

"You grew up on a world without much technology or science," he said. "I sometimes forget."

She rolled her eyes. "Yes, I'm just the ignorant desert peasant."

"That's not what I meant," Bay said. "You know a lot more about magic than I do."

"I told you, Bay, aether isn't magic." She groaned. "It's just as logical as your chemistry and physics."

"All science is like magic to those who don't understand it," Bay said.

He tugged off another vine, scattering blue beetles that glimmered like gems, and revealed a fleck of silver on the cliff. He removed more vines and moss, uncovering lines engraved into the limestone, coiling, forming sigils, filled with flecks of silver.

"Coral, come take a look," he said. "Somebody engraved something here and filled it with silver."

She approached and touched the engraving. She spoke in an awed voice. "This is not silver, Bay. This is aetherstone. The solid form of aether. Help me clear off all this greenery."

They worked quickly, scraping off moss and vines. More engraving came into view.

A doorway.

A doorway was engraved on the cliff, its borders filigreed, branching off into runes. Smaller runes appeared within the doorway, still filled with flecks of aetherstone. The twin waterfalls, flowing from the statue's eyes far above, framed the door.

Bay frowned. He ran his fingers across the engravings.

"This isn't a real door," he said. "No hinges, no knob. This is just a giant rune shaped like a door."

Coral pressed her hand against the stone. She closed her eyes and spoke softly. "This door has no hinges or knob, but it can be opened. This is an aetherstone door. To open it we—"

She grimaced, cried out, and pulled back.

"Coral!" Bay reached toward her.

She doubled over, trembling. She took deep, heavy breaths through a clenched jaw.

"Coral, what's wrong?"

She looked up at Bay. Her eyes filled with fear.

"I sensed something," she whispered. "When I touched the aether. Danger. Evil." A tear rolled down her cheek. "Great evil."

Bay stiffened. "Then let's get the hell out of here. I ain't opening no portal to hell."

"Not in there," Coral said. "Danger above." She glanced up to the sky and bit her lip.

Bay took a deep breath and reached for Lawless, his rifle. "Scorpions."

"I think so," Coral said. "Many of them. Filled with such anger. Such cruelty. Such evil." She shuddered. "We must act quickly."

She brushed more moss off the center of the door, revealing words engraved in the stone.

She frowned. "It's a poem. I can't read this. I think it's an old human tongue."

Bay's eyes widened.

"That's an ancient dialect," he said. "From two thousand years ago."

Coral looked at him, frowning. "You can read this?"

He nodded. "Yeah, of course. I used to watch old movies on the Earthstone all the time. I grew up with this language. It's what Rowan speaks too. Hell, just a while back, Rowan made me watch all three *Lord of the Rings* movies in this dialect."

For an instant, anger flashed across Coral's eyes. "Well, read it!"

Bay nodded and read the poem, translating it into their modern dialect.

Welcome, traveler
And rest your weary feet
For your road has been long
And filled with tears
Born in fire and tempered in water
You have crawled and climbed
Through mud and rain and shadow
To reach my door
Speak the reason you're here
And enter my hall

As Bay read the words aloud, three runes began to glow under the poem. Each was shaped like a keyhole.

He looked at Coral.

"Is that it?" he said. "We just need to tell the door why we're here, and it'll let us in?"

Coral bit her lip, considering. She spoke carefully. "It seems so. The ancients bestow runes upon those they deem worthy. Every rune on my body—I earned it by proving both my worth and need. Gadriel, the Weeping Weaver, was closest among all weavers to the ancients. He too wants to judge the worth and need of everyone who enters his guildhall."

Bay cleared his throat. He began to tap on the cliff. "There's gotta be some electronic device in here. A microphone to hear a password spoken. We might be able to hack it."

"You'll find none of your science here, Bay," Coral said. "This passageway was built of aether. Same as the wormholes. We must prove our worth and need. As the poem says, we must tell the Weeping Weaver why we're here. Only then can we enter."

"Well, we both know why we're here," Bay said. "But you better tell our weeping friend." He lowered his voice to a whisper. "It'll sound better coming from a fellow weaver and all."

Coral nodded. "I hope this works."

"Of course it'll work," Bay said. "And if it doesn't, Brooklyn will blast the door open with her cannons."

Coral rolled her eyes. She took a deep breath, then took a few steps back. She faced the door and craned her head back, gazing up at the statue's head high above.

"Wise sage!" she cried out, loud enough to send animals scurrying away from the trees. "I am Coral Amber, Journeywoman of the Weavers Guild. I have traveled through many dangers to come here. I come seeking the Godblade! Will you welcome me into your hall?"

They stared at the wall, waiting.

One of the three keyhole runes dimmed.

Bay frowned. He shoved against the door, instantly feeling silly. Nothing but a cliff.

"What went wrong?" he asked Coral.

She cringed. "I'm not sure." She pointed at the two keyholes that still shone. "It seems like we have two more tries."

Bay frowned. "But we told the truth, didn't we?"

Coral sighed. "Yes. But maybe I didn't present my case convincingly enough."

"Try again," Bay said. "And put some drama into it this time! Some emotion, some tears. Make it Shakespearean. Showmanship, baby!"

She placed her fists on her hips. "The wisest weaver of the ages, the sage who forged the Godblade and founded this guildhall, would not appreciate some dog and pony show."

Bay looked at the door, then back at Coral. "Maybe we need to have sex again."

She rolled her eyes. "You wish."

"Hey!" He bristled. "It was your idea last time."

She took a deep breath. "I need time to think. To meditate. To reflect. I—"

Thunderclaps sounded above.

Shrieks tore through the sky.

Bay and Coral looked up.

"Muck," Bay muttered.

He unslung his rifle from across his back. He stared up, inhaling sharply.

Hundreds of ships flew above, still distant, mere specks from here. But when Bay zoomed in with his minicom, his suspicions were confirmed.

"Strikers," he said. "A goddamn battalion of them. The shield should hold them back, but—"

Above, the strikers opened fire.

Their rounds slammed into the invisible shield enclosing the planet. Flames spread across the shield, blanketing the sky. The earth shook. Trees cracked. Stones cascaded down the cliff. The roaring fire was deafening. The sky sounded like cracking bones and avalanches.

Coral reached out and grabbed Bay's hand. The bombardment continued, a firestorm that rocked Elysium.

"The shield is holding!" Coral said.

"It might not hold much longer!" Bay shouted over the storm. "We gotta find this Godblade and get the hell out of here. Try to open the door again!"

"I don't know how!" Coral said.

"Improvise!"

Bay stood by her, rifle raised, ready for a swarm of scorpions to descend—not that a single rifle would be much use. Coral took a deep breath, faced the towering statue, and tried again, shouting over the raging assault above.

"Sage Gadriel! I am Coral Amber, a weaver. The galaxy is in danger. The cruel Hierarchy invades world after world, conquering, butchering, destroying civilizations. You see their wrath above us now! They've murdered millions of humans already, and if we cannot stop them, they will murder the rest, and the galaxy will fall into darkness. I am a servant of the ancients, a wielder of the light! I fight for truth and peace! I've come seeking the Godblade—not for power, not for vainglory, but to defeat this evil that even now assaults Elysium. Will you let me enter?"

Above, the scorpions detonated a massive explosive.

White light blazed, searing across the sky, blinding.

A nuke, Bay thought. *They lobbed a Ra damn nuke.*

The ground shook. Coral fell to her knees. Bay wavered, nearly falling too.

Above them, the shield cracked.

Bay and Coral stared at the door.

The second keyhole dimmed. The door remained closed.

"Damn it!" Bay shouted. "What the hell?"

Coral rose to her feet. She stared at him, eyes wide. "I thought it would work. I thought I'm worthy, that—"

Another nuclear explosion rocked the sky.

The sound was deafening. Bay and Coral screamed and covered their ears. A shock wave slammed into them, knocking them down. Trees fell. Brooklyn screamed in the distance. Cracks raced across the cliff.

But the door remained shut.

Bay looked to the sky, and he saw fire spreading across the shield, curling it open.

Another explosion blazed.

The shield trembled, flickered, and vanished.

And the strikers began swooping.

Coral winced. She grabbed Bay's hand.

"We'll have to flee!" she said. "We failed. Let's get into Brooklyn—and out of here!"

Bay stared at the swooping strikers. They were shrieking across the sky. Within minutes, maybe only seconds, they would be here.

He stared back at the cliff.

"Bay!" Coral cried, tugging his hand.

"Wait," he said.

"We're unworthy! We—"

"Wait!" he said.

He stared at the door. He stared at the fossils in the cliff—trilobites at the bottom, rising to dinosaurs, finally to mammals near the cliff top. He looked back down and reread the poem engraved onto the door.

"Your road has been long," he said softly. "Born in fire, tempered in water. Crawled through mud and shadow." He gasped. "Speak the reason you're here." He spun toward Coral. "That's it, Coral! We have to tell the door the reason we're here!"

The strikers stormed downward.

They were instants away now.

Their cannons were blazing hot.

"I did!" Coral said.

He shook his head. "No you didn't. Not like the poem means." He walked toward the door. As plasma began to rain, he shouted at the top of his lungs. "Evolution!"

Plasma bathed the treetops.

Flame and smoke spread across the land.

The door in the cliff shone bright and slid open.

Bay and Coral ran inside. The door closed behind them and melted into the stone, sealing itself shut, leaving them in shadows.

CHAPTER TWENTY-FOUR

Outside, Elysium thundered as the strikers bombarded the land. Inside the Weeping Guildhall, cold shadows rolled like a calm midnight sea.

Bay stood in the darkness, his heart thundering. He had dodged the plasma by seconds. It took a moment for him to realize: *I'm still alive.*

"Bay, are you all right?" Coral whispered beside him.

Bay couldn't see her, but he felt her clutch his hand.

"I'm fine." He took a shuddering breath, trying to slow his pulse. "Just rattled. That was a close one."

He could hear the smile in her voice. "Is it ever anything else?"

More than ever, Bay wished he had two working hands. He ached to keep holding Coral's hand in his; her skin was soft and soothing. Reluctantly, he pulled his hand free, reached into his pocket, and fished out his minicom. He tapped a few buttons, and a beam of light illuminated the hall.

His eyes widened. "Well I'll be damned."

Coral whispered a few words under her breath, then opened her palm. She cast her own beam of light from a rune shaped like a sun. Her eyes widened too.

"It's an orrery!" she said.

Behind them, the wall rattled.

Both jumped.

Bay spun around. There was no more door, only a sheer wall of stone. But he could hear the muffled shrieks of scorpions.

"They're pounding the statue," he said. "Damn it. They'll nuke the whole place."

Coral shook her head. "No they won't. The scorpions want the Godblade. They can't nuke the guildhall without destroying the artifact." She patted the wall. "It's protected with aetherstone. I can feel the power surging through the wall, filling it. Conventional explosives won't get them in. They'll have to solve the riddle, same as you did."

"You might be underestimating their weapons," Bay said. "They bombed their way through the shield. They can bomb their way through this wall. But we might have a few minutes."

"Or a few hours," Coral said. "Or a few seconds. Depending on how clever they are. Or how powerful their bombs are."

Bay winced. "Even if we can beat them to the Godblade, how the hell do we get out?"

She looked at him, a strange light in her eyes. "Bay, if we find the Godblade, nobody will stand in our way."

He shuddered. "I don't know why, but that creeps me out."

"Me too," Coral confessed.

The wall shook again. The strikers were firing on it. The wall trembled, shed dust, but stood. For now.

"Let's hurry," Bay said.

They turned back toward the hall.

The chamber was as large as a cathedral's nave. Mosaics of stars and galaxies covered the walls, floor, and ceiling, formed from millions of black and silver stones.

But most impressive was the orrery in the center of the chamber.

The clockwork machine towered, rising nearly to the vaulted ceiling. It was a mechanical solar system. Brass gears covered the floor. Rings rose across the chamber, so large that warships could have flown through them. Each ring represented a planet's orbit. Metal planets moved along these rings like carts along rails. Some planets were small, no larger than an apple, while others were the size of watermelons. The planets were studded with shimmering gemstones—there was a yellow planet, a red one, a couple of blue ones. Around each planet spun smaller rings, and little moons moved along them.

A massive sun rose in the orrery's center, as large as a carriage, coated with shimmering red and golden stones.

As Bay stepped toward the orrery, it came to life. Light flared inside the mechanical sun, beaming through the golden gemstones, illuminating the room with firelight. The planets began to move along the tracks, the moons around the planets.

Bay gazed in wonder. "It's *our* solar system." He laughed. "I recognize it from the Earthstone. I've seen images of it. This planet here, the large one with the ring system? It's called Saturn." He pointed. "That huge one is Jupiter."

Coral gasped and held his hand again. Her eyes shone with tears. "It's home. Our home. Of course it is." She looked at Bay, smiling. "Sage Gadriel came from Earth, after all."

She bit her lip. Bay stared into her eyes. They turned around together and ran closer to the mechanical sun.

They found it.

The third planet from the sun.

It flowed along its orbit, the size of Bay's fist, shimmering blue and white.

"Earth," he whispered.

Coral looked at him, smiling—a huge, bright smile that showed her teeth.

A boom sounded from outside. The cavern trembled, and dust rained from the ceiling.

"That was a bomb," Bay said. "A big one. Our scorpion buddies are going for brute force."

Coral pointed. "Look. A doorway at the back."

Leaving the orrery, they approached the second doorway. It too was locked.

Bay groaned. "Great." He pointed. "Another riddle."

Words were engraved into this doorway too, filled with aetherstone. Unlike the words on the outer door, these were still crisp, untouched by the centuries of wind and rain. The words shone in the orrery's light.

"What does it say?" Coral said.

Bay read the words. "In times of love and war, darkness falls."

She frowned. "That's it?" She tilted her head.

"That's it."

Behind them, a series of blasts slammed against the cliff. The chamber shook. Bay and Coral swayed and fell. Dust flew and cracks spread across the ceiling. Stones fell from above. Bay thought the entire guildhall would collapse. By the time the barrage ended, cracks spiderwebbed the walls.

"I thought you said there's aetherstone in the walls," Bay said.

Coral pushed herself up, hair in disarray. She shivered. "There is. But even aetherstone can only withstand so much."

Outside, scorpions were screeching. He heard a high, whirring sound, and more dust filled the air.

"Great," Bay muttered. "They brought drills. We might only have a few seconds here." He took a deep breath. "Gotta think. Time of love and war, time of love and war …"

"This is a time of love and war," Coral said. She slipped her hand into his. "Maybe we do need to have sex again."

Bay let out a mirthless laugh. "You wish." He shook his head. "No, it's not that. The first riddle—the Weeping Weaver wanted us to prove our knowledge. Not our worth, not our love, not the justice of our cause, but our *knowledge*. This too is such a riddle."

Coral frowned. "In times of love and war … I'm lost."

Bay paced. "The sage was a human, right? He made sure everyone who came here would know that. His humanity was important to him. He carved himself—the figure of a human—on the cliff. And inside the guildhall, he built this orrery, showing the solar system humans come from." Bay nodded. "He left clues for the first riddle—the fossils in the cliff, showing evolution. The orrery, Coral! It must be a clue."

He approached the orrery, then swayed and fell as more blasts hit the wall. The enemy's drills shrieked. A drill's tip broke through.

"Bay!" Coral cried. "The drill!"

"I see it, I see it." He frowned, trying to ignore the drills, the blasts, to concentrate. "A time of love and war, love and war …" He spun toward Coral. "I remember! Old mythology from Earth. Venus was the goddess of love, and Mars was the god of war."

Coral's eyes widened. "A time of love and war—a planetary alignment! Which ones are Venus and Mars?"

He pointed them out. Coral pulled the planets along their tracks, aligning them with Earth.

Bay and Coral spun toward the door to the second chamber.

It remained closed.

Bay ran toward it. He leaned against the stone. The door wouldn't budge.

"Muck!" he said. "We got it wrong. Coral, we—"

Across the hall, the wall shattered.

Boulders flew, slamming into Uranus, Neptune, and Saturn. Dust filled the hall. Rocks hit the orrery gears.

And the scorpions swarmed in.

Coral screamed.

Bay fired the rifle.

His bullet slammed into one scorpion's head, knocking the beast down. But a dozen more raced across the debris, cackling. Stingers rose and sprayed venom, and Bay leaped aside, dodging the spray. He fired again, hit another scorpion, but he knew he couldn't fight them all.

"Darkness falls," Coral said. "In a time of love and war, darkness falls."

A scorpion vaulted over the orrery and flew toward Bay. He fired. His bullet hit the alien, knocking it against the orrery sun. The creature burned. More scorpions scuttled around the burning corpse.

Coral raced toward the aliens.

"Coral, stand back!" Bay said.

But she kept running. A scorpion raced toward her, and she raised her palm. A blast of air flew out, slamming the scorpion against the wall. Another beast pounced, and Coral spun toward it, casting a funnel of air, knocking it back. She leaped forward and landed by Earth.

She grabbed the small, round jewel that represented the moon. She tugged it along its track, placing it between Earth and the sun.

"Darkness falls," she said. "A solar eclipse."

The stone door creaked, then slid open. The planets moved along the tracks, rearranging themselves.

"Coral, get in there, I'll cover you!" Bay shouted, loading and firing Lawless.

She ran past him and bounded through the doorway. A scorpion raced after her, and Bay fired from point-blank range, blasting it back. He ran through the doorway, and the scorpion followed.

The door slammed shut, crushing the creature, cracking the shell, snapping the alien in half. The scorpion's upper half twitched and still reached with its pincers, trying to kill Bay.

He fired Lawless into its screeching jaws, silencing the beast.

He shuddered and panted, heart pounding.

"You all right, Coral?"

She was trembling, her hair tangled, her eyes wide. But she nodded. "I'm fine." She flashed a shaky smile. "As close as it gets, as always."

Already, they heard the scorpions slamming at the wall.

"And it won't be long until they break through this doorway too," Bay said. "Not with those drills. Let's find this Godblade."

CHAPTER TWENTY-FIVE

As the scorpions pounded at the door, Bay and Coral went deeper into the Weeping Guildhall.

Before them spread a vast, shadowy hall. As they walked, glowing orbs came to life, hovering in the air, casting silvery light.

Their eyes widened.

"It's beautiful," Coral whispered, tears falling. "It's so beautiful."

Bay whistled appreciatively. "Could put the Sistine Chapel to shame."

Murals covered every surface. Artists must have spent years painting these masterpieces. Clouds, stars, and suns covered the ceiling. Mosaics spread across the floor, depicting animal life evolving from fish to reptiles to mammals.

But the walls, Bay thought, were the most impressive. They depicted scenes, larger than life, of old Earth.

He stepped toward one mural. It depicted a family on Earth, gathered around a baby, sheltered in a humble home. As Bay kept walking, he reached another mural. This painting depicted a child playing on the streets of an Earth city. Skyscrapers rose in the background. A few paces more, and the child was a youth, wandering a forest, communing with animals, meditating on a mountaintop.

"What is this?" Bay said.

"It's him," Coral said, gazing with wonder, awe in her voice. "The sage. Gadriel the Good. This is his life story."

Bay nodded. "Not bad. I need one of these when I die. Maybe a comic strip would be more appropriate for me."

The walls shook. Metallic screeches sounded. The scorpions were drilling again.

Bay glanced toward the back of the room.

"I don't see another doorway," he said. "This must be the last room. The Godblade must be somewhere in here."

Coral nodded. "Let's look for it."

They explored the hall, but they found no artifacts. In fact, the room was empty aside from the floating orbs of light.

"There's nothing here, Coral." Bay groaned. "Damn it."

She frowned. "There are murals. The murals must contain a clue—same as the fossils and orrery did. Let's go back to the first mural, then follow them through the room. There's a story here."

The drills were still working.

"Coral, we don't have time for stories," Bay said.

"Pretend it's a comic strip."

"Comic strips have babes in bodysuits."

Coral rolled her eyes. "I'll wear a bodysuit for you later. Now help me find a clue."

They examined the murals again. Once more, Bay looked at the progression of baby to child to young man. Bay kept following the murals. As he walked across the hall, the murals revealed more of Gadriel's story. The young man worked on a lume, weaving rugs. In another panel, he discovered how to embroider runes, to speak to the ancients in the Empyrean Firmament. In another panel, the sage—now an older man, his hair white—was teaching the art to younger weavers.

The walls trembled. A crack raced across the floor. The drills spun.

Bay and Coral hurried. They reached panels that showed the Hydrians, a race of alien squids, attacking Earth. Cities burned. Countless died. Gadriel fled the burning planet, weeping for the fate of the world. In exile, he sought a new world, a place of solitude, a place to meditate, to learn from the ancients. On the distant planet Elysium, he formed a colony, and he taught many weavers there—some human survivors, most aliens.

"Nothing here about a Godblade," Bay said, glancing toward the doorway they had entered. The wall was shaking. Dust was flying. Cracks raced across the stone.

Coral gasped. "Look."

She pointed at another fresco. It depicted Hydrians finding an aging Gadriel on Elysium. Even in his old age, the sage was mighty. He fought them, beating them back. Yet in another panel, the squids grabbed Gadriel's apprentices, held them hostage.

Bay and Coral kept walking, viewing more of the story. They were near the end of the artwork now.

The sage approached the squids, hands raised, face stoic.

"He's surrendering," Bay said.

Coral's eyes filled with tears. "He's giving his life for theirs. He's sacrificing himself for his apprentices."

Indeed, in the next panel, the squids released the apprentices and grabbed the sage.

And they tortured him.

Bay grimaced.

"Awful," he said.

Several panels depicted the torture of the sage. The squids nailed him onto a wagon wheel, cut him open, removed his organs. Gadriel wept, dying on the wheel.

"The Weeping Weaver," Bay said softly.

"He's weeping not for himself," Coral whispered, "but for Earth."

She pointed. Above the images of the tortured sage appeared Earth, now destroyed, the squids gripping the planet with their tentacles.

They reached the penultimate panel, and Coral gasped.

"He's rising again," she whispered.

The artwork here was massive, larger than life, depicting the ancients descending from the Empyrean Firmament and resurrecting the sage. Gadriel rose, healed and whole, clad in white robes.

Drills burst through the far wall.

The scorpions roared.

Bay and Coral reached the final panel. The artwork showed the sage standing upon a mountain, raising a crystal sword. A rune shone on his hand, shaped like a serpent swallowing its own tail. Light flashed from Gadriel's blade, slaying the squids, destroying their starships.

"The Godblade," Bay whispered.

Coral gasped. "That's how the Hydrian Empire fell. The sage destroyed them! It was too late. Earth had already fallen. The last human survivors were exiled. The sage smote our enemies, but too late …" Her tears flowed.

"Not too late." Bay inhaled deeply. "We can still go back. We can reclaim our world. We're still here. And the Godblade is here, somewhere in this Guildhall. It will destroy the scorpions like it destroyed the squids."

Coral frowned and pointed at the mural. "There are words there. In ancient human language. Can you read them?"

Bay nodded and stepped closer. The words appeared beneath the sage with the sword.

"Only one who has died in agony, and who has risen again, may gain the ouroboros rune. Only such a weaver, one who has known the pain of death and joy of life, may bestow life or death upon nations."

As soon as Bay uttered those words, a door at the end of the hall materialized and opened.

At the opposite end of the hall, the drills finally demolished the wall, and the scorpions poured in.

Coral and Bay ran through the new doorway, plunging deeper into the guildhall. The door vanished behind them, leaving only a wall.

They rested for a moment, panting.

"As close," Bay whispered.

"As it gets," Coral said, wiping sweat off her brow.

They stood in a shadowy room. It was too dark to see ahead. For a moment, they just stood still, catching their breath.

"An ouroboros rune," Coral whispered. She trembled. Her eyes dampened. "He had an ouroboros rune."

Bay frowned. "The snake?"

Coral stared at him. A tear flowed down her cheek. "Remember what I told you about artifacts?"

He nodded. "Yeah. Powerful objects. Like your dagger. Like the looms the old weavers used. Like the shield around the planet. Every one requires a special tattoo."

"And the Godblade requires an ouroboros rune," Coral said. "I saw it in the mural."

"All right," Bay said. "So you pray to the ancients, and you get one."

"Bay!" She grabbed his arms. "Weavers have been praying for an ouroboros for thousands of years. I've never seen a weaver earn one! It's the rarest of all runes. As far as I know, nobody since Sage Gadriel himself has earned an ouroboros rune."

He winced. "And without this rune …"

"Even if we find the Godblade, I wouldn't be able to use it. Not without dying." She lowered her head.

"What?" Bay frowned. "Dying?"

"You read the words on the mural, Bay." Coral trembled. "That's how Gadriel earned an ouroboros rune. By dying and rising again. To earn such a rune, I would need to die and be reborn."

Bay inhaled sharply. "But—Coral! You can't just die and rise again. You're not some mythical sage."

She clenched her jaw. She looked into his eyes. "If I must, then I will die. A human can die for several seconds, then be brought back. We can stop my heart. Have a doctor restart it. I can—"

"Coral, I won't let you die!"

"And I won't let humanity die!" she shouted, tears on her cheeks. "I will do whatever I must to save humanity, to destroy the scorpions. If I must die, I will die. And I will rise stronger."

"And if you don't?" Bay whispered. "If you can't be brought back?"

She embraced him. "We'll cross that bridge when we come to it, all right? We haven't even found the Godblade yet. Come, I hear the scorpions drilling. Let's go get the damn sword."

They stepped deeper into the darkness. When they lit their lights, they found a tunnel sloping downward. They walked into the depths. The air grew colder, and the sound of the scorpion drills echoed.

A hundred steps later, the tunnel opened up into a new chamber. Bay and Coral stepped inside, raising their lights.

Coral gasped. "A tomb," she whispered, holding up her glowing palm. "The tomb of the sage."

Bay stepped forward, pointing his minicom's flashlight. Compared to the splendor of the other chambers, this place was simple. The walls were unadorned, carved from the living rock of the mountain. There was only one mural—an ouroboros painted on the ceiling, a serpent forming an infinity sign, biting its own tail.

In the center of the room rose a sarcophagus. The stone coffin was painted blue and adorned with silver runes. Its lid was sculpted into the shape of a man—the same man carved into the cliff, the same man painted on the murals. The stone engraving seemed peaceful, though tears were painted flowing down the cheeks. Here rested Gadriel, the sage, the Weeping Weaver. His hands were placed upon his chest, holding a stone blade.

"The Godblade," Bay said, touching the stone.

Coral knelt before the sarcophagus and whispered prayers. She rose and looked at Bay.

"The blade you touch is only a sculpture. The true Godblade will be inside the sarcophagus. Help me lift the lid."

The tomb shook as the scorpions drilled above, cutting through the last barrier. Bay and Coral grabbed the sarcophagus's stone lid. It was too heavy to lift, but they shoved, strained, and scraped it across the coffin. Finally they had to pause, and Coral activated runes on her arms, giving her extra strength. They managed to lower the stone lid to the floor, then rise, aching and panting. Coral especially seemed winded. Using aether always took a lot out of her.

The sage rested inside the sarcophagus, mummified.

A human born on Earth, Bay thought, staring in morbid fascination.

Gadriel's skin was papery, clinging to the skull. He wore faded blue robes. Silvery runes were still visible on his skin, even now, two thousand years after his death. His emaciated hands rested on his chest, as they appeared on the sarcophagus lid.

But the sage's real hands were empty.

They held no sword.

Coral let out a strangled gasp.

"It's gone!" she said. "The Godblade is gone!"

Bay frowned. He leaned over the mummy, squinting. He could just make out the faded outline where a sword had once lain. The mummy's robe was a darker blue there, the discoloration shaped like the blade.

"There's a note in his hand," Bay said. "Paper would have decayed. This note is new."

He plucked the paper from the mummy's knobby fingers. He unfolded it and read aloud.

"I've taken the Godblade. Please forgive me, spirits of the guildhall. But I cannot allow this weapon to fall into the wrong hands. It must be destroyed. Forgive me. Forgive me."

Bay looked up at Coral.

"It's signed with a single letter," he said. "D."

Coral stared back, eyes huge and terrified.

Stones rumbled.

Dust flew.

The scorpions came racing down the tunnel toward the tomb.

"Coral, get behind the coffin!" Bay shouted, aiming Lawless.

She stood, shocked, eyes wide. "It's not here," she whispered. "How could it not be here?"

"Coral, incoming!" Bay shouted and fired his rifle.

A scorpion burst into the tomb.

Bay's bullet slammed through its head, splattering brains.

More scorpions climbed over the corpse and scuttled into the chamber.

There was no other door here. This was a dead end. Bay and Coral were trapped.

Bay fired again, knocking back a scorpion, but another one of the aliens reached him. Pincers snapped, and Bay fell back, swinging Lawless, desperate to hold it back.

Coral cried out, snapping out of her daze. Her runes shone, and she lifted the heavy sarcophagus lid, then slammed it down onto the scorpion, crushing the creature. Its shell cracked, and its innards oozed. As more scorpions swarmed, Coral hurled the lid at them, knocking them back. Not pausing for breath, she leaned forward, arms outstretched, and blasted air from her palms.

Bay kept firing, but he was running low on ammo. He could not hold off the beasts forever.

"Humans, humans!" they chanted. "Filthy pests! Skin them! Break them! Eat them! Skin the filthy pests!"

One scorpion lashed at Coral, and she fell, bleeding. Another knocked Bay against the wall, and he fired Lawless, sending a bullet through its jaws. More kept rushing in, filling the tomb.

Bay reached into the coffin, pulled out the mummy, and tossed the corpse aside.

Coral gasped. "Do not desecrate the sage!"

Bay groaned. "Sweetheart, these scorpions are about to do worse than desecrate an old mummy. Come on, help me!"

He grabbed the sarcophagus, struggling to lift it. Coral helped, and they were able to flip the coffin over. They knelt, lowering the stone over their bodies, leaving just a few centimeters for air.

The scorpions surrounded them, clawing at the stone, trying to reach underneath. Bay tried to rise, to walk forward with the coffin over them, but the scorpions shoved against it, knocking them back down, nearly overturning the stone shield.

"I'm sorry, Coral," Bay said, kneeling, his head bowed. The sarcophagus weighed down on his shoulders. "I didn't want it to end this way."

Tears flowed down her cheeks. Coral kissed him. "I love you, Bay Ben-Ari. Goodbye."

Engines roared.

The smell of smoke and oil filled the tomb.

"Dudes!" rose a voice. "I'm here, dudes!"

Bay gasped. "Brooklyn!"

Explosions sounded. Firelight flared, and tongues of flame reached under the sarcophagus. Scorpions screeched. Smoke filled the tomb, and more blasts shook the chamber, deafening.

"Bay, Coral!" cried the voice. "Get in here, hurry!"

Bay and Coral rose, shoving off the stone coffin.

Brooklyn was there, nearly filling the entire tomb. Dead scorpions oozed beneath her.

"How the hell did you fit in here?" Bay said.

"The damn scorpions blasted the walls down," the starship said. Her airlock hatch popped open. "Get in quick! There are more!"

They entered the small starship. Brooklyn spun around in the tomb, denting her hull against the fallen coffin, then blasted forward into the tunnel.

Or at least what remained of the tunnel. The scorpions had demolished the guildhall. The walls were crumbling, the ceiling shedding dust. The aliens were everywhere, hissing from cracked walls, from boulders on the floor, spraying venom from their stingers.

Brooklyn charged toward them, cannons firing.

The starship plowed through the beasts, scattering their shells. She burst into the hall of murals. The front and back walls had fallen, and dust coated what paintings remained. A drill came at them, spinning, shrieking, showering sparks. Brooklyn cried out, bounded over the drill, and slammed onto the floor beyond, crushing scorpions. They raced over the ruins of a fallen wall and into the main hall, where the orrery lay shattered. More scorpions awaited them here, and Brooklyn roared forward, ramming into them, her afterburner blazing.

They surged through dust into the open air.

The idyllic scenery was gone. The front of the cliff had shattered. Chunks of limestone were strewn across the landscape, crushing trees. The sage's stone head lay by the river. The waterfalls gushed over burnt grass. All around, the world of Elysium burned, and smoke curtained the horizons. Strikers filled the sky.

"Brook, get us into space!" Bay shouted.

The starship hurtled onward. "Soon."

"Go up!"

"Forward!" Brooklyn said, racing toward a cloud of smoke. "We gotta lose pursuit first."

Strikers swooped toward them, plasma firing.

Brooklyn plunged into the cloud of smoke. They stormed through the veil. Strikers screamed all around, and streams of fire cut the smoke like blades. Brooklyn flew faster, vanishing in the darkness, skimming the ground.

Coral huddled in her seat, knees pulled to her chest, trembling. She seemed barely conscious, drained of aether and energy.

"It wasn't there," she whispered, eyes fluttering. "The Godblade is gone."

"Hold on tight, we're soaring!" Brooklyn shouted.

The starship changed direction. She flew upward through smoke and clouds and burst into a dark sky. Strikers were here too. Brooklyn barrel rolled, flying upward, whipping around the barrage of plasma. She breached the atmosphere and soared into space.

The strikers followed.

"We gotta go to warp speed!" Bay said.

"We're too close to the planet!" Brooklyn said. "If we bend spacetime, the gravity will crush us."

Bay grabbed the joystick. "Let me fly. We'll slingshot."

Brooklyn relinquished control. A hundred strikers were charging after them, firing their plasma. A bolt grazed Brooklyn's stern. The ship rocked, nearly cracking open. Bay turned and dived back toward the planet, letting the gravity tug them. He shoved the throttle down, flying as fast as he could.

This'll be close …

He winced and turned, skimming across the atmosphere, letting the gravity hurl them over the horizon and into deep space.

They shot forward, propelled by Elysium's force, flying much faster than Brooklyn could on her own.

The starship rattled. Fire blazed around them. Behind them, a few strikers attempted the maneuver too, only for three to crash onto the planet, and for the others to careen wildly into deep space, missing Brooklyn by thousands of kilometers.

Brooklyn charged forward, leaving the planet behind.

"All right, we're good!" Brooklyn said. "Warp speed in three, two, one ..."

Spacetime bent around them, forming a bubble.

Bay cringed. Making the jump always felt like a vise crushing his skull.

The stars stretched into lines, and they shot forward. Within instants, Elysium was just a speck behind them, then gone.

Bay took a shuddering breath.

"Brooklyn, are you all right? Can you keep ahead of them?"

Her camera turned toward him. "I'm flying fast. We have a head start of a few million kilometers. But those strikers are fast bastards. I can't outrun them forever."

Bay cursed. His belly curdled. "Fly back toward Concord space. Fast as possible. We're small and hard to detect. We can lose them."

Her camera bobbed. "We'll be fine, dude. I promise." But there was uncertainty in her voice.

Coral rose to her feet. Silent, she stepped into the hold. Bay followed and found her sitting on the bed, hands on her knees, staring ahead blankly.

"Coral, you're bleeding," Bay said. "Let me bandage you and—"

"We failed." The weaver looked at him, eyes haunted. "We failed, Bay. The Godblade is gone. The galaxy will fall."

Her tears flowed. Bay sat beside her and pulled her into an embrace.

"We'll figure it out," he whispered. "If the Godblade is still around, we'll—"

He froze.

He leaped to his feet.

"Of course," he whispered.

His head spun. He clutched his temples and had to sit back down.

"Bay!" Coral glared at him. "What is it?"

He gave a mirthless, crazed laugh. The hold spun around him.

"The Godblade," he said. "The one painted onto the guildhall wall. The one engraved onto the sarcophagus. I've seen it before."

Coral gasped. It was her turn to leap up. She grabbed his shoulders. "What?"

With a trembling hand, Bay brushed back his hair, then reached for his minicom. He loaded up his gallery of photos and began scrolling through them.

"It was years ago," he said. "I almost forgot. Back before David Emery left us. Back when Jade still lived among us, just a little girl. She was good friends with Leona." He laughed again, a pained laugh. "She was my friend too."

Coral shook him. "Bay, what are you talking about?"

He pulled up the right photograph. He showed it to Coral.

"This is a photo from seventeen years ago, back when we were children. When we all lived together." He pointed. "This girl with the curly dark hair, holding a wooden sword? That's Leona. This boy holding a plastic gun? That's me. And this?" He pointed at a girl with blond hair, holding a crystal sword. "This is Jade

Emery before the scorpions kidnapped her, before they implanted machines in her skull, turning her hair blue, turning her into a monster. She was our friend." He looked into Coral's eyes. "And she's holding the Godblade."

CHAPTER TWENTY-SIX

A nightmare.

It had to be a nightmare.

This place could not be real, not even in hell.

Ayumi stood in the Red Hospital in the heart of the gulock, gazing upon purest pain.

"Come, child." A nurse clattered toward her. "Do not be afraid."

Beneath her white uniform, the nurse had the body of a woman. A human. Yet instead of feet she had curving scorpion claws. A mask covered her mouth and nose, but her eyes were inhuman. Small. Perfectly round. White. Sunken into depressions. They looked like white marbles at the bottom of cups.

"Who are you?" Ayumi whispered. She stood barefoot on the cold hard floor, naked and bleeding and trembling. "What are you?"

"Do not be afraid," the nurse said. "Maybe you will be like me. I will help you."

The nurse reached out. Her fingers were long, twice the length of normal human fingers. Ayumi saw the stitches.

Fingers stitched onto fingers, she thought.

The deformed hand coiled around Ayumi's arm. Another nurse approached, clattering on her claws, and grabbed Ayumi's other arm. More nurses moved about the room, gazing with white marble eyes.

"Please," Ayumi whispered. "I can work hard. I can work the wagons. Or the chimneys. Not here. Please. Not here."

"Do not be afraid," said one of the nurses. "I will help you. Maybe you will be like me. Come now. Fear not."

They pulled Ayumi through the hospital. She walked with them, head lowered. She didn't want to look, but they pulled her head up. And Ayumi saw.

"Do not be afraid," the nurses said. "See? Maybe you will be like them. Come now. Fear not."

Prisoners filled the hospital. Dozens of them. Barely human. Barely alive.

The doors were open. She saw. She was afraid.

In one room, a group of children sat on benches, their skin burned off. They looked at her with huge eyes, nailed into their seats.

In another room, people hung on the walls from meat hooks. One man had two heads, one his true head, the other stitched on and blinking. One man was two men. Each split down the middle, sliced vertically, stitched together, forming rotting conjoined twins. In one room, a child sat in a bucket of ice water, shivering and blue, staring, wires puncturing his skull. In another room a boy hung from the ceiling, embers crackling below him, cooking him alive. One woman had several torsos, stitched together, turning her into an elongated scorpion with many arms. One room was labeled a maternity ward, and a woman lay inside, pregnant, surrounded by nurses with notepads, giving birth with her thighs tied together.

A nightmare, Ayumi thought. *Just a nightmare. It can't be real.*

"You are most lucky," said a nurse. "These experiments help our masters study our bodies. With these experiments, they learn how to win the war. You are serving the Hierarchy, child. Are you happy?"

"Who are you?" Ayumi whispered, voice trembling. "Are you human?"

"Do not be afraid," said the nurse. "Maybe you will be like us. I will help you. Fear not."

They took her past these horrors. Past these weeping, begging humans. In one room, nurses were slicing a man open, pulling out his organs as he screamed. In another room, a woman was nailed to a table, carved open like a frog to be dissected and poked. In one room a man wept as the nurses sawed open his skull, then plugged electrodes into his brain.

Just a nightmare. Just a nightmare. Fear not. They will help you.

The nurses finally led Ayumi to a room at the back of the Red Hospital. A stark white room, the lights searing and unforgiving. When they lay her on the examination table, Ayumi fought them. But the nurses were so strong. They strapped her down, shone the lights upon her, told her not to fear. In the struggle, one nurse's mask fell off, revealing a face with no lower jaw.

Ayumi lay on the table under the stark lights, shaking, praying to die.

Please, ancients, she thought. *If you're alive, let me die.*

The nurses pulled tubes and needles from their toolkits. They ran tubes into Ayumi's arms. They shoved a tube down her throat. They pricked her body, drew blood, attached electrodes. On a tray, they arranged scalpels and rib spreaders and hammers. They gave her no anesthetics.

Please, ancients. Please. Kill me. Please.

Her tears fell. Her father had been a weaver. He had woven a marvelous rug with birds that flapped their wings, with rivers that gurgled, with mountains capped with snowy cotton that was cold to the touch.

We lived in an enclave, she thought. *We were happy. My father knew you, ancients. You gave him the aether, the magic to weave rugs of splendor. I am the daughter of a weaver. Please hear me. Please pity me. Please kill me.*

A nurse stuck her with a final tube.

"The doctor will see you now," she said. "Fear not. I will help you."

The nurses stepped toward the door, pulled it open, and the doctor entered.

He was a scorpion, but not like the others. The warrior scorpions had black shells, but this one was yellowish, the color of pus. Warts covered his shell like a coat of barnacles. An apparatus was attached to his head, a crown of many magnifying glasses that moved on gears. The doctor had the same eyes as the humanoid nurses, small round marbles, no pupils or irises, just white spheres sunken into his skull.

"Well, well, what have we here?" the doctor said, voice raspy and high-pitched. "Lovely specimen." He clattered closer, reached up a pincer, and stroked Ayumi. "How old are you, child?"

"Thirteen, I think," she said. "Please, sir, they said I can work with the wagons."

The doctor seemed to smile, though it was hard to tell with a scorpion. "Ah, you are afraid. I understand. You should be, you know. This will hurt. Quite a bit, I'm afraid." His smile was almost kindly. "But you are a human, after all. You live to feel pain."

The doctor lifted a scalpel.

And he cut her open like a fish.

Ayumi screamed.

She flailed against her bonds.

She prayed.

Please, ancients, please, ancients, please …

The tubes pumped her with fluids. And the doctor cut. Snipped. Pulled out her womb, her ovaries, placed them aside, filled her with liquid.

And she screamed.

And she wept.

"Keep her alive," he said to the nurses. "Seal her up. Stitch her up. More tomorrow."

The nurses pulled out steel thread. "Fear not."

Ayumi screamed as they worked.

She passed out, woke again, stitched together. Bleeding. Dying.

A nightmare. Just a nightmare.

White eyes in the shadows, marbles in cups. Tears, hot and bloody.

He wove me a rug of many colors. Of birds that flew and mountains that soared. I flew on a blue bird through the night, a bird with small white eyes.

In the darkness, she flew on the magical beast again, holding his blue feathers. The bird that had died in her attic. Naked and afraid. He had grown strong, grown his blue feathers, risen again into the sky. They flew toward a distant star. To Sol. And the sunlight seared her.

Dawn came. And the doctor came. And he smiled.

"Good morning, my child! Are you ready? This will hurt, I'm afraid."

And he ripped her stitches open. And he cut. And she lashed at her bonds until the straps dug to the bone, and she screamed until she tore her throat. And he cut, removing pieces, filling her with fluid.

"Fear not," said the nurses, great naked birds, looming above her, bodies pink and wet. "Maybe you will be like us."

Her eyes rolled back, and she flew on her blue bird through the night, a bird like a whale, taking her through darkness, blind but leading her home.

"You bathe in pain," whispered the doctor, taking out organs, planting new organs, working as she trembled and wept. "How beautiful. How beautiful, the human agony."

She slept in pain.

She screamed.

She stood on a rooftop, and all around her the enclave burned, and baby birds lay at her feet, curling up, consumed by fire. The reptiles feasted. Her toes fell off. Her toes became baby birds. The reptiles ate them. They lived inside her. Breeding, cutting, bursting out, and she was a bloated corpse of bustling lizards.

A star in the distance. Shining in the night.

Sol.

A soul.

A dying light.

A tunnel to light.

She fell into shadow.

Her heat stilled.

Laughing, the doctor placed defibrillator paddles on her chest. Electricity coursed through her. She awoke, gasping, heart racing.

The doctor kept cutting.

Ayumi flew.

She was a freezing bird, trampled, broken. Grains of wheat spilled from her split belly.

She was a barren desert.

She was meat on a spine.

She was maybe like them.

She was eyes in a cup.

She was in darkness, rising, screaming, falling again. Flying.

She was a scrap of cloth, embroidered with metal thread, a trapped bird.

Earth. A soul. A world. Ahead—a pale blue dot. And Ayumi flew.

She slept, nailed to the wall, stitched shut with rusty metal. She woke on the table, cut open.

"So beautiful inside." The doctor leaned above her, magnifying lenses on his eyes, cutting, removing, taking out all her pieces, all her secrets. "So wet and red and lovely."

Her heart cracked and fell still. The defibrillator crackled, and she jolted up, screaming. And he worked again.

She was torn apart. She hung on a wall, a frog, splayed open, dissected. She gazed upon the searing lights. Upon a blue world in the darkness. Upon Earth.

I will see it again, Father. I promised. I promised.

And still the doctor cut her, snipping her spine.

And the pain flowed away.

She floated in space. In the darkness among the stars. Heading toward light.

Silence.

All was silent.

No more pain. Only death.

"Ancients," she whispered.

Above her rolled a sea. Deep blue and indigo. Another plane. A realm of light, casting shadow. They swam above her, beings with no forms.

"I must see Earth," she said, flying in the blackness.

Sadness fell upon her like the rain. Colors swirled above, and voices spoke in her mind.

You may rest, child. Let go. Flow into death. There will be no more pain.

She shook her head. "I cannot die. I promised my father. To see Earth. To see home. He wove me a rug." Her tears flowed. "A rug of Earth."

She raised the scrap of the rug, the piece that had survived the fire. On it appeared her bird, flapping its wings.

These are threads of aether, said the voices.

"For I am a daughter of aether," whispered Ayumi. "Let me live."

Life will hurt, child.

"I do not fear the pain."

A rumble beyond, grainy. *She is dead. Lived longer than I thought. Toss her out with the others.*

The nurses lifted her corpse. No pain. No memory. Falling into darkness.

Ayumi reached out toward the ancients.

"Please."

Life is fragile, child. Do you not fear dying again?

"I will never fear this place." Ayumi smiled through her tears. "For you are here."

Light.

Light glittered across her, silvery and warm.

On an examination table, a warty scorpion pressed a defibrillator's paddles against a mutilated corpse.

Electricity coursed through her, jolting her heart.

Light. Light everywhere like motes of stardust.

On the table, Ayumi's eyes opened.

She gasped for air.

Above her—searing white light.

Around her—organs on trays. Her organs. And yet a heart still beat in her chest. On her hand—a glowing rune.

The doctor hissed and scuttled back, eyes wide, stinger raised.

"Impossible!"

The nurses screamed.

Her bonds tore. Ayumi rose, whole and healed.

She was naked, pale, pure. Reborn. Alive. Alive.

Shakily, she raised her palm. A rune shone there, shaped like a snake biting its tail. A weaver's rune.

The doctor shrieked and lunged toward her.

Ayumi grabbed a scalpel and tossed the blade, hitting his eye.

The doctor fell back, eyeball bursting, screeching, tail flailing.

She walked toward him, eyes dry. The doctor hissed, curling up, eye gone.

"How is this possible?" he screeched.

Ayumi grabbed the defibrillator paddles from the table. The machine he had used on her so often, bringing her back to life again and again.

"You brought me back so many times," she whispered. "But not this time."

She turned on the machine. She cranked the dials up to the max. The defibrillator hummed and hissed and crackled. She placed the paddles against the doctor.

The creature screamed.

Ayumi stood, eyes dry, holding the paddles against him, driving the electricity into the creature. Murdering. Murdering him. His shell cracked open. His insides gushed out, burning. He twitched like a doll on a string, and when she removed the paddles, he fell.

The nurses looked at her. Half human. Half beasts. Scorpion eyes and scorpion claws. Slowly, they removed their masks.

"Free the others," Ayumi said. "Take them off the walls. Take them off the tables. Take them outside."

She walked out of the hospital, leading the most miserable and courageous humans who had ever lived.

Nurses—deformed and sliced and stitched together.

Patients—sawed open, burned, frozen, cut and reformed.

Experiments—barely alive, swaying, blinking in the sunlight. They were like broken hatchlings, trembling, rising from shells. They stepped, limped, crawled away from the hospital into the gulock. Blinking, they moved past the pile of skinned bodies toward the huts. Never had such pitiful, deformed creatures walked together. Never had braver warriors walked into the fire.

The scorpions saw them. The creatures shrieked and charged at them.

The patients did not flee.

They had endured medical experimentation. The loss of their families. The loss of their humanity. They welcomed death.

The scorpions reached them, ready to kill.

And the patients fought.

With scalpels. With rocks. With tooth and nail—those who still had teeth and nails.

"For Earth!" they cried, those who could still speak.

And on the rocky ground of a foreign world, light-years from Earth, they died.

The scorpion claws cut them. The stingers stung them. The venom coursed through their veins. They died far from home, twisted, deformed, but not alone. They died with brothers and sisters. They did not die in labs, experiments on tables and walls.

They died as heroes.

"Kill them all!" shrieked the scorpions. "Kill every last pest in this camp!"

The arachnids swarmed. They burst into huts and tore the prisoners apart. They laughed, ripping through corpses, not bothering to skin them.

The prisoners cried out. They died. Thousands died.

But thousands fought.

Even those who had not endured the Red Hospital were barely human. Starving. Skeletal. Reduced to an animal state. Yet as they rose one last time, as they fought with stones and sticks, they were the finest of humanity.

Ayumi walked at their lead. She raised her hand, and the rune glowed. A weaver's rune. A gift from the higher plane. The scorpions saw and hissed, blinded, and scurried back.

As death sprawled around her, Ayumi reached the gates of the gulock. Towering gates. Iron and black and sharp. Human skins hung from them, faces still attached. She looked up at those lurid curtains, and tears filled her eyes.

Her own skin hung there.

She had been skinned whole. Face and hair. Flapping above the gate.

But I'm healed. The ancients healed me. I will not die today. She raised her eyes, and between the clouds, a patch of night sky shone. *I will see Earth.*

The gates were locked and electricity buzzed across the fence. Prisoners tried to climb, to flee, only for the electricity to course through them. They died on the fence, limbs slung between the crackling bars. The last hospital survivors gathered around Ayumi.

"We will climb the fence," they said.

"The electric shock will kill you," Ayumi said.

They nodded. "It will. We will burn on the rods. But you will climb over our bodies. You will be free, Ayumi-san. You will be free. We will all be free."

She knew they were dying already. She knew they could not survive the damage the doctor had already done.

They climbed the fence.

They screamed as the electricity filled them.

Nurses and patients, human again. As they died, they were human again.

As behind her the scorpions were butchering the thousands, Ayumi climbed over the bodies of her friends. She climbed to the top of the crackling, buzzing fence, and she remembered climbing the walls of the enclave, gazing from their top upon the city of Palaevia. From up here, Ayumi gazed upon a different land. Upon a dark, cold wilderness, a hinterland of boulders and distant white trees. A planet whose name she did not know. A planet so far from home.

But her rune shone on her hand. She was not alone.

The top of the fence was tall. She knew the fall would likely kill her.

But she was not alone.

She would see Earth again.

Ayumi jumped off the top of the fence.

She jumped into darkness. To freedom.

She landed in a pile of ashes. Ashes of burnt humans. Their deaths had saved her today.

Ayumi ran into the darkness, naked and beaten and covered in blood, scars in her heart, scars in her mind. A glow on her hand. A gift that shone. Behind her rose the screams of the dying, of those she could not save, and Ayumi knew that she would forever hear those screams. She ran into shadows, and she flew on her bird, traveling in the night to a distant star.

CHAPTER TWENTY-SEVEN

Rowan sat in the shadowy hold, working on the script to *Dinosaur Island II*, when the alarms blared and doomsday arrived.

She bolted up, scattering pages of her script.

The klaxons wailed across the ISS *Byzantium*. Red lights strobed. A robotic voice cried out: "Enemy incoming! Enemy incoming!"

Rowan leaped to her feet. Even though she stood inside the *Byzantium*, a great warship, she clutched her pistol as if scorpions were already on board. When she looked out the porthole, she could see the rest of the Inheritor fleet orbiting Helios. They were changing position, placing the local star to their sterns, assuming battle formation.

It's here, Rowan thought, heart thudding. *Doomsday. The great battle which will win or lose the war. My sister is here.*

She ran across the *Byzantium*'s hold, boots thumping and echoing inside the cavernous tanker. The *Jerusalem*, the flagship of the fleet, was filled with bunks and rooms and corridors. The *Byzantium* was the same model tanker, refitted for war with the same shields and cannons. But on the inside, the *Byzantium* was a vast empty chasm, used in her older days to ship gasses and liquids across space.

Today, the *Byzantium* was masquerading. On the outside, she looked like exactly like the *Jerusalem*, even painted with her colors and name. But the true flagship was now hidden behind Helios, the hot and verdant moon below. And the *Byzantium*, this ship is disguise, was a trap prepared to spring.

A company of soldiers filled the freighter, two hundred men and women, brave Inheritors ready to kill and, if they must, die for their cause. Some were only teenagers, no older than her seventeen years. Others were elders with white hair. They were haggard warriors, their uniforms old and ratty, their hair shaggy, and they bore an assortment of weapons—rifles, pistols, even swords and clubs. The Heirs of Earth were not a true army, just a group of refugees and rebels. But in these warriors' eyes, Rowan saw more courage than she had ever felt.

As she ran by them, they saluted her.

"Godspeed, Rowan!" one man cried.

"Earth's light shines upon you, Rowan!" said another Inheritor, an old man with brown skin and two white braids.

"Kick some ass, kid!" said another, a young man with laughing eyes.

Rowan reached the door to the bridge, then turned to face the others. These men and women, two hundred in all, would help her spring the trap. If Rowan failed, if she could not capture Jade, it would be this company tasked with capturing her—or killing her. Her eyes strayed down to their weapons.

I must not fail.

She looked back up, facing them.

"Earth calls us home, friends," she said. "For Earth!"

"For Earth!" they cried, voices thundering.

Rowan ran onto the bridge. Emet was at the helm, turning the *Byzantium* away from the sun. Rowan took position at the gunnery station. She couldn't see the enemy fleet yet, but the monitors showed a swarm of green dots approaching—fast.

There were thousands.

Thousands of strikers.

"Holy Flying Spaghetti Monster," Rowan muttered, feeling faint.

Her head spun. Her hands shook. She could barely hold the triggers to the cannons. She panted and she worried she would have another panic attack, like the one she had suffered in the engine room.

Emet looked at her. He nodded and gave her a small smile.

"Ready, Corporal Emery?"

There was warmth in his eyes. There was comfort.

She looked at him. A tall lion of a man. He wore his old blue coat and black cowboy hat. His shoulders were wide, and his rifle hung across his strong back. He seemed like a force of the universe, impossible to topple.

You are like a daughter, Emet had told her in the engine room, embracing her. And this was what she needed now. Not just the strong, confident leader. But also the father. Also love.

"Ready," Rowan said, her fear fading.

The Inheritor fleet faced the darkness. Frigates hovered in the center, the core of the fleet. Corvettes surrounded them, a shield of fury. Starfighters formed the third layer, a heliosphere of speed and vengeance. Their supply barges and refugee carriers retreated to hide behind the nearby gas giant, a handful of starfighters accompanying them.

To their right, the Menorian fleet arranged itself for battle. The geode-ships, each the size of a frigate, formed a wall in space, their crystals shining. Rowan had grown up devouring books by Marco Emery and Einav Ben-Ari, great heroes of the old wars, and she knew they had fought alongside these tentacled aliens. Rowan was proud to fight with them too.

I will make you proud, my ancestors, she thought. *I promise. I will win back Earth, the planet you fought for. Your sacrifice will never be forgotten.*

Movement caught her eye. Rowan turned to the left and gasped.

"Ships from our port side! The enemy misled us, they—" She frowned, then her eyes widened. "Concord ships! A Concord fleet, come to help!"

She watched in awe. Hundreds of warships came to join them. Their hulls were cylindrical, winged, and filled with water, and fish swam within them, lavender and blue. Rowan recognized them. Here flew the Gouramis, wise and brave aliens from an ocean world. These beings too had fought with her ancestors, had come to honor their ancient alliance with Earth.

"We have allies," Rowan whispered, tears in her eyes. "Earth is not alone." She wiped away her tears. "Humanity still has friends."

The Concord fleet faced the darkness together, united, as Helios spun below.

And from the darkness they came.

Thousands of strikers.

The scorpion fleet was here.

CHAPTER TWENTY-EIGHT

The strikers stormed forth, thousands of them, filling space with their wrath.

The human fleet and their allies hovered in place, facing them, waiting, shields up, cannons hot, hearts strong.

Rowan stood on the bridge of the *Byzantium*. She gripped the cannon controls, hands on the triggers, ready to aim and fire. Her heart pounded. Her knees shook. And yet her head felt surprisingly clear.

I'm ready. I'm a warrior. I will fight.

She inhaled deeply.

"Warriors of Earth!" Emet said, standing at the helm, transmitting his words across the fleet. "Show them no fear. Show them no mercy. Show them human pride! For Earth!"

From across the fleet, the voices rose. "For Earth!"

The strikers stormed closer. Closer still. At their lead flew a massive, triangular dreadnought. Rowan recognized it, and her heart fluttered. Here flew the *Venom*.

Jade's warship.

"The trap is set," Rowan whispered.

For an instant—silence.

She held her breath.

Then the thousands of strikers opened fire.

Rowan screamed and pulled her triggers.

A hailstorm of plasma hit the Concord fleet, blazing across the shields, blinding Rowan. She cried out and nearly fell as the *Byzantium* shook.

Rowan's cannons pounded. Her shells flew toward the enemy and slammed into the *Venom*, exploding against the hull.

An instant later, the rest of the Concord fleet fired their own guns

The human cannons pounded the enemy with blazing, hypersonic artillery. The Menorians' geode ships spun madly, and light gathered between their crystal hearts, then blazed outward with searing beams. The Gouramis' water-ships unfurled cannons like blooming sprouts. The slender guns spun, then hurled balls of crackling photons.

The barrage slammed into the strikers with fire and light and twisting metal. Several strikers fell back, crashed against other ships, and split open. Other strikers shattered under the impact. Scorpions spilled out, twitching, dying, then falling toward Helios and burning in its atmosphere.

Yet thousands of strikers remained. They kept charging and more plasma flew, a typhoon of fire.

As the inferno washed across the Concord fleet, Rowan screamed.

The *Byzantium*'s shields superheated. Alarms blared. Warnings flashed across monitors. One of the cannons curled up, burning, melting. The ship rocked, and two Firebirds burned before them, falling apart in the blaze.

"Heirs of Earth—charge!" Emet cried.

The admiral shoved down the throttle.

The *Byzantium* roared forth, breaking through the wall of fire.

Around them, the other warships charged with them.

They stormed across space, cannons firing.

Plasma bolts slammed into them. Firebirds burned. A warship tore open. A corvette exploded, raining shards on nearby ships. Dozens died. Hundreds died. But still they flew, cannons firing, storming toward the enemy.

With explosions like supernovas, with shrieking sound and shattering metal, the two fleets slammed together.

The battle burst and expanded into a swarm of thousands of starships, swerving around one another, firing cannons, raining metal onto the moon below.

Rowan kept firing her remaining cannons. Emet flew the ship, zigzagging around the enemy. Their shells and missiles flew from all sides, tearing through strikers. A geode-ship fell apart at their side, showering crystal shards. A Gourami vessel cracked open, spilling water and floundering fish. A corvette rammed into a striker, shoving it against another scorpion vessel, until both enemy ships exploded. Husk after husk fell toward Helios, burning in the moon's atmosphere.

"Sir!" Rowan said, firing at a charging striker. "Should we fall to Helios?"

"Not yet!" Emet said. "Not until she sees us."

Rowan looked around, seeking her through the battle. Where was the *Venom*? Where was her sister?

A striker roared toward them. Rowan unleashed five missiles. They curved around the striker, turned, and entered the exhaust. The striker exploded seconds before it could hit the *Byzantium*. The pieces that remained hammered against their shields. Two other strikers flew from their starboard side. Rowan took out one, but the other rammed the *Byzantium*, denting the hull, nearly ripping off the shields. Drills began carving through the hull.

"Sir! They're trying to board us! Should we—"

"Not yet!" he said.

Rowan kept firing, but she was running low on missiles. All around, space swirled and burned with battle. Humanity's starfighters streaked around her, afterburners blazing, leaving trails of fire. Warships lumbered forth, cannons pounding the enemy. The strikers stormed everywhere, unleashing hellfire.

Metal, glass, blobs of water, and burnt corpses floated through space. Helios kept grabbing debris with its gravity, tugging it down, then burning it in its atmosphere. Forests blazed on the moon's surface.

Drills whirred.

Behind Rowan, soldiers cried out, voices echoing in the cavernous hold of the *Byzantium*.

Scorpions screeched.

Gunfire rang through the tanker.

Rowan glanced over her shoulder. Her heart froze and shattered. The scorpions were racing into the hold, leaping onto the company of Inheritors.

"Rowan, fire those cannons!" Emet said.

"But the men—"

Emet glowered. "Concentrate on your task!"

She turned away from the battle in the hold. Ahead, strikers raced toward the *Byzantium*. Rowan grimaced and fired her last missiles. The projectiles swerved through space, hit the strikers from behind, and shattered them. The *Byzantium* plowed through the wreckage. Rowan was down to shells now—deadly yet crude explosives with no heat-seeking capabilities. She kept firing, and the *Byzantium* roared through the battle, seeking their prey, seeking the *Venom*. All the while, the battle continued in the hold, marines and scorpions screaming and killing and dying.

Finally—there!

"I see her!" Rowan shouted and pointed. "Up there! Behind the company of geode-ships!"

Emet nodded and raised their prow, rumbling up toward the sun. The *Venom* flew there, pounding the Menorian ships, scattering their crystals. Several smaller strikers flew around the dreadnought, battling human starfighters. Rowan narrowed her eyes, prepared to pound the enemy. To draw Jade's attention.

On the monitor ahead—a rising reflection. A creature behind her.

Rowan spun around, drawing Lullaby.

The scorpion pounced.

Holding the heavy pistol with both hands, Rowan fired.

Her bullet tore through the scorpion's skull and embedded itself in the bulkhead.

Two more scorpions raced onto the bridge. Behind them, Rowan glimpsed more of the aliens battling the marines in the hold. Lullaby vibrated, gears turning, as the railgun recharged. She fired again, the recoil nearly knocking her back, and took down another scorpion. A third beast leaped through the air. Rowan fired. Her bullet smashed through the scorpion's stinger, and venom sprayed across the cockpit, burning the bulkheads.

The alien, stinger shattered but jaws still snapping, slammed into Rowan.

She cried and fell against her dashboard, and the ship shook as all cannons fired.

Gripping the yoke with one hand, Emet turned and aimed his double-barreled rifle. He fired, knocking the beast off Rowan. Her ears rang. She rose in time to see more scorpions race onto the bridge. Emet and Rowan fired again and again, taking a few down.

One of the aliens reached Rowan. She fired several bullets through its torso, but it managed to scuttle toward her. Its pincers snapped, grabbed Lullaby, and tore the pistol from her grip.

Rowan gasped and retreated until her back hit the dashboard.

The scorpion reared above her, claws raised. Its jaws opened in a lurid grin, dripping saliva. Emet was battling two other aliens nearby, unable to help. Venom had sprayed his shoulder, eating through his shirt to blister his skin.

"Rowan Emery," the scorpion hissed. Its saliva burned holes through the deck. "My mistress told me to fetch you alive. She will torture you herself. Your skin will hang in her hall."

Rowan stared into the eyes of the beast. Evil. There was pure evil there. These were creatures that delighted in torment, in agony. In its eyes, Rowan saw the death of humanity, saw herself flayed and dripping and dying, and her heart barely found the courage to beat.

You are ready.

You are strong.

You are a warrior of Earth.

She reached over her shoulder. She felt the cylindrical container that hung across her back.

She pulled out the electric cape.

As the scorpion lunged at her, Rowan unfurled the cape and swung it around the creature.

The cape snapped shut, crushing the scorpion, snapping limbs and claws, constricting the alien. Its head was still free, twitching, screeching, snapping its jaws.

Rowan lifted the fallen Lullaby and pulverized that shrieking head.

With another blast, she slew the scorpion Emet was fighting. The admiral nodded to her, then leaned against a wall, clutching his burnt arm, his jaw clenched.

In the hold behind them, the soldiers were slaying the last invaders and plugging the hull breaches. Rowan stared through the viewport. Above, she saw it—the *Venom*. The Skra-Shen dreadnought loomed, cannons blasting, taking out starfighter after starfighter.

The *Byzantium*, disguised as the *Jerusalem*, flew up to meet it.

The *Byzantium* was a full-sized frigate, the largest class of warship humanity owned. But the *Venom* was a dreadnought, a class above, a warship that could destroy worlds. There were only a handful of dreadnoughts in the galaxy, terrors of engineering. The *Venom* loomed twenty times larger than the *Byzantium*, and it turned to face the frigate.

The human starship hovered before the beast, a hornet before an eagle.

If we judged her right, Jade will try to take us alive, Rowan thought. *If we're wrong, she'll shoot us out of space.*

Around them, thousands of starships still battled. For an agonizingly long moment, the human and scorpion ships faced each other, still, two old enemies in a silent standoff.

And the *Venom* did not fire.

Rowan opened a communication channel.

A video feed appeared on her monitor, showing the *Venom*'s bridge.

Rowan stared, eyes damp, heart pounding.

"Jade," she whispered.

Her sister sat on a throne upholstered with human skin. Hands, faces, and tufts of hair were still attached. Jade lounged lazily, one leg tossed across an armrest. She wore her suit of dark webbings. Her hair was shorter but still a striking blue, synthetic and glimmering like fiber optic cables, and her skin was like porcelain. The round implants buzzed and flashed on the shaved side of her head. Hundreds of scorpions filled her starship, scuttling around her.

"Hello, little Rowan, my lovely pest!" Jade said, raising a mug carved from a skull. Red liquid that looked disturbingly like blood swirled inside. "And hello, Emet, Old Weasel, commander of this vermin swarm. Are you ready to scream?"

Rowan stepped closer to the viewport. She stood right before the monitor, and it felt like standing face to face with Jade. Her sister was powerful, mighty, sitting atop a throne with an army of scorpions around her. Rowan felt much smaller, younger, and weaker, a mere girl with a secondhand uniform and an old pistol, flying inside a rusty old tanker. But Rowan stared steadily into her sister's eyes.

"You will never catch me alive, Jade," Rowan said. "You are human. Do you hear me, *you are human.* Nothing but a pest!"

Emet cut the transmission.

The admiral looked at Rowan. She nodded.

Emet shoved the throttle forward and charged toward the *Venom*, cannons firing.

Rowan hopped into her seat, snapped on her seatbelt, and fired a handful of shells.

They could not hurt the *Venom*, no more than a paper cut could take down a prizefighter. They knew it. But they attacked nonetheless.

The trap was sprung.

They rammed into the *Venom*, and its plasma fired, and the *Byzantium* trembled, and the galaxy seemed to burn.

CHAPTER TWENTY-NINE

As Emet charged in the *Byzantium*, attacking the far-larger *Venom*, the madness of his plan struck him.

I'm going to die today.

He rammed again into the scorpions' dreadnought.

Rowan will die.

The *Venom*'s plasma washed over his ship, cracking their shields.

We will all die.

Emet clenched his jaw. The inferno blazed across the *Byzantium*. In the holocaust, he saw all those he had lost. His dying wife. His dying soldiers. Visions of a dying Earth. As the *Byzantium* shook, as their shields cracked, and the *Venom* pounded them, Emet saw the death of humanity.

No.

He sneered and tugged the ship aside, scraping the prow against the *Venom*, raising clouds of sparks.

No!

Rowan fired her shells, hurling the *Byzantium* back into space, until the stern slammed into another striker, and more plasma pounded them.

NO!

Drills slammed into their hull, whirring, spinning, and the enemy prepared to board, to capture them, to flay them alive.

"No," Emet whispered.

He reached toward the control panel at his side. Rowan nodded and reached out too.

They pressed the button together.

A nuclear warhead—no larger than a matchbox—flew from their cannon and exploded.

White light.

Silence.

Raging inferno without a note of sound.

All around them, the strikers careened backward, melting.

The *Byzantium*'s shields shattered, melted, burned off, revealing the inner hull of an old tanker.

And *Byzantium* fell.

She fell from the battle, spinning, tumbling, bathed in white light.

Emet dropped back into his seat. Rowan clung to her own seat, eyes screwed shut, jaw clenched, the light washing over her.

They barreled through burning starships, knocking them aside.

Helios appeared through the devastation. The gravity caught the *Byzantium*, began tugging her down through the floating debris. The ship shook. Emet's teeth knocked together. His spine rattled. He clung to his control board, only his seat belt preventing him from slamming against the bulkhead. The light faded above. The shock wave was still knocking starships aside.

In the middle of the devastation, he saw the *Venom*.

As they had calculated, running the numbers again and again, the *Venom* still flew.

The dreadnought's shields were cracked open. Her hull had been breached. Burns spread across her, and a section of the prow was gone.

But the flagship of the scorpion army had been built to withstand even a nuclear assault. Jade was still alive.

And her flagship swooped, following the falling *Byzantium*.

The trap is sprung, Emet thought. *You will be ours, Jade.*

They crashed through floating debris and slammed into the atmosphere.

Fire blazed around them.

The *Byzantium* shook madly. Whatever remained of the shielding tore off. Wind shrieked through the starship. Control panels cracked. Monitors shattered. Rowan's seat tore free, and she screamed, flew through the cockpit, and Emet reached out and caught her before she could hit the bulkhead. He pulled her against him, wrapped her in his arms, and clung to his vibrating seat. He could barely see. His teeth, his bones, his brain all shook. He could no longer see anything but fire. Behind him, soldiers cried out, but their voices soon faded under the roar of denting, screeching, cracking metal. The hull was bending inward. The tanker, built only for travel in a vacuum, was crumpling like a tin can.

We will not die today.

Holding Rowan with one arm, Emet squinted and reached out, hand shaking. The G-forces seemed ready to rip off his arm. It took all his strength to grab the controls.

They were tumbling straight down now, shrieking through the sky, plunging toward the ground.

Roaring, Emet tugged the yoke back.

Their prow rose.

The G-force slammed into them like the hammer of a god.

Rowan lost consciousness.

A black veil fell. Emet was blind. He was losing consciousness too.

He forced in a breath, and the shadows cleared.

Holding the unconscious Rowan, he grabbed the throttle and shoved it forward.

Fire blazed from their exhaust pipes on full afterburner.

They stormed forward, ripping the sky, leaving a trail of flame that rained down onto the trees.

Helios was burning. The wreckage of other starships lay across the hills. More starships were raining from the sky, breaking up in the atmosphere, falling as flaming debris. Helios had been beautiful once. Now it was hell.

Rowan was waking up. The atmospheric entry had left her with swollen, bloodshot eyes. But she came to quickly, inhaling sharply, staring ahead.

"There." She pointed. "The canyon."

Emet saw it. The ravine snaked across the land. The place where they had drilled so often. The place where a hidden tunnel and shuttle awaited. The place where they would trap Jade.

He flew haphazardly, feigning loss of control. It had to look like a crash, not a landing. It wasn't hard to fake. Half their engines had gone out. The ship was careening, the hull punched with holes. The *Byzantium* was never meant to fly in an atmosphere period, let alone like this. Emet wasn't even sure he could land without killing everyone on board. Holding the yoke felt like wrestling a wild boar.

He glanced up, seeking pursuit. Smoke covered the sky, but he heard the shrieks of strikers.

"Jade is following," Emet said. "Good."

Rowan nodded, lips peeled back. "Let's do this."

Emet gave another boost to the engines. They plunged downward, rattling, losing more pieces of their hull, falling apart. Debris rained behind them, burning the trees below. Leaving a trail of black smoke, the *Byzantium* stormed toward the canyon. Closer. Closer. They grazed the trees along the ledge, shattering branches.

Rowan grimaced.

Emet winced and gritted his teeth.

Silence.

He held his breath.

They prepared to land inside the canyon, to screech to a stop right beside the hidden tunnel and escape shuttle.

A striker burst out from the smoke above.

Bolts of plasma flew toward the *Byzantium.*

Emet cried out, cursed, tried to dodge the attack. Rowan screamed and fired her cannons. Plasma bolts slammed into the *Byzantium*, knocking the ship aside, and they spun in the air, flipped upside down, and righted themselves again. Their cannons blazed, taking down the striker, but a last bolt of plasma hit them, destroying an engine, and they were falling, crashing.

"Hold on!" Emet shouted. "Rowan, ho—"

They slammed onto the ground above the canyon.

They tore through dirt, trees, and boulders.

The *Byzantium* came to a halt—hundreds of meters away from the canyon, from the trap they had set.

Their engines gave a last moan, then died.

CHAPTER THIRTY

The *Byzantium* lay on the ground, smoldering, her engines dead.

Rowan and Emet stared at each other, silent for a moment.

Then Rowan leaped from her seat, raced out of the cockpit, and into the hold. Devastation awaited her: half the company of Inheritors was dead, lying on the deck amid scorpion corpses. For now, Rowan ignored the fallen, ignored the horror. She raced through the carnage, reached the airlock, and burst outside.

She stared around her.

They had landed a hundred meters, maybe more, away from the canyon.

A tremble seized her.

We need to land inside the canyon, she thought. *We need to trap Jade near the hidden tunnel we drilled into the cliff. We need to take her to our escape shuttle.* She took shaky breaths. *Up here, we will fail.*

Rowan looked above her. Smoke and clouds hid the sky. On the horizon, starships were tumbling down, wreathed in fire, slamming into a burning landscape. The battle thundered. Any moment now, Rowan knew, Jade would descend with her strikers.

Up here we're dead. Just like our damn engines.

Emet raced outside toward her. Blood dripped from a gash on his chin.

"We'll trap her here," he said. "We'll figure it out."

Rowan shook her head. "We'll continue as planned. Get back onto the bridge, sir."

She left him, hurried back into the ship, and yanked open the hatch to the engine room. The shaft plunged downward. The last time Rowan had climbed this hatch—at least the identical one on the true *Jerusalem*—panic had seized her, and memories of bonecrawlers and marshcrabs had spun her head. Today Rowan climbed down with a single thought: *Get those engines back up and running.*

She entered the engine room.

Last time Rowan had seen such a room, she had marveled at it, wandered among the machinery, found beauty and elegance in its design. It seemed far larger and more complex now.

She pulled out her pocket watch and pressed its button.

"Fillister," she said, "I'm going to need your help. And fast."

"Right-o, guvna!" said the dragonfly.

The small robot shot forward and buzzed around, scanning the engine room. Rowan joined him, looking for damage.

"There!" She pointed. "That turbine is busted. It's jamming the engine."

"And these cables are toast," Fillister said.

"Ignore those, those are just cooling cables," Rowan said. "We just need a single burst of speed, that's it. Can you grab me that screw? Damn it! We're going to need to patch up the coils there too—you do those, and reattach the spark. I'll get the turbine unjammed! Hurry!"

They worked furiously. With every heartbeat, Rowan worried that Jade would arrive, would burn them down. Yet her fingers were steady. Her mind focused, nearly in a trance. She didn't need to fly. She didn't need anything to last longer than a second—just that single burst of power.

She yanked the jammed turbine free. Fillister reconnected the coils and cables.

Rowan hit the comm on her lapel. "Admiral, sir, I'm going to give you a burst!"

His voice emerged. "Roger that, Corporal, I'm on the bridge and holding the yoke."

Rowan inhaled deeply and pulled a lever.

Fire blazed.

She screamed, knocked back.

The engine gave a single burst of fury, and then the bad turbine tore free and flew across the room, slamming into pipes before crashing down.

It was enough.

The *Byzantium* screeched across the ground, engines—what remained of them, at least—sputtering.

Rowan raced up the ladder into the hold. Her teeth rattled. She fell, rose again, and clung to a handle by a porthole.

The *Byzantium* rumbled forward, ripping up grass and soil, uprooting trees, and finally reached the edge of the canyon.

The last fumes burned inside what remained of the engines, pushing them over the edge.

They roared down into the canyon, and Rowan screamed and clung with all her might.

* * * * *

The *Byzantium* dived into the canyon.

They fell a few meters, sputtered forward, then slammed against a cliff. Boulders tumbled. Their starboard hull tore open with a spray of sparks and a cascade of stones.

Smoke and dust and rocks filled the ship. Klaxons wailed, then fell silent as the speakers fell from the bulkheads.

Emet shoved down on the brakes. He realized he was screaming.

They swerved, hit the other side of the canyon, cracking the hull, rose with a burst of fire, then slammed down hard.

Emet's seat tore free. He flew toward the ceiling, slammed against the metal, and fell. He banged his shoulder against a control panel and roared in agony. What remained of the *Byzantium* skidded across the canyon floor, ripping up stones, banging between the walls. Boulders rained behind them. Rocks slammed into the roof, denting the metal. Ahead, through the storm of dust, Emet saw the red boulder rising along the canyon's ledge—his marker.

He hit the reverse thrusters with all his strength.

The starship screeched along the stone. The engines were dead but momentum shoved them onward. Sparks showered. Dust and bits of stone flew. They scraped forward, tearing open, until half the hull was gone, exposing the canyon walls.

In a cloud of dust, the *Byzantium* fell still.

They were only a hundred meters off target.

Emet jiggled the throttle, giving them a tiny burst of power, just a wisp of a fume.

They jerked forward, then were still again.

They were right beside the secret tunnel in the canyon wall—the place they would drag Jade into, the place where their armored shuttle awaited.

"Rowan?" Emet spoke into his comm. "Rowan, are you all right?" Silence from the engine room. "Rowan?"

She groaned through the speaker. "Sir. Ow. I broke every bone in my body. Even bones I didn't know I had. Just kidding. But I did fall down on Fillister. Thank goodness I only weigh as much as a pancake."

Emet couldn't help but smile. He exhaled in relief.

He left the cockpit and entered the hold. A nightmare awaited him. Half the marine company had perished in the battle and crash. Corpses and blood were everywhere. Rowan stumbled across the deck, bleeding from her elbows and a gash to the head. Emet limped toward her, every muscle and bone aching.

"Rowan," he rasped. "Rowan, look into my eyes. Are you all right?"

She raised her head. She looked into his eyes. Her face was bruised, blood dripped down her temple, and her lip was split. But she stared at him steadily.

"We're inside the trap," she said, voice hard. "We're alive. We're ready." She smiled crookedly, though terror filled her eyes. "Now we wait for Jade."

CHAPTER THIRTY-ONE

Rowan stood in the crashed starship, waiting for her sister to arrive.

She took a deep, shuddering breath. She placed her hand on Lullaby's handle, seeking comfort from the pistol, then pulled her hand away.

I don't want to kill you, Jade. I want to bring you home.

The canyon was eerily quiet. The engines on the *Byzantium* were dead—for good this time. Rowan could still hear the battle far above, but the explosions were muted, limited to a handful of starships that were falling toward the planet, crashing beyond the horizon. Here in the canyon, the wind moaned, and a few severed cables crackled.

Rowan ran across the hold of the ship. Dead scorpions and humans lay on the bloody deck, corpses mangled. The bulkheads were torn open, revealing craggy canyon walls. The airlock door had fallen off, and Rowan stared outside. She could see the curtain of vines on the cliff, hiding the tunnel where her shuttle awaited.

A hundred Inheritors had survived the battle and crash. Silently, the soldiers stepped through the airlock into the canyon, then hid behind trees, boulders, and veils of moss—hiding spots they had pre-prepared.

Rowan stood in the center of the hold, taking deep breaths. Emet came to stand at her side.

Together, they waited inside the shattered starship, facing the airlock, silent.

Rowan reached over her shoulder for the canister. She pulled it down so it hung at her side. Within an instant, she knew, she could pull out the cape and toss it. The movement had become as natural as breathing.

They kept waiting.

Silence.

"Sir?" Rowan whispered.

"Corporal?" Emet said.

"If I die today, sir—"

"You are not dying today, Corporal."

"But if I do, sir," Rowan said, "it has been an honor."

Emet nodded. "The honor is mine, Corporal. But now focus on the task. Jade will soon be here."

They stood in silence for another moment, waiting.

She won't come, Rowan thought. *Oh God, she's not coming. She thinks we're dead already. Or she suspects a trap. Or—*

Engines rumbled far above.

Rowan stepped outside the airlock onto the canyon floor. She looked above.

Three small strikers were descending.

Her breath caught. She turned to look at Emet, who still stood in the fallen *Byzantium*'s airlock.

"It's not the *Venom*," she said, then instantly realized the foolishness of her words. "Of course not. The *Venom* is too large for an atmosphere." She stared back at the sky. "Landing craft. Three of them."

Emet beckoned her. "Come, Rowan, back into the *Byzantium*."

His voice was calm, in control, but Rowan heard the underlying tension. Even Emet was scared.

She took a shaky breath. The engines rumbled above. They had planned to meet Jade inside the hold, reasoning that the bulkheads offered more protection, but suddenly Rowan desperately wanted to be outside in the canyon. Better yet, they should have remained above the canyon, up there in open space. Rowan was too constricted down here. She was trapped. She was trapped like in the engine room, like in the ducts of Paradise Lost, and the monsters were approaching in the darkness, and—

Calm yourself.

She took a deep breath.

You are ready.

The engines roared outside, and smoke filled the canyon.

Through the cracked hull, Rowan saw three small strikers—each was no larger than a bus—land in the canyon.

Rowan gulped and struggled not to draw her pistol.

The strikers were motionless. Their engines purred. For a long time nothing happened.

"Jade!" Rowan suddenly blurted out. "Jade, I'm here!"

From outside—silence.

She suspects a trap, Rowan thought. *She knows. Oh God, she knows.*

She clenched her fists.

"Jade, come talk to me!" Rowan said. "We'll work this out!"

Atop the canyon, Rowan knew, other Inheritors were hiding among the boulders, aiming rifles. A hundred more hid across the canyon. A dozen waited inside the concealed tunnel with the shuttle.

The canyon remained silent. Not a man or scorpion moved.

Then—she heard thumps. Rowan glanced outside and saw a hatch open on a striker.

A cannister rolled out onto the canyon floor.

"Grenade!" Rowan cried.

She leaped back and covered her head with her arms.

But no explosion followed.

A static crackling sounded.

Rowan removed her arms and stared outside. A light projected from the cannister, and a holographic image of Jade appeared. The astral huntress smirked.

"Hello, Rowan!" the hologram said. "You didn't truly expect me to come down there into your trap, did you? Such a silly little pest."

Rowan inhaled sharply. She ran to the edge of the airlock and stared at the hologram. "Sister! Listen to me. We must talk. Face to face. Come down to me! We will speak." Her eyes filled with tears. "We're sisters, Jade, you must believe me, you—"

"Silence!" the hologram shrieked. "I've had enough of your mind games, you pathetic little liar. You tried to trap me. To hunt me." Jade cackled. "But now you've become the hunted." The hologram turned toward the scorpions in the canyon. "Scorpions! Bring her to me. Bring her alive and every other human you find. Sin Kra will torture them himself."

And from the strikers' hatches, the scorpions emerged.

Rowan screamed and opened fire.

The scorpions leaped toward her. Dozens were pouring from their ships. The smoke parted above and more strikers descended, hovered over the canyon, and spewed hundreds of scorpions into the gorge.

Jade's hologram stared into Rowan's eyes, smiled crookedly, and vanished.

Rowan fired in a fury, bullet after bullet, taking out scorpions until she ran out of ammo. As she knelt to reload, Emet stood over her. With one hand, he fired Thunder, his double-barreled assault railgun. With the other hand, he fired Lightning, his electric pistol.

The rest of the Inheritors fought with them. They ran out of the *Byzantium*'s hold, firing rifles and pistols, swinging swords and clubs, roaring for Earth. They emerged from their hiding spots inside and above the canyon, hammering the enemy. They fought with all the courage of humanity.

We are humans, Rowan thought as she fired her pistol, shouting, blasting down the leaping scorpions. *We survived war after war, invasion after invasion. We survived the centipedes, the spiders, the grays. We survived the squids that destroyed our world. We survived two thousand years of nightmares in the dark. For thousands of years, courage has been our torch. Courage now!*

"Courage now!" she said. "For Earth!"

"For Earth!" the soldiers cried. "For Rowan Emery! For Emet Ben-Ari!"

Here in the canyon, as hundreds of scorpions descended upon them, they fought with the greatest courage of Earth, with their homeland's light shining within them.

And in the canyon, they fell.

Soldier after soldier tumbled down the cliffs, died on the ground, burned in the ruins.

For every scorpion slain, several Inheritors fell. The aliens cackled, skinning wounded soldiers, devouring the flesh within, laughing. Laughing with cruelty as the blood splashed them.

Rowan watched them die. Men and women she had trained with, befriended. The last free humans in the galaxy. They had followed her here, believed in her. And around her, they died.

"Jade!" Rowan cried, but nobody answered. The hologram was gone. Jade was still in the *Venom* high above, waiting.

Rowan kept firing until her gun clicked, out of bullets. She reached into her pocket for another magazine, found that she was out.

The scorpions surrounded her. Two of the creatures pounced. Their claws grabbed her. Rowan screamed, flailing.

Bullets slammed through one scorpion's head, shattering the skull, splattering brains. A bolt of lightning slammed into the second scorpion, knocking it back. Rowan saw Emet standing nearby, holding his rifle and pistol, their muzzles smoking.

"Rowan, into the tunnel!" Emet cried.

Rowan looked toward the cliff wall. The curtain of vines had burned away. She saw the stone door there. One Inheritor keyed a code into a hidden panel, and the round door slid open, revealing the tunnel. A spray of venom hit the man, and he crashed down, head melting. Other Inheritors knelt above the corpse, firing railguns at the scorpions, breaking the beasts into shards of hot exoskeleton.

Emet walked over corpses toward the tunnel, firing both weapons with every step.

"Rowan!" he shouted. "With me! Into the tunnel! We're getting out of here."

She stood by the *Byzantium*'s airlock. She stared at him. The battle seemed to spin around her. More Inheritors died at her feet. A man fell down the cliff and thumped onto the ground nearby, and scorpions leaped onto the corpse.

"But I haven't met Jade yet," Rowan said.

Emet fired his rifle, knocking a scorpion back, and reached the tunnel. He stood by the entrance. Rowan stood across the gulf, still by the *Byzantium*'s airlock. The distance between them was only a few steps, but it seemed a light-year.

"Rowan!" Emet reached out toward her. "Rowan, come—"

A stinger sprayed his arm with venom.

Emet howled and pulled his sizzling arm back. He ripped off his coat, roaring in agony, slapping off the acidic droplets. Already his arm was blistering. He tried to step toward Rowan, only for a scorpion to leap onto him, to knock him back. He fired Lightning, and the pistol tore through the scorpion, hurling it against the wall.

"Rowan!" Emet cried again, reaching across the distance. More and more scorpions were scuttling into the canyon now. More and more Inheritors were dying. "Rowan, to me! Run! I'll cover you. Run! To the tunnel!"

She stared at him, daring not leave the airlock.

"I have to talk to Jade," she whispered. A tear flowed down her cheek. "Emet, I have to."

He placed one foot into the tunnel. "Rowan! To me, Corporal! That is an order! We have to run, to live to fight another day. We're getting out of here!"

Emet tried to run toward her again, but three scorpions leaped onto him. They slammed him down. Rowan gasped and let out a sob as their claws tore into Emet. She stepped back into the airlock, knelt by a dead Inheritor, and grabbed a rifle. She fired, slaying the scorpions that were cutting Emet.

"Sir!" she cried.

He rose, bleeding, deep gashes on his limbs. He stared into her eyes.

"I'm not leaving you, Rowan," Emet said. "I am not leaving you! We're getting out of here. Both of us."

He began walking toward her again through the sea of scorpions.

He's going to die for me, Rowan thought.

She cried out, jumped out the airlock, and ran toward him across the gulf.

The enemy was everywhere. Dozens, hundreds all around, thousands scurrying above the canyon, countless strikers in the sky. The beasts filled the gorge like a river. Barely any humans still fought. Rowan ran, trampling over corpses, until she reached Emet.

He grabbed her arm, firing his rifle with his free hand.

"Now come on, Rowan!" he shouted, pulling her.

They ran toward the tunnel, firing in every direction as the enemy swarmed in.

Emet reached the tunnel first and leaped inside. Several other Inheritors were waiting in the shadows. Behind them, Rowan saw the waiting shuttle, the vessel that could take them back into space. Standing in the shadows, Emet beckoned Rowan.

"Corporal!" he cried.

She stood outside the tunnel on the canyon floor.

He stared into her eyes, and he understood.

"Rowan!" he shouted.

"I'm sorry," she whispered, tears in her eyes, and shoved the tunnel door.

He tried to reach her. He was too slow. The round stone door slammed shut, sealing Emet inside. Before he could open it, Rowan fired her gun, burning the control panel. The door remained locked.

Rowan spun around, her back to the door, and faced a hundred scorpions in the canyon. They covered the cliffs, the ground, the fallen *Byzantium*. The other Inheritors all lay dead. Rowan faced the enemy alone.

"Rowan!" Emet was shouting behind the door, pounding on it. His voice was muffled. "Rowan, damn it! Rowan!"

Chin raised, eyes damp, she stepped toward the scorpions. She dropped her pistol, and she raised her hands. The aliens crept near, staring, hissing.

Images flashed before Rowan's eyes—visions of herself hanging in chains, tortured, dying for the amusement of Emperor Sin Kra.

And memories.

Memories of her childhood. Playing with Jade. Hugging her. The humanity she had seen briefly in Jade's eyes in the *Jerusalem*'s airlock.

Courage now. Courage for my sister. For Earth.

"Take me to her," Rowan said. "I am Rowan. Take me to Jade."

The scorpions grabbed her. They stared with burning eyes, licking her, cutting her. They dragged her away from the cliff, up a hatch, and into a striker.

"Rowan!" she heard Emet cry. He was still trapped in the tunnel.

Rowan stood inside the striker. The scorpion claws wrapped around her arms and legs. The aliens slammed the striker's door shut, and darkness flowed over her world.

Engines rumbled.

The striker rose.

Rowan stood in the shadows, trapped in the scorpions' grip, and took a deep breath.

"Jade," she whispered, "I'm coming back to you. We'll be together again."

CHAPTER THIRTY-TWO

The darkness spread before them.

The ISS *Nazareth* floated through the black. A single starship in the void. A lone survivor. Heading to Earth. Heading home.

Leona stood in her cabin, silent, staring into a mirror.

"Who do you see?" she whispered to herself.

A tall woman. Olive-toned skin. A wild mane of curly brown hair. Brown trousers, a blue overcoat, a pistol on her hip. Three stars on her shoulders—a commodore. A warrior. An Inheritor.

"Who do you see?" she repeated, softer now.

A leader. A leader of two hundred men and women. Perhaps they were all that remained. Perhaps she led all of humanity.

She looked closer.

She saw a bride, broken, bleeding.

She saw a girl, exiled, dreaming of slaying her enemies.

A dreamer. Yes. She saw a dreamer.

She pulled back her sleeve and looked at the tattooed letters on her arm.

"I love to sail forbidden seas," she whispered.

A line from an old book of Earth. Leona had always dreamed of seeing her homeworld again, of saving humanity, of rebuilding her species on their ancestral planet. But she had dreamed deeper dreams too. Smaller, more personal, perhaps more powerful. Dreams of sailing the ocean, not the darkness of space. Dreams of feeling the sun on her back, of sailing from port to port, of exploring the forbidden seas from the tales.

She looked at her model ship in a bottle, and she touched the seashell that hung around her neck. It was smooth under her fingers. A piece of home. A gift from Earth.

"We're close now," she said to her reflection. "Closer than we've ever been. And I'm afraid. I'm afraid of what we'll find."

Would Earth be desolate, awash with radiation and disease?

Would their homeworld be a frozen wasteland, a swamp, a desert like Mars?

Were the basilisks now colonizing Earth, and were their starships patrolling its orbit?

In the Earthstone, Leona had seen a clement Earth, beautiful and lush with life, a world of misty valleys, flowering meadows, and warm seas. But that had been thousands of years ago. Within weeks, she would be there. She would see.

I'm a dreamer, she thought. *But will this turn into a nightmare?*

A pounding came at her cabin door.

Leona spun toward it. Her heart pounded just as hard.

She opened the door, and a young private stood there, panting. He was a boy of fifteen, eyes wide, still filled with some light, some innocence, despite the horror they had all lived through.

"Commodore Ben-Ari!" he said. "Commodore, quick!"

Leona's heart pounded against her ribs.

"What is it?" she barked. "Scorpions? Somebody else?"

"It's …" The private opened and closed his mouth several times, lost for words.

Leona grabbed his shoulders. "Speak!"

The boy was shaking, cheeks flushed.

"A star!" he finally blurted out. "A star, ma'am. *Our* star. It's Sol. It's rising in the distance."

Leona rushed out of her cabin, raced down the corridor, and burst onto the bridge. Mairead and Ramses were already there, standing at the viewport, gazing out into space. Leona ran to join the two captains.

"Look, Commodore," Ramses said softly. "Look.

"It's beautiful," Mairead whispered. Tears filled her green eyes.

The *Nazareth* was flying at warp speed. The stars at their sides were blurred, stretched out like the tails of asteroids. But directly ahead was their destination. Their lodestar. Their port of call.

There before them, a single pale dot, it shone.

"Sol," Leona whispered. "Our home star."

She had seen it before with Rowan's powerful telescope—a mere pixel on a small monitor.

This was different.

Now Leona was not just viewing a pixel, a processed image filtered through cables and microchips, displayed electronically on a screen.

She stood, gazing upon the sun with her naked eye.

A mote of luminous dust. A speck so small she could barely make it out. It was the sunrise, and it was the most beautiful thing she had ever seen.

"For the first time in two thousand years," Leona whispered, "human eyes gaze upon the sun."

Tears flowed down her cheeks. Other officers and soldiers joined her on the bridge. The news had spread across the warship. Around Leona, the others wept. A few fell to their knees. A few whispered prayers. They stood on the bridge, a handful of humans, perhaps the last, but also the first of a new era.

That star was one in trillions. It was the most important star in the cosmos. It was still weeks away. It still lay across enemy space. It was as close and real as a beloved memory of childhood.

Leona grasped her seashell pendant, her relic from home. The others gathered around her, wonder in their eyes. They placed their arms around one another. They stood together in awed silence, shedding tears in the light of a distant dawn.

The story continues in

An Echo of Earth

Children of Earthrise Book 3

NOVELS BY DANIEL ARENSON

Earthrise:

Earth Alone
Earth Lost
Earth Rising
Earth Fire
Earth Shadows
Earth Valor
Earth Reborn
Earth Honor
Earth Eternal

Children of Earthrise:

The Heirs of Earth
A Memory of Earth
An Echo of Earth
The War for Earth

The Moth Saga:

Moth
Empires of Moth
Secrets of Moth
Daughter of Moth
Shadows of Moth
Legacy of Moth

Dawn of Dragons:

Requiem's Song

Requiem's Hope

Requiem's Prayer

Song of Dragons:

Blood of Requiem

Tears of Requiem

Light of Requiem

Dragonlore:

A Dawn of Dragonfire

A Day of Dragon Blood

A Night of Dragon Wings

The Dragon War:

A Legacy of Light

A Birthright of Blood

A Memory of Fire

Requiem for Dragons:

Dragons Lost

Dragons Reborn

Dragons Rising

Flame of Requiem:

Forged in Dragonfire

Crown of Dragonfire

Pillars of Dragonfire

Misfit Heroes:

Eye of the Wizard

Wand of the Witch

Kingdoms of Sand:

Kings of Ruin

Crowns of Rust

Thrones of Ash

Temples of Dust

Halls of Shadow

Echoes of Light

Alien Hunters:

Alien Hunters

Alien Sky

Alien Shadows

Standalones:

Firefly Island

Flaming Dove

The Gods of Dream

KEEP IN TOUCH

www.DanielArenson.com
Daniel@DanielArenson.com
Facebook.com/DanielArenson
Twitter.com/DanielArenson